Anita feared what Hawk might be about to tell her.

"What is it?" Anita looked into his dark eyes and felt her throat tighten. Her heart was beating so rapidly she felt sure he could hear it.

Hawk stroked her cheek with the back of his free hand. "I admire you for wanting to be independent, but please don't shut me out of your life just to prove you don't need anyone."

Anita shivered at his touch. Hawk's voice, his words, the intense way he was looking at her—they all suddenly overwhelmed her. *I could never shut you out of my life, Hawk. I am afraid I am falling in love with you, and I do not know how to deal with it.*

Unwilling to say what was really in her heart, Anita stammered a reply. "I. . .you are wrong. I do not mean to shut you out. I cannot thank you enough for being a friend to Juanita and me. You will always be an important part of our lives."

Hawk frowned. "You think of me only as your friend? I hoped—" He sounded troubled, and Anita feared what he might say next.

"Please understand. Juanita and I have had no one to help us for so long—it is not easy to break old habits."

"In time, do think you might change your mind about me?"

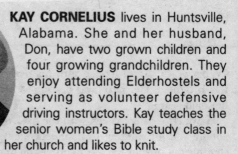

KAY CORNELIUS lives in Huntsville, Alabama. She and her husband, Don, have two grown children and four growing grandchildren. They enjoy attending Elderhostels and serving as volunteer defensive driving instructors. Kay teaches the senior women's Bible study class in her church and likes to knit.

Books by Kay Cornelius

HEARTSONG PRESENTS
HP 60—More than Conquerors
HP 87—Sign of the Bow
HP 91—Sign of the Eagle
HP 95—Sign of the Dove
HP130—A Matter of Security
HP135—Sign of the Spirit
HP206—Politically Correct
HP561—Toni's Vow

Anita's Fortune

Kay Cornelius

Heartsong Presents

To Carol Benjamin, Peggy Farmer, Lee Marsh, Edna Waits, and Ellen Woodle, fellow writers and faithful friends, with affection and appreciation for everything we have shared through the years.

Muchas gracias to Marjorie Masterson, Spanish teacher and former exchange teacher to Barranquilla, Colombia, for her considerable expertise.

A note from the Author:
I love to hear from my readers! You may correspond with me by writing:

Kay Cornelius
Author Relations
PO Box 719
Uhrichsville, OH 44683

ISBN 1-59310-123-6

ANITA'S FORTUNE

Our mission is to publish and distribute inspirational products offering exceptional value and biblical encouragement to the masses.

All Scripture quotations are taken from the King James Version of the Bible.

All of the characters and events in this book are fictitious. Any resemblance to actual persons, living or dead, or to actual events is purely coincidental.

PRINTED IN THE U.S.A.

one

"Tell me about Christmas when you were a little girl, Mama."

Anita Muños de Sanchez smiled at her daughter, Juanita, whose dark eyes shone in anticipation of the story she never tired of hearing.

In the tones of "Once upon a time," Anita began to recite how their house in Colombia filled with fun and laughter, and aunts and uncles and grandparents brought gifts of candy and books and clothes. Her mother cooked for days, making the special treats they had at no other time of the year. They went to church for special programs and made a manger scene in the house to celebrate the Christ Child's birth. Then, the day after Christmas, Anita and her brother took some of their gifts to an orphanage as a way of giving thanks for everything they had received.

"I wish we could have Christmas like that now," Juanita always said at the end of the story.

"We have our own special Christmas, and one day you will be telling your little girl stories about making cookies for the people in the homeless shelter and wearing pretty wings as an angel in the pageant."

"I wish I had aunts and uncles and grandmothers to talk about," Juanita said.

"You can tell your little girl about all our friends at church," Anita said. "For now, it's time for prayers and bed."

Later, sitting alone in the living room, illumined only by the lights on their small tree, Anita recalled the last Christmas she had spent at her childhood home. For the first eighteen years of her life, Christmas had been a happy time. Surrounded by a loving family who understood the true meaning of the celebration of the birth of the Christ Child, she had nothing but happy memories of the holidays, which her evangelical parents kept as true "holy days." She was willing to share the stories of those days with her daughter, but Juanita knew nothing of the tragedy that had followed the happy times.

Looking back, Anita realized the signs that all was not well had been beneath the surface for some time. Sometimes her parents quit talking when she entered the room. Strange telephone calls came at all hours, including the middle of the night. "Wrong number," her mother would say the next morning, but even after her father chose to have their home telephone number unlisted, the calls continued. Maria Borda de Muños's usually cheerful countenance often looked sad and drawn, and Ricardo Muños spent more time away from home "on business" than ever before. Yet when Anita asked them what was wrong, they assured her everything was fine. Her older brother must have noticed something strange was happening, but when she shared her concerns with him, Enrique told Anita she was imagining things.

"Study hard and do not worry about anything else," her mother told Anita when she entered her senior year at American High School. "God will care for us."

Anita liked school, and she always made good grades. Her human physiology teacher, Señora Marjorie Ledford, an exchange teacher from Virginia, took Anita aside one day and asked if she had any career plans. Everyone assumed Anita would go on to a university, as most of American High School graduates did. Some even traveled long distances to attend colleges and universities in the States, but Anita had no desire to leave Colombia.

"My brother is taking a general diploma at the Atlantico. I suppose I will do the same."

"Enrique will work in your father's warehouse business, so that is fine for him. But with your great aptitude for the bio-logical sciences, you should consider a medical career."

Dr. Anita Muños. Anita imagined herself in a white lab coat, a stethoscope around her neck, saving lives. *Maybe I could become a medical missionary and bring the good news to many who have never heard of the Great Physician.*

However, when Anita mentioned she might like to study medicine, her parents exchanged a strange look and said they would have to look into it. A few weeks later, they told her they had enrolled her in a nursing school in Bogotá.

"If you still want to be a physician after that, we will see what can be done," her mother said.

Anita had welcomed her parents' decision; medical school would take years and years, but as a nurse, she could start helping people much sooner.

Before Anita left for her first term in a large teaching hospital in Bogatá, Ricardo Muños gave her a notebook-sized metal lockbox attached to a length of chain with a separate lock.

"Put your valuables inside this box and chain it to a heavy piece of furniture like your bed frame in such a way it cannot be easily removed. Keep the keys on a chain around your neck at all times."

"Are you sure such a thing as this is necessary?"

"I am sure. The sealed envelope inside is to be opened only in case of a dire emergency. Do you understand?"

Anita had a few pieces of heirloom jewelry she had planned to leave in her room at home, but her father told her to put them in the lockbox. She guessed the fat envelope inside contained a fairly large sum of money. The whole business made her feel uncomfortable, but Anita did as she was told. She chained the box to the metal frame of her bed in the nurses' dormitory and wore the key around her neck under her uniform.

First-year students were allowed a brief vacation the week before Christmas. When Anita called to tell her parents when her flight would arrive, her brother answered the telephone. In a strained voice, he told her not to come home.

"Stay in Bogotá, 'Nita. I will let you know when it is safe to come here."

Anita had tried to find out what was wrong, but Enrique hung up after repeating, so urgently that she had to believe him, that she must not come home.

After the initial shock wore off, Anita called her mother's older sister, her favorite aunt. When she repeated Enrique's message, Aunt Rita told Anita it did not surprise her.

"Your parents are having problems. Enrique is right. You must stay where you are."

Anita found it impossible to consider that her parents' marriage could be in trouble, yet Aunt Rita refused to give any more information. "Can I stay at your house, then?"

"No, that cannot be." Anita heard the fear in her aunt's voice and shivered. "Stay in Bogotá," Aunt Rita said again, then hung up abruptly.

Something is going on, and I must know what.

Anita made several more vain attempts to contact her parents, both at home and her father's office, before she decided to go to Barranquilla despite being warned to stay away.

The next twenty-four hours were forever branded into Anita's memory. She had prayed for her family all the way from Bogotá to Barranquilla, yet when she saw the burned-out hulk of what had been her home and was taken to the morgue to identify the bodies, Anita felt so abandoned by God she could not even attempt to pray.

Her family was dead, and nobody seemed to care. Certainly not the authorities, who quickly ruled her parents and brother and a servant had perished in a fire of unknown origin. She could not reach any of her relatives; her aunts and uncles and grandparents seemed to have disappeared into thin air.

Everyone was suddenly afraid of Anita, including her oldest friends. After quick expressions of sympathy, they closed their doors to her. Anita went to Señora Ledford's apartment near the American school, but the doorman told her the teachers had left for the holidays. Pastor Robales refused to take her in even temporarily, advising her to leave the city immediately. "Go with God," he added as he closed his door. Anita realized the bitter truth. The life she had always known was gone forever, and she had nowhere to turn.

When Anita tried to find out who was investigating the fire, she was told the case was closed. On her way out of the police headquarters building, a detective took her aside and offered chilling advice.

"Leave Colombia as soon as you can, Señorita. The people who did this to your parents and brother will not rest until they kill you too."

"What people? My parents did nothing wrong. I have done nothing—"

"Ricardo Muños did not cooperate with some very influential people—that is all I can say. Trust me in this. You are in great danger. You must get away immediately."

Anita flew back to Bogotá as soon as she could get a flight. At night, she retrieved the lockbox from beneath her bed and left the nurses' dormitory without saying good-bye to anyone. Instinctively, Anita realized others could also be in danger because of her.

Let them think what they will. I will not pass this way again.

An hour later, in the privacy of a stall in the ladies rest room at the Bogotá airport, Anita opened the lock box. Her eyes blurred with tears when she saw her father's familiar handwriting on the envelope. *Soledad por Emergencia.*

With trembling fingers, she had opened it. . . .

"Mama!"

Jolted back to the present, Anita turned to see her daughter holding the infant Jesus that belonged to the manger scene.

"Is it time for the baby Jesus to be born yet?"

Anita glanced at her watch's luminous dial. "It is not quite midnight, but if you promise to go right back to bed, you may put Him in His crib now."

Juanita nodded. Carefully, she placed the Christ Child into the manger atop the dried grass she and Anita had gathered for the purpose. "Sleep well, Baby Jesus," she whispered.

Anita carried her daughter back to her bed and kissed her good night. "Sweet dreams, *Muchacha.*"

"Sweet dreams to you, *Mamacita,*" Juanita murmured drowsily.

Anita returned to the living room and glanced at the manger scene. She treasured her daughter's love for Jesus and prayed that Juanita's faith would grow as she matured, as her own had. In the dark days after her eighteenth Christmas, her belief in God had been tested as never before.

Thinking back to that time, Anita marveled at her father's foresight. His envelope contained American money, as she suspected, but beyond that, Ricardo Muños had given Anita detailed instructions on what she should do and concluded by saying she should always ask God to help her. "Remember Hebrews 13:5-6. 'He hath said, I will never leave thee, nor forsake thee. So that we may boldly say, The Lord is my helper, and I will not fear what man shall do unto me.'"

At the bottom he had added these words: *Todo se pasa. Dios no se muda.*

Anita repeated the words from St. Teresa of Avila she had memorized as a child: "Everything passes. God does not change."

Even though her life had been turned upside down, Anita still had the assurance of her faith. "Go to the American embassy in Bogotá," her father's note instructed. The officials there knew about his death and did not seem surprised to see her. They cut through the customary red tape to get her out of Colombia quickly. She would fly to the United States and be enrolled in a nursing program at an Arizona hospital.

"When can I go back to Barranquilla?" she asked.

The embassy official shook his head. "I'm afraid it may never be safe here for you, Señorita. You are young, and you speak English well. You have a rare opportunity to make a new life in the United States. I advise you to take advantage of it."

I tried to do that, Anita told herself.

But the embassy hadn't warned her about men like Juan Sanchez.

two

Anita knew she should turn off the Christmas tree lights and go to bed, but she couldn't get Juan Sanchez off her mind. She had been in Arizona for almost a year when he appeared at her apartment house and tried to engage her in conversation. She had every intention of ignoring him, just as she had other men who showed interest in her, but about that time Anita started getting disturbing notes. Written in Spanish, they were filled with vague threats. When the authorities dismissed them as a prank and refused to take any action, she had told Juan about it.

"I am a private investigator with connections in the highest places, and I can help you," he said, and Anita believed him. Juan was handsome and charming, ten years older than Anita and a refugee from Guatemala. When she told him her family had been killed by men she suspected were bigtime drug dealers, he convinced her they were probably after her, as well. However, he was willing to help her escape their clutches.

"Come with me away from this place. Here, your every move is known. I will take care of you. Trust me."

Unfortunately, she had. Juan seemed so sincere, so interested in her welfare, Anita never suspected he might have set her up. She didn't love Juan, but she was grateful for his help, and when he asked her to marry him, it seemed the best way to escape from her family's killers.

In Anita's childhood dream, she would be married in her church, surrounded by her family friends. She expected to wear a traditional white wedding gown and veil and carry her mother's bridal Bible. In reality, Juan stopped in New Mexico just long enough to get a justice of the peace to perform the hurried ceremony.

"You are safe now," Juan told her, but Anita soon realized that was not the case. Eventually, she learned the truth: knowing Anita was the only surviving child of wealthy parents, Juan had thought she must surely have a fortune stashed away somewhere, and he wanted to get his hands on it. They never stayed in one place very long. Sometimes Juan had money, but more often he did not. When he drank, he had a tendency to become violent, and occasionally he struck her.

Long before their first anniversary, Anita realized marrying Juan had been a terrible mistake.

Except for Juanita.

The child sleeping in the next room had been a gift from God. Loving and caring for Juanita had kept Anita going during the long months after Juan had been sent to prison.

Juanita had just begun to walk then, and she had no memory of her father. When she was old enough to ask about her daddy, Anita told her he had to go away for awhile and would come back one day.

She both counted and dreaded the days until he would be released on parole. Then, a week before Juan would have come home, a violent riot broke out in his prison block, and Juan was killed. Anita tried to console herself that he might have been trying to stop the riot, since a man about to be released would have no reason to cause trouble. In any case, Anita Muños Sanchez had become a widow with a four-year-old daughter to support. She told Juanita the father she didn't remember was in heaven and they were going to live in San Antonio, Texas. In San Antonio, Anita had found a nursing school that would let her work for her tuition while she finished the requirements to become a registered nurse.

She had found something else there—a church much like the one she had known in Colombia, whose members accepted and supported Anita and her daughter. Now Juanita was a happy and healthy first-grader.

I have much to be thankful for this Christmas. May I never forget my many blessings.

⁂

Anita had not meant to, but she fell asleep in her chair. When she awoke, the lights still burned on the little Christmas tree, and Juanita was tearing into the small store of presents beneath it.

"Look at my huggy doll, Mama! It's just what I wanted."

Anita grabbed her daughter and held her close. "And you're *my* huggy doll!"

The soft-bodied doll had long black hair just like Juanita's. She wore a blue print dress, detachable blue shoes, and a permanent smile. "I can't wait to show Dora to Beth," Juanita said. "Can I go over there now?"

"Wait until after breakfast. So you named your huggy doll Dora?"

"Yes, 'cause I just *adore* her. I picked out her name a long time ago."

"Dora is also a short form of 'Theodora,' which means 'gift of God,'" Anita said. "Remember the Bible verse you learned last week?"

Juanita wrinkled her brow. "Something about every good and perfect gift."

"Close. 'Every good gift and every perfect gift is from above.' That's from the book of James. And what is the greatest Christmas gift ever?"

Juanita pointed to the manger scene. "Jesus. Everybody brought Him gifts, but He's the bestest present."

Anita hugged her daughter again and wished, as she so often did, that her parents had lived to see their precious grandchild. But of course, if they had lived, Anita wouldn't have come to be in this place.

"You haven't opened your presents, Mama. The one in the

red paper's from me."

Anita knew Beth's mother had helped Juanita shop; she was not surprised to see the white sweater.

"This will be perfect to wear on a chilly winter night. Thank you."

"Dora and I are hungry," Juanita said a few minutes later.

"So am I. Which do you want, pancakes or waffles?"

Juanita held up her doll. "Dora says she likes pancakes best."

"Then pancakes it will be. You can help mix the batter."

æ

Beth lived a few hundred yards away in the next building of their apartment complex, but Anita never let Juanita walk there or back alone. She visited for awhile with Beth's parents, Tim and Amy Sherrod, who were also fellow church members, then excused herself.

"Call me when you're ready for Juanita to come home."

"We'll drop her off on our way to my folks' house," Amy said.

Back at her apartment, Anita cleared away the Christmas wrappings, leaving the opened gifts displayed around the tree. She had just picked up a book of devotions, a gift from her nursing supervisor, when the telephone rang.

"Sanchez residence," Anita said.

"Mrs. Juan Sanchez?" a male voice asked.

Anita drew her breath in sharply. She had been careful not to use Juan's first name in San Antonio; very few people knew it. "Who is this?"

"A friend of Juan's. We need to talk."

His voice grated like fingernails on a chalkboard, and Anita felt a chill of fear. "I do not talk to people I do not know."

"You should know me. Juan Sanchez was my partner."

"Partner in what?"

"Like I said, we need to talk."

"About what?"

"You sure do ask a lot of questions. I'll be there in fifteen minutes."

"I do not want to see you," Anita said, but the caller had already hung up.

She replaced the receiver and brought her hands together in an attitude of prayer. Anita did not recognize the man's voice, but whoever he was, she wanted nothing to do with anyone who claimed to be Juan's partner.

As far as she knew, Juan worked alone—if deception and stealing could be called "work." He never told Anita where he was going or what he was going to do. When the police came to arrest Juan on a theft charge, he denied any wrongdoing. It was all a misunderstanding, he insisted. But the evidence had been enough to bring him to trial and persuade the jury hearing the case and the presiding judge to the contrary.

Through it all, Anita never heard Juan or anyone else say he had not acted alone.

What could this man want?

Anita glanced at the clock. Whoever he was, she did not want Juanita to see him. She probably had an hour before the Sherrods brought her daughter back home. If he really got there in fifteen minutes, he should be gone before Juanita returned.

Even though she expected it, the sound of the doorbell startled Anita. Through the peephole in the front door, she saw a fair-skinned, sandy-haired *Americano* of average height and weight. Even after years in the United States, Anita still automatically registered everyone she met as *Latino* or *Americano*. In all the places she and Juan had lived, there had been many Latinos. This man was a stranger, and as Anita opened the door as far as the chain lock allowed, she wondered if Juan ever had anything to do with him.

"*Feliz Navidad,* Señora Sanchez. I trust you are having a pleasant holiday."

Anita spoke through the narrow opening in the door. "I do

not know who you are or what you want. I doubt my husband knew you either."

"Oh, he knew me all right. Like I said on the phone, we worked together. My name is Bill Rankin; I need to talk to you."

Bill Rankin. The name stirred a faint near-memory, but she could not attach it to anything substantial. "You have five minutes. After that, I expect you to leave."

"I understand."

Anita unchained the door to admit Bill Rankin. Observing people had become second nature to her from work as an emergency room nurse, and Anita noted he had watery blue eyes and a faint, crescent-shaped scar over his left eye, possibly made by a broken beer bottle.

She remained standing, determined to make this man's visit short and uncomfortable.

"What really brings you here, Mr. Rankin?"

"Cut right to the chase, don't you? Juan warned me you were that way."

"You have less than five minutes now. I am listening."

"Maybe we ought to sit down."

"No. Get to the point."

Rankin's eyes searched the living room, and too late Anita realized her daughter's gifts were still on display. "Juan said you had a kid. Must be four or five years old by now, right?"

Anita swallowed hard and hoped Rankin didn't notice the fear she felt for Juanita. "Whatever you have to tell me, do so and leave."

Rankin shrugged. "The fact of the matter is, I never got my cut from our last partnership. Juan said you would give it to me."

Anita tried to disguise her alarm. "I have no idea know what you are talking about. My husband is dead. He left me nothing."

"Yeah, I heard about that prison riot—tough way to go. But Juan Sanchez didn't die broke."

"I told you I know nothing. I want you to leave now."

Rankin picked up a Bible puzzle book from beneath the Christmas tree. "Juan said you went to church a lot. Last I heard, lying is still a sin. I believe you need to think real hard about that, Anita."

His use of her first name reddened her cheeks, but Anita forced herself to speak calmly. "I am not lying. You have not told me what it is you think Juan owes you."

Rankin's lips compressed. "No, think about it, Juan Sanchez cheated me out of a fortune. We both had a key to the storage unit where we stashed it. We was going to split it after things calmed down, but then I got collared on a parole violation and Juan got sent up on some other robbery thing. I got out last week and went to the unit, but my key didn't work. The manager said a dark-haired woman cleaned it out months ago. The way I figure, it had to be you. Half that stash is mine, and I intend to get it."

Anita shook her head. "I never rented a storage unit, and I do not have what you want. You are mistaken."

"And you're mistaken if you think you can get away with this, Lady. Juan said his wife was smart. If that's so, you'll cooperate with me."

Despite her inner turmoil, Anita spoke with calm assurance. "I cannot give you what I do not have. Please leave now."

"All right, but don't think this is over. I'll be back. One way or another, I intend to get what's mine."

Anita closed and chained the door behind Bill Rankin and leaned against it. Her heart pounded and her head swam from the enormity of what she had just heard.

Bill Rankin obviously believed she had collected some sort of fortune her husband had denied him. Yet, Anita had told the truth. She had never known Juan to rent a storage unit, nor had she taken anything from one.

One way or another, I intend to get what's mine, the man had said.

The doorbell rang and Anita shuddered, fearing Rankin had returned.

"Mama, let me in," Juanita called out. Relieved, Anita unchained the door and swept her daughter into her arms. Then she had a chilling thought: Bill Rankin hadn't been gone very long. He could have seen Juanita coming to the apartment door.

Dear Lord, show me what I must do to keep my daughter safe.

&

After Juanita went to bed, Anita assessed her situation. Bill Rankin was convinced Juan Sanchez's widow had something of value that belonged to him. In an attempt to get it, he could be more than willing to harm Juanita. Calling the police would be a waste of time. Even if the authorities took his implied threats seriously, Bill Rankin had not actually harmed them, nor had he broken any law. By the time he did so, it might be too late.

As she always did when faced with a problem, Anita turned to the Scriptures. Her Bible still lay open to the second chapter of Matthew's Gospel, where she had read Juanita the story of the coming of the Wise Men, ending with the twelfth verse. She continued reading the passage, which suddenly took on new significance:

> And when they were departed, behold, the angel of the Lord appeareth to Joseph in a dream, saying, Arise, and take the young child and his mother, and flee into Egypt, and be thou there until I bring thee word: for Herod will seek the young child to destroy him. When he arose, he took the young child and his mother by night, and departed into Egypt.

Anita buried her head in her hands and prayed earnestly. *Be with me, Lord, and help me protect my child. Grant me the wisdom to know what to do and the strength to carry it through.*

three

The next few days were the longest in Anita's life. With God's help, she had made a good, secure home for her daughter in San Antonio. Now, a stranger from her husband's past threatened to destroy everything. He would be back, that was certain. She had no choice—she and Juanita would have to leave, and soon.

But where could they go?

Anita still kept her valuables in the lockbox her father had given her. Of its original contents, only a few pieces of jewelry remained, and those only because Anita had refused to let Juan pawn them. She had a small amount of cash on hand and not much more in a savings account in the credit union of the hospital where she worked. The rent on her furnished apartment was not due until mid-January. Her ten-year old automobile had long since been paid for, although she had used part of her reserve cash to keep it running. The car could hold their absolute necessities; the rest of their belongings would go to the homeless shelter supported by her church.

Anita had enough monetary resources to leave, but she lacked a destination. She had no desire to return to any of the places she and Juan had lived before he went to prison. It was better to make a fresh start. She and Juanita would head east, but no one in San Antonio must know the real reason.

"We are going to take a trip in the car to a new place," she told Juanita when nearly all the arrangements had been made.

"Can Beth come with us?"

"No, Sweetie. We might not be back for awhile. You can take as many of your toys as you can fit in this duffel bag. We will give what is left to the boys and girls at the rescue mission."

Juanita was accustomed to giving away her old toys, but she found it hard to part with some of the newer ones. In the end, Anita let her pack another small suitcase with things she could play with while they traveled.

Anita gave the apartment manager notice she would not be renewing her lease and resigned from her hospital job by telephone. She left the phone connected, however. If Bill Rankin called again, she did not want him to know she had left town. She told her pastor and Beth's parents that she and Juanita were going to visit relatives and might not return to San Antonio. They were surprised, but no one seemed to doubt her. The last thing Anita needed was for someone to report her and Juanita missing—and then to be found by Bill Rankin.

Finally, all the arrangements were in place. In the predawn darkness of the Saturday after Christmas, Anita dressed her sleeping daughter and carried her to the car. For the second time in her life, Anita Muñoz Sanchez headed into the unknown, guided only by her faith.

❧

"Where are we going, Mama?" Juanita asked when she awoke.

"Toward the sunrise," Anita replied.

"Where's that?"

"I can show you on the map when we stop for breakfast."

A hundred miles later, Anita pulled into a fast-food restaurant and opened the map she had marked the night before. "We are here," she said, "and this is where we are going."

Anita's finger traced the route, east on Interstate 10 through Houston and Baton Rouge, then northeast on Interstate 59 and Interstate 81 into Virginia.

"Will we get there today?" Juanita asked.

"No, it will take several days."

Juanita held out her huggy doll. "Dora's hungry."

"So am I. We will have a nice breakfast."

❧

As mile after weary mile unfolded, Anita began to doubt the

wisdom of attempting to travel all the way to Virginia. She had picked that destination in part because she remembered it was the home state of Señora Ledford, her American school teacher, but mostly because it was so far from any connection with Juan Sanchez.

What Juanita had initially welcomed as an adventure turned into an endurance contest after the novelty of travel lost its appeal. Anita drove as many hours each day as she dared, stopping only to eat, sleep, and buy gas. In that manner, she reached the mountainous terrain between Birmingham and Chattanooga shortly after noon on the third day. Anita turned off the interstate in a steady, cold rain and pulled into a truck stop for gas. When she went inside to pay the cashier, she overheard truckers talking about the ice storm that was rapidly working its way south.

"How is the road to Chattanooga?" she asked one of them.

"Probably not very good, Ma'am. A semi's already jack-knifed outside Chattanooga, and it wouldn't surprise me if they close the interstate."

"Is there any other way to get there?"

"U.S.11 runs parallel to the interstate. It's still open, but it'll probably get icy too."

Anita dug the map from her tote bag. "Show me where we are now."

The trucker jabbed his finger at an unnamed interstate exit. "Go back over the interstate and take the first left. It'll get you to Chattanooga, but it has a sight more curves than the interstate."

Anita thanked him and returned to the car. She had planned to get at least as far as Chattanooga that night, and since the rain had let up, she decided to use the alternative road.

"Where are we now, Mama?" Juanita asked when she saw they weren't returning to the interstate.

"I am not sure, Sweetie, but we are headed in the right direction to get to Chattanooga."

A few minutes later, Anita thought the rain had stopped and turned off her windshield wipers. Soon she realized the precipitation had merely changed to sleet, which was forming a thin sheet of ice over everything. Anita had driven on many mountain roads before but never when they were coated with ice. She ran the blower on the defroster at full speed and turned the wipers back on, but they were fighting a losing battle against the gathering ice.

Anita weighed her options. She had seen little traffic on this road, and if she stopped, she might be stranded on it. She did not know how far Chattanooga was, but it seemed obvious she could not get there any time soon.

Ahead on the right, a state road sign pointed to Rockdale. She pulled over and finally found the town on her map. Rockdale was not as large as Ft. Payne, which lay to the south, but it was the only place of any size in the vicinity.

Cautiously, Anita turned onto the Rockdale road. Even narrower than the one she had just left, it descended in a series of curves. Although the turns were well banked, the accumulating ice made them treacherous. Anita felt her car fishtailing in the first few turns and managed to steady it. Then another, deeper, curve caught her off guard, and she felt the car skidding. On one side, a thin guardrail separated the shoulder of the road from a sharp drop-off. On the other, a solid bank of rock rose vertically. Anita kept her foot off the brake in hopes the car might slow on its own. But the turn tightened, and when she touched the brake lightly, she felt her tires losing traction. She did not trust the fragile guardrail to keep her vehicle from plunging over the embankment, but she did not want to collide with the massive rock bluff either.

Knowing she was about to lose control of the vehicle, Anita clenched her jaw and gripped the steering wheel.

Help us, Lord, she prayed, just as the car spun around sickeningly and skidded off the road.

૨૦

Weekday shifts were usually quiet for Rock County Deputy Sheriff Hawk Henson. On a normal day, he might serve a few subpoenas, investigate a few citizens' complaints, and enforce traffic laws in the jurisdiction. But from the moment the National Weather Service in Birmingham issued a Winter Storm Watch about ten that Monday morning, Hawk knew the day would be far from routine.

A steady rain had fallen all morning and saturated everything. Now the drops encountered an Arctic cold front that had broken through the high-pressure barrier that would normally have kept it away. When such a storm occurred in the mountains of northeastern Alabama, the rain often turned to sleet, causing ice to build up on every exposed surface from bridges and overpasses to trees. Ice-coated tree limbs were beautiful, but all too often they broke beneath the unaccustomed weight and fell onto power lines, leaving thousands of people without electricity. Sometimes it was days before households in remote areas had their power restored. As a member of the county's Emergency Response Team, part of Hawk's job was to see that people who needed it had help.

"Looks like we're in for a bad one," Sheriff Lester Trimble said when he came back to the courthouse after lunch.

"I'm afraid so," Hawk agreed. He had sensed this storm brewing for several days, but he knew better than to tell his new boss. *That's just more of that Injun superstition of yours,* Sheriff Trimble would have said. Trimble, formerly the chief deputy, had been elected to the post in November, when Asa McGinty, the longtime sheriff who had hired Hawk, retired.

Fresh out of the army after serving in the military police for eight years, Hawk could have joined any number of big city law enforcement agencies. However, he had come back home to Rock County, where his Cherokee ancestors had lived since finding sanctuary from the Trail of Tears. In the years since, the mountains that had protected the Cherokee survivors had also furnished many of them with a living.

"Word just came that I-59's closed south of Chattanooga. An eighteen-wheeler jackknifed in the rain. State troopers are trying to keep everyone from driving on the roads around Lookout Mountain," Hawk reported.

"Yeah, so I heard. Tom Statum had the radio on at the restaurant. There's enough warning out now. People know not to drive in this kind of weather."

"Locals do, but we should check the road coming into town."

Sheriff Trimble shrugged. "Anybody fool enough to be trying to drive on it in this weather deserves what they get. Unless it's an emergency call, you should stay put."

That wasn't an order, Hawk told himself when Lester Trimble left for the day an hour later. The sheriff lived on the side of Warren Mountain; his wife was there alone, and he wanted to make sure she could start the emergency generator if their power failed.

"Call me if you need me," the sheriff said in parting, but Hawk knew he really meant: *It's all yours now. Don't bother me.*

"You can leave too if you want," Hawk told Sally Rogers, the sheriff office's receptionist and dispatcher for more than twenty years.

"Thanks, but I'll stay until the end of my shift," she said.

Hawk looked out of the office window at the darkening sky. Sleet rattled against the windows, and the top of the hills surrounding Rockdale were already turning white.

Check for traffic on the road into town.

Hawk jerked his head around, for a moment convinced that someone had spoken the words aloud. But Sally sat quietly at her desk, and no one else was in the office.

Similar cautions had been given to Hawk several times over the years. The voice he heard so clearly usually warned him of danger to himself or someone else. The first time it happened,

Hawk had told his mother about it. *It is a gift from God*, she said. *Do not be afraid to listen and heed what it tells you.*

Hawk Henson took his leather jacket from a hook near the door. "Hold down the fort, Sally. I'm going to make a final traffic check on the road into town."

She looked surprised. "Shouldn't be anything out there by now."

"Maybe not, but it won't hurt to look. You can forward my calls to the cruiser."

Hawk left Sally shaking her head and walked, head down against the peppering sleet, to his Rock County Sheriff's Department vehicle. The weather was worsening. Sally was probably right. *No one in their right mind would still be on that road.*

Hawk glanced at the mountain rising above the town.

But if anyone up there needs help, I'm on my way.

❧

Anita heard her daughter's scream and added her own at the same instant her car made contact with, then scraped along the guardrail until it jolted to a halt. Even though Anita's car did not have an air bag, her safety belt held her in place. Securely strapped into the back seat, Juanita wailed in shock and fright.

Shakily Anita got out of the car. "Do not cry, Sweetie. Everything's all right." She quickly satisfied herself that her daughter was largely unhurt. Anita's left elbow sported a bruise, while Juanita had escaped with only a tiny scratch on her arm.

Juanita clutched her huggy doll. "Dora didn't like that."

"Neither did I. But God is looking after us. He kept us safe, and He will send someone to us soon."

Anita cautiously walked around to the passenger side of the car to survey the damage. Her heart sank when she saw the crumpled fender and broken headlight. The right front tire was flat, but even worse, the rear of the car partially blocked the roadway. Anyone coming around the curve might not see her wrecked vehicle in time to avoid it. She feared being hit, but sleet still fell, and the car was their only shelter.

"You and Dora can sit up front with me, and we will keep each other warm," Anita said. She had turned off the ignition immediately after the crash and did not want to risk starting the motor to run the heater unless it became absolutely necessary.

"It's getting dark, Mama," Juanita said after a few minutes.

"The skies are just cloudy. It is still a long time until night."

Juanita's lower lip trembled. "Suppose nobody comes?"

"Someone will. Let us close our eyes and thank God for keeping us safe so far and ask Him to send help. You go first."

Minutes after Anita added her petition to her daughter's, she heard an approaching automobile.

"It's a policeman, Mama," Juanita said when the black-and-white vehicle rounded the curve, slowed to a stop, and turned on its blue light bar.

Sheriff, Rock County, Alabama, Anita read on the side of the cruiser. *We will not make it to Tennessee tonight.*

A man in a dark brown uniform came toward Anita as she got out of the car. "Are you all right?" he asked.

Even in the waning daylight, she saw he had dark skin and hair. Not *Latino* exactly, but not the usual *Americano* either. *Native American*, she guessed.

"Yes, but the car is not."

"So I see." He returned to the cruiser and spoke into the two-way radio at some length before returning. "A wrecker's on the way from Rockdale. I reckon that's where you were headed."

Anita nodded. She was accustomed to hearing South Texans, but this man's speech had an unexpected softness. "Actually, I wanted to go to Chattanooga, but a trucker told me the interstate might be closed."

"It is, but you couldn't get to Chattanooga on this road, either."

"I know. I was on US 11. When the weather turned bad, I decided to stop in Rockdale instead. I did not know I would have to go down a ski slope to get there."

He smiled and extended his hand. "I'm Hawk Henson, Rock County deputy sheriff. Something told me to check on this road before I clocked out."

"That was God," said Juanita, who had scrambled out of the car in time to hear his last remark.

"I am Anita Sanchez, and this is my daughter, Juanita."

Hawk Henson's eyebrows rose perceptibly, and Anita could imagine what he must be thinking. It would not be the first time that her Hispanic name had caused people to regard her with a mixture of curiosity and repulsion.

The deputy sheriff released Anita's hand and shook her daughter's. "In any case, you're getting chilled out here. Hop in the back seat of my car, Miss Juanita. It's nice and warm, and I'll take you and your mother to town after the wrecker gets here."

"That is very kind of you, Deputy," Anita said.

"Just call me Hawk. Get what you need for the night from the car. Everything else will be safe for now."

Anita took their overnight bags from the back seat and handed them to the deputy. "How large is Rockdale?" she asked when he had stowed their things in his patrol car.

"It's no Chattanooga, but we have several nice places to stay. I recommend the Rockdale Inn. It's not fancy, but it's near everything, including Hovis Batts' repair shop. And speaking of that, here he comes."

In short order, the affable garage man had hooked Anita's car to his wrecker and started back down the mountain to Rockdale.

"I hope you don't wreck your car too," said Juanita as the deputy eased down the road, keeping a safe distance from the wrecker.

He glanced at her in the rearview mirror and smiled. "That would put us in a pretty pickle, wouldn't it?"

Juanita giggled. "I never saw a pretty pickle. I don't like pickles."

"Neither do I," Hawk agreed. He continued to drive slowly, and several times during the drive to Rockdale, the radio crackled, followed by a spate of unintelligible words.

"I suppose you must be used to driving on ice," Anita said.

"Nobody ever gets used to ice, Ma'am. Best thing is not to drive on it at all, but this cruiser has special tires, and I know the danger spots. That curve that did you in is the worst one on the road."

"I was not expecting ice in Alabama," Anita said.

Hawk seemed amused. "Obviously, south Texas is a lot different from northeastern Alabama."

"How do you know where we live?" asked Juanita.

"I don't, but your car is licensed in San Antonio, Texas, and it isn't stolen."

Anita considered his words. "You must have called the tag number in on your radio."

"Yes, Ma'am. Don't take it personal, though. That's routine when a traffic call involves an unknown subject."

An unknown subject. As far as Rockdale, Alabama knew, Anita was completely unknown.

She found that thought comforting.

four

The moment Hawk Henson stepped from his patrol car, he knew the petite brunette standing beside her wrecked car wasn't a local. Her first words combined with her appearance to place her into a broad frame: *Hispanic.* Hawk Henson had been stationed at Fort Hood long enough to recognize the ethnic source of the young woman's dark hair and eyes and clear olive skin.

He was not surprised when he heard her last name. Sanchez was a common Mexican name, both in Texas and, for several years now, on nearby Sand Mountain in Alabama. The majority of those Mexicans were males who worked hard in niche jobs, kept to themselves, and sent most of their pay back to their families in Mexico. However, he was almost certain that this Anita Sanchez had no connection with them. She had an air of refinement, and the formal way she spoke English without using contractions suggested she had studied the language, rather than learning it by ear after coming to the United States.

The little girl looked just like her mother and had the same lilt to her voice. They were different, all right, and Hawk had no trouble determining he would do all he could to help this intriguing young woman and her soft-eyed daughter.

❧

"When are we going to get there?" Juanita asked when they had been in the patrol car for a short while.

"Look, Sweetie. The sign says 'Welcome to Rockdale,'." Anita said. Soon, they crossed a bridge, and Anita realized the mountain's trees and rocks had been replaced by houses and businesses, and rain had replaced the sleet. The roads in the valley were wet but apparently had not yet iced over.

"Here we are in Rockdale, Alabama," Hawk Henson

announced. "That big building yonder is the Rock County courthouse." He turned left and slowed down in front of Hovis Batts' Garage. "There's the wrecker. Hovis will take your car around to the back lot for the night. The Rockdale Inn is right down the street. I can take you to the inn and bring the rest of your luggage over later."

"I suppose we should not leave anything in the car." Anita had not thought that far ahead, but she was glad to have someone else helping her to make decisions for a change. Even before Juan went to prison, Anita had borne most of the responsibility for their household.

"Yes, Ma'am. Most of the folks around here aren't likely to steal, but it's not good to put temptation in their path."

Hawk Henson slowed to a careful stop up in front of the Rockdale Inn and removed their overnight bags from his patrol car. "Watch out. Those stone steps are probably getting slick."

"They just look wet," Anita said, but her first step convinced her he was right.

"You can't see glare ice. We get that kind of black ice around here a lot, and it's dangerous to drive or walk on, either one. Here, I'll help you."

The deputy steadied Anita's arm with his until she reached the top step, then he went back and carried Juanita and her huggy doll up the steps and into the inn. The lobby was deserted, but when Hawk rang the bell on the counter, a plump woman wrapped in a purple sweater emerged from a door marked "Office." She glanced from Anita and Juanita to Hawk Henson, obviously trying to make some connection.

"Hello, Deputy. What can I do for you?"

"Evening, Mrs. Tanner. These folks had some car trouble on their way down the mountain, and they need a place to stay."

"For how long?"

"Until my car is fixed," Anita said.

Mrs. Tanner glanced at the deputy. "When do you reckon that'll be?"

"We don't know yet. Hovis Batts just towed it in, but from the looks of it, it could take awhile."

Mrs. Tanner pointed to the rates posted on a sheet under the glass countertop. "You can pay by the day or week. If you give me a charge card, we can work out the details when you know more."

Anita felt a stir of uneasiness. "I do not have a charge card."

The deputy frowned. "I hope you don't carry a wad of money around."

"No. I have traveler's checks."

Mrs. Tanner's grin showed a gold tooth Anita hadn't previously noticed. "That's good as cash any day of the week in my book. Let's get you registered and into a room."

Instead of the kind of single registration card Anita had been filling out at motels along the way, the Rockdale Inn used a bulky guest register ledger. While she filled in the necessary information, Hawk Henson took the luggage to room 115, at the rear of the ground floor. He returned and gave Anita the key but did not leave.

"You can get breakfast here, but you'll have to go somewhere else for your other meals. Statum's Restaurant has good food and it's close, but the sidewalks will be getting slick. I'll clock out and come back and take you to the restaurant."

Anita hardly knew how to respond to the deputy's offer, which sounded almost like an order. Perhaps Hawk Henson was merely doing his duty as a deputy sheriff, but she detected at least a glimmer of personal interest.

"Dora and I are hungry, Mama," Juanita said.

Anita noticed the fatigue in her daughter's voice and sighed. "Thank you, but we don't want to put you out. We can take a taxi to the restaurant."

Both Hawk Henson and Mrs. Tanner, who had been listening to their conversation, laughed. "Honey, there's one taxi cab in this whole town, and I guarantee it won't be running in this kind of weather," Mrs. Tanner said. "You'd better take the deputy up on his offer before he changes his mind."

"All right," Anita said.

The deputy turned to Mrs. Tanner. "I'll bring some rock salt for those steps. Somebody could break a leg out there tonight."

"I didn't know it was getting that cold," Mrs. Tanner said.

Anita and Juanita started down the hall, and Hawk called after them, "I'll be back in fifteen minutes."

Anita turned and waved. "We will be ready."

❧

Statum's Family Restaurant, usually crowded by five-thirty on a weekday evening, held only a handful of diners when Hawk Henson led Anita and Juanita to a booth near the back, beyond the cold, plate glass windows.

The worsening weather was the universal topic of conversation among the few patrons. The waitress who came to take their order asked Hawk what he knew about road conditions.

"Hi, Rita. The roads are bad and getting worse on Lookout Mountain. It's warmer in the valley, but I suspect we'll get some ice here tonight too."

Anita saw that the attractive, young, red-haired waitress seemed to be trying hard not to stare at her and wondered if the deputy noticed. She was glad he did not feel he had to introduce them, but from the curiosity in his own glance, Hawk Henson inevitably would raise questions. Although long accustomed to evading men who wanted to know her better, Anita braced herself for the encounter.

"What can I get you this evening?" Rita asked.

"I'll have the blue plate special," Hawk said. "It's usually good," he added to Anita.

"All right, I will take that too, with water to drink. Do you have a child's plate?"

The waitress pointed to the bottom of the menu. "Chicken fingers or a small hamburger with fries and applesauce."

"She will have the chicken, but leave off the fries and bring her a glass of milk."

Juanita looked distressed. "I don't want to eat *fingers.*"

"You will not be, Sweetie. It is the same as chicken planks. You like those."

The waitress looked at Hawk. "Will this be on separate checks?"

"Yes," Anita said quickly. "I will pay for ours."

Rita nodded and tucked the order pad into her apron pocket. "I'll be right back with your drinks."

"So you were on your way to Chattanooga," Hawk said as if resuming a previous conversation. "Business or pleasure?"

That is none of your concern. Anita hesitated to say so, however; after all, the deputy had rescued them from the storm and been nothing but kind since. She could be polite, at least.

"Neither. Chattanooga seemed to be a good place to stop for the night."

"We're going to Ginny," Juanita said.

Hawk raised his dark eyebrows in the gesture of inquiry she'd noticed before. "Ginny? Is that in Tennessee?"

"She means Virginia," Anita said reluctantly.

"You still have a long way to travel, then."

Anita nodded but said nothing. From experience, she had learned not to volunteer information.

The waitress brought their drinks, and Hawk immediately took a sip of his steaming hot coffee. Rita hadn't furnished any creamer; apparently she knew Hawk took his coffee black.

"You ought to have coffee. It'll warm you up in a hurry," he said. "Ice water only makes you feel colder."

"I am quite comfortable," Anita said. She could not tell him why she always ordered water. In addition to coffee's extra cost, no brew in the States had ever tasted as good as the coffee she remembered in her native Colombia.

Hawk glanced at the thin gold band on Anita's left hand. "I suppose your husband couldn't make the trip with you?"

"No," Anita replied, truthfully enough. She felt no sentimental attachment to Juan Sanchez's wedding ring, but she continued to wear it. She didn't want anyone to think Juanita's mother hadn't been married. The band also protected Anita from men who might think any single woman was fair game.

Juanita set her glass of milk on the table. "Mama doesn't have a—" She stopped when she saw Anita's warning glance.

Never tell strangers anything personal. Anita had repeated the warning for many years, and Juanita seldom forgot. Obviously, her daughter already considered the deputy to be their friend—and that could be dangerous.

Tom Statum, the restaurant's owner, emerged from his office and came over to greet Hawk. "Don't tell me Sheriff Trimble's got you working the second shift now."

"No, Sir. I've clocked out for the night."

Tom Statum looked at Anita and Juanita, then back to Hawk. "Who do you have here? I don't remember seeing these young ladies in here before."

"This is Anita and her daughter, Juanita, and Juanita's daughter, Dora. Their car had a little problem with ice on the road into town this afternoon."

"I hear it's bad from here to Lookout Mountain," Tom said. "I'm thinking of closing early, before it gets any worse here."

"That might not be a bad idea. I checked with Emergency Response about thirty minutes ago. They don't expect much trouble here in town, but the power company trucks are ready to go if they're needed."

"If it gets much colder, they will be." Tom moved away from the booth as the waitress approached with a laden tray. "Here comes your food. I'll let you folks eat in peace." He nodded to Anita and Juanita. "Nice to meet you ladies," he added.

Had Tom Statum noticed the deputy had not mentioned their last name? Anita was almost certain Hawk had not forgotten it, but whatever his reasons, she was glad for the omission. It made her feel safe to be anonymous, at least for the present.

The waitress dealt out their plates and put extra napkins on the table. "Holler if you need anything else."

Juanita put her huggy doll's soft arms together and nudged Anita. "Look, Mama. Dora wants to say the blessing."

Hawk's eyebrows rose, but he made no comment.

"Fine," Anita said. Without looking at Hawk, she laid her right hand over Juanita's and bowed her head.

"Thank You, God, for everything. Bless our food. Amen."

"Dora, that was a very nice table grace," Hawk said.

"It was a *blessing*," Juanita corrected.

"That is the same thing, Sweetie," Anita said.

Hawk smiled. He was obviously comfortable around Juanita, and he seemed to enjoy her insistence on praying in the restaurant. Anita busied herself, helping Juanita with her food and giving her a portion of the vegetables from her own blue plate special.

As they ate, Hawk talked about the usual winter weather in this part of Alabama. "How do you like the food?" he asked when he exhausted that topic.

"It is very good."

"I see Miss Juanita isn't eating much," Hawk said.

"She is tired. This has been a long day."

"Travel isn't easy for little kids," Hawk said, although Anita doubted he had any firsthand knowledge.

When the waitress returned to refill Hawk's coffee mug, both refused her invitation to try a dessert.

"No, thanks, Rita. I'll take the check now," Hawk said.

Anita noticed the waitress went out of her way to hand her bill to her directly, as if afraid the deputy might try to take it if she left it on the table. It was obvious to Anita that Rita regarded Hawk as more than a regular patron of Statum's Restaurant, but the deputy seemed blissfully ignorant of the waitress's interest.

"Y'all take care tonight," Rita said. The words were plural, but addressed directly to Hawk.

"You too. Tom said he'd close early. You should go home and stay there."

Rita smiled. "I won't be having any late dates tonight, that's for sure."

Anita reached the cash register first. When she opened her billfold, she had the distinct impression that Hawk Henson might be looking over her shoulder at her driver's license.

The deputy seems to be trying to figure me out, Anita thought, almost too tired to care.

"The sleet seems to have stopped," Hawk observed when they left the restaurant.

Anita wrapped her cloth coat around her and shivered. "The air seems much colder."

"So it does. Let's get your luggage before the weather turns worse."

"Is he still here?" Anita asked when Hawk stopped at Hovis Batts' Garage. A single overhead light burned in the office, but both garage bay doors were closed.

"Hovis is always here. He lives in an apartment upstairs."

Hawk called the garage man on his cell phone, and a few seconds later, the outside floodlights came on and Hovis Batts opened the gate to the back lot.

"Stay in the warm car, Sweetie. We will be back in a minute," Anita directed. Juanita was already curled up like a kitten, so nearly asleep she barely nodded.

"Here it is," Hovis said unnecessarily. Anita's car had been removed from the wrecker, and, in the glare of the floodlights, it looked even worse than she remembered.

Anita dreaded hearing his answer, but she had to ask the question. "How much will it cost to fix?"

Hovis stroked his chin and cocked his head to one side. "Hard to say before I can get it inside the garage for a better look. Offhand, I'd say you're looking at anywhere from a couple hundred to a couple thousand dollars."

Anita's heart sank. His words were not unexpected, but she did not understand the dollar spread.

"What's the bottom line?" Hawk asked.

Hovis shrugged. "If all the lady wants is to get back on the road, it could cost as little as the price of a new headlight assembly and tire. I doubt anything major's messed up under the hood, but I won't know until get a better look. Repairing the body damage would cost a lot more." Hovis looked to Anita. "Do you have insurance?"

"Just liability."

"I don't reckon the guardrail will sue you for running into it," Hovis said.

Hawk ignored the garage man's attempt at humor. "Open the trunk. I'll get the rest of their luggage out of your way."

Anita had filled every usable inch of the automobile's spacious trunk. Hawk's eyebrows lifted in surprise when he saw all the suitcases, cardboard boxes, and plastic bags to be removed.

"My patrol car won't hold all of this. I'll take what I can now and come back for the rest of it."

"I am sorry to be so much trouble," Anita said.

"You're not. It's all in a day's work."

"I never seen a trunk packed with so much stuff," Hovis commented. "Looks like you're moving."

Anita made no comment and avoided looking at Hawk, who must have reached a similar conclusion. When the deputy found the metal lockbox, Anita could almost see the suspicion in his eyes.

There are no drugs inside, she wanted to say, but denying an unspoken charge might only make her appear guilty.

He gave Anita the box. "You'd better take this."

"My traveler's checks are in it," she said.

Hawk's eyebrows raised again, and Anita wondered if he believed her. "Looks like you'll be needing them."

And then some.

Forty-five minutes later, Hawk had finished transferring everything from the car to room 115 at the Rockdale Inn. Mrs. Tanner was nowhere in sight, for which Anita was thankful.

"Thank you," she said when the deputy piled the last of the luggage into the room. "I do not know what we would have done without your help."

Hawk spoke as if reading from a cue card. "I'm glad I could be of service, Ma'am."

Are you really?

Even as Anita locked the door behind the deputy, she had the distinct impression she would see him again.

Anita wrestled her sleeping daughter into her nightclothes and tucked her into one of the room's two double beds, then she knelt to pray.

As bone-tired and half asleep as she was, Anita would not rest until she had thanked God for keeping them safe and delivering them into what appeared to be good hands, then she concluded with her perennial plea for guidance.

Continue to be with us, Lord, and help me to know what I should do.

⁂

A few blocks away, Hawk Henson let himself into his rented duplex, chosen for its proximity to the courthouse. Removing only his shoes, he stretched out on the bed. The threat of bad weather had lessened, but if an emergency arose, he wouldn't have to waste time getting dressed to respond.

Hawk pillowed his hands under his head and peered into the darkness. His bedroom wall became a screen for the film produced by his mind, a replay of the hours he'd spent in the company of Anita Sanchez and her daughter.

Hawk had never been attracted to anyone he met in the line of duty, but then he'd never run across anyone like Anita Sanchez. Despite her beauty, she'd made no attempt to flirt with him. She seemed independent yet vulnerable, and Hawk found himself wanting to put his arms around her and assure her he would take care of her. Although his law enforcement experience strongly suggested she probably had something to hide, Hawk's instincts made him doubt she could be guilty of any sort of criminal behavior.

Given the damage to her car, she would likely be around for awhile. One way or another, Hawk Henson determined he would find out more about Anita Sanchez.

five

"Look, Mama, the sun's shining."

Anita struggled awake and opened the covers to let her daughter crawl into bed beside her. "So it is. Did you and Dora sleep well?"

Juanita nodded and kissed her huggy doll. "Dora had a bad dream, but then she went right back to sleep. Now she's hungry."

Anita glanced at her wristwatch and was surprised to see it was almost eight o'clock. "Get dressed, Sweetie. After breakfast, we will come back and have our baths."

Mrs. Tanner sat in the lobby, drinking coffee and watching a television news channel. She pointed toward the adjacent breakfast room. "Help yourselves."

"What is the weather forecast?" Anita asked.

"Clearing and warmer. Even Lookout Mountain should be thawed out soon."

"That is good news," Anita said, thinking it would be even better if she could get into her car and drive away.

Surveying the Rockdale Inn's array of dry cereal, milk, juice, coffee, and cinnamon rolls, Anita realized Dora was not the only hungry one.

After she filled their plates, Anita sat at one of the small tables and held hands with Juanita while she thanked God for the food. When she raised her head and saw Mrs. Tanner watching, Anita did not look away. Recalling the way the people in the restaurant had regarded them, Anita decided staring at strangers must be a major source of entertainment in Rockdale.

"I hope you have a nice day," Mrs. Tanner said when Anita and Juanita started back to their room.

"It is good to see the sun again, at least." Anita hesitated, then decided she should tell Mrs. Tanner about the extra luggage in the room. "Deputy Henson thought I should not leave anything in my car, and last night he helped me bring the rest of our things to my room. I thought you should know in case the maid might say something."

Mrs. Tanner looked interested. "The maid doesn't work nights. If anyone saw you and the deputy going into your room, it wasn't Millie."

"I did not mean that," Anita said quickly. "It is hard to move around the room for all the luggage. We have no need for daily room service, anyway."

Mrs. Tanner shrugged. "Whatever you say. Just let me know when you find out how long you'll be here." *And the sooner you leave, the better I will like it,* Anita thought her tone suggested. More than once, in ways both subtle and open, landlords had let her know "her kind" were unwelcome. While she had long since steeled herself to ignore such slights, they still hurt.

Anita returned to the room and tried to view their things as the innkeeper might. By volunteering unnecessary information, she had practically insured that Mrs. Tanner would snoop around the room as soon as they left. She didn't think the woman would take anything, but that would not stop her from drawing unwelcome or inaccurate conclusions.

Anita left the bathroom door open while Juanita played in the tub. She made up both beds, then got down on her hands and knees to chain the lockbox to her bed frame. Satisfied it was hidden by the dust ruffle, she replaced the box's key on the gold necklace around her neck.

Having done all she could to protect their possessions, Anita said a silent prayer, asking God to be with her and Juanita through whatever the day might bring.

❧

"Where are we going, Mama?" Juanita asked when they left the Rockdale Inn about an hour later.

"To the garage to see about the car."

The midmorning air was brisk but not uncomfortably cold. Anita turned her face up to the sun, enjoying the welcome warmth. With Juanita's hand in hers, they walked past a variety of buildings in the direction of Hovis Batts' Garage.

Adjacent to the Rockdale Inn parking lot, an old frame house had been converted to a law office. On the other side was a vacant brick store with a For Sale sign in one the large front windows. Then came a dry cleaning business, a parking lot, and another vintage frame house now used as a boutique. After crossing a side street, they came to a combination gas station and convenience store, another parking lot, and a hardware store. Anita walked slowly, partly so as not to tire Juanita, but also so she could take everything in. Anita had never lived in a small town, and she was curious about this place in which they had found shelter from the ice storm.

"Are we there yet?" Juanita asked after they crossed yet another side street.

"Almost, Sweetie."

The garage had not seemed so far when they had ridden to the inn from it the night before, and Juanita was not the only one glad to see the Batts Garage sign halfway down the next block.

Hovis Batts sat at a cluttered rolltop desk in his office, entering figures into a calculator. When Anita entered, he stood to greet her and Juanita. "'Morning, Ma'am. Hello there, little lady."

"Have you looked at my car yet?" Anita asked.

"Did that first thing, knowing you was anxious to get back on the road. Would your daughter like to go to the customer lounge? Little ones usually like watching the tropical fish swim around the aquarium."

Juanita looked to her mother for permission, and Anita nodded.

"How bad is it?" Anita asked after Juanita left.

"The good news is everything under the hood looks okay, and you can drive it just fine without fixing the body damage." He paused.

"What is the bad news?"

"Not as bad as it could be, but probably not as good as you'd like. You already know you need a new tire and headlight. The A-frame suspension, front shocks, and part of the headlight housing all need to be replaced. I checked around, and nobody local has all the parts on hand."

"Can you order them?"

"Sure, but it'll take awhile to get here, and you'll need to pay up-front before I order anything."

"How much?"

"I was just figuring all that up. A new headlight assembly runs about two fifty, but you might be able to get one from a junkyard. Add the shocks and new tire and the labor—this is just a rough estimate, but I'd say you're looking at around twenty-five hundred dollars."

Anita had braced herself for bad news, but this figure was worse than her expectations. She knew to the penny how much money she had. When she left Texas, Anita figured she would already have found a job in Virginia before her savings ran out. Wrecking her car had not been part of her plans.

"I cannot pay that much all at once," she said.

"You can use plastic. I take all the major credit cards."

Anita shook her head. "I do not have a charge card."

The garage man looked surprised. "These days, I thought everybody had at least two or three. Maybe you could ask somebody to wire you money? I used to send my boy cash that way all the time."

I have no one to ask. That was a truth Anita did not care to reveal.

"How much money will you need to order the parts?"

"Five hundred down would do it."

"How much is the towing charge?"

Hovis Batts seemed embarrassed. "You don't have to worry about that. Deputy Henson's already been in this morning and taken care of it."

It was Anita's turn to be embarrassed. "He has?"

"Yes. He said to tell you he's on duty today if you need anything."

Anita spoke as much to herself as to Hovis Batts. "I suppose I should thank him. Do you know where I can find the deputy?"

"The sheriff's department works out of the courthouse. He'll be there unless he's out on a call."

"I remember seeing the courthouse yesterday. It is back that way, is it not?"

Hovis Batts jerked his thumb in the general direction of the square. "Two blocks down and two to the left—you can't miss it. About that up-front money—the sooner I get it, the quicker I can order the parts."

"Will you take traveler's checks?"

"No, but you pass the Rock County Bank on the way to the courthouse. They can cash them for you there, for sure."

Anita called to Juanita. "Come on, Sweetie. Time to go."

"Is the car fixed?"

"Not yet, but Mr. Batts is working on it."

"Can I come back and see your fishes again?" Juanita asked him.

"Any time." Hovis Batts looked at Anita. "Whenever I get uptight about things, I go in there and look at those fish. Calms me down every time."

"Maybe I should try it myself," Anita said.

Yet, as they walked to the courthouse, Anita realized she did not feel as tense as she probably could given the circumstances. She had asked God to help them and guide her, and she believed He would. The sun was shining, and she and Juanita had found at least one friend in Rockdale.

For these blessings, Lord, accept my thanks.

&

The sheriff's department occupied cramped quarters on the ground floor of Rock County's aging courthouse. Signs in front of a half-dozen parking spaces around the building proclaimed they were reserved for the official vehicles of the sheriff and his deputies. VIOLATORS WILL BE FINED. Rock County Sheriff's Department cruisers occupied three of the places, leaving the others vacant.

"Look, Mama, there's Deppy Hawk's car," Juanita exclaimed when she saw the cruisers.

"Deputy," Anita corrected automatically. "All the patrol cars look alike. His might not be there."

"The dep'ty is nice. I hope we get to see him again."

So do I. "We can go inside and see if he is here," Anita said.

Only a few steps into the courthouse Anita saw heavy black lettering on a frosted door:

ROCK COUNTY SHERIFF'S OFFICE
LESTER TRIMBLE, SHERIFF

Anita opened the door and went inside. At one of the four desks in the room, a balding deputy sat with his back to her, talking on the telephone; the other desks were empty. A woman in a uniform similar to Hawk Henson's sat at a desk, surrounded by a switchboard and several computers. SALLY ROGERS, DISPATCHER, according to her nameplate.

She looked up when Anita approached the desk. "Can I help you?"

"I would like to see Deputy Henson."

"He's out on a call, but Sheriff Trimble's here."

"When do you expect the deputy to return?"

The dispatcher glanced at a notebook on her desk. "That's hard to say, Ma'am. He could be back soon, if you care to wait."

Anita looked around. The only available seating, a hard wooden bench, did not look at all inviting, but they were already here, and she still wanted to thank Hawk Henson. "Come on, Sweetie. We can sit over there and rest a minute."

The balding deputy was still talking on the telephone. From where they sat, Anita couldn't see the nameplates on the other desks, but she noticed all but one of the desks was strewn with papers and empty food containers. Anita felt almost certain Hawk Henson's work space would be the neat and orderly one.

"Look at the big fishie, Mama." Juanita pointed to a mounted fish on the wall behind the desks.

A trophy fish, body curved, had been captured by the taxidermist in the act of jumping out of the water.

Poor thing. "I have never seen a fish like that," Anita said aloud.

Other examples of a hunter's attempt to preserve his kill lined the walls. Anita recognized a many-antlered buck deer, then shuddered along with her daughter at the hideous head beside it. She had never seen one alive, but from its curved tusks and pig-like face, Anita guessed the trophy to be a wild boar.

The dispatcher saw them looking at the heads and spoke with pride. "All those came from right around here in Rock County."

Anita wondered if Hawk Henson had killed them and tried to think of a tactful way to ask. "Someone who works here must be a good hunter," she said.

The dispatcher nodded. "Most every man in the county likes to hunt and fish. See that boar's head over there?"

How can we miss it? Anita wanted to say but simply nodded.

"A ten-year-old boy bagged that one bow-hunting."

Juanita's eyes widened. "Like an Indian's bow and arrow?"

"No, he used a crossbow."

The dispatcher might have told the stories of the other trophies, but the door to the sheriff's private office opened, and a large, mostly bald, middle-aged man came out. He stopped and stared at Anita.

"Who do we have here?"

"The dispatcher said we could wait for Deputy Henson."

The sheriff's eyes narrowed in appraisal. "What business do you have with him?"

"I want to thank him for his kindness to me and my daughter."

"And what might that be?"

"My car wrecked on the road into town yesterday. The deputy came to our rescue."

The sheriff's blue eyes gleamed. "So you're the one. What were you thinking about, driving in that kind of weather? My deputy could have lost his patrol car up there on that mountain."

The sheriff's tirade shook Anita, but she was determined not to show her discomfort. "I assure you I did not have the accident on purpose, Sir. I was trying to find a place to spend the night, and Rockdale was the closest town."

"Where are you from? You don't sound American."

Had the sheriff smiled or said the words lightly, Anita could have dealt with them in the same way. Yet however much his rudeness and implied prejudice stung, Anita knew she could not afford to lose her temper.

"I have lived in Texas for many years." *The last time I looked at the map, it was still in America.*

He spoke under his breath, but Anita still heard his words. "Wetback, huh. Might have known it."

Anita was still biting her tongue when Sally Rogers called to the sheriff, and he turned away.

"Sheriff Trimble? Your wife's on line one."

"I'll take it in my office."

The sheriff glared at Anita once more, then closed his office door with a great deal more force than necessary.

"Mama, why is that man so mad?"

"Some people are just naturally angry. We must pray for them and not become angry ourselves."

Juanita thought about her mother's words for a moment. "That's hard to do."

"I know, Sweetie. That is where the praying part comes in."

"Dora doesn't want to stay here," Juanita said.

Neither do I. Anita still intended to thank Hawk Henson, but she had worn out her welcome with Sheriff Trimble, and she wanted to hear no more from his sharp tongue.

"We can see the deputy later," Anita said.

"You decided not to wait?" Sally Rogers asked when they stood to leave. Anita thought she detected a gleam of sympathy in the woman's eye and knew she must have heard the sheriff's comments.

"We need to be going," Anita said.

"I'll tell Hawk you came by, Mrs.——?"

"He will know," Anita said.

And he knows where to find me.

six

Anita returned to the Rockdale Inn to retrieve her cache of
traveler's checks. She was about to leave the lobby to go to the
bank when a Rock County Sheriff's Department cruiser
stopped in front of the inn.

"Look, Mama, it's the dep'ty," Juanita said.

"So it is." Anita glanced at the empty reception desk, glad
Mrs. Tanner was elsewhere at the moment.

Hawk Henson hurried up the steps, head down, and Anita
noted his surprise when he opened the door and saw her and
Juanita standing in the lobby, wearing their coats.

"Looks like I caught you just in time," he said. "Sorry I
missed you earlier. Sally said you came by the office. Is something wrong?"

"No. Mr. Batts told me you took care of the towing bill. It
was kind of you to do so, but I intend to pay you back."

Hawk's lips compressed, and Anita saw her words dis-
pleased him. "I wanted to do it. I expected nothing in return,
so please say no more about it."

Anita had been brought up to accept gifts graciously, but it
had been such a long time since anyone had given her anything, she was out of practice. "In that case, Juanita and I
thank you."

Juanita held out her huggy doll. "Dora thanks you too."

Hawk took one of the huggy doll's limp hands in his and
shook it. "I am glad to see Dora has good manners." He
looked back at Anita. "Can I give you ladies a lift?"

"I want to cash some traveler's checks. The bank is close
enough for us to walk there."

"It's also less than a block from the sheriff's office, which is where I'm heading. You might as well ride while you have the chance."

"Dora and I like your car, Dep'ty Hawk," Juanita said.

"I hope you are not breaking any rules," Anita said when she saw several passersby gaping at the sight of Deputy Henson assisting his unusual passengers into the patrol car.

"Not one," Hawk said, but Anita doubted Sheriff Trimble would agree. "Hovis Batts tells me it might take awhile to get your car fixed," Hawk said when they passed the garage.

And a lot of money. Although Hawk did not say so, Anita realized the garage owner had no doubt shared that news as well.

"He has to order some parts," she said.

"I know. It would save you a chunk of money if we can find a headlight assembly on a junked car, though."

We? Anita swallowed hard. "I would not know how to find a junked automobile."

"I know enough for both of us. I'm off tomorrow, and I have nothing better to do. I'll make a few calls first, then check out likely salvage yards. There are several around Ft. Payne and more up on Sand Mountain."

I should not let this man put me any further in debt to him. Even so, Anita pushed the thought aside. "If you are willing to do that, I would be grateful."

Hawk smiled, and once more Anita noticed how white his teeth were. "I'll tell Hovis to hold up on ordering that part."

"I can tell him myself, since I have to take the money to him when I get the checks cashed," Anita said.

"Fine." Hawk pulled into the bank parking lot and turned off the ignition. "I'll come in with you and then take you to the garage."

Anita raised her eyebrows. "Are the streets here that unsafe?"

"No, but it doesn't pay to take unnecessary chances." Hawk looked as if he might say more had Juanita not been present.

The few people in the bank lobby looked up when they

entered, and Anita guessed they wondered what business one of their deputy sheriffs had with the unfamiliar woman and child with him. Hawk walked over to the far teller window, where a dark-haired, dark-eyed teller greeted him warmly. DEBORAH HAWK, her nameplate said.

"Hi there, Chief. What can I do for you this morning?"

"Nothing for me, Princess. But this lady wants to cash some traveler's checks."

The teller looked at Anita, then back at Hawk. "I don't reckon I need to ask if she has an account with us."

"Doesn't matter," Hawk said. "Traveler's checks are just as good as cash, aren't they?"

The teller ignored Hawk to look at Anita. "I'll have to see some ID."

Anita opened her purse and handed over her driver's license. "Will this do?"

"Texas, huh? By way of the Rio Grande?"

"That's none of your business." Hawk made his words a mild reprimand, and the teller surprised Anita by sticking out her tongue at him.

Behind her, Anita heard Juanita's quick intake of breath and was grateful her daughter did not blurt out what she probably thought. *How come that lady stuck out her tongue at Dep'ty Hawk? Doesn't she know that's not nice?*

"Just give her the money," Hawk said.

"I will, but she has to sign the checks in my presence first. How many checks do you want to cash, Ms. Sanchez?"

"Five, each for one hundred dollars."

"How do you want the money?"

"Give her a cashier's check made out to Hovis Batts," Hawk said before Anita could reply.

"What kind of scam you got going with Hovis?" the teller asked, her tone making it clear she was teasing.

"The lady's car needs parts, and he's got to have up-front money before he'll order them. Oldest scam in the world."

"Car trouble takes a bundle of money, all right," the teller said. "That fender-bender I had two months ago cost me over three thousand dollars and ruined my insurance rating."

"It would help if you didn't drive like a maniac," Hawk said.

"That last accident wasn't my fault, and you know it. Those crazy Mexicans—"

"Never mind," Hawk interrupted. "Shouldn't you be making out the check?"

"Thanks for telling me how to do my job," Deborah Hawk said dryly. "The drill is I have to wait until all the traveler's checks are in my possession before I can legally negotiate them."

"Here is the last one." Anita pushed the signed checks toward the teller, who made a display of inspecting each before she put them inside her cash drawer and turned away to the check-writing machine.

"Debbie's my cousin," Hawk said as if answering a question Anita had not asked.

"Hawk is a family name?"

"Yes. My mother and Debbie's father were brother and sister, and we grew up together. She has a sharp tongue at times, but she's all right. Next time you come in here, she'll take good care of you."

"I hope I will not have to ask her to cash many more checks," Anita said.

"I suppose that depends on how long you intend to stay," Hawk said, almost making it a question.

"Or on how long my money lasts."

"Here you are, Ms. Sanchez. Hovis can cash this any time he likes without a waiting period."

Anita inclined her head. "Thank you."

"Thanks, Princess. Watch that lead foot, now."

"You watch out too, Chief."

Something about the way the teller looked at Anita suggested that she might be warning Hawk about her.

Do not take offense where none is intended, Anita reminded herself. She had first heard those words from her mother, and many times since leaving Colombia she had taken them to her heart as a talisman against the hurt of being considered "different."

When Anita handed Hovis Batts the cashier's check, she thought she detected a new respect in his eyes. "I'll get on ordering the parts right away."

"Hold off on the headlight assembly," Hawk said. "I'll try to find one locally."

"All right. When will you be able to look?"

"I'm off tomorrow. If nothing turns up, I'll let you know."

"How long will it take the parts to get here?" Anita asked.

"That's hard to say with New Year's coming up. I'd say it'll be at least four or five days."

Anita did some mental arithmetic and arrived at an inevitable conclusion—given that and the time it would take Hovis Batts to install the parts, it could be a long while before she could resume her journey.

The pager on Hawk's belt beeped, and he sighed. "It's back to the office for me."

"Can we go with you, Dep'ty Hawk?" asked Juanita.

"I'm afraid not. But I'll give you and your mama a ride back to the inn if she'll let me."

Anita shook her head. "No, thanks. We can walk from here. Thank you again for all your help."

"That's a nice young man," Hovis Batts said when Hawk left. "If he can find a headlight from a junker, it'll save you quite a bit of money."

"I hope he can," Anita said.

"Dora's hungry, Mama," Juanita said when they left the garage.

Anita glanced at her watch, surprised to see that the morning was nearly spent. Aware that each passing day would cost more of her savings, she decided to pick up sandwich makings at the convenience store near the garage.

"We can have a picnic in our room. Let us see what we can find to eat."

Anita was glad to discover this particular convenience store had a fairly extensive food section. "What kind of jelly do you want with your peanut butter?" she asked Juanita.

"*Dora* wants grapen."

"Grape, not grapen." Anita made the correction almost automatically. She picked up a loaf of bread and a flat of bottled water, then added a couple of apples to her basket. Seeing Juanita eyeing them with longing, she also took a box of animal crackers. Not exactly a feast, but enough to tide them over until supper—when, she supposed, they would eat in the only restaurant within walking distance of the Rockdale Inn.

The clerk looked up from her tabloid magazine when Anita placed her choices on the counter. "Will that be all?" she asked.

"Yes." Anita opened her purse, her hand on her billfold.

"We don't take checks—just cash or major credit cards," the clerk said, pointing to a large sign to that effect.

Why does she think I am going to give her a check? Anita quickly dismissed the sudden edge of irritation. "How much do I owe?" she asked instead.

The clerk said the sum slowly, took Anita's money without comment, failed to add the standard "Thank you and come back," and immediately returned to her reading.

"That lady wasn't very nice," Juanita observed when they left the store.

"She was reading something interesting, and we took her away from it," Anita said. Privately, however, she suspected the clerk had simply not liked their looks.

Neither had Hawk's cousin. Anita realized if Hawk had not gone into the bank with her, she might have had trouble getting her traveler's checks cashed. She was a stranger in town, true enough, but Anita felt there was more to it than that.

Why did so many people in Rockdale seem to mistrust her? She would ask Hawk Henson the next time she saw him.

❧

When Hawk returned to the office, Sally Rogers told him the sheriff wanted to see him.

"He had another round with Mrs. Trimble while you were gone, and he's not in a very good mood," she warned.

"Thanks for the heads up."

Hawk paused at the sheriff's office door, mentally bracing himself. Sheriff Trimble was unpleasant most of the time, but when he was in a really bad mood, sparks flew and his deputies tried to find some excuse to leave the office. Hawk knocked and announced himself, then was greeted with a roar from within.

"Come in, Henson."

The sheriff remained behind his desk as if to remind Hawk he was in charge. "I hear you've been messing around with that fool woman who wrecked her car during the ice storm. I don't want her and that kid of hers hanging around my office."

As he so often had to do in the sheriff's presence, Hawk recalled a familiar verse from Proverbs: *A soft answer turneth away wrath: but grievous words stir up anger.*

"Mrs. Sanchez and her daughter had an unfortunate accident. She came to thank us for helping them. I doubt if you'll see her around here again."

"*Sanchez.* If there's one thing this town don't need, it's a bunch of *Sanchezes* moving in. I don't want what happened on Sand Mountain and Ft. Payne repeated in Rock County. Those Mexicans come in illegally to begin with, and then the next thing you know, you've got three, four families living in one house, taking jobs away from decent people, carousing around, and causing all kinds of trouble."

Hawk ignored most of the sheriff's tirade, only part of which he knew to be true, but he could not let Anita go undefended. "Mrs. Sanchez is not an illegal Mexican immigrant. She and her daughter are American citizens, and they have just as much right to be here as anyone else."

"How do you know she's legal? Just because she batted her pretty brown eyes at you don't mean anything she told you is true."

Hawk hesitated, wondering how much he dared say to the sheriff. "Mrs. Sanchez didn't tell me she's a citizen. I found that out when I ran a routine check on her car tag. According to Texas records, she is a native of Colombia, South America."

"I wouldn't be surprised if she didn't come up here to run drugs. When's she leaving town?"

"I don't know, but her car is in pretty bad shape." Hawk paused, then decided to give the sheriff something to consider. "Rock County can't afford a discrimination lawsuit. If Mrs. Sanchez should decide to stay here, we don't have the authority to make her leave."

Sheriff Trimble scowled. "We don't have to ask her to stay either. Get it, Henson?"

"I think we understand each other," Hawk replied levelly. It was not the first time he and his boss had locked horns, and given each man's temperament, Hawk knew it would not be the last.

"Fine. Tell that woman to stay out of my department."

"Don't worry. After the way I suspect she was treated this morning, I doubt that will be a problem."

⁂

After lunch, Juanita yawned and announced that Dora wanted to take a nap. Anita tucked them both in and put the food away in the cooler she had retrieved from the car the night before.

Juanita fell asleep almost immediately, and Anita sat at the small table and opened her Bible. She needed time to think about everything that had happened that day and to consider what she should do next.

Virginia was still a long way off, and the chance she could find her former teacher was slim. In addition, she did not know how long it would be before her car was ready to drive—and by then, even more of her savings would be gone.

Anita had made a clean break from San Antonio, and she felt sure Bill Rankin could not track her. For her purposes, Alabama would serve as well as Virginia, and from what she had seen of Rockdale, it could also be a good place to bring up her child.

That is, if the people could get over the prejudice some of them seemed to harbor against her.

Anita bowed her head and prayed for guidance. She had felt the strong presence of the Lord on every step of her journey, even when she wrecked her car.

Send me a sign, Lord. Let me know what I should do.

seven

Although Anita half-expected Hawk Henson to call or come by, he had not done so by the time Juanita announced that Dora was getting hungry.

"Put on your coat, Sweetie. We will walk over to the place where we had supper last night."

"Will the dep'ty be there?"

"I doubt it," Anita replied.

However, they had no more than been seated when Hawk Henson entered Statum's Restaurant and immediately spotted them.

"Is this seat taken?" he asked Juanita, who giggled and obligingly scooted over to make room for him in the booth.

"You look different," Anita commented. Hawk had exchanged his uniform for a brown cardigan worn over a sports shirt with a buttoned-down collar, blue jeans, and hand-tooled cowboy boots.

"Better or worse?" he asked.

"Neither—just different."

The same red-haired waitress from the previous night came to take their order, but this time Hawk made it clear he would be paying.

"It seems I am always having to thank you for something new," Anita said when the waitress left.

"I can afford it," he said easily. "You'd be surprised how much a Rock County deputy sheriff pulls down these days."

"How hard is it to get work around here?" Anita found herself asking.

"It depends. What kind of work do you have in mind?"

Anita lowered her head. She had already said more than

she had intended, but she trusted Hawk to tell her the truth. "I am a nurse, but I could take a fast-food job if necessary—anything to make a little money."

Hawk's eyebrows lifted in surprise. "What about your husband? Can't he send you something?"

Anita glanced at Juanita, who seemed more interested in a little girl who had just come in with their parents than in her mother's conversation. "No," she said simply. "That is not an option."

"I see," said Hawk. "You're running away from him, right?"

"No," Anita said, then stopped before she made matters even worse.

"Look, Mama. That little girl has a huggy doll almost like Dora," Juanita said.

"So she does, Sweetie."

The children looked at each other, and when Juanita raised one of Dora's hands in a wave, the other huggy doll waved back.

"That's Jack and Cynthia Tait," Hawk said. "Jackie's about Juanita's age."

"I wish I could play with her," Juanita said wistfully.

"That could probably be arranged." Hawk slid out of the booth and went to the Taits' table.

Anita could not hear what he said, but in a moment the family came to the booth, and Hawk made the introductions.

"So you're at the Rockdale Inn?" Cynthia Tait asked Anita.

"For now, at least," Anita said.

"Jackie's getting restless, and with another week of Christmas vacation left, I'd be happy to have your little girl come over to play."

"I am sure Juanita would like that, but I have no way to get her there at the moment," Anita said.

Cynthia Tait waved her hand, displaying a number of rings on each finger. "I can come after her. How about ten o'clock tomorrow morning? I'll bring her back about two, if that's all right."

Juanita turned pleading eyes to her mother. "Puhlease, can I go, Mama?"

Anita smiled at her daughter's eagerness. "It is kind of you to ask, Mrs. Tait. Juanita and I thank you."

"Just call me Cynthia," the woman said.

"And I'm Jack," her husband added.

"That worked out well," Hawk said when the Taits returned to their table. "Juanita has a new friend, and her Mama can help me look for a headlight assembly tomorrow."

Anita started to protest, then thought better of it. *Why not go with Hawk?* It would give her a chance to tell him as much of her background as he needed to know.

Besides, Anita had come to enjoy his company.

❧

December 31.

Anita looked at the date on her calendar and thought about how much had happened in the last few weeks. Until Bill Rankin had come along, it had been a good year. Since then, just about everything that could go wrong, had. But tomorrow, another year would begin. Each day was a gift from God, another new chance to change her life.

Even now, on this last day of the old year, Anita had something to look forward to. A trip to a junkyard did not sound very thrilling, but if it saved any of her precious store of money, it would be well worth it.

Juanita was excited about playing with her new friend, and her eyes shone as she kissed her mother good-bye and went off with Cynthia Tait.

When her daughter left, Anita returned to their room to dress for her junkyard expedition. Hawk had told her to wear old clothes, but when she came into the lobby in the coveralls she kept in the car in case she had to change a tire, he seemed surprised. With her hair in a ponytail beneath a baseball cap, she knew she must look quite different from the young woman Hawk was accustomed to seeing.

"Will this do?" she asked.

"Sure, but I hardly knew you in that getup. You look like a teenaged boy ready to work on his hot rod."

Although Hawk smiled when he said it, Anita felt oddly embarrassed, as if she had broken some unwritten rule. "I can change—"

"No need for that—you look fine. Let's go."

"I must be back before Cynthia Tait brings Juanita home."

"Don't worry about that. If we're delayed, I can call Cynthia and ask her to keep Juanita there. Besides, a lot of places close early on New Year's Eve. We should be finished by noon. I brought a thermos of hot chocolate and a couple of sandwiches for lunch."

"I hope your vehicle has a heater," Anita said when she saw how much colder the air had become since the day before.

"It's a Jeep 4x4—and yes, it has a heater. I also keep a few blankets and extra jackets in back. The weather around Lookout Mountain can go from good to terrible with little warning."

Hawk opened the door for Anita, then walked around and started the engine.

"Where are we going?" Anita asked.

"To a junkyard in Georgia first."

"All the way to another state?"

"Tennessee, Alabama, and Georgia all come together not far from here," Hawk said. "If the first place doesn't work out, we'll try a salvage yard on Sand Mountain."

They had been climbing out of Rockdale for several minutes when Hawk slowed and pulled to the side of the road. He pointed to the dented guardrail that had stopped Anita's car. "Look familiar?"

Seeing the scene on a clear, sunny day, Anita shivered, realizing how easily her accident could have been much worse. "Without that guardrail, I would probably not be here now. God was with us."

Hawk nodded. "I agree."

He drove on, from time to time pointing out sites of interest along the way—strange rock formations, then an everlasting spring that gushed from the side of the mountain only to disappear into a supposedly bottomless pit a few feet farther on.

"The spring never runs dry, even in the worst drought," Hawk explained. "The Cherokee say it is a gift of God."

Hawk slowed, then turned into a narrow dirt lane guarded by a No Trespassing sign on the trunk of an oak tree. He pulled in beside a long-abandoned log structure.

"This is called a 'dog trot' cabin because dogs slept on the wide-open hall between the rooms. When I was a kid, I spent a lot of time here."

"It looks very—" Anita paused, searching for a word that would convey her meaning without insulting Hawk.

"Primitive?" Hawk supplied. "It was. No electricity, and the water comes from a spring. My great-grandfather built a better house down the road a ways, but I still like this place best."

"You do not still live up here?"

"No. We came down from the mountain when I was twelve, but the house is still back there. I check on it from time to time."

Anita imagined Hawk as a young boy growing up in what seemed to be a wilderness. "I think you would still like to live here."

Hawk nodded. "In a way, I would, but it's too far from town."

He pulled back onto the highway, and before they had gone much farther, Anita saw a flash of tan in the underbrush beside the road. She felt her body lunge forward as Hawk braked heavily, just seconds before a magnificent buck deer loped across the road, followed by a couple of does.

"Sorry for the sudden stop, but if we'd hit those deer, my Jeep would be in even worse shape than your car."

Seeing the deer, Anita was reminded of the trophies in the sheriff's office. "Do you hunt them?"

Hawk nodded. "Occasionally, but not for sport."

"So the buck's head in the sheriff's office is not yours?"

"No. My father taught me to respect all animals. It's part of my Cherokee heritage. God gave them to us, and He expects us to use them wisely. When I kill deer, I dress the meat and cure the hide."

"I suppose you did not catch the fish on the wall either."

Hawk laughed. "No. I eat my catch."

After they climbed out of the valley, Hawk turned onto the road that Anita knew led to Chattanooga, then turned onto another road. A few minutes later, he stopped at a dilapidated salvage yard in the middle of nowhere. PETE SCOTT—BEST JUNKERS IN GEORGIA, the crude, hand-lettered sign announced. A chained Doberman barked to announce their arrival, bringing the owner out of the shack that passed for his office.

"Howdy, Hawk. It's been awhile. Good to see you."

Hawk shook the man's hand and nodded toward Anita. "Pete, this lady needs a right headlight assembly for her Olds. You told me over the phone you have one."

"Yep, but that car come in some time ago, and it's pretty well buried out back."

"We'll find it."

Hawk took a sack of tools from the Jeep, and Anita followed him through the weed-choked lot. Hundreds of wrecked automobiles lay where they had been dumped, some little more than rusty hulks, others fairly new models. "How will you ever be able find anything in here?" she asked.

"By looking. You can help. Pete said the car was blue. Be careful of sharp edges," Hawk added when a jutting fender threatened to rip a hole in Anita's coveralls.

After fifteen minutes, she was ready to give up, but Hawk persisted. "I think I see the car. Stay where you are, and I'll check it out."

Hawk disappeared behind the yellow hulk of an ancient school bus, then emerged moments later, shaking his head. "I found the car, all right, but the right headlight's cracked."

"It cannot be used?"

Hawk shook his head. "No, but all is not lost. I have another prospect on Sand Mountain."

"Where is that?"

"On another ridge not far from here."

"You are very kind to go to all this trouble for me," Anita said after they pulled away from the junkyard.

"It's no trouble. I should thank you for giving me a good excuse to prowl junkyards again. It's been awhile since I allowed myself that pleasure."

"You call it pleasure? I would call it hard work."

"As a kid, I used to help my father rebuild wrecked cars."

"Was that his business?" Anita asked, immediately regretting she had asked such a personal question.

"One of them. Mostly, he ran a bush hog."

Anita had no idea what a bush hog was, but she refrained from asking. Something in his voice gave Anita the feeling Hawk's father was dead, and that he still grieved the loss. *As I do for my father and mother and family and always will.*

Anita shivered, and Hawk reached over to turn up the heater fan. "Warm enough now?" he asked after a few minutes, and she nodded.

After making several more turns onto narrow, winding back roads, Hawk reached US Highway 431, a busy four-lane route. "We're on top of Sand Mountain now," he announced. "We should find your headlight here."

A tall fence surrounded the salvage yard where Hawk stopped next. Once more, the owner greeted him like a long-lost friend, and again Anita followed Hawk through a tangle of auto bodies and parts. Eventually, they reached an Oldsmobile Anita thought could be the twin of hers, even to the paint color. The back of the car had been badly mangled ("Train hit it," the salvage owner told them), but the front was intact.

"This will do," Hawk announced, and for the next few minutes, Anita served as mechanic's assistant, handing him

the requested tools and helping him remove the headligh
assembly.

While Hawk took the part to his Jeep and stowed hi
tools, Anita paid the salvage man, grateful to find the cos
was only a fraction of what Hovis Batts had quoted for th
same new part.

"Now, for lunch," Hawk said when they were back in th
Jeep. "If you want more than a sandwich, we could stop a
one of the many restaurants along this road."

Anita glanced at her coveralls and shook her head. "I ar
not properly dressed to go to a restaurant. Your sandwiche
will be enough."

"You look better than half the people you'd see inside,
Hawk said, then let it go at that.

This part of Sand Mountain was built up, with one tow
seamlessly melding into another. Anita noticed the area ha
many small Mexican restaurants and *grocerias,* and most o
the other businesses had prominent *Se habla Español* signs.

"Why do so many places say they speak Spanish?"

"Because so many Mexican immigrants live here now. I
started as a trickle with migrant labor in the summers; then
new chicken processing plant opened. When word got aroun
they were hiring Mexican workers, more and more poured in.

"Do the local people accept them?"

"Some do, others don't. The Mexicans tend to keep t
themselves."

Hawk had not said, nor had Anita asked, but she sus
pected enough of these newcomers were illegal aliens t
make them all be viewed with suspicion. *Perhaps that is wh
so many people in Rockdale look at me in such a peculiar way—
they think I am one of these immigrants.*

"I am not from Mexico," Anita said aloud.

Hawk parked in a deserted roadside park and turned t
face her. "I already know that. But I don't believe you have
husband."

Anita felt her face warm. Hawk Henson had been extremely good to her—far better than any other man she had met in America. She did not want to lie to him, but she could not share the real reason she had left Texas with anyone.

Anita took a deep breath. "I will tell you about Juan Sanchez."

eight

Seeing the pain reflected in Anita's eyes, Hawk almost wished he hadn't said anything about her husband. *Juan*. Of course Juanita Sanchez must have been named for her father. Hawk wondered why he hadn't already guessed that himself.

Anita paused as if searching for the words to tell him about this phantom husband. Hawk opened the thermos and poured her a cup of hot chocolate. She looked at him with gratitude, then took a sip. She gripped the cup tightly, then spoke slowly, in a voice devoid of emotion.

"I married Juan Sanchez soon after I came to America. He had trouble finding work, and we moved around a lot. After he died, I moved to San Antonio. After Christmas, I decided to visit a teacher I knew when I lived in Colombia." Anita paused and took another sip of chocolate.

"You were on your way to Virginia to see this teacher when you had the accident?"

"Yes."

Hawk's heart twisted in sympathy at the sorrow in her eyes when she lifted her head. It was obvious Anita Sanchez didn't want to talk about her late husband, and Hawk resolved not to question her further about him. But the supposed friend in Virginia was another matter.

"Have you tried to contact this person since the accident?"

Anita shook her head. "No. I—I really do not know where she lives."

Hawk leaned back against the window and shook his head. "Let me get this straight. You took off from San Antonio with everything you own packed into your car without knowing where you were going?"

Anita looked him in the eye. "I know it must sound strange, but that was the way of it. I had to leave San Antonio."

"Too many memories?"

Anita nodded. "Yes. It was not a good place for us anymore. I planned to start over in Virginia, but nothing worked out as I expected."

Hawk barely resisted the impulse to reach out and comfort Anita her in her obvious distress. He would never take advantage of a grieving widow, but this woman obviously needed someone's help. Even if Anita Sanchez was still hiding something from him, as he suspected, Hawk couldn't turn away from her.

"You can start over anywhere. Let's talk about it while we have our lunch."

❧

By the time Hawk dropped Anita off at the Rockdale Inn, her head was spinning with the ideas he had proposed. He had spoken quietly, answering every objection she had raised with logic and gentle persuasion.

Not only did Hawk Henson believe Rockdale was an ideal place for Anita to make a new start, he knew people who could help her every step of the way.

Glad to have some time alone before Juanita returned from playing with Jackie Tait, Anita took off her junkyard garb and stepped into the shower. Her body felt tired, but Hawk's words had lifted her spirits. He had not insisted on knowing more about Juan Sanchez, for which Anita was grateful. Then when Hawk started talking about the possibility she might stay in Rockdale permanently, he had made it all sound so possible, so—Anita searched for the word—so *right*.

She had asked God for a sign, and she believed He might have given her one.

You can find peace in this valley, My child.

The words had not been spoken audibly, but Anita's heart heard them clearly.

Show me what You want me to do, dear Lord . I am Your servant.

&

When Hawk returned in the evening, he took them to a pizza restaurant, much to Juanita's delight. She loved pizza, but their budget seldom allowed it. The music was too loud for much conversation, but Juanita obviously was having a glorious time.

"I'm sorry we can't celebrate New Year's Eve properly, but I have to try to keep the drunks off the road tonight," Hawk said when they left the restaurant.

"Juanita and I could never stay awake until midnight, anyway," Anita said.

When they reached the inn, Hawk accompanied Anita and Juanita into the lobby. "I can stay a little while longer," he told Anita. "Can you get Juanita settled and come back? We need to talk."

When Hawk had left her at the inn earlier that day, Anita had promised to think about the possibility of establishing a new life in Rockdale, and she suspected he wanted an immediate answer.

Anita listened to her daughter's prayers and silently added one of her own. *Let me say what I should. Let my decision also be Your will.*

When Anita returned to the lobby, Mrs. Tanner was talking on the telephone behind the registration desk. Anita suspected as soon as that conversation ended, the innkeeper would probably try to overhear theirs.

"We can sit in the breakfast area," Anita suggested.

Hawk took a chair opposite her at one of the small tables and leaned forward. "What about it? Are you ready to stay in Rockdale?"

"I cannot make that decision now—it is too soon. I have always prayed to know God's will for my life. I have to trust Him to show me if I should stay."

"Show you how?"

"It is hard to say. Ever since I left Texas, I had the feeling God was guiding us. If He means me to stay here, I believe I will know if I can find a job and a place to live."

"I can help you with both."

"I appreciate all you have done for us, but I must stand on my own two feet."

Hawk frowned. "If you think I expect anything in return for helping you—"

"No, no, it is not that. I do not wish to become dependent on anyone. I—I think it would be better if you did not do so much for me."

Hawk's lips compressed. "Speak for yourself, Anita."

It was the first time Hawk had addressed her by her first name when they were alone, and somehow he managed to make it a verbal caress. Anita made herself look directly at him and hoped he would not notice how much his simple use of her first name had affected her.

"I do speak for myself—and for my daughter."

Hawk sighed and reached into his shirt pocket for a small notebook. He wrote a couple of names, then removed the page and offered it to her. When their hands brushed, Anita knew she was right to insist on keeping her distance from Hawk Henson. The attraction she had felt for this man from the first had steadily grown. His touch kindled sparks that traveled all the way from Anita's hand to her heart. As much as she enjoyed the sensation, Anita knew she could not afford to have it repeated. She had trusted one man and had been badly hurt. She did not intend to allow herself to make that mistake a second time.

"These are the people you told me about today?"

"Yes. Toni Trent heads the local Department of Human Resources office. She can tell you what services are available and how to get them. Phyllis Dickson does the hiring at the hospital. You can walk to the DHR office from here, but the hospital is a couple of miles on the other side of the courthouse."

"To me, that is also walking distance." Anita looked at th names and noted Hawk's handwriting was exceptionally nea She tried to imagine what would happen if she asked thes women for help. *They might take one look at me and tell me to g back to Mexico.*

"The DHR office and just about everything else will b closed tomorrow, but you can see Toni first thing on Frida I'll call tomorrow and tell her you're coming."

"Are you sure—"

"They'll treat you right," Hawk interrupted. Seeing he hesitation, he wrote several telephone numbers on anothe sheet of paper and pushed it across the table. "Let me kno how it goes. Here are the numbers where I can be reachec The top one is my cell phone, then the sheriff's office, an the last one is my home number."

"Will you have to work tomorrow also?" Anita asked.

Hawk smiled without humor. "Yes. Sheriff Trimble mad out the holiday work schedule according to the football bow games he wants to see. It's no holiday for law enforcemer though. A few people always get hurt shooting fireworks, bu drinking causes most of our New Year's calls, ranging fror drunk driving to domestic violence."

Yes. I had my share of bad holidays when Juan Sanchez drank It was not a subject Anita cared to remember.

"You cannot see the football games yourself, then?"

Hawk shrugged. "Football is almost a religion to som people around here, but it's just a game to me. I can watc the portable TV in the office between calls. What will yo and Juanita do tomorrow?"

"We like to watch the parades before the football game After that, we will rest and count our blessings."

"That's not a bad way to spend any day." Hawk glanced a his watch and stood. "I have to go now. Call me on Friday?"

"I will."

As soon as the door closed behind Hawk, Mrs. Tanne

called to Anita. "Any idea how much longer you'll be here, Mrs. Sanchez?"

Anita thought Mrs. Tanner's emphasis on "Mrs." spoke volumes. *She must believe I am a bad woman, up to no good with Deputy Henson.* However, she spoke politely.

"I do not know, but I can pay you now for this week if you like."

Mrs. Tanner waved her hand. "That's all right. You can wait until Friday to take care of the bill."

"I will give you the money then. Good night." When Anita turned to leave, Mrs. Tanner spoke again.

"Happy New Year, Mrs. Sanchez."

"The same to you, Mrs. Tanner."

Back in her room, Anita considered the timeworn phrase. *Happy New Year.*

With God's help, it would be a happy year.

And soon she would take the first steps to make it so for her and her daughter.

❧

"Do you have any plans for the day?" Mrs. Tanner asked when Anita and Juanita finished their breakfast.

"We will probably stay in our room and watch the parades on television," Anita replied.

"You might as well watch them on the big-screen TV out here," Mrs. Tanner said. "I don't care about the football games unless Alabama or Auburn are playing, but I enjoy the pretty floats and all the music."

"Can we, Mama?" asked Juanita, as if she feared Anita might refuse.

"Of course, Sweetie. Thank you, Mrs. Tanner."

Mrs. Tanner popped corn for them around lunchtime, then surprised Anita by inviting her and Juanita to have supper with her in the cramped apartment behind the inn's registration desk.

"I don't suppose you know about eating black-eyed peas

and hog jowl for luck on New Year's," the innkeeper said when they were seated around the small table.

"Hog jowl?" Anita repeated, unsure what that meant.

"The meat around a pig's jaw—but I cook my peas with a ham hock. They taste even better that way."

Juanita eyed the main dish warily. She had been trained not to make comments about food she was served, but Anita guessed the source of her concern. *Do I have to eat those dirty-looking peas?* Juanita's eyes asked.

"See the black dots in the middle of each pea? They look like little eyes, do they not? That is why they are called black-eyed peas," Anita explained.

"So you have had them before?" Mrs. Tanner sounded almost sorry she would not be the first to introduce the peas to Anita.

"I have seen them in the frozen food section at the market, but I do not know their taste."

"Now's your chance." Mrs. Tanner put the rest of the food on the table—a tossed salad and a pan of cornbread hot from the oven—and sat down. "You want to say a blessing?" she asked Juanita, who had already folded her hands.

Suddenly shy, Juanita shook her head. "This is your house. You do it."

Mrs. Tanner imitated Juanita by folding her hands and bowing her head. "We thank You for this food, Lord," she said after a pause.

"Amen," added Juanita.

As they ate, Mrs. Tanner confided that she didn't like her first name (Lois) and recounted in some detail the story of how she had met and married Mr. Tanner, who had left her the inn at his death some years ago.

"We never had any children. Your little girl must brighten your life, Mrs. Sanchez," she concluded.

"Please, call me Anita. Yes, Juanita is a gift from God."

"She's getting sleepy," Mrs. Tanner observed. "Maybe you should take her on to bed now."

Anita felt a twinge of guilt for not helping her hostess with the dishes, but she could see Juanita was tired, worn out by the unusual events of the past week. "Thank you for the meal," Anita said. "We enjoyed it very much."

Mrs. Tanner looked embarrassed. "I knew everything was closed for the holiday, and I couldn't let anyone under my roof go hungry. Besides, eating alone isn't much fun."

That I know, Anita could have said. On the way back to their room, Anita realized she had been wrong about Mrs. Tanner. She had thought the innkeeper to be a nosy busybody, but now she realized she was probably lonely. If Anita had misunderstood this woman, it was no wonder that so many others also misunderstood her.

Judge not, that ye be not judged. The verse, a favorite of her mother's, came to her mind unbidden. *Never become so concerned with others' faults that you do not see your own.*

"I will try to do better," Anita said aloud.

"What, Mama?" Nearly asleep, Juanita spoke in a whisper.

"Nothing, Sweetie. I was thinking out loud."

"It sounded like you were praying," Juanita said.

"In a way, I suppose I was." Anita unlocked the room and closed the door behind them. "Brush your teeth and wash your face. When you're ready for bed, I will hear your prayers."

The preparations took the edge off Juanita's sleepiness, and when Anita leaned over to kiss her goodnight, she smiled up at her. "You know what, Mama?"

"No, what?"

"I think we are in a good place."

"So do I, Sweetie."

Thank You, Lord, for bringing us here.

nine

Hawk called Toni Trent around four o'clock in the afternoon on New Year's Day. From the background noise, he guessed she and David had probably invited several friends over. She put him on hold until she could pick up a telephone in a quieter room.

"I hope this isn't a child endangerment call," Toni said.

"No, things have been pretty quiet so far. Men don't usually start beating up their families this early in the day. I have a friend who needs a favor, though. She'll be coming to the DHR office tomorrow, and I wanted to give you a heads up."

Toni reached for the notepad and pencil she kept beside every telephone. "Would this friend happen to be the beautiful brunette you've been seen with several times lately?"

Hawk groaned. "Where did you hear that?"

"Where didn't I hear it? Tom Statum was the first to mention it, I think—anyway, who is this friend, and what can I do for her?"

"Her name is Anita Sanchez. She's a widow with a young daughter. She wrecked her car in the ice storm the other day, and it'll be awhile before Hovis Batts gets it put together again. She doesn't have much money, and she can't afford to stay at the Rockdale Inn much longer."

"Her name is Sanchez?" Toni repeated.

Hawk sighed. "Yes. What about it?"

"I just wondered if she would be eligible for Food Stamps. The rules are rather strict."

"I don't know about that, but I doubt she'd take anything she thought was charity."

"Food Stamps aren't charity—they are a federal government

entitlement for people in need."

"Whatever you say. If you can help her find a place she can afford, it would be a great start."

"I'll see what I can do." Toni paused. "It's about time you had a lady friend. I hope this one works out. Happy New Year, Hawk."

"Hey, wait a minute," he protested, but Toni hung up before he could deny Anita was his "lady friend." Silently he rehearsed the arguments in his imaginary defense. *Anita Sanchez and her daughter need help, that's all. What kind of person would I be if I failed to do what I could to make their lives a little better?*

Hawk sighed. He could assure everyone else his motives were entirely pure, but deep down, he realized Toni Trent was closer to the truth than he cared to admit.

It's about time you had a lady friend. Toni could have been teasing, but he knew she wasn't. Ever since his return to Rockdale, Hawk had earned the reputation of being a loner. He had dated several women, but he seldom went out with the same one more than two or three times, and those not consecutively.

It was a fact: In the few days he'd known her, Hawk had already spent more quality time with Anita Sanchez than with any of the forgettable women he'd dated in the past few years.

Maybe it's just as well Anita believes I'm doing too much for her. Hawk tried to tell himself he should keep his distance to quiet the gossip, but he didn't care about that.

Hawk Henson had never made a New Year's resolution in his life, but at four-fifteen on the afternoon of the first day of the new year, he decided to continue to help Anita Sanchez—and to see her as often as she would allow.

❧

Bill Rankin was not having a happy New Year's Day at all. As he sat drinking beer in a smoky bar in San Antonio, he decided it was probably among the most miserable days of his life. Worst of all, he had no one to blame but himself. He now realized he had handled Anita Sanchez badly. If he had it to do over, he would have tried to befriend her first and make her believe he wanted to help her get all the money she was due from her no-good husband.

Bill shifted his weight on the barstool and sighed. He had been too impatient to claim the fortune that was rightly his to take the time to charm her into giving it to him. *I could have done it that way,* Bill told himself. He had talked more than one lonely woman out of her money, but something in Anita Sanchez's eyes warned him she would never allow herself to be such an easy mark. *Why, then, didn't I figure she would try to run?*

"I thought she'd stay here because of the little girl," Bill mumbled. He had badly misjudged Anita Sanchez, and as a result she had managed to slip away—and no one would tell him where she had gone.

She and her fortune, the money that was rightfully his.

Bill raised his beer and made his own private New Year's resolution. *I will find Anita Sanchez and her brat, and I will get every penny she owes me.*

The daughter would be the key to Anita's fortune. Her mother had shown she would do anything to protect her—even if it meant giving up everything else.

I will find her. The trail was cold now, but sooner or later, Anita Sanchez would make a mistake which would lead him straight to her.

Comforted, Bill raised his mug again and toasted his inevitable victory.

❧

Anita had expected to take Juanita with her to the DHR office, but when Mrs. Tanner found out where she was going, she offered to let Juanita stay at the inn with her until Anita returned.

"Juanita has some new coloring books. She could use them at one of the tables in the breakfast area, if that is all right."

"Even better, she can stay with me right here behind the counter," Mrs. Tanner offered. "I'll clear a space for her."

Juanita seemed so pleased with the idea, she scarcely waved good-bye when Anita left.

The morning air was brisk but not unbearably cold. The night's light frost had melted in the morning sun, and the cloudless sky promised a lovely day.

May it be a good day for Juanita and me as well. Anita fingered the plain gold cross hanging from a delicate gold filigree neck chain. According to family legend, the first Muños man to seek his fortune in Colombia many generations ago had brought the chain with him from Spain. When she was sixteen, her father put it around Anita's neck and reminded her of its history. *The cross is not a worldly bauble to be worn with pride, my daughter, but a reminder to be humble in remembrance of the price the Savior paid for your salvation.*

Anita had removed the cross from the lockbox that morning to wear as a symbol of the source of her courage and strength. Along with it, she took the document certifying Anita Muños Sanchez to be a naturalized citizen of the United States of America.

At the DHR office entrance, Anita stopped and took a deep breath. *Be with me now, Lord,* she prayed, then went inside.

The receptionist looked up when she entered, but before she could ask Anita's business, a woman emerged from a door marked "Director" and greeted her.

"Good morning, Mrs. Sanchez. Hawk Henson told me to expect you."

Anita had imagined the DHR director would be old and gray or perhaps fat and frumpy. However, the young woman who extended her hand to Anita was trim and attractive. From her short brown hair to her tailored brown business suit and sensible pumps, she looked every inch a professional. Yet her smile was warm, welcome proof she truly cared for others.

"I am pleased to meet you, Mrs. Trent."

"We can talk in my office. Alice, hold my calls, please."

Anita sat on the edge of the chair Mrs. Trent offered. Instead of going behind her desk, the DHR director pulled up another chair to sit beside Anita.

"I understand you could use help," Mrs. Trent said.

"I do not know what Deputy Henson told you, but my daughter and I need a place to live. I cannot afford to stay at the Rockdale Inn much longer."

"Yes, Hawk said housing was your main problem. Can you tell me a little about yourself, Mrs. Sanchez? If you're a qualified alien, you might be eligible for several benefits."

Anita felt her face warm. *Why do so many Americanos automatically presume anyone with a Latino name must be an illegal alien?* She opened her handbag and removed the precious paper. "I am a naturalized citizen of the United States. Here is the proof."

Mrs. Trent looked uncomfortable. "I'm sorry—it's my job to ask. You're eligible for several programs, including Food Stamps."

Anita shook her head vigorously. "I still have some savings. I need a job and a place to live. I have not come here to beg for Food Stamps."

"I understand. We usually refer clients who need work to the State Employment Office. However, I believe Deputy Henson said you're a nurse?"

"Yes. I have emergency room experience."

"In that case, you should see Phyllis Dickson—she's the hospital's head of personnel. For a place to live, I can refer you to Harrison Homes, Rockdale's only low-rent apartment units. What do you have in mind?"

"Something small for my daughter and myself. We have no furniture."

Toni Trent made a note on the legal pad. "I'll talk to the rental agent and get back to you. Tell me about your daughter."

"Juanita is six years old."

"You'll want to register her for school. I can help you do that too," Toni added, seeing Anita's stricken look.

"There are so many things to consider in a new place," Anita said.

"I know. I came to Rockdale as a stranger once myself." Toni asked a few more questions and made notes on a yellow legal pad. "I believe I have everything we need," she said, then paused. "Unofficially, I'm curious about why you decided to come to Rockdale."

"The deputy did not tell you?"

"No. He said you were a friend who needed help, that's all."

Anita touched her gold cross. "I was caught in an ice storm a few days ago. My car wrecked on the road into town, and Deputy Henson found me. He has been helping my daughter and me since."

"So you have decided to stay here because of the deputy?"

Anita hesitated, then shook her head. "Not really. I know it might sound strange, but I believe God might have led me to this place."

Toni Trent did not seem surprised or taken aback. "I noticed your beautiful cross. You and your daughter would be welcome at our church Sunday."

"Thank you, but my car has not yet been repaired."

"I suspect Deputy Henson would give you a ride."

Anita tried to suppress her alarm. She did not want to be seen in Hawk's company anywhere else. "Maybe later, after we are settled," she said.

Toni stood. "It has been a pleasure to meet you, Mrs. Sanchez. I'll talk to the rental agent and let you know about an apartment."

"Thank you very much. I would like to see the lady at the hospital now, if you will please tell me how to get there."

"I can do better than that." Toni Trent led Anita from her office and stopped at the reception desk. "Where are the abuse report forms for the hospital?"

The receptionist pointed to her "Out" box. "I was going to mail them when I went to the post office."

"I'll hand-carry them. If anyone calls, I should be back in forty-five minutes." Toni turned to Anita. "You can ride to the hospital with me."

"That is not necessary. I do not mind walking," Anita said.

"When you see how far it is to the hospital, you'll be glad you rode."

"Hawk told me it was about two miles," Anita said, then wished she had not used his first name.

Toni smiled. "Men aren't always accurate about distances."

They got into Toni Trent's SUV, and after they had traveled a few blocks, Toni pointed out a series of one-story red brick buildings. "That's the Harrison Homes apartment complex. It's a low-rent housing development where most tenants behave and take care of their apartments. Dwight Anders is a good manager."

Anita looked at the monotonous sameness of the apartments, typical of all government-sponsored housing projects. She and Juan had lived in such places, and Anita had been very happy to get out of them. Still, the smallest apartment here would be better than their cramped room at the Rockdale Inn. "They look very nice."

A few blocks later, Toni pulled into the parking lot of the Rockdale Hospital, a three-story yellow brick building which occupied the entire block. *A one hundred-bed hospital,* Anita guessed. An ambulance stood on the emergency-room apron, its doors open as its occupant was removed. *The patient will be taken to a cubicle for evaluation and treatment. Those first few minutes will be important.* ER procedures were universal, and Anita could already picture herself working there. *Let there be a place for me here if it is Your will,* she prayed.

Anita realized Toni Trent was addressing her. "The personnel office is on the right as we go in. I'll take the abuse report forms to the administrator and meet you in the lobby after you see Mrs. Dixon."

Seeing Anita enter with Toni Trent, the receptionist quickly ushered her into Phyllis Dickson's office. Had the social worker not been with her, Anita doubted she would have been granted such speedy access.

The personnel director at the San Antonio hospital had been a stern and large-boned, middle-aged woman with iron-gray hair. Anita was pleasantly surprised when Phyllis Dickson turned out to be an attractive blond, and she hoped she would be as kind as Toni Trent. However, from the moment the personnel director laid eyes on her, Anita had the feeling she was being weighed in the woman's private scales and found wanting.

"You say you are a nurse?"

Anita nodded. "Yes. I trained in Arizona and Texas. I worked as an emergency room triage nurse in San Antonio."

"Do you have proof of past employment and an Alabama nursing license?"

"I can give you the address of the hospital where I worked until after Christmas, and I have a copy of my Texas license."

"At the present, money is short. We aren't hiring nurses."

Anita tried not to show her disappointment. Everything else had gone so well that day, she had hoped this would, also. "Is there any kind of work I can do?"

The personnel director looked through a slender stack of papers on her desk. "A temporary position will be available in the day surgery area when one of the staff goes on leave in a couple of weeks."

"I will take it."

"It's janitorial work," Mrs. Dixon said. "Do you still want it?"

Janitorial work. The most menial job, with the worst pay, in any hospital. Anita swallowed hard and tried not to show her distress. *It is only temporary, and perhaps a nursing job will open soon.*

Anyway, in her position, Anita did not have many choices.

"I need to work. Whatever the job is, I will do it."

ten

Toni Trent was waiting in the lobby when Anita emerged from Mrs. Dixon's office. "Does she have anything for you?"

"A woman in day surgery goes on maternity leave in a couple of weeks. I will take her place for a couple of months."

"Day surgery," Toni repeated. "Nursing?"

"No—cleaning."

"At minimum wage?"

"A little over. It is not what I hoped for, but it is a start."

"Good. Mrs. Dixon's certifying you will be employed will help with your housing application."

"How long does it usually take to get an apartment?" Anita asked when they reached Toni's SUV.

"That depends on whether there's a waiting list. Since we're so close already, let's find out."

Toni turned into Harrison Homes and parked in front of the housing office. "Wait here. If Dwight Anders isn't in his office, I can still get a housing application."

A short time later Toni returned to the car, accompanied by a rather stout man Anita judged to be around forty. "Mrs. Sanchez, this is Dwight Anders. He's going to show us a one-bedroom apartment."

Anita got out of the car and joined them. "Is the apartment available now?" she asked.

"It will be after we finish cleaning and painting it. The last tenants left before Christmas, and what with the holidays and all, we haven't had a chance to get the work done."

Dwight Anders led them to the unit, one in a row of seemingly identical apartments. When he unlocked the door and motioned them to step inside, Anita was surprised to see

Toni Trent put her hands to her face, apparently overcome with some emotion.

"I know this apartment well. Being in it again brings back a lot of memories."

"Why? Did the DHR have to come here for some reason?" Dwight Anders asked.

"No. I stayed here with April Richardson part of the time when I was fifteen. We kept our bikes against that wall over there."

The manager looked blank. "April Richardson?"

"You probably know her as April Winter, Congressman Jeremy Winter's wife."

Dwight Anders looked impressed. "She once lived here? No wonder the congressman is so willing to help us get the funds to repair and update the units."

"This one looks as if it could use some help," Toni said.

From the small living room, Anita could see almost the entire apartment. The kitchen was to the left, open to the living room. The bedroom was straight ahead, with the bathroom behind the kitchen. Small as it was, Anita would be glad to live in it, except for one thing.

"There is no furniture?" Anita asked Mr. Anders.

"No, this unit rents unfurnished."

"Do you have anything you could put in it?" Toni asked.

"Only bits and pieces tenants left when they moved—mostly junk. The unfurnished units rent for less," he pointed out.

"Then don't try to furnish it," Toni said. "Assuming Mrs. Sanchez qualifies, when could she move in?"

"That depends on the paperwork. The apartment should be ready in a couple of weeks." Dwight Anders turned to Anita. "Get your application in as soon as you can, Mrs. Sanchez. The larger units have a waiting list. You're lucky you can use a small apartment."

The Lord's plan has nothing to do with luck, Anita wanted

to say. "Thank you, Mr. Anders. I will start on the papers right away."

The housing director returned to his office, and Toni and Anita got back into the SUV. "What do you think about the apartment?" Toni asked as they drove away from the Harrison Homes. "Is it large enough for you and your daughter?"

"Oh, yes, thank you. But I cannot afford to buy much furniture."

"You won't have to. I stored a set of twin beds and matching dresser last fall when my stepdaughter got new furniture for her room. My sister-in-law is about to replace a sofa. We'll be glad to see them put to good use."

"I do not think finding furniture for me is part of your job," Anita said.

"My job is to help others any way I can, just as I have been helped. I was a messed-up teenager when I met April Richardson. I'm in social work now because of people like her and my sister-in-law, who for many years had the job I have now."

Looking at the poised DHR director, Anita found it hard to picture Toni Trent as a troubled teenager. "I became a nurse to help others, myself," she said. "I hope I will yet be able to do that in Rockdale."

"So do I." Toni stopped in front of the Rockdale Inn and handed Anita her business card. "You can call my cell phone if you have any questions about the housing application. Bring it to my office Monday, so I can review it before we turn it in."

Anita regarded Toni Trent with gratitude. "I wish I had the words to tell you how much I thank you, Mrs. Trent."

"You don't need words—your eyes speak for you. I'll see you Monday?"

"Yes, Mrs. Trent."

When Anita entered the lobby, Mrs. Tanner and Juanita were nowhere in sight, and for a moment she feared something might have happened to Juanita.

She was about to knock on Mrs. Tanner's apartment door when she saw it was slightly ajar. She heard Mrs. Tanner say something indistinguishable, followed by the welcome sound of her daughter's laughter.

"Mrs. Tanner? I am back," Anita called.

The innkeeper came to the door, wiping her hands on a kitchen towel. Behind her stood Juanita, enveloped in an apron which covered almost her entire body.

"That took less time than I expected," Mrs. Tanner said. "Juanita and I are making soup."

"It's veg'able soup, Mama, and I put in the words," Juanita said.

"The words?" Anita repeated.

"Small pasta letters, actually—to make it alphabet soup," Mrs. Tanner explained.

Anita hugged her daughter. "I know it will be good, then."

"Come back around noon, and we'll have it for lunch."

"Thank you, we will. And I also thank you for watching Juanita."

"It is my pleasure," Mrs. Tanner said, obviously meaning it.

Later, when Anita said grace, her heart felt lighter than it had for days. She welcomed the opportunity to thank God, not only for the soup, but for all the other blessings the day had brought.

తు

After lunch, Juanita needed little persuasion to lie down for a rest. After her daughter fell asleep, Anita returned to the lobby and gave Mrs. Tanner a capsule version of the day's events.

"I hope to get into an apartment at Harrison Homes soon, but that will probably take another two weeks," Anita concluded. "How much will I owe you in all?"

"Pay me for the first two weeks, and we'll call it even," Mrs. Tanner said. "I know you and Juanita need more room, but I'll be sorry to see you leave."

"I want to pay the entire bill. I do not like to be in debt to anyone."

"You won't be if you'll agree to sit behind the desk and answer the telephone while I'm out. It would be a big help to me."

"I suppose I could," Anita said. "Until I start working at the hospital, I will not have anything else to do."

"It's settled, then."

"One more thing," Anita said. "I promised to let Deputy Henson know what I found out today, but Juanita is sleeping, and I do not want to awaken her."

"You can use the phone in my apartment. It's a private line. Do you know his number?"

"Yes, thank you."

Mrs. Tanner led Anita into her neat combination sitting room and bedroom and pointed out the telephone beside her recliner. "Take your time," she said, then closed the door behind her.

Presuming Hawk would be at work, she tried his office number. "May I speak to Deputy Henson?" she asked when Sally Rogers answered.

"He's out on a call. Is this Mrs. Sanchez? He said to tell you he'll call you when he has the chance."

Anita thanked her and hung up. She was not surprised the receptionist recognized her voice, but she wondered what Sally Rogers thought when Hawk told her Mrs. Sanchez would call him, and she felt frustrated she had not been able to tell Hawk her news. After all, if it had not been for him, her life could well have taken a totally different turn.

"That was a short conversation," Mrs. Tanner commented when Anita returned to the reception desk.

"The deputy is out of the office," Anita said.

"I always liked Hawk Henson. Some folks around here act like they're ashamed they have Indian blood, but Hawk's family has never been like that."

"From what he said, he has kept up some of the old ways. That cannot be easy in these days."

"I suppose not." The inn telephone rang, and when Mrs. Tanner went to answer it, Anita waved and returned to the room.

Juanita stirred when she opened the door, then sat up and announced she had slept long enough. "Can we go outside, please, Mama?"

"We can walk to the garage. I want to see how the work is coming along on our car."

"And I want to see the fishes."

٢٥

Hovis Batts greeted them warmly and assured Juanita the fish had been waiting for her return.

With her daughter engaged in fish watching, Anita asked about her car. "Was the salvage headlight all right?"

"Perfect—even down to the color. In fact, I put it on this morning. The parts I ordered ought to come any day now. You'll be back on the road again before you know it, Mrs. Sanchez."

"I have decided to stay here, at least for awhile, but I will need the car when I start working at the hospital."

Hovis Batts' face registered surprise, then curiosity. "I thought you was anxious to get out of here. What made you change your mind?"

Hawk Henson. But Anita knew he was not the only reason.

"The people where I was headed might not be as kind as those I have met here. Besides, I would have run out of money by the time I could have gotten there."

"I suspect people are about the same everywhere, when you get down to it. Some folks around here won't give you the time of day, but don't let them bother you none."

Sheriff Trimble for one, Anita thought. But Hovis Batts was right: anyone looking for a slight would be sure to find it, no matter where they lived.

"Let me know when the car is ready."

"I will, but I hope you'll bring the little lady here anytim you like. My fish like to have visitors."

"In that case, I will watch them with my daughter fo awhile and let you get back to work."

Juanita sat in front of the aquarium, transfixed. "Look Mama," she said when Anita entered the room. "That on mean fish is chasing all the others. See how scared they look?"

"Yes. But look, here comes another fish to chase that one."

"I want the good fish to win," Juanita said.

"So do I, Sweetie."

They watched the chase for several minutes, until both fis tired of their sport and retired to the elaborate underwate castle, leaving the other aquarium inhabitants to go abou their business.

For some reason, the aggressive fish reminded Anita of Bi Rankin. A few weeks ago, she had run away like one thos poor fish to escape a man she felt to be evil.

Now, praise God, Bill Rankin was half a continent awa and no longer able to hurt her and Juanita. And in Haw Henson, they had a champion who would protect them.

Now, we are safe. May it always be so.

eleven

"Henson? Come in here," Sheriff Trimble bellowed from his office.

Hawk hung his coat on the rack beside the door and sighed. He had spent much of the day driving all over Rock County on a wild goose chase. An informant claimed knowledge of a crystal methamphetamine lab operating in the wilderness, but Hawk had found nothing. He knew meth labs were out there, all right—they had replaced the growing of marijuana as the major source of local illegal activity throughout northeast Alabama. Rock County law enforcement officers were increasingly faced with problems the rural county had never had before and for which they were largely unprepared.

Now what? Hawk hoped the sheriff wasn't about to send him out on another patrol. "Yes, Sir. What is it?"

"Sit down. Find anything?"

"Not in any of the places I looked—and I covered a lot of territory."

"I'm not surprised. We don't know enough about all this new stuff. Asa McGinty applied for several drug training grants before he retired. I reckon that's why we got this letter."

Hawk skimmed the paper the sheriff handed him. A narcotics training academy in North Carolina had accepted the Rock County Sheriff's Department application to send an officer for extensive training. He returned the letter to the sheriff and nodded. "That sounds like a good course. When will you go?"

Sheriff Trimble snorted. "Never. I'm too old for that kind of stuff. I'm giving them your name. They'll let you know when the next class starts."

Only recently Hawk would have embraced the opportunit to attend such a school, not only for the training, but also t get away from Rockdale for awhile. A change of scene neve hurt, and every time he left it, he always returned refreshe and with a new appreciation of his beloved county.

But things had changed. Hawk realized he didn't want t go anywhere now. Since Anita Sanchez had come into hi life, nothing had seemed exactly the same.

"Shouldn't you send one of the other deputies? They hav more seniority."

"Maybe so, but they all say you are the best one to go, an I agree."

Hawk understood perfectly. *Nobody else wants to do this, s I'm stuck with it.* Having to make do with everyone else's left overs was nothing new to Hawk, but he resented the sheriff' easy assumption he would automatically agree to do anythin he was asked. "Suppose I don't want to go, either?"

Sheriff Trimble scowled. "If we don't use this grant, it won' look good when the time comes to ask for more trainin money, and the druggies will keep on outsmarting us. Turnin down training like this won't look good on your record, either.

"I never said I wouldn't go. How long is the course?"

"I'm not sure since they have more than one. Most are fiv days, others are longer. It'll take you a day to get there an another day to get back. You'll get your regular salary and a expenses, including travel."

"You can turn in my name. Is that it?"

"Not quite." Sheriff Trimble leaned back in his chair an folded his arms across his chest in the manner of a man abou to deliver a reprimand. "Your foreign girlfriend called you her while you were out. This is a business office. Tell her not to d that again."

Hawk forced back an angry reply. It had been a long day and he was tired, but that was no excuse to lose his temper. "I you mean Mrs. Sanchez, she isn't my girlfriend, and she isn' 'foreign.' I asked her to call me, not the other way around."

"I don't imagine she's 'Mrs. Sanchez' when you're alone, is she, Henson? Like I said before, we don't need her kind around here. For all you know, she could be a drug runner herself."

"Anita Sanchez is a widow who's had a hard time lately. She is no more a drug runner than you are, Sheriff."

"I reckon that remains to be seen, Henson. Close the door when you leave."

❧

As the afternoon passed and Hawk did not call, Anita began to wonder if something could have happened to him. In San Antonio, she had worked with a woman whose husband was in law enforcement. Although her friend accepted the fact he had a dangerous job, Anita noticed her anguish when he went undercover and disappeared for days at a time.

Anita had experienced similar pain with Juan, except when her husband left for a long period of time, it usually meant he was either in trouble or looking for it.

What would life with Hawk be like?

Anita cut the thought short, upset she had allowed herself to think of Hawk as anything more than a friend. He had been good to her, but he had his own life. She and Juanita were not a part of it now, nor would they ever be—

The telephone rang, startling her. It was almost as if thinking of Hawk had caused him to call, and Anita took a steadying breath before she picked up the receiver.

"Hi, Anita. Sorry I couldn't get back to you sooner, but this is the first chance I've had to call all day. What did you find out?"

"Quite a bit." Briefly, Anita told him about her day.

"You already have a job offer and a place to stay? That's great. We should celebrate tonight."

"It is too early for that. The job isn't very good, and it does not start for a couple of weeks. I might not be approved for the apartment, either."

"Don't borrow trouble. We'll talk about it tonight if you

and Juanita will have dinner with me."

Anita hesitated. She meant it when she told Hawk they should not be seen together so much, but she had much to tell—and ask—the deputy. "I would rather go out of town."

"So would I. There's a restaurant in an old house near Mentone. It's not a fancy place, but the food is good."

"Where is Mentone?"

Anita sensed Hawk's smile. "Out of town a ways. I'll be by for you ladies at six o'clock."

❧

Although she kept trying to convince herself Hawk was just a family friend, Anita felt fluttery as a teenager on her first date when she dressed for the evening. She had a limited wardrobe, in part because she had always worn uniforms to work but also because she spent most of her clothing budget on her growing daughter. She had one dress for special occasions and a couple of other everyday outfits, plus several separates, all suited for the San Antonio climate. Taking Hawk's word that the place they were going was not fancy, Anita decided to pair her black slacks with a long-sleeved white blouse and her only woolen jacket.

Juanita had several like-new hand-me-down outfits her friend Beth had outgrown, including a few long dresses she loved. Bypassing the ones with ruffles and bows, Anita chose the red-and-green plaid dress Juanita had worn to church the Sunday before Christmas.

"You look pretty, *Mamacita*," Juanita said when both were ready.

"So do you, Sweetie."

"Looks like somebody's going to a party," Mrs. Tanner observed when Juanita twirled in front of her, showing off her dress.

"Dep'ty Hawk's coming to get us," Juanita said.

Mrs. Tanner glanced at Anita. "Where's he taking you this time?"

"To a restaurant in an old house in Mentone, I think he said."

Mrs. Tanner raised her eyebrows. "Mentone, eh? There's some high-class inns and eating places around there."

"He said it was not a fancy place."

"If it's the one I think, it's got a real pretty view, but of course you won't be able to tell that at night."

"Mama, here he is!"

Hawk greeted Mrs. Tanner, then helped Juanita put on her coat. "Isn't Dora going with us?" he asked.

"No. She's tired. She has to stay here and sleep."

Hawk directed his attention to Anita. "Will that jacket be enough?" he asked, seeing she did not have her coat.

"It will if the car is warm and we will not have to walk very far."

"My heater works, and it's only a few steps from the parking lot to the restaurant—but it's another cold night."

"Good-bye," Mrs. Tanner called after them. "Have a good time."

"You have a good time too!" Juanita responded, leaving the innkeeper smiling.

❧

Once more they climbed out of the valley onto Lookout Mountain and traveled on a series of winding, two-lane roads. With the dark asphalt pavement beneath and an almost starless sky above, they rode through a tunnel of light made by the Jeep's headlights.

"It sure is dark out here," said Juanita.

"We'll come back in the daytime so you can see everything." Hawk waved his hand toward invisible sites. "DeSoto State Park and Little River Canyon are just over there, and Sequoyah Caverns is nearby."

"Are those caves?" Anita recalled the thousands of bats she had seen in a New Mexico cave and shuddered.

"Yes. The caverns are named for the Cherokee who made

an alphabet for the Cherokee language. We know Sam
Houston visited the caverns—he left his name on one of the
pillars in 1830."

"Sam Houston from the Alamo?" Juanita asked.

"The same. The caverns belong to the Echota Cherokee
Tribe, so in a way, I'm one of the owners."

"Can we go there tonight, Dep'ty Hawk?"

Hawk chuckled, a rich sound that started low in his throat
and grew into a full laugh. "It's closed at night, but I'll take
you there some weekend soon, all right? For now, look at all
these lights."

Many Christmas decorations were still up throughout the
area, and in the resort town of Mentone, clear lights festooned
nearly every building and twinkled in the still night air.

"Pretty!" Juanita exclaimed. Although it was far too dark to
see it at night, Anita took Hawk's word that Mentone
offered a magnificent view from the bluff on which it sat.

"I'll show you our ski resort next time."

"Skiing in Alabama?" asked Anita. "Surely it is not cold
enough here for that."

"The mountain elevations get more snow than Rockdale,
but it wouldn't be enough without a little help. It's interesting to watch the machine make snow."

"Do you ski, Dep'ty Hawk?" Juanita asked.

"No," Hawk said emphatically. "I'd rather keep both my
feet on solid ground."

Hawk slowed and turned into a narrow graveled driveway
beside a Victorian frame house. In addition to lights around
the circling verandah, a single candle shone in every window.

"Look at all those pretty lights, Mama!"

"I see them, Sweetie."

The display reminded Anita of the San Antonio Riverwalk,
and for a moment she felt a pang of loss for the culture she
had left behind. Being Hispanic in San Antonio, she was one
among many, and no one noticed she spoke English with an

accent. In Rockdale, however, everyone knew she was not one of them, often before she said a word.

Live in the present, she reminded herself. This day, which had been good so far, was not yet over. Perhaps the best was yet to be.

The full parking lot made it appear they might have a long wait for a table. However, when they entered the wide entrance hall, a dark-haired hostess in a long red wool dress hugged Hawk and led them to a table in what had been the house's library. Shelves filled with a mixture of books and unglazed pottery rose to the tall ceiling, and a cheerful fire blazed on the hearth.

Even as Anita speculated the hostess might be Hawk's girlfriend, he introduced her as his cousin, Amitola.

"That's a pretty name," Juanita said.

"It means 'rainbow' in Cherokee," Hawk said. "Amitola, these are my friends, Anita and Juanita Sanchez."

The girl nodded to acknowledge the introductions. "Do you live in Rockdale?"

"We are there at the present," Anita said.

"Sorry I don't have time to visit—we're really busy tonight. Your server will be along in a minute."

"You made it sound like you're in Rockdale temporarily," Hawk said when Amitola left.

"We may be. I do not even know if we will have a place to stay in Rockdale."

"I wouldn't worry about that. Toni Trent has been known to work wonders when it comes to finding housing."

"She is a wonderful lady. Thank you for speaking to her on my behalf."

"Toni would have welcomed you even if I hadn't called her first. You're right—she is a great lady. We came back to Rockdale about the same time after being away for awhile. Our paths crossed when DHR needed a deputy to help remove a child from an unsafe situation. It turned out to be the first rescue case for us both, and we've been friends ever since."

"Who's DHR?" Juanita asked.

Anita's look flashed a warning for Hawk to watch what he said. She did not want Juanita to be concerned about children being taken away from their homes.

"The DHR is a place where people go for all kinds of help," Hawk said.

"You went there this morning, didn't you, Mama?"

"Yes, Sweetie. Mrs. Trent is in charge there. She took me to the hospital, then to see an apartment."

Juanita's eyes grew large and her lower lip trembled. "Is she going to take me away too?"

"Of course not!" Anita reached over to hug her daughter.

"No one is going to take you away from your mother," Hawk said. "I won't let them."

The server appeared with the menus, diverting Juanita's attention. Even though she said nothing more about her fears, Anita realized she had not protected her daughter as well as she thought; Juanita had probably known more about their sometimes precarious situation than she had let her mother know.

Someday, when Juanita was old enough to understand, Anita would tell her daughter the truth about her life in Colombia and her marriage to Juan Sanchez. For now, she wanted her to be happy and feel safe in their new life in Alabama.

☙

Prompted by Anita's questions about Cherokee history, Hawk did most of the talking during dinner, but he volunteered no information about himself.

"You seem to have many cousins. You must have a large family," Anita said.

Hawk smiled. "All the Cherokee around here consider ourselves to be kin, whether we're close blood relatives or not. The girl at the bank is my true first cousin. Amitola and I are third cousins, I think. The Old Ones somehow kept up with it all. I never have tried."

Do Cherokee have to marry within their tribal family? Anita would not ask the question, but her daughter came close.

"Dep'ty Hawk, do you have a Cher'kee wife?"

The question seemed to amuse him. "No, Miss Juanita. I have never had a wife of any kind."

"Amitola's pretty. Why don't you marry her?"

"Juanita! You should not say such things," Anita protested.

Hawk smiled. "I don't mind. I can't marry Amitola because she already has a husband. In fact, she and Joel have a three-year-old boy and a girl about your age."

Anita had repeatedly told herself Hawk Henson could never be more than a friend, yet she felt foolish relief at his reply.

"I'd like to play with Amitola's little girl," Juanita said.

"That would be hard to arrange, since she lives on the other side of Mentone. You'll have lots of kids to play with when you start school, though."

Juanita looked excited. "I like school. When can I start?"

Anita wished he had not brought up the subject, since she had done nothing about enrolling Juanita. "We will talk about that later, Sweetie."

Mercifully, their server arrived with the bill at that moment, and they left the restaurant and started back to Rockdale without further conversation.

"I think we just lost a passenger," Hawk said a few minutes later when a glance in the rearview mirror revealed Juanita had fallen asleep.

"It is past her bedtime, but riding in a car always makes her sleepy. When she was a baby, it was sometimes the only way to get her to fall asleep."

"What about your husband? Was he still living then?"

Anita hesitated. She could not lie to Hawk, but neither was she ready to tell Hawk where Juan Sanchez had been during that time. "Yes, but he was not with us very much."

"It's hard to raise a child alone," Hawk said. "My mother did her best, but she was never the same after my father died."

"How old were you then?"

"Twelve. Mother would have liked to stay on the mountain, but we had to move back to town when he got sick."

Anita tried to picture Hawk at twelve. "You did not want to leave?"

"Not at first, but I knew we had no choice. I thought we'd return when I got old enough to do all the heavy work. But by then, my mother wasn't well enough to go back."

"She is not still living?"

"No. She died on my eighteenth birthday." Hawk cleared his throat and glanced at Anita. "What about your folks?"

From long practice, she had learned to be brief and matter-of-fact. "I lost them both when I was eighteen."

Hawk took his right hand from the steering wheel and briefly touched Anita's arm in a gesture of sympathy. "What happened?"

They were murdered because they would not cooperate with a drug ring. Anita could not bring herself to speak the whole truth, so she said as little as possible. "Our house burned while I was away in school."

"That must have been terrible for you. You came to America afterwards?"

"Yes."

Hawk considered her words for a moment before he spoke again. "You lost your family and then your husband, yet you didn't give up. You're a brave lady, Anita."

Hawk's praise disturbed her. She had not told him the whole story, and she felt completely unworthy of Hawk's admiration. "When I was a little older than Juanita is now, I asked Jesus Christ into my heart. I have faith He will help me, and He always has."

Hawk nodded. "Some Power was definitely with you during

that ice storm. Most women would have fallen to pieces after wrecking their car, but you didn't."

If I were really as strong as you seem to think, I would never have agreed to see you tonight. Anita smiled ruefully. "I know I have been blessed, but I am still feeling my way in this place. Some things have worked out, but much still has be done."

When Hawk glanced at her again, Anita lowered her head, embarrassed. "You know I will do whatever it takes to help you any way I can," he said."

"Yes, and I appreciate the offer. But as I told you, I must do as much as I can on my own."

Hawk seemed ready to pursue their conversation further, but as they crossed the bridge back into Rockdale, the glare of the street lights woke Juanita.

"Where are we?" she asked drowsily.

"Almost home," Hawk said.

When they stopped in front of the inn, Hawk carried a groggy Juanita through the lobby. After Anita unlocked the door, he laid the girl on a bed inside the room.

"Good night, Hawk. Thank you for a wonderful evening."

Anita's hand was on the door, ready to close it after him, until Hawk covered her hand with his and took a step toward her.

"Come back out after you put Juanita to bed. I have something to say to you."

Anita started to ask what it was, but his intent look silenced her. "I won't be long."

Shortening her daughter's usual bedtime ritual, Anita helped Juanita into her nightgown and tucked her into bed.

What does Hawk want to say to me? Her heart beating unaccountably fast, Anita squared her shoulders and left the room.

twelve

When Anita entered the hall, Hawk took her hand and led her to a nearby alcove containing the ice and vending machines. It offered relative privacy.

"What is it?" Anita looked into his dark eyes and felt her throat tighten. Her heart was beating so rapidly she felt sure he could hear it.

Hawk stroked her cheek with the back of his free hand. "I admire you for wanting to be independent, but please don't shut me out of your life just to prove you don't need anyone."

Anita shivered at his touch. Hawk's voice, his words, the intense way he was looking at her—they all suddenly overwhelmed her. *I could never shut you out of my life, Hawk. I am afraid I am falling in love with you, and I do not know how to deal with it.*

Unwilling to say what was really in her heart, Anita stammered a reply. "I. . .you are wrong. I do not mean to shut you out. I cannot thank you enough for being a friend to Juanita and me. You will always be an important part of our lives."

Hawk frowned. "You think of me only as your friend? I hoped—" He sounded troubled, and Anita feared what he might say next.

"Please understand. Juanita and I have had no one to help us for so long—it is not easy to break old habits."

"In time, do think you might change your mind about me?"

Hawk sounded so wistful it was all Anita could do not to throw her arms around his neck. She had never had such strong feelings for a man, but Anita could never forget the hard lessons she had learned when she misplaced her trust in

Juan Sanchez. Her heart told her Hawk was different, but her mind was reluctant to believe it.

"Perhaps it does not need to be changed." Anita rested the palms of her hands on his shoulders and stood on tiptoe to brush his cheek with a light kiss. "I promise to pray about it."

Hawk looked startled, then he smiled faintly. "I will be doing some praying myself. For now, promise to call me if you need anything or when you can stand to have me around again—whichever happens first."

Reassured by his teasing tone, Anita returned his smile. "I will."

Hawk hugged her in the same brief, almost impersonal way he had earlier embraced Amitola. "Take care, Anita," he said, then walked away.

Anita stayed in the alcove for a moment, considering what had passed between them. While her heart urged her to confess her true feelings for Hawk, her mind warned her it would be too soon for both of them.

She believed God had led her to this place, and perhaps to this man. *Dear Lord, if You mean for us to be together, let me know it in Your own time.*

As Anita returned to the room where her daughter slept, she felt as if a burden had lifted from her shoulders. Many important things would require her full attention in the next few days, and while she was resolved not to allow Hawk Henson to distract her, she thanked God for this man's willingness and ability to help her.

❧

Toni Trent had offered to help Anita complete the Harrison Homes application. Anita did not know how to answer some of the questions, so she took Juanita with her to the DHR office. After Toni showed Anita how to finish the form, she turned her attention to Juanita.

"If you're like the little boy at my house, you're probably ready to start back to school."

Juanita looked to her mother, uncertain how she should answer.

"I have not enrolled her," Anita said.

"This would be a good time to get that done." Toni glanced at her watch. "I don't have to be in court for almost an hour. I can take you to Rockdale Elementary. You can walk back to the inn from there," she added, seeing Anita was about to protest.

At the school while Anita filled out the registration papers, Toni Trent conferred with the principal. She came out of the office looking pleased.

"Juanita will be in Mary Oliver's class. She's an excellent teacher. My stepson had her for the first grade, and he loved her."

"Miss Oliver is in her classroom, working on materials for the next term. I've called her on the intercom," the principal said.

After Toni greeted the teacher and introduced Anita, Miss Oliver stooped to shake Juanita's hand.

"I am happy to meet you, Miss Juanita Sanchez. Would you like to see our classroom?"

Anita was reassured by the woman's warm, motherly manner, but a suddenly shy Juanita nodded and said nothing. However, when she saw the names of the other students above their material cubbyholes, Juanita broke into a big smile.

"I know her!" She pointed to Jackie Tait's name. "I played at her house."

"You'll soon know all the other boys and girls too," Mary Oliver said. "Let me show you some of the things we'll be doing."

While her daughter was thus occupied, Anita turned to Toni with a new concern. "Juanita stayed at her Texas school until I could pick her up after work. Is that kind of day care available here?"

"Not yet, although several parents have asked the school

board to look into starting it. However, I know someone who might keep her for you."

When they left the school a few minutes later, Toni drove to a nearby condominium and introduced Anita and Juanita to Mrs. Tarpley, an older woman who reminded Anita of her grandmother.

"What a pretty little girl!" Mrs. Tarpley exclaimed. "How old are you, Darling?"

Juanita's shyness seemed to have evaporated. "I am six years old. I'm in the first grade."

"She'll be in Mary Oliver's class," Toni said. "When her mother starts working at the hospital in a few weeks, she'll need a place to stay for a few hours after school."

"I reckon Josh would be glad to have some company. We can try it for awhile and see how it goes."

"Thanks," Toni said. "We'll get back to you about it in a few days."

"I like her," Juanita commented when they left.

"So do I," Anita agreed. "Once again, I do not know how to thank you," she told Toni.

"Think nothing of it. As I may have mentioned, I know what it's like to be a stranger in Rockdale."

Not really, Anita wanted to say. *At least no one ever thought you were an illegal alien.* "Most people here have been kind," she said instead.

"I'm glad to hear it. As for those who haven't welcomed you, give them time. Old notions sometimes die hard."

Anita knew about those "old notions." Not only in Rockdale, but almost everywhere she had lived in America, a few ignorant people always seemed ready to judge her and Juanita according to their preconceived notions of Hispanics.

"Such people do not bother us," Anita said, hoping it would continue to be true.

૨ઍ

The next week passed in a blur. Juanita started school and

appeared to be making a good adjustment, and Anita appeared before the Harrison Homes housing council for a formal interview. Despite her concern she might not have made a good impression, her application was approved a few days later. That news added to Anita's feeling that their staying in Rockdale was in God's will.

She stayed at the inn most of the time, filling in for Mrs. Tanner. Anita had seen Hawk only briefly since the night they went to Mentone, but he called almost daily. When Hovis Batts finished the repairs on her car, Hawk checked it out to make sure it was safe for her to drive.

"Hovis did a good job," he said when he delivered the vehicle to the inn. "You'll need to get an Alabama car tag and driver's license soon," he added.

Anita groaned. "Add that to the utilities and telephone deposit, and my first paycheck will be gone before I even start working."

"Your Texas tag doesn't expire for a few months, so you can get by with keeping it awhile longer. You have thirty days to get an Alabama driver's license, but for ID purposes, you might not want to wait that long."

"Where do I go to get a driver's license?"

"The office is in the courthouse. You'll have to take a vision test and show a valid ID."

Anita went to the courthouse the next day, but the form required a permanent address, and she did not know the street name or number of her Harrison Homes apartment. "I will have to come back when I have all the information," she said.

The clerk raised her eyebrows. "She probably can't reada the Engleesh," she heard the woman tell another applicant.

With their laughter still ringing in her ears, Anita walked past the sheriff's office. She thought about stopping to see Hawk, but not wanting to risk a repeat of her encounter with the Sheriff, she went on.

On the Thursday before Anita was to report for work at

the hospital, Dwight Anders called to tell her the work on her apartment had been completed. "The keys are in my office. Since you've already paid the deposit, you can move in anytime you like."

Anita called Hawk's cell phone to deliver the good news.

"Great. I have Saturday off. I'll be there at eight o'clock to help you move."

"It should not take long. You know we have very little."

"That doesn't matter. I can't think of a better way to spend my day off than with you and Juanita."

It will be good to see you again too. "Thank you," she said instead.

To Anita's surprise, the Trents arrived in David's truck about the same time as Hawk. "We do not need this much help," she protested.

"Many hands make light work," Toni said. "David got a key yesterday and moved the furniture I told you about. I can't wait for you to see it."

When Anita finally stood in the living room of her new home, the sight almost overwhelmed her. "You told me about the beds and sofa. What about all this other furniture?"

A small dinette set, a couple of chairs, a pair of end tables, lamps, even a small television set filled the apartment. In addition, a dozen cartons were stacked on the kitchen counter and against the walls, waiting to be unpacked.

"The seekers class at Community Church rounded up some things we thought you might need, and Hawk donated the end tables and a couple of chairs," Toni explained.

Tears came to Anita's eyes as she examined the contents of the boxes. They were filled with sheets, towels, kitchen utensils, and dishes—many of the things she had planned to buy when she had the money.

"All this—it is too much," she finally managed to say. "You know how I feel about taking charity."

Toni shook her head. "This is not charity. Most of it is

used, and everything here was offered in the spirit of Christian love. Please accept it in the same way, and help someone else one of these days."

"I will," Anita said. "Please tell your friends I thank them from my heart."

"When you get settled, I hope you will come to Community and tell them yourself," Toni said. She glanced at Hawk. "That goes for you too."

"You know I have to work a lot of Sundays. I've used my lunch break to come to the worship service, but there's no way I can get to Bible study as long as Sheriff Trimble makes out the work schedules."

"You two go to the same church?" Anita asked.

Hawk nodded. "Yes. In fact, one of my mother's cousins donated the land Community Church sits on."

"That must mean you're related to Jeremy Winter," Toni said. "I didn't know that."

"Hawk has many cousins." Anita and Hawk's exchanged smiles did not go unnoticed.

"It seems you're getting to know our deputy pretty well," Toni said.

"He has been very good to Juanita and me," Anita said.

"All in the line of duty, of course," David Trent teased.

"Mama, which bed is mine? Dora wants to take a nap."

"You decide, and I will find sheets for it."

With the help of Hawk and the Trents, the unpacking went rapidly. At noon, David went out for pizza. Anita was touched when his thanks for the food included the request that God would bless this home she and Juanita were establishing.

When they had done all they could, Toni and David Trent left, and soon afterward Juanita fell asleep on her chosen bed with her huggy doll clutched in her arms.

"She was too excited to sleep much last night," Anita said.

"You look exhausted yourself. Try to get some rest."

Anita walked to the door with Hawk. "I know you must be

tired of hearing me say it, but again, thank you for your help."

"I could never get tired of hearing you say anything, Anita."

Hawk's eyes looked into hers, and Anita's breath caught in her throat as he bent his head to hers. When their lips met, Anita's arms circled his neck almost as if they had a will of their own.

"Thank *you*," Hawk whispered against her cheek. He held her close for a moment, then released her. "Call me if you need anything."

"I will."

Anita watched him walk away, more certain of the bond they shared. Juan Sanchez had only pretended to be concerned about Anita's welfare so he could take advantage of her. From the first, however, Anita had instinctively known Hawk Henson was different. She had come to believe she could trust him with her life—and perhaps, even her heart

The Lord has truly been my Shepherd. The words of the Twenty-third Psalm came to her mind. Only recently, she had walked in the valley of the shadow of death. Now, in so many ways, Anita could say with the psalmist, *My cup runneth over.*

Yet, even as she praised God for her blessings, Anita knew she should never take them for granted.

thirteen

The Rockdale Hospital day surgery was the most recent addition to a building that had been added onto several times since it opened in the 1930s. Anita reported to work on the first day with mixed feelings. She was grateful to be employed at all, but working in a hospital setting without being able to use her training was frustrating. Her orientation had dealt with standard hospital procedures for safe handling of bodily wastes, the meaning of various codes, and the like, things she already knew.

However, when head custodian Jean Vinson presented Anita with a detailed list of her duties, Anita felt far less at home. The woman's attitude indicated she doubted if anyone with a Spanish accent had the intelligence to follow her directions.

"Your job is to keep the entire day surgery area as clean as possible at all times, but you must never go in an operating area when it is in use."

After a few more instructions, Jean Vinson took Anita to the janitorial supply closet and showed her the cleaning supplies. "Don't even think about taking any of this home. Everything is checked out from central supply, and you'll have to pay for any shortage. Understand?"

Anita inclined her head. "Yes, Mrs. Vinson, I understand."

"I hope so. If you can't handle this job, lots of local people would like to have it."

"I will do my best. I want you to tell me if I do anything wrong."

Mrs. Vinson blinked, taken aback. "No doubt you will," she muttered. "Here's a cart. Take it to your area and get started."

The first week was the worst. Strong physically, Anita was no stranger to hard work, but it was a challenge to clean such a large area both thoroughly and quickly. She did her job without calling attention to herself and spoke only when spoken to.

Hawk stopped by to see Anita several times during the first week. She did not think his work usually brought him to the hospital so much, and she suspected he had come to offer moral support.

On Tuesday of her second week at the hospital, Hawk invited Anita to have lunch with him in the cafeteria.

"What is the occasion?" she asked.

"The prisoner I brought to the ER for treatment was admitted for surgery. I don't have to go back to the office for awhile. How are things going? You look tired."

"Everything is fine. Juanita enjoys school, and she likes staying with Mrs. Tarpley until I get off."

"You shouldn't be doing janitorial work when the ER really needs you."

"Why do you say that?"

"My prisoner had to wait in the ER far too long before anyone saw him. The desk clerk said someone had called in sick and a couple of others have quit lately, so they're understaffed."

"Mrs. Dixon told me the hospital was not hiring nurses."

"They ought to be. My prisoner's appendix almost burst this morning. I'm going to register an official complaint."

Anita appreciated Hawk's righteous indignation, but she doubted the personnel director would. "Please do not mention me in any way. Mrs. Dixon could think I asked you to complain because I think I am too good to scrub floors."

"I don't intend to. As part of the county's emergency preparedness team, it's my duty to make sure the hospital is prepared for any kind of disaster. At the moment, the ER can't handle even routine cases."

Anita considered Hawk's words. "Mrs. Dixon knows I

have ER experience. I wonder if she has checked my references yet?"

"If she hasn't, I predict she will soon."

⁊⧫

Anita was cleaning the rest room in the day-surgery waiting room a couple of days later when word came that Phyllis Dickson wanted to see her immediately. She prayed all the way to the personnel office. *Whatever happens, let me accept it.*

This time, Mrs. Dixon seemed almost cordial. "I have checked your credentials, Mrs. Sanchez. The Alabama Nursing Board has agreed to accept your Texas license on a temporary basis, pending approval of your application. If you're still interested, we have an immediate opening for a triage nurse in the ER day shift."

Anita checked the impulse to hug Phyllis Dickson, but she could not keep from smiling at her. "Oh, yes, I want the job."

"You can start Monday. In the meantime, I'll have to find someone to cover your day-surgery duties." Phyllis Dickson's expression softened. "Mrs. Vinson says you're a hard worker. She'll be sorry to lose you."

"I did not think she liked me," Anita said.

"She liked the way you did your job, and that's what matters around here. Go back to day surgery now, and I'll send payroll the change right away."

⁊⧫

When she got home that evening, Anita called to thank Hawk. "If you had not complained to Mrs. Dixon, I would probably still be a cleaning lady."

"I can't take all the credit. I wasn't the first to bring the situation to her attention. It was only a matter of time before she would have had to hire more nurses."

"I am happy it was sooner rather than later."

"And I am happy for you."

Anita thought Hawk's voice sounded strained. "Is something wrong?"

"Not exactly. I have paperwork to finish tonight, but I'd like to come by around nine o'clock, if that's all right."

"Of course. I will leave the outside light on for you." *Something is bothering Hawk,* Anita thought as she hung up the phone, and she wondered what it could be.

"Is Dep'ty Hawk coming to see us?"

"Yes, Sweetie, but not for awhile. Wash up and you can help me set the table."

Juanita wanted to stay up until Hawk arrived, but after doing her homework and taking a bath, she let Anita hear her prayers and tuck her into bed. "Tell the dep'ty to come back in the daytime," she said sleepily.

"I will. Good night, Sweetie."

Hawk arrived shortly after nine o'clock, still in his uniform.

"You must have had a busy day," Anita said.

He nodded. "You might say that."

"Would you like something? I have hot chocolate and soda."

"No, thanks." Hawk sat on the couch and patted the cushion beside him. "Sit down."

Anita had never seen Hawk look so serious. "You seem troubled tonight. What is wrong?"

"Nothing—but I have to be away for awhile."

"Why?"

"The sheriff's department got a grant to send an officer to North Carolina for drug enforcement training, and Sheriff Trimble decided I would be the one to use it."

"That sounds like a good thing," Anita said.

"Oh, the training will be great, and we need all the help we can get in learning to deal with illegal drugs. I just wish someone else had wanted to take it."

He does not want to leave because of me—and I do not want him to go, either. "How long is this training?"

"Five days plus travel time. I leave tomorrow."

Anita felt relieved. "You will be away only a week?"

"I don't like to be out of touch that long. I'll have my cell phone, but from the course description, we'll be in the field most of the time."

"Juanita will miss having you around. She wants us all to go to Mentone again."

The intense way Hawk regarded Anita made her realize he was about to say something highly personal. He smiled slightly and squeezed her hand. "I'd like to think her mama might miss me just a little bit too."

I will miss you a great deal, Hawk. I cannot imagine a day without seeing your face or hearing your voice. Anita could not bring herself to say the words aloud, but she returned his smile. "Of course I will."

"When I come back, we'll make a day of it—we'll see Sequoyah Caverns and the ski slopes and then have dinner at another mountain restaurant."

"I will tell her. And we will pray for your safe return."

Hawk put his arms around Anita. "I will pray for you too, Anita," he whispered against her hair. Releasing her, he stood. "Take care of yourself."

Anita smiled faintly. "It is what I have always done."

At the door, Hawk turned and lightly kissed Anita's forehead. "That's for Juanita. " He cupped her face in his hands and looked into her eyes. "And this is for you."

Hawk's kiss was long and sweet, and Anita gladly returned it.

"See you soon," he said and was gone.

Anita closed the door behind her and leaned against it, her knees suddenly weak. *He loves me—and I love him.*

The words had not yet been spoken, but in her heart Anita knew as surely as she had ever known anything that they would be.

☙

Anita's first day of work in the ER was not physically exhausting, but her coworkers were not enthusiastic about adding the cleaning woman from day surgery to their staff. Tom Duffey, the male charge nurse, let Anita know she would be reassigned if she didn't work well with the ER team.

It was a fairly light day, and Susan Endicott, the female emergency medicine doctor who supervised the ER, had time to check Anita out on the use of various life-saving equipment and pose hypothetical questions about ER cases.

By the end of the day, secure in the knowledge she had earned Dr. Endicott's approval, Anita breathed a prayer of thanks.

Except for missing Hawk, her life could hardly be better.

❧

"You say you are investigating Mrs. Anita Sanchez?"

Janet Foster, a junior personnel assistant at the San Antonio hospital where Anita Sanchez had last worked, leaned back in her chair and considered Detective Martin's request. It was her first day of filling in for the absent chief of personnel, and she didn't like the way this burly detective was trying to intimidate her.

"Yes. Mrs. Sanchez was under suspicion for drug trafficking when she left town with a large sum of stolen money. We need your help to find her."

Janet Foster picked up a file jacket tabbed SANCHEZ, A. M., and scanned the contents. "Mrs. Sanchez had good evaluations, but it appears she resigned without the usual notice."

"Like I said, she was in a hurry to get away from the law."

"I'm afraid we can't help you, Detective. Mrs. Sanchez left no forwarding address."

"What about her last salary check? Where was it sent?"

"The staff was paid for their work to date at the end of the week before Christmas. No other money was coming to her."

Detective Martin leaned over the desk. "Are you sure there's nothing else in that file?"

Janet Foster turned the jacket upside down, and a telephone memo fell out. "Apparently someone from another hospital called to verify her past employment."

"When was that?"

"About a week ago."

The detective was obviously excited. He took a pen and notebook from his coat jacket. "Exactly where was the call from?"

"I don't know. It just says 'Rockdale Hospital.'"

"Thank you, Miss Foster. You have done the public a great service. I'll see that you are commended for this."

The detective left the office hurriedly, and Janet Foster replaced the Sanchez file in the jacket.

❧

In the privacy of his cheap hotel room, Bill Rankin put his fake ID card and detective's badge in an envelope, then sealed it and stuck it in his breast pocket. The fake credentials had cost an arm and a leg, but they had been worth every penny. Now, thanks to them and the help of a not-too-bright hospital paper-pusher, he knew where to begin to look for Anita Sanchez. There couldn't be many Rockdale Hospitals in the United States. Soon, he would find her—and the fortune she had stolen from him.

fourteen

Hawk's drug enforcement course covered a great deal of territory and was much more demanding, both mentally and physically, than he had expected. Anita Sanchez was on his mind all week, but he had no opportunity to call her from the field. The hour was late when he got back to the base of operations Thursday night, and he didn't want to risk waking her.

Friday morning, Hawk discovered his cell-phone battery had died. He borrowed a cell phone from his roommate but hung up when he got Anita's answering machine. It wasn't quite eight o'clock in Rockdale, but he realized Anita would already have left to take Juanita to school.

After the brief graduation ceremony on Friday morning, Hawk started the long drive back to Rockdale. He felt an odd sense of urgency, prompted not only by his desire to see Anita, but also by a feeling something might be wrong. He knew it was unreasonable—Anita took pride in being able to take care of herself and her daughter, and everything seemed to have worked out for her. *Anita has a good job and a place to live, her car has been repaired—and I think she knows how I feel about her.*

"If she doesn't, she soon will," Hawk said aloud.

❧

"Mrs. Sanchez? Mrs. Dixon wants to see you right away," the ER receptionist said when Anita came back from lunch Friday afternoon.

Anita's heart sank. Had someone complained about her? Although Tom Duffey still regarded her with suspicion, she felt her first week in the ER had gone well.

"You asked to see me, Mrs. Dixon?"

"Yes, Mrs. Sanchez. Come in and close the door behind you."

Phyllis Dickson pointed to Anita's personnel folder. "Your application for employment states you are a widow. Is that correct?"

Anita nodded, mystified. "Yes. My husband died several years ago."

"His name was Juan Sanchez?"

Again Anita nodded. "Why do you ask?"

"I just had a telephone call from a man who claimed to be your husband. He asked if you worked here."

For a moment, Anita could not speak. "It could not be my husband."

"I didn't think so. This man didn't have a Mexican accent."

"Did he call himself Juan Sanchez?"

"No. He said his name was John Martin, and he needs to get in touch with you concerning your child."

Bill Rankin. Somehow, that man has found me. Anita was almost afraid to ask, but she had to know. "What did you tell him?"

"Nothing. Hospital personnel records are private."

Anita released her breath in a long sigh. "Thank you."

"Do you know who this man is?" Mrs. Dixon asked.

"I think it is someone Juan Sanchez once worked with. Do you know where he was calling from?"

"No. The reception faded a few times. I suppose he was using a cell phone."

Anita shivered. *Bill Rankin could be on his way to Rockdale this very minute.* "Thank you for letting me know."

Phyllis Dickson stood, signaling the end of the interview. "I don't want any trouble at the hospital."

"Neither do I."

Mrs. Dixon's warning numbed Anita. She did not want to lose her job because of Bill Rankin, but knowing her daughter could be in danger from him was far worse. *If only Hawk were here—he would know what to do.*

Anita prayed for a calm spirit and the wisdom to make

correct decisions, and when she could do so in privacy, she called Toni Trent.

"I believe a man I knew in Texas is coming here. I am afraid he might try to harm Juanita."

Thankfully, Toni did not seem surprised or press her for personal details. "Give me his name and a general description."

After Anita did so, Toni promised to call the school and Mrs. Tarpley. "They'll make sure that no one has access to Juanita that they don't know personally. Local law enforcement should know about him, as well."

"Hawk is still out of town. I do not think Sheriff Trimble would listen to me."

"I'll call him, and I won't mention your name. I'll also talk to Earl Hurley, the Rockdale chief of police."

"Thank you. It might turn out to be nothing, but—"

"Better safe than sorry," Toni finished for her. "Call me right away if anything else comes up."

Somehow, Anita made it through the rest of her shift and picked up Juanita at the usual time. The girl's happy chatter made Anita even more determined to protect her daughter from Bill Rankin. As soon as she was sure Juanita was asleep that night, she tried again without success to call Hawk. His cell phone was out of calling range or he was unavailable, the robotic voice at the other end repeated each time.

When her own telephone rang a few minutes later, Anita hesitated to answer it, although she had asked for an unlisted number. Her answering machine was programmed with an anonymous male voice, and she let it take the call.

"Anita, this is Toni. If you're there, pick up."

"Hello, Toni. I was afraid it might be—someone else."

"Has the man contacted you yet?"

"No, and as I told you, I do not know for certain he will."

"Earl Hurley found no outstanding arrest warrants for anyone named Bill Rankin. Unless he actually commits a crime, their hands are tied."

"Perhaps this will come to nothing. He is not here yet—he might not even be planning to come. As the Bible says, 'Sufficient unto the day is the evil thereof,'" Anita quoted.

"That's a fine Scripture, but you must be careful, Anita. I've dealt with domestic violence, and I know how ugly it can get. Women should never be too afraid or ashamed to ask for help."

I should have done that when I was married to Juan, but domestic violence is not my problem now. Anita realized the social worker must think her current problem was related to domestic violence, but she could not deny it without telling Toni the whole sordid story of Bill Rankin's connection to Juan Sanchez—and she did not want to do that.

"God is with us. I will be all right. Good night, Toni."

❧

Hawk made better time coming back than he had going to North Carolina, but it was still almost midnight when he crossed the bridge into Rockdale, too late to call Anita.

I'll see her first thing tomorrow, Hawk promised himself.

Road-weary, he fell into bed and slept deeply until the insistent ringing of the telephone jarred him awake. He managed to pick it up just before his answering machine clicked. He was surprised to see it was almost eight o'clock.

"Henson," he said.

"Hawk—I thank God you are back. I thought I would have to leave a message on your answering machine."

Anita's voice sounded strained, and he sat up in bed, now fully awake. "What is wrong?"

"I need to talk to you."

"Has something happened to Juanita?"

"No. She is with Toni Trent. I will tell you why when I see you."

"I'll be over right away."

Hawk showered and dressed quickly, speculating all the while what could make the normally calm Anita Sanchez sound so afraid.

Whatever it was, Hawk prayed he would be able to help her.

⁂

"Thank you for coming." Anita said when she opened the door to admit him.

Hawk looked at her closely. Anita didn't appear to have been crying, but she was clearly troubled. "I intended to come by this morning, but I got in late last night, and I overslept."

"You have not had breakfast?"

Hawk made a gesture of dismissal. "I'm not hungry. What's wrong?"

"It is too long a story to hear on an empty stomach. I will make you breakfast."

Seeing Anita was determined to feed him, Hawk sat at the table and watched her move efficiently around the kitchen, pouring juice and coffee and whisking eggs to make an omelet.

Hawk wanted to tell Anita how much he had missed her, but the misery in her eyes silenced him.

"I didn't think you drank coffee," he said when Anita poured a cup for herself and joined him at the table.

"It is not as good as the coffee I had in Colombia—but this brand is acceptable."

"Thanks for that great breakfast. Now tell me what's going on."

When Anita lowered her head momentarily, Hawk thought she might be praying. Then she looked at him and squared her shoulders. "There are some things about me you do not know," she began.

⁂

Anita started at the beginning, briefly recounting the tragic events that had led her to leave Colombia. She traced how Juan Sanchez had persuaded her to marry him because he could protect her from the people who had killed her parents.

"I now believe Juan made up the threats himself. He thought I could claim my parents' fortune as my own until he realized it no longer existed. He turned to petty crime and was arrested and sent to prison. He died there in a riot not long before he would have been released."

As heartbreaking to hear as her story was, Hawk knew Anita was telling the truth. He reached across the table to take her hands in his. "I had no idea you have had that many terrible things happen to you."

Anita shrugged. "God has helped me through it all. Juanita and I had a good life until a man Juan had done robberies with showed up on Christmas Day. He claimed I stole a fortune belonging to him."

"You didn't, though?"

Anita shook her head. "I knew nothing about it. He said a woman who looked like me took his share of the money from a storage unit before he got out of prison. He wanted me to give it back."

"That's why you left San Antonio—you were running away from this guy?"

Anita nodded. "I did not think he could find us, but Mrs. Dixon said a man claiming to be my husband called the hospital Thursday to ask if I worked there. It has to be Bill Rankin. He knows where we are. I am afraid he will try to harm Juanita when I tell him I cannot give him the money."

No wonder she looks so troubled. "I had a feeling you were hiding something, but I never suspected anything like this. You should have told me."

"I would have when I knew you better, but I feared you might think less of me if you knew the whole story."

"Why? You shouldn't be ashamed of what Juan Sanchez did. You've risen above a lot of bad things in your life. If anything, I admire you even more, Anita."

Her face reddened. "I am so glad you are back," she whispered.

"Come here." Hawk stood and opened his arms, and Anita entered into his embrace. "Everything will be all right." He stroked her hair and comforted her as he would a child. He was willing to let her cry into his shoulder as long as she liked, but soon Anita pulled away and faced him, dry-eyed.

"What happens when Bill Rankin comes here looking for me?"

As a man in love, Hawk wanted to tell Anita he would protect her, no matter what. But as a law enforcement officer, he knew Rankin could be a dangerous foe. "The first thing is to keep Juanita away from him. You say she's at the Trents' now?"

"Yes. I called Toni yesterday, and she offered to take Juanita today. She also contacted the sheriff and the Rockdale police chief. He told her Bill Rankin is not currently wanted for any crime, and they cannot do anything unless he commits one here."

"You did well to call Toni, and she took the right steps. How much does she know about the situation?"

"I told her Juanita might be in danger from a man from my past. She does not know why I fear him."

"That doesn't matter—the main thing is, Juanita should stay away for the time being. Pack a suitcase with enough clothes to last her a few days, just in case, and I'll see that Toni gets it this afternoon."

"What about me? What should I do?"

Hawk glanced around the apartment. "Rankin mustn't know Juanita lives here. If he asks about her, say she's still in Texas. Take her artwork off the refrigerator and hide her toys.

"Then what?"

"We wait for him to show up. And we pray—a lot."

fifteen

Anita reached Toni by her calling her cell-phone number. "We've been shopping, and we're about to come home for lunch. Juanita can stay with us as long as necessary," Toni assured her.

"Thank you, Toni. Hawk has Juanita's suitcase. You can get it from him later today."

"I'm glad Hawk's back. He's a good man to have on your side in a crisis."

"I know," Anita said. She hung up and turned to Hawk. "Toni said Juanita can stay there indefinitely."

"I thought she would. Toni's a good woman to have on your side in a crisis."

Anita managed a feeble smile, her first in many hours. "That is exactly what Toni said about you. Juanita and I are blessed to have such good friends."

"Toni and I have worked together on several crisis situations involving children."

"I wish you could stay here," Anita said when Hawk stood to leave.

"So do I, but I have work to do at the sheriff's office, and I must get a new battery for my cell phone. It quit on me in North Carolina."

"I do not want to be out of touch with you, especially now."

"Don't worry, I'll borrow a phone if I can't get mine fixed. If you can't reach me, call Toni."

"I will."

Hawk kissed her briefly, and when he left, Anita locked and bolted the door behind him.

She felt the need to pray, yet she could not concentrate

enough to frame an effective prayer. *God knows what I need. I must trust Him to provide it.*

❧

Anita had never known time to go by so slowly. When the telephone rang, her heart hammered, and she waited in dread for the answering machine to take the call.

"Pick up, Anita."

"Where are you?" she asked, relieved to hear Hawk's voice.

"At my desk in the sheriff's department. I have a new battery for my cell phone, but it'll be awhile before it's charged up enough to use. In the meantime, you can call me here at the office."

"Yes. I will let you know if anything happens."

"Are you all right? I can barely hear you."

Anita cleared her throat and tried to speak louder. "I am fine."

"Stay that way. I'm working on a plan to deal with this guy. I'll talk to you again in a little while."

Anita hung up the telephone, but in minutes it rang again. She waited warily until she heard Toni Trent's voice.

"Hi, Anita. Somebody here wants to talk to you."

"Guess what, Mama!" Juanita exclaimed as she got on the phone. Without waiting for Anita to speak, she continued in a rush. "We had hot dogs and, then Miss Toni took me and Josh to her church, and she played a tape in a big machine and tried out this real pretty song. She's gonna sing it tomorrow. She says I can stay over here tonight and go to church with them and hear her sing if you'll let me. Can I, Mama?"

Hearing her daughter's excitement, Anita thanked God for a friend like Toni Trent, who had the ability to keep Juanita safe without letting the child know she was in danger. Now it was up to Anita to play her part. "Are you sure it is all right with Miss Toni?"

"She wants to me stay."

"Let me speak to Miss Toni."

When Toni came on the line, Anita thanked her for the invitation as normally as she could. "Hawk has her suitcase. He was at the sheriff's department when he called a few minutes ago."

"David can pick it up—he's going out again, anyway. Let me know when you want us to bring Juanita home."

You mean, when it is safe to bring her home. "I will." *And dear Lord, let it be soon.*

№

The third time the telephone rang an hour later, Anita took a deep breath and braced herself, certain this time the call would be from Bill Rankin.

"It's Hawk. Any word yet?"

"No. You must wonder if Bill Rankin even exists."

"He's real, all right—I looked up his record. Rankin was released from prison on parole in December and supposedly returned to the Houston area."

"We lived in Houston when Juan went to prison."

"That makes sense. That's probably where the money he thinks you have was stashed away."

Anita shivered. "What will happen when he finds me?"

"Nothing, if I have anything to say about it. My guess is he'll drive here. He probably won't get here before Sunday evening. I have to work until eleven tonight, but I'm off Sunday. I'll be over tomorrow morning. If you need me before then, call my cell phone. Try to get some sleep tonight."

"Thank you, Hawk."

№

Before she went to bed, Anita read through many of her favorite psalms. Gradually, the peace which passeth all understanding allowed her to have a restful night. She felt much calmer when she opened the door to Hawk around ten o'clock on Sunday morning.

"You look much better today," Hawk commented after embracing her briefly.

"I prayed a lot, and I slept well last night. Now I wonder if

Bill Rankin is really coming here."

"I'm almost certain he'll show up. I dug around in the Texas records a bit more. Juan Sanchez and an unknown accomplice committed a robbery in Dallas. Juan went to prison, the other man got away, and the money they took was never recovered."

"Juan was already in prison before I knew about the robbery. I never heard how much money was involved."

"The company they robbed didn't make the amount public, but I found it in the police records. If they agreed to split the money, Rankin's share would be twenty-five grand."

Anita's eyes widened. "I had no idea it was so much. I wish Juan had never told that man he had a wife."

Hawk squeezed her hand. "I know you hoped you'd never see this Rankin again, but if he comes here, we'll make sure he's put away where he can't bother anyone again."

"I just want him to go away and leave me alone."

"That won't work. Rankin tracked you to San Antonio, and he knows you're in Rockdale. When he gets here, you have to let him into the apartment and talk to him. It won't take him long to incriminate himself."

"It will be my word against his," Anita said.

"Not this time. I'm getting you a remote recording device called a wire. Every word you and anyone near you says will be sent to a receiver and recorded."

"Where?"

"In my Jeep."

Anita thought of what lay ahead and shook her head. "He believes I have his money. When I keep telling him I do not, I think he might hurt me."

"I won't let that happen. I'll hear every word Rankin says and watch every move he makes. If he even looks like he wants to lay a hand on you, I can have him in handcuffs in a matter of seconds. But I doubt that will be necessary, because you won't tell him you don't have the money."

"Then what—"

"Here's the plan." Hawk spoke earnestly, answered Anita's questions, then asked her to repeat what she was to do when Bill Rankin arrived. "If he calls first, get him to come to the apartment. I'll stay here until I know he's on the way."

"What if he should come here directly?"

"He won't see me—I'll have time to go out the back door."

"You seem to have thought of everything," Anita said.

"I hope so. Juanita will have to stay at Toni's again tonight. I'll get the equipment together and come back later."

Anita followed Hawk to the door. "You know I can never tell you how much what you are doing for Juanita and me means to me."

Hawk smiled faintly. "As you recently pointed out, you've done a good job of taking care of yourself. But until Bill Rankin is back behind bars where he belongs, I'm glad you're letting me help."

≈

Knowing the Trents usually went out to eat after church, Anita waited until Sunday afternoon to call Toni.

"How is Juanita?" she asked.

"She's having a really good time. She enjoyed going to Bible study and church with us. The question is, how are you?"

"I am afraid I might be coming down with something. I do not want to expose Juanita to it."

"I understand," Toni said. "We'll be glad for her to stay over tonight, and I'll take her to school tomorrow."

"Let me tell her—I do not want her to worry about me," Anita said.

After a brief conversation that reassured Anita her daughter welcomed staying with the Trents another night, she hung up the phone with the hope it would be the last time she had to make such a request.

As much as she dreaded seeing Bill Rankin again, Anita

was more than ready to face him if it meant he would be out of her life forever.

෧

Hawk returned to the apartment around three o'clock with a small plastic case containing a tangle of wires, a small battery, and a miniature microphone. He showed her how to put it on, then directed her to test it by talking.

"I'll be in the Jeep, checking to make sure it's working."

Anita entered the bedroom to untangle the wires. She wrapped them around her waist, then put on a bulky turtle-neck sweater to make sure the wires were hidden, the battery was accessible, and nothing would muffle the microphone.

Back in the living room, Anita looked out the window at Hawk's Jeep and waved. "I have this thing on, but I do not know if it works."

In a moment, Hawk returned to the apartment. "I heard you loud and clear. You can turn off the battery for now— you're ready for Mr. Rankin."

෧

Tom Duffey worked as charge nurse for the Rockdale Hospital ER day shift four days a week and every other weekend. Compared to the more dramatic Saturday night cases, Sunday nights were usually calm. Shortly after seven o'clock on this Sunday, Tom was doing paperwork at his desk in the charge nurse's office when the receptionist called him.

"A man with a badge wants to see you," she said.

"What kind of badge?"

"Detective."

"Where's Dr. Drew?" Tom asked, referring to the Birmingham medical school resident who worked in the ER on weekends.

"The doctor said you should talk to him."

Tom sighed. "Send him back."

The man who approached Tom's desk didn't fit his idea of a detective. His clothes looked as if he'd slept in them, he needed a shave, and his horn-rimmed glasses gave him a peculiar, owlish look. However, he opened his billfold to reveal a detective's shield with "Martin" printed across it.

"I'm Detective John Martin. I want to see the charge nurse. Where is she?"

Tom was accustomed to people who didn't know male nurses existed and had long since stopped taking it personally. "You're looking at him. What can I do for you?"

"I need to question one of your nurses about an investigation—a young woman named Anita Sanchez."

Tom heard the name with mixed feelings. Professionally, he knew he wasn't supposed to reveal information about hospital employees, but personally, he hadn't trusted the Sanchez woman from the start, and he was curious to know why the detective wanted her. "Is she in some kind of trouble?"

"No, but she may have important knowledge about a current police investigation. Where can I find her?"

"I can't give out that information."

Detective Martin snapped his billfold shut and leaned over the desk. "Look, Mr. Duffey, don't make this hard. If I have to come back here with a warrant, interfering with a police investigation won't look good on your record."

Tom raised his hands in mock surrender. "No need for a federal case." Tom opened his desk drawer and withdrew the card marked SANCHEZ, ANITA M., from the file box. "She lives in Harrison Homes—the apartment number isn't listed." Tom copied the information on a memo sheet and handed it to the detective.

"This is just what I need. Have a nice night, Mr. Duffey."

The man almost swaggered as he walked away. *He didn't say where he was from,* Tom realized the moment the detective left. Everyone in law enforcement anywhere around Rockdale had been in the ER on business at one time or another, and Tom knew them all. Belatedly, he thought he should have checked the man out with the local police.

However, to say anything now would be like locking the barn door after the horses were long gone.

He called Anita Sanchez a young woman—he must know her. Tom briefly thought he should alert Anita Sanchez about the man, but he didn't want to get on the wrong side of the detective.

"What did he want?" the ER receptionist asked when Tom returned from his office.

"Nothing important."

sixteen

The pale winter sun set early, and Anita turned on a single lamp beside the couch. Hawk brought in pizza, and after they ate, they remained at the kitchen table, near the back door. Although the blinds were closed, they could see the headlights of every car entering Harrison Homes. They watched at the window to see if any of the automobiles would stop in front of Anita's apartment.

"This place has a lot of traffic for a Sunday night," Hawk commented after the tenth car went on without stopping.

"For public housing, it is still a quiet place."

"Dwight Anders makes sure of that, but you and Juanita should have a better home."

"Getting this apartment was an answer to prayer. It is more than enough."

Hawk regarded Anita intently. "I know, but you and Juanita deserve to have the best of everything."

At the moment he moved to take her into his arms, another automobile turned into the apartment complex, then slowed to a crawl. The car passed the apartment, then the driver braked and backed up.

Anita whispered, even though no one outside could hear her, "It must be Rankin."

The automobile eased into a parking place between Hawk's Jeep and Anita's car. When the headlights went out, Hawk gave Anita a quick hug.

"Turn on the battery before you go to the door. He has no idea you know he's coming, so act surprised. You know what to do?"

"Yes."

"Remember, I won't let you get hurt."

Hawk closed the back door behind him just as a knock sounded at the front door. Anita switched on the battery and earnestly prayed she would be able to do what Hawk had told her.

Anita turned on the outside light and peered through the blinds. At first, she did not recognize the man standing there. His hair was a strange color, and he wore odd, horn-rimmed glasses. Once she looked at his features, however, Anita knew Bill Rankin had, indeed, found her. Taking a deep breath, she opened the door.

"Hello, Mrs. Sanchez." He jerked a thumb toward her car. "Looks like you ran into a little trouble on the way from Texas."

Anita had no difficulty looking shocked. "What are you doing here?"

Bill Rankin smiled smugly. "You know very well. I want no more than I did before—and I won't take less. Aren't you going to let me in?"

Anita shrugged and opened the door wider to admit him. "It will not do you any good. I have nothing to say to you."

"Is that why you left town in such a big hurry?"

"What I do is not your business. Please go away and leave me alone."

"Not until you show some cooperation. Tell me, how does that pretty little girl of yours like Alabama?"

She glared at him. "My daughter is not here. I left her with friends in Texas."

"Even if you did, I can find her. You don't want to make me have to do that, do you?"

Rankin's smirk told Anita he enjoyed her discomfort.

She folded her arms and regarded him steadily. "If you do not leave, I will have you arrested."

Rankin's laughter was chilling. "Sure, you will. Look, Anita, you know we have to settle this sooner or later. If you try to run away again, I'll just follow you. I'm a reasonable man. Give me what is mine, and you won't see me again."

"You have never told me what, exactly, you want."

"Don't try to play dumb with me, Girlie. We both know what Juan Sanchez did with my money. You beat me to Dallas and took it all from the storage unit. Now, I want my share."

"In San Antonio, you told me you did a robbery with my husband. He did prison time for it, and you did not. I do not think you deserve anything."

"I don't see it that way. You should know by now I mean business. You have my money, and I want it."

"If I had taken your ten thousand, would I be living in public housing?"

Bill Rankin's face reddened. "You have a lot more than that, and we both know it."

"I know no such thing. But. . ." Anita paused for a moment. "How much money would it take for you to go away and leave me alone?"

Rankin relaxed visibly. *He thinks he has me now.* Anita's heart beat faster. *I must keep my nerve.*

"All I ask is my share of the take—for thirty thousand, you'll never see me again."

Anita shook her head. "I will not be cheated. Your share was less than twenty-five."

Rankin's smile made him look almost pleasant. "So you do have the money! I knew it." He glanced around the apartment as if looking for a possible hiding place.

"You will find nothing here," Anita said hastily.

"So where is it?"

Anita pulled her necklace from beneath the turtleneck and showed him the key attached to it. "This opens a safety deposit box at a local bank."

Rankin looked skeptical. "You would have to rent more than one box to hold a suitcase full of cash."

"No. Inside the safety deposit box is the key to a storage unit."

Bill Rankin folded his arms and shook his head. "You expect

me to believe you went to all that much trouble to hide the money in this jerkwater town?"

"Believe what you like. The bank opens at nine. I will get the key and meet you at the Store-More on Rockdale Boulevard."

"Try any tricks, and my contacts in Texas will take care of your daughter. I don't think you want that to happen."

"What I want is to be rid of you, Mr. Rankin. That matters more to me than the money."

"Smart girl. See you tomorrow. Sleep well, Mrs. Sanchez."

Anita followed Rankin to the door and leaned against it, drained.

As soon as Rankin's car was out of sight, Hawk reentered the apartment through the back door. "You can turn off the microphone now."

"Did it work?" she asked.

"Perfectly. You were great."

"Is it enough to arrest him?"

"We have Rankin's verbal threats on tape, but when he shows up at the storage unit, it'll prove beyond all doubt he intended to extort money from you."

"What happens then?"

"The Rockdale Police will be on hand to arrest him." Hawk glanced at his watch. "I need to set things up with Chief Hurley tonight. Will you be all right here alone?"

Anita allowed herself a small smile. "I am accustomed to being by myself, but I am never alone—God is with me."

"I think you'll be safe tonight. I doubt Rankin will come back, but if he should, call me immediately—and don't let him inside."

Anita nodded agreement, and Hawk gathered her into his arms for a brief kiss. "Everything will be all right. Soon all of this will be over."

When Hawk left, Anita closed and locked the door behind him. His words had reminded her of her father's favorite quotation from St. Teresa. *"Todo se pasa—Dios no se muda."*

Everything passes—but even more important—*God does not change.*
    God will supply all the courage I need to play my part well tomorrow.

❧

Bill Rankin left Harrison Homes and headed toward the Courthouse Square. He was pleased with the way the evening had gone, but fatigue from his long drive from Texas was beginning to take its toll. He had originally planned to spend the night in his car, watching Anita Sanchez's apartment to make sure she didn't try to run out on him. However, his negotiations with her had gone so well, Rankin no longer thought that precaution was necessary.

Mentioning her kid had done the trick, he decided. Anita Sanchez might like to keep all the money, but even more than that, she wanted her daughter to be safe—and she knew Bill Rankin was smart enough to find her. Tomorrow, all his hard work would pay off.

In the meantime, he needed a place to sleep. Rockdale wasn't exactly overrun with motels, but Bill remembered a billboard on the edge of town advertising a place on Main Street, "in the heart of Rockdale." He reached Main Street and turned right. A few blocks later, he saw the Rockdale Inn, a square, two-story red brick building. From the few cars scattered around the parking lot, Bill Rankin figured he could get a room without any trouble. "This is your lucky day, my man," he said aloud.

The lobby was empty when Bill entered, but when he rang a bell on the counter, a woman emerged from a room marked "Office" and greeted him. *Lois Tanner, Manager,* he read on her name tag.

"I need a single room for tonight."

Mrs. Tanner quoted a lower price than he expected.

"In that case, I'll pay cash."

"Sign the register, and I'll get your room key."

Welcome to the dark ages, Bill thought when the innkeeper

pushed the large ledger toward him. He hadn't seen one of those in a hotel for years. He had just written "John Martin" after the current date when a name at the top of the opposite page leaped out at him. *Anita Sanchez*. She had signed this very register only a few days after Christmas.

"I see a familiar name," Bill said.

"Oh? Who would that be?"

"Someone I knew in San Antonio—Anita Sanchez. Nice-looking brunette lady with a pretty little girl."

Mrs. Tanner beamed. "That would be Juanita. I hated to see them leave."

"They're still in town, though?"

"Oh, yes. Anita Sanchez works at the hospital. You can look her up there tomorrow, Mr.—" The innkeeper turned the ledger around to read his name. "Mr. Martin."

"I might do that. I suppose Juanita is going to school here?"

"Yes—Rockdale Elementary. She's a bright little girl." Mrs. Tanner rummaged around under the counter for a moment and brought out a photograph of a little girl with long, black hair, wearing an oversize apron. "I took this one day when she was helping me make soup."

"She still resembles her mother," Bill said.

"Isn't that the truth! Here's your key, Mr. Martin. Room 116's on the right. It's just across the hall from where the Sanchezes stayed."

"Thanks." Bill Rankin walked away from the registration desk, his fatigue suddenly replaced by anger. Anita Sanchez had lied to him. *Her daughter is here in Rockdale, after all.* There had been no sign of her in the apartment—Bill was certain of that. Someone must have tipped off Anita Sanchez.

She knew I was on her trail, and she played me for a sucker.

Bill entered his room, his mind racing. He didn't know what game Anita Sanchez might think she was playing, but she was about to lose—and her daughter would be Bill Rankin's winning card.

seventeen

Anita slept fitfully Sunday night and awoke long before dawn. She watched the sun rise in a cloudless sky on Monday morning and rehearsed the day ahead.

In a few hours, she and Bill Rankin were to meet one last time, and she prayed everything would go according to Hawk's plan. Anita did not know what the future might hold for her and Juanita after this morning, but she had no doubt Hawk Henson would play a large part in it.

When her telephone rang around seven o'clock, Anita answered right away, thinking it must be Hawk.

"Hello, Mamacita. Are you feeling better?"

Hearing her daughter's voice, Anita smiled. "Hi, Sweetie. Yes, I am much better. I will not go to work this morning, but I will see you after school."

"All right. Here's Miss Toni. She wants to talk to you. 'Bye, Mama." Juanita made a kissing sound, and Anita could hear her daughter hand the receiver to Toni Trent.

"Good morning," Toni said. "Juanita and I wanted to know how you're getting along."

"As I told her, I will not go to the hospital this morning. I plan to pick her up after school, though."

Anita heard Toni cover the telephone while she talked briefly to someone, then she returned to the line. "The kids are making so much racket packing their lunches I could hardly hear you. They've closed the kitchen door, so we can talk in peace. Is everything really all right?"

"Yes. Hawk has the situation under control."

"I'm glad. If there's anything I can do, I hope you'll let me know."

"I will. Thank you for keeping Juanita. I know she has had a good time."

"The pleasure was ours. I should warn you—Mandy French-braided Juanita's hair last night."

"French braid?"

"You might have another name for it—her hair is plaited close to her head. French braids can stay in place for days. Mandy's Aunt Evelyn taught her how to do it, and she loves to practice on anyone with long hair. I hope you don't mind."

"Not at all. Tell Mandy I might let her braid my hair sometime too."

"I will." The call-waiting tone sounded on Toni's line. "Oops—I need to take this call. I'll check with you later."

Anita hung up, feeling much better. Her daughter was happy and safe, and soon she would see Hawk again.

When Bill Rankin was out of the way for good, life would be close to perfect.

❧

"I hope you slept well, Mr. Martin."

Bill Rankin looked up from his breakfast and belatedly realized he was the Mr. Martin the innkeeper was addressing. "Yes. I like a quiet place like this."

"Business is slow this time of year. If you want to stay longer, I can give you a very good rate."

"I'll keep that in mind. By the way, do you have a Rockdale map?"

Mrs. Tanner laughed. "It's hard to get lost around here, Mr. Martin. I can tell you how to get to just about anyplace hereabouts."

"I want to make note of some area addresses. A map would help."

Mrs. Tanner returned from the reception desk and handed him a dog-eared Chamber of Commerce map with the town of Rockdale grid on one side and Rockdale County roads on the other. "It's not new, but then not much else around here is."

"Thanks. I'll return it in a few minutes."

"Take your time. Checkout's not until noon."

Back in the room, Bill Rankin opened the map and began to make notes. He glanced at his watch, satisfied he had time to find Juanita Sanchez and still meet Anita at the Store-More.

Anticipating the look on the woman's face, Bill smiled in satisfaction. His situation was looking better by the minute. Not only would he get his cut of the money, but probably Juan's as well.

Bill patted the fat envelope in his briefcase. In a matter of hours, John Martin's passport and airline tickets would take Bill Rankin out of the country to a place where he could live like a king on almost nothing.

But first, he had to find Juanita Sanchez.

&

Bill Rankin noted the location of the elementary school on Mrs. Tanner's map. Although it was within easy walking distance of the Rockdale Inn, he drove his car to within a block of the school's main entrance and parked. From his vantage point, he could watch every child enter. Even if he didn't see Juanita Sanchez go into the building, Bill Rankin believed the girl would be there that morning.

Just after eight o'clock, he would go inside, flash Detective John Martin's badge, make up a story about Juanita Sanchez being in danger, and walk out with his prize. On the way into town, he'd noticed a long-abandoned log cabin near the road. He would have enough time to take the girl there and still meet her mother at nine o'clock.

While he waited, Rankin idly watched the seemingly endless procession of vehicles depositing waves of children in front of the school. A pickup truck pulled to the curb in front of him and stopped. A boy and girl got out, and the male driver pulled away from the curb immediately and turned left into a cross street.

He must be in a big hurry, was Rankin's first thought. Then he looked at the children and felt a rush of adrenaline. He quickly dismissed the boy, who looked about eight or nine years old, and focused his attention on the petite dark-haired girl clutching a cloth doll. Her hair was in braids, but her features definitely matched the picture the innkeeper had showed him.

If that little girl isn't Juanita Sanchez, I'll eat my hat.

The boy walked rapidly toward the school, leaving his companion behind. Quickly, Rankin got out of the car and started after the girl. He saw a doll-sized blue shoe on the sidewalk and picked it up.

About the same time, the little girl stopped and turned around, apparently realizing her doll had lost one of its shoes.

Rankin smiled and held out the small blue object. "Hello, Juanita. I believe I have something that belongs to you."

eighteen

"Good morning, Anita. Any problems last night?"

Hawk's welcome voice made Anita smile. "No. Everything has been very quiet. Dr. Endicott knows I will not come to work today. I plan to be at the bank at nine o'clock."

"Good. Bill Rankin might not be trailing you, but you know what to do."

"Yes. I will stay in the bank a few minutes. Then I go to the Store-More on Rockdale Boulevard."

"Correct. Rankin will show up there for sure, and when he does, we'll be ready."

"If he has reason to believe I have called the police, I do not know what he might do."

"He won't see us—besides, his mind will be on the money."

"I want this man to be out of our lives."

"We're almost there, Honey. Hang on, and I'll see you shortly."

Anita stood holding the receiver for a moment, reviewing their conversation. Hawk had called her "honey," not in the way Southern clerks and waitresses did as a matter of course, but with genuine affection. Having to deal with Bill Rankin had preoccupied them both and postponed the time when their feelings for one another could be openly discussed. Now, Anita had yet another reason to play out the rest of her charade with Bill Rankin.

At twenty minutes before nine on Monday morning, Anita Sanchez entered the Rockdale bank where she had recently opened a checking account.

Almost immediately, Hawk's cousin called to her. "Hi, Ms. Sanchez. You're getting an early start. What can we do for you?"

"Good morning, Debbie. I would like to have my paycheck from the hospital sent here directly. Can I do that?"

"Sure, if you have an account with us."

"I opened a checking account last week, but I have not used it."

"I can give you the form to request direct deposit. It's very simple."

As Debbie Hawk got the form, Anita half-turned so she would see anyone entering the bank. She did not expect Rankin would come inside, but if he did, she would pretend to have been coming from the bank's safety deposit boxes.

"Here you go," Debbie said a few moments later. "I put your account number on the top line. Fill out the rest and take it to the hospital payroll office."

"Thank you." Anita took the form and had started to leave when Debbie spoke again. "I haven't seen my cousin around lately. Is he all right?"

The teller's casual presumption that she would know about Hawk both embarrassed and pleased Anita. "Hawk was out of town for a week. He is back now."

Debbie smiled. "The next time you see him, tell him I said hello."

"I will."

Her conversation with the teller temporarily distracted Anita, but when she emerged from the bank into the glare of the sun, she thought about what lay ahead and sighed deeply. With God's help, the nightmare Bill Rankin had brought into her life would soon be over.

❧

Wearing uniform coveralls provided by Rockdale Moving and Storage Company, Hawk and Rockdale Chief of Police Earl Hurley waited in the Store-More office for the subject of their stakeout to arrive. The third member of their team, Sheriff Trimble, was stationed inside a storage unit containing, among other things, the decoy suitcase.

Getting them together early on a Monday morning, especially with such short notice, had taken all of Hawk's powers of persuasion. Aware of past arguments over jurisdiction between the city and county law enforcement units, Hawk presented the situation as an exercise in interagency tactical training. Chief Hurley welcomed the opportunity to defend his town's turf, and Sheriff Trimble agreed to participate so he could claim some of the credit for capturing a dangerous criminal. Since neither routinely worked stakeouts, Hurley and Trimble were quite willing for Hawk, who had the most tactical experience, to take charge of the operation.

Early Monday morning, they met in the warehouse of a moving company owned by one of Hawk's cousins. After a brief run-through, the men put coveralls on over their uniforms and drove a small moving van to the storage facility.

"What happens if Anita Sanchez loses her nerve?" Earl Hurley asked Hawk.

"I don't think she will. In any case, she's an innocent victim and must be protected."

"She doesn't look all that innocent to me," Sheriff Trimble muttered. "If it wasn't for her and her kind, our jobs would be a lot easier."

Hawk wanted to defend Anita, but he knew he'd be wasting his breath on a man unwilling to part with his deep-rooted prejudices.

"Our job is to catch bad guys," Chief Hurley reminded the sheriff, "and I hope we can close the book on this one."

When the time neared for Anita and Rankin to meet, Hawk felt a rush of adrenaline. As he always did when facing a potentially dangerous situation, Hawk closed his eyes and offered a silent prayer for protection.

"Someone's coming," Earl Hurley said in a stage whisper, and Hawk opened his eyes to see Anita's car pull into the Store-More.

❧

Bill Rankin's errand had taken a little longer than he expected, but it would be well worth it. He had Anita Sanchez exactly where he wanted her, and very soon, he would have her money as well.

Rankin got back to Rockdale as the clock on the court-house struck nine times. He spotted Anita's car in the parking lot of the bank and congratulated himself. *Perfect timing, Rankin. You ought to do this for a living.*

Chuckling at his wit, Bill Rankin drove toward the place he and Anita were to meet. Seeing a grocery store, he pulled into the parking lot and put Dora's shoe into a Rockdale Inn envelope, sealed it, and stuck it in his pocket. He waited a moment after Anita's car passed before he eased back onto Rockdale Boulevard. He didn't think she had alerted the police to follow her, but he'd done time more than once for taking too much for granted. He could smell a setup a mile away, and if anything looked out of the ordinary, he wouldn't even stop at the storage unit.

Seeing the Store-More sign ahead, Bill Rankin slowed even more. Although Rockdale Boulevard was a busy, four-lane road, the Store-More units were tucked away at right angles to the street, somewhat shielded from curious passersby. Except for an unattended moving van and Anita's automobile, the place was deserted.

Since everything looked legitimate, Bill Rankin smiled in anticipation as he turned into the parking area. If all went as well as he expected, Anita Sanchez was about to lose her fortune—and he was about to claim it.

❧

When Hawk had explained his plan to Anita the night before, it had sounded simple. Anita would meet Rankin near the Store-More office and lead him to a nearby unit where she would show him a suitcase supposedly containing the money. When Rankin took the suitcase, the law enforcement officers would come out of their hiding places and make the arrest. At no time would Anita be in danger. The case against Bill Rankin would stand up in court, and he would go to prison on a number of different charges ranging from a Texas parole violation to attempted extortion.

Now that the time had come to carry out the plan, Anita prayed for the ability to play her part well. Knowing Hawk was nearby reassured her. Although she could not see him and was not sure where he was, Anita knew he would protect her. When Rankin pulled in beside her, she did not hesitate to get out of the car and wait for him to join her.

"Good morning, Señora Sanchez," he drawled. "I presume you're here on this lovely day to do a little business."

"What kind of business is that?"

"The same as we agreed to last night. Something of mine is in one of these units, and when I have it, you'll get something you want."

"You will go away and leave me alone, yes?"

"That is not the only thing you want." Rankin reached into his pocket and pulled out an envelope with a pronounced bulge in the middle. "Take this."

"What is it?"

"Look and see."

Anita's fingers trembled slightly as she opened the envelope. When she saw the small blue object it contained, her heart lurched, and she felt dizzy. *Dora's shoe.* Juanita had taken her doll to the Trents' house. *Wherever Dora was, Juanita would likely be.*

"How did you get this?"

"That doesn't matter. You lied when you said your pretty little girl was in Texas. You'd better not be lying about the money. Give me what I want, and you'll get what you want—that's the deal."

"Where is my daughter?"

"In a safe place—for now. The quicker I get the money, the sooner you'll have her back."

Anita hesitated, her mind whirling. She knew Hawk was probably watching from the office, too far away to have seen Dora's shoe or heard Rankin's words. And even if he did, what could Hawk do differently? Bill Rankin had changed the script, but Anita had no choice but to play the part she had been assigned and pray everything would work out as originally planned. When that happened, Rankin would no longer be a threat to anyone.

"How do I know you have Juanita?"

"How do I know you have the money?"

"You will see. The suitcase is in that unit."

Rankin followed Anita down the line of identical storage units until she stopped at number seven. He looked around as if to assure himself they were alone. "Unlock the door and get on with it."

"That has already been done. It is open."

Bill Rankin frowned. "How did you have time to do that before I got here? This had better not be a trick."

Anita stood silent as Rankin seized the handle and raised the unit door. Hawk told her he would put an old brown leather suitcase underneath several boxes and other household items. In the time it would take Rankin to get to it, the officers would be in position to make the arrest.

When daylight flooded into the cubicle, Anita noticed a mattress leaning against the wall moved slightly and guessed one of the law enforcement officers was hiding behind it.

Fortunately, Rankin had not seemed to notice the movement. He glanced at the unit's contents and shook his head. "Where did all this stuff come from?"

"Different places," Anita replied truthfully enough. The unit was Hawk's and contained assorted odds and ends of furniture and household goods belonging to him and his late parents. She spotted the decoy suitcase Hawk had described, one of several pieces of luggage half-hidden beneath several cardboard boxes.

Silently Anita pointed to it, then stood back and held her breath, expecting Rankin to reach for the suitcase.

Instead, he pointed to a nearby dresser. "Put the suitcase up there and open it."

Anita hoped the officers would come forward and arrest Rankin at any moment, but no one approached as she wrestled the suitcase free and laid it on top of the mirrorless dresser.

"Open it," he demanded.

Anita pressed her thumbs against the latches. They snapped open with a loud click, and she stepped away. "You do the rest," she said.

Rankin put both hands on the lid, ready to lift it.

Where was Hawk? Although the winter morning was unusually warm, Anita felt cold. She folded her arms across her body and grasped her elbows. She had no idea what, if anything, the planted suitcase contained, but she knew it was not the fortune Rankin expected, and she feared what might happen if he looked inside before he could be arrested. Only when he could not lift the lid did Anita notice the small key-hole in the center of the suitcase.

Rankin scowled. "It's locked. Where's the key?"

"I—I don't have it," Anita stammered.

Enraged, Rankin pushed Anita's jacket aside and reached for her neck. His hand encountered the necklace, and roughly he jerked it free and held it up, revealing the dangling lock-box key.

"What do you call this, then?"

nineteen

"I don't know what's going on, but I don't like it," Hawk said moments after Bill Rankin arrived.

Earl Hurley peered through the binoculars he used at Alabama football games and had thought to bring at the last minute. "The guy just handed her some kind of envelope. She's in the way—I can't see what's in it."

"They're spending too much time talking. I should have wired Anita."

"I can't read lips, but Rankin looks like he thinks he's got the situation under control."

"He'll soon find out otherwise."

When Anita turned away and started toward the storage unit, Hawk alerted Sheriff Trimble by walkie-talkie. "They're on the way. Don't make your move until Rankin has the suitcase in his hand."

The sheriff's voice sounded muffled and far away. "It's about time. I just turned off my flashlight, and I can't see a thing."

"There will be plenty of light when they open the door." Hawk switched off the walkie-talkie and stood. "Let's go. It shouldn't take Rankin long to find the suitcase."

Although they had agreed not to use weapons unless absolutely necessary, Earl Hurley and Hawk had concealed their revolvers in the side pocket of their coveralls, and Hawk assumed Sheriff Trimble had done the same. Neither man spoke as they approached unit seven.

"Put the suitcase up there and open it," they heard Bill Rankin tell Anita.

Rankin and Anita had their backs to them as she lifted the suitcase onto an antique dresser and opened the side clasps.

Hawk and Earl Hurley exchanged a concerned glance.

This isn't the way we planned it. Where is Sheriff Trimble, and what will he do?

They were still a couple of yards away when Bill Rankin tried to lift the suitcase lid, then snatched Anita's necklace. Hawk started running toward them, and at the same time, Sheriff Trimble stepped from his hiding place behind the mattress, which fell over and hit Rankin and Anita.

"Hands up!" the sheriff cried, waving his pistol wildly.

Rankin pushed the mattress back toward the sheriff, knocking him off balance. Grabbing the suitcase, he turned and ran into Hawk and Earl Hurley.

"Not so fast," the police chief said.

Bill Rankin's face reddened in fury. "What's going on here? Movers are robbing me in broad daylight? Where are the police?"

"We're right here." Hawk grabbed one of Rankin's arms, and the police chief held the other. Rankin continued holding onto the suitcase, and Anita's necklace dangled from his hand.

Sheriff Trimble joined them, holding his revolver with both hands. "It looks like you're the robber here," he said.

"You might as well drop the suitcase," Hawk said. "You won't find any money in it."

Anita remained inside the rental unit until Rankin was finally in custody, then she came out and stood beside Hawk.

"If you're the law around here, arrest this woman," Rankin loudly protested. "She's the thief, not me."

"That's not the way we heard it," Hawk said.

Chief Hurley cleared his throat to make a formal arrest statement, but Anita interrupted him. "This man has my daughter. Make him tell us where she is."

All three law enforcement officers stared at Anita. "What makes you think he's telling the truth?" Chief Hurley asked.

"This." Anita opened her shoulder bag and removed the envelope Rankin had given her.

Hawk recognized its contents immediately. "That shoe belongs to Juanita's doll. How did you get it, Rankin?"

"I found it," he said. "I don't know where the girl is."

When the men increased the pressure on their grip, Rankin winced and moved his shoulders to indicate his captors were hurting his arms. "Can we talk about this somewhere else?"

"Cuff him, and I'll call for a patrol car," Chief Hurley said. "If he's a kidnapper, the feds need to be informed right away."

Anita was closer to tears than she had been at any time since Bill Rankin found her. She looked from the chief to the sheriff in turn, her eyes pleading even more than her voice. "Please help me find my child—I have to know she is all right."

Hawk looked at Anita as if he wanted to take into his arms and comfort her. "Don't worry. We'll find her."

Sheriff Trimble was obviously skeptical. "This man told you flat out he has your daughter?"

"More or less. He said he had something I wanted and he would give it to me in return for the money."

"Before we jump to any more conclusions, let's make sure the girl's really missing," Chief Hurley said. "Where is she supposed to be?"

Anita forced herself to speak calmly. "Juanita spent the weekend with the Trents. She should be at school now."

Earl Hurley jerked a thumb toward the moving van. "My cell phone's on the front seat. Call the school and see if she's there, then bring me the phone."

"Check with the Trents if she's not," Hawk added. "They might just be running late. Do you have the numbers?"

"Yes." Anita climbed into the moving van cab and called Rockdale Elementary School from the list she always carried in her handbag. Waiting for someone to answer, she prayed to hear good news. *Maybe Bill Rankin really did find the shoe, or more likely, he managed to steal it to frighten me into giving him the money. If so, Juanita will be at school. . . .*

"Rockdale Elementary, Mrs. Hurst speaking."

Anita had met the school secretary when she enrolled Juanita, and she remembered how patiently the woman had helped her fill out the paperwork. "Mrs. Hurst, this is Anita Sanchez. I need to know if my daughter, Juanita, is at school today."

"Just a moment and I'll check."

Anita heard the sound of papers being shuffled, followed by a long silence and a muffled conversation before the secretary returned to the phone.

"Mrs. Sanchez? Miss Oliver reported her absent. No one tried to check her out from the office—apparently she never got here today."

Anita's eyes filled with tears, but she managed to steady her voice. "She spent last night with the Trents. Is Josh also absent?"

"I'll find out."

In the silence, Anita tried to tell herself everything was probably fine. *Toni Trent sometimes has emergency calls. Perhaps such a call this morning delayed her.*

After another long pause, the secretary returned to the telephone. "Josh is here, Mrs. Sanchez. He says his mother had an emergency call, and his father took him and Juanita to within a block of school and let them out to walk the rest of the way. Josh went on ahead and thought Juanita was behind him. Perhaps you should tell the police."

"Thank you. I will do that."

Numb with worry, Anita left the van. Hawk, Sheriff Trimble, and Chief Hurley had removed the moving company coveralls and were in the process of putting Bill Rankin into the back seat of a Rockdale police cruiser.

Hawk turned as Anita approached. "What did you find out?"

"Juanita is not in school. Josh Trent is, but Juanita never got there." Anita brushed past Hawk and went to the patrol car where Bill Rankin sat in the back seat and addressed him in a voice choked with emotion. "What have you done with her? Where is Juanita?"

Even in custody and wearing handcuffs, Bill Rankin remained defiant. "Where is my money?"

Hawk reached inside and grabbed the lapels of Rankin's coat. "Aren't you in enough hot water already? Tell us where to find the girl, or you're going to be in a whole lot more trouble."

"Let me go. I can't tell you where she is."

Hawk stepped back, but there was no mistaking the fury in his eyes. "Can't, or won't?"

Bill Rankin leaned back against the seat as if considering his options. "I might be able to show you a place where a child could hide."

Anita's eyes pleaded with Chief Hurley. "Let him take us there."

"Not until we book him."

Hawk spoke earnestly. "Look, Chief, this man kidnapped a six-year-old child this morning. Getting her back is more important at the moment than taking his fingerprints."

"I don't know what you're talking about," Rankin said sullenly. "Anita Sanchez robbed me. I haven't hurt anybody."

"That part had better be the truth," Hawk said.

"Where is my daughter?" Anita repeated.

Rankin jerked his cuffed hands in the direction of the mountain. "Up there."

"That's Rock County's jurisdiction," Sheriff Trimble said. "We'll go in one of our patrol cars."

"Mine is at the warehouse," Hawk said. "I'll drive the moving van there and be right back."

"Please hurry," Anita said.

Chief Hurley obviously didn't want to turn over any part of the investigation to Sheriff Trimble, but his jurisdiction technically ended at the city limits. "My patrol car will follow as backup, but I'll ride in the county car with the prisoner," the chief told Sheriff Trimble.

While Hawk was gone, the chief used his cell phone to report the incident to the FBI. "We have the situation under control," Anita heard him say, and she prayed it was so.

Some ten minutes later, they were on their way up the mountain. Hawk drove his Rock County patrol car, with Anita in the front seat. Still in handcuffs, Bill Rankin sat in the rear, wedged between Police Chief Hurley and Sheriff Trimble. Two city policemen followed in a Rockdale police cruiser.

Rankin had agreed to point out where they might find Juanita without admitting he had taken her there against her will, but he refused to answer any questions. "I know my rights. I'm supposed to have a lawyer. I don't have to talk to you."

"That's right, Rankin," Hawk said. "You don't have to say a word to show us where Juanita Sanchez is—just point in the right direction."

Bill Rankin chuckled as they drove past the guardrail crumpled by her car, and Anita's heart sank. *Juanita would have noticed that. Maybe she even said something to him about it.*

Hawk's quick glance told Anita he had noticed the guardrail as well and also remembered it as the place they had met. *How long ago that now seemed. . . .*

"There's nothing much along here except woods and logging trails," Sheriff Trimble said a moment later. "Did you take the girl to DeSoto State Park?" he asked Rankin.

When he remained silent, Hawk spoke. "I doubt he would go there. It's too public and too far."

"We must be getting close," Anita said. "He could not have gone very far this morning. He was at the storage unit just after nine o'clock."

"Good point," Hawk said. "Maybe you should consider a career in law enforcement, Mrs. Sanchez."

Hawk had spoken lightly, but Sheriff Trimble did not. "That's all we need, another fox to guard the henhouse."

Anita was not certain what the sheriff's statement meant, but she knew it was not complimentary. The sheriff had made his dislike for her plain enough.

"In a case like this, we need all the help we can get," Chief Hurley said.

Rankin remained silent, but a moment later he leaned forward and peered ahead, then raised his cuffed hands in the direction of a NO TRESPASSING sign on the right.

Anita and Hawk exchanged a quick glance of recognition but remained silent.

"How do you suppose Rankin found this place?" Sheriff Trimble asked as Hawk turned into the narrow lane.

"He probably noticed it on the way into town and thought it would make a good hideout," Chief Hurley said.

"Chances are he was planning to kidnap the girl all along," the sheriff said.

"No," Bill Rankin said, apparently forgetting he had said he wouldn't talk.

As the patrol car slowed in front of the log cabin that had been Hawk's ancestral home, Anita leaned forward and clasped her hands. *Let Juanita be all right,* she prayed, as she had from the moment she had seen Dora's shoe.

Anita wanted to run into the cabin, but even before the patrol car came to a complete stop, Hawk stayed her arm. "Wait outside. The sheriff and I will go in first."

Chief Hurley remained in the back seat with Bill Rankin, and Anita stood by the cabin door until, moments later, she heard a welcome voice from inside.

"Hello, Dep'ty Hawk. Have you seen Mama?"

Anita brushed past the men and knelt to sweep Juanita into her arms. The tears she had not shed in her anguish now flowed freely in her joy. "I am right here, Sweetie."

"Don't cry, Mamacita," Juanita said when her mother finally released her. "God took good care of me, just like you said He would."

Anita threw back the blanket and cried out when she saw rope binding her daughter's thin ankles. "Hawk, look at this."

Hawk's eyes darkened when he saw the circle of rope burns

around Juanita's ankles. "We'll have these off in a jiffy," he assured her.

To distract Juanita while Hawk loosened the ropes, Anita produced Dora's missing shoe and helped her slip it onto the huggy doll's foot. "There now. Dora has two shoes again." Then Anita took a closer look at the doll's hair. Once long like Juanita's, it was matted together. "What happened to Dora's hair?"

"I tried to do it in French braids, but it got all tangled."

Anita knew Mandy Trent had braided Juanita's hair, but she had not realized how much difference the French braids made. Having her hair pulled back made Juanita's face appear thin, and she looked older. "Don't worry, Sweetie. We can fix it when we get home."

"All set," Hawk said. Having freed Juanita, he unhooked the other end of the rope and coiled it. "This will be added to the evidence against Mr. Rankin."

Anita examined Juanita's ankles, relieved the damage seemed superficial. As painful as they must be, the burns would have been much worse if Juanita had struggled against the rope. Although it must have seemed like an eternity to the child, Anita thanked God Juanita had been in the cabin a relatively short time.

"Let's get you home." Hawk scooped Juanita into his arms and carried her outside.

The Rockdale policemen were transferring Bill Rankin to the back seat of their cruiser when Anita came out of the cabin. Seeing her, he stopped and yelled, "You may think you can keep your fortune, but when I tell the police where it came from, you won't have a dime."

"I thought you weren't going to talk," Chief Hurley said.

Bill Rankin shrugged. "Anita Sanchez may have everybody in this hick town fooled, but believe me, she's no saint. That's all I'm saying until I get a lawyer."

Hawk was buckling Juanita in the back seat of his patrol

car when Rankin made his outburst, and Anita hoped her little girl had not heard it. However, when Anita got in beside Juanita, she saw the girl looked troubled.

"That man said he was your friend, Mama, but he doesn't act nice at all. Dora's shoe fell off, and he took it and wouldn't give it back. He said he was taking me to see you, but you weren't here. Then he tied me up so I couldn't go outside and get chased by a bear. I wish he would go back to Texas and leave us alone."

"So do I, Sweetie. We must ask God to keep him from bothering us again."

"That's one prayer request I believe God will grant," Hawk said.

twenty

After they let Sheriff Trimble out at his office, Hawk offered to take Anita and Juanita directly to their apartment and return their car later in the day. "I imagine you ladies could use a little rest."

Anita shook her head. With the Lord's help, she and Juanita had walked through the valley of the shadow of death and come out unscathed. She had stayed strong then, and she intended to remain that way until she had seen the incident with Rankin through to its conclusion.

"Thank you for the offer, but I can drive myself home."

"I'm not tired," Juanita said. "You can take me back to school now, Dep'ty Hawk. Dora's s'posed to be my Show and Tell."

Anita smiled, grateful Juanita had apparently not been traumatized by the morning's events. "You can take Dora to school another time, Sweetie. We need to get home and put medicine on your ankle."

Juanita nodded. "All right. Dora's a little tired, anyway. She's had a very bad morning."

So have we all, Sweetie.

When they reached the Store-More, Hawk helped Juanita into the back seat and fastened her safety belt. "There you go, Princess."

He closed Juanita's door and joined Anita, who stood beside her car with her keys in her hand, looking down the line of storage units.

"This is not over yet, is it?" Anita's eyes asked Hawk to assure her their ordeal was completely finished, but he could not.

"When the FBI gets here, you and Juanita will be questioned.

You'll probably have to testify before a grand jury and at Rankin's trial, but I don't think he'll ever be in a position to bother you again."

"What about the money?"

Hawk looked puzzled. "What do you mean?"

"None of this would have happened if my husband had not helped Rankin commit a robbery. I would like to help the police find the money and restore it to the rightful owner."

"I have an idea who might have taken it, but the money has probably long since been spent."

"You can tell me about it later," Anita said.

Hawk glanced around, and seeing no one in the vicinity, he put his arms around Anita and pulled her to him. "Yes. I have several things to talk about. Go home and get some rest, and I'll come by after work."

❧

Anita went home, but resting was another matter. Soon after Anita entered the apartment, Toni Trent came by with Juanita's suitcase.

Toni hugged Anita and Juanita in turn. "I couldn't believe you got her back so fast," Toni said after Juanita took the suitcase to her room and started to unpack.

"The Lord was with us," Juanita said.

"Just about everyone in town was praying for both of you. David was in Statum's having coffee when he heard about it. He thought it was just a rumor at first."

Juanita came out of the bedroom, looking puzzled. "Mama, all my toys are gone. Did that man take them too?"

It will be a long time before she can forget Bill Rankin. "No, Sweetie. I put them away in the closet. You can get them out now."

"I can't tell you how sorry we are about what happened," Toni said when Juanita left. "David is devastated. The children were in sight of the school, and he had an important eight o'clock appointment. It never occurred to him anyone would snatch a child off the sidewalk in broad daylight in our little town."

"Please do not let your husband blame himself," Anita said. "I still do not understand how Rankin found out Juanita was in Rockdale."

"Perhaps he was already here, watching you even before he called the hospital."

"There are other things that do not make sense," Anita said but then was interrupted by the ringing telephone.

"I'll get it," Toni offered. "You don't need to be answering a lot of questions just now." Anita nodded consent, and Toni picked up the receiver. "Sanchez residence, Toni Trent speaking."

"Hello, Toni. This is Lois Tanner. Is it true that Juanita's been found and she's all right?"

"Yes on both counts, praise God."

"I felt just awful when I heard that sweet little girl was missing. It's funny—I was going to call Anita today, anyway—a man who registered at the inn last night said he'd known her in Texas."

"What was his name?" Toni asked, instantly alert.

"John Martin. He seemed to know Anita well. I showed him a picture I took of Juanita when they were living at the inn."

"Did he ask you questions about them?"

"Not that I recall—oh, he did ask if Juanita was with Anita and wanted to know if she was going to school."

"Lois, the police are going to want to talk to you. Call Earl Hurley and tell him what you just told me."

"Why?"

"That man could be the one who took Juanita."

"Oh, no! He seemed so nice—you know I would never willingly do anything to harm Juanita."

"Of course you wouldn't. We all know that. But you can help build the case against him."

"I'll call Earl Hurley right away. Tell Anita I'm sorry. I don't know what else to say."

"That's enough."

"If there's anything else I can do, I hope you or Anita will let me know."

"We will. Good-bye, Lois."

Anita had heard enough of the conversation to guess its content even before Toni repeated it. "One more mystery solved," she said. "The man who called Phyllis Dickson said he was John Martin too."

"He is very clever," Toni said. "I suppose that's what attracted you to him in the first place."

"What?" Anita asked, then she realized she had never told Toni Trent the reason she feared Bill Rankin. "I want you to know what really happened. Maybe it will help me to understand it better myself."

"What about Juanita?" Toni asked.

Anita looked into the bedroom and saw her daughter had fallen asleep on her bed, Dora in one arm and her next-favorite doll in the other. She closed the door and rejoined Toni in the living room.

"This could take awhile. I will make coffee."

❧

After all the personnel in the sheriff's office who were involved in the day's operations had given their statements to the FBI agent dispatched from Huntsville, Sheriff Trimble called Hawk into his office. He was pleased with the way things had turned out, especially since the FBI agent had been quite complimentary of him and his department.

However, Sheriff Trimble seemed convinced that the morning's events, precipitated by Anita Sanchez, signaled the start of a massive crime wave.

"I still think that woman has some connection with drugs. She might be clean now, but she and her husband must have been involved with all kinds of drug dealings in Texas."

"No. Juan Sanchez never had anything to do with drugs. He had a criminal record, but she didn't know that when she married him."

"What about her relationship with Rankin? You know the old saying—a person who lies down with dogs gets up with fleas."

Hawk sighed, exasperated by the sheriff's attitude. "She had no relationship with Rankin. As I told you, she was trying to get away from him. Despite all the bad things Anita Sanchez has been through, she is a fine woman."

Sheriff Trimble shook his head. "It's obvious her pretty face has you completely taken in. Once the hullabaloo is over, I hope the woman will return to her own kind and let Rockdale get back to normal."

"If I have anything to say about it, Anita Sanchez won't be going anywhere."

Sally Rogers stuck her head into the sheriff's office. "Your wife's on line one, Sheriff."

Leaving the sheriff's office, Hawk clocked out and picked up his jacket.

"I was praying for the little girl," Sally said. "I'm happy she turned out to be all right."

"So am I. But keep the prayers coming, please. She and her mother still need all the help they can get."

❧

Knowing Hawk was coming over, Anita decided to cook dinner for him. She knew everyone in Rockdale would be talking about the day's events, and she did not want to burden Juanita with the added attention they would receive if they appeared in public so soon.

Even more than that, Anita wanted to be alone with Hawk so she could thank him for all he had done for her and Juanita. At the same time, she felt she had to make it clear she expected nothing more from him.

By late afternoon, Juanita was restless and looking for

something to do, so Anita wrapped an apron around her and set her to work in the kitchen. By the time Hawk arrived, Juanita had tired of playing cook. She greeted him warmly, then pulled off her apron and handed it to him.

"Here, Dep'ty. You can help Mama now. Dora and I are going to practice our letters 'til it's time to eat." Juanita picked Dora up from the couch and went into the bedroom, closing the door behind her.

Hawk smiled. "I was going to ask how she is doing, but I think I just got my answer."

"Juanita does not really understand what happened today. We talked about what she will do if anyone ever again tries to make her go with them. I also told her Bill Rankin was only pretending to be our friend."

"For now, that is enough. She is a remarkable little girl—and blessed with a wonderful mother."

"Oh, Hawk—Juanita and I owe you so much. Please know you do not have to do anything else—"

Hawk stepped forward and took Anita into his arms. His lips stopped her carefully rehearsed speech with a knee-weakening kiss. Then he looked into Anita's eyes and said words already written on Anita's heart.

"I love you, and I want to marry you. I know I don't have much to offer—"

Anita put her hand across Hawk's mouth. "Do not say such things. You have much more to offer than I could ever deserve."

Hawk covered her hand with his and moved it to his cheek. "Does that mean you'll consider marrying me?"

"There is nothing to consider. I married Juan Sanchez for the wrong reasons. I hoped I would grow to love him, but it never happened. From the first time I saw you, I believed with all my heart that God sent you to help us. I appreciated what you did for Juanita and me in friendship, but when I got to know you better, I began to understand what real love should be like, and I realized I had never known it. Now I do."

Hawk reached into his pocket and brought out a small black jeweler's box. "In that case, this is for you."

Anita was close to tears when Hawk opened the box and revealed a ring set with a small solitaire diamond. Although she had never had an engagement ring before, she knew one when she saw it.

Anita held out her left hand and removed the wedding band from her marriage to Juan Sanchez. "I have continued to wear this ring for Juanita's sake. It stands for a vow I made in good faith, but I am no longer bound by it."

Hawk's hands shook slightly when he took his ring from the box and slipped it on Anita's finger. "I'm glad you feel that way."

"I do."

Hawk smiled. "I do too, and I can't wait for the world to know it."

"Neither can I."

Hawk grinned widely, then embraced Anita again. They stood together, content in each other's arms, until the stove timer chimed. Startled, Anita pulled away and smoothed her apron.

"The food is ready. Tell Juanita to wash her hands and come to the table."

"Is there anything else I can tell her?"

"Not yet. Wait until after dinner—otherwise she will be too excited to eat."

Hawk kissed Anita's forehead and smiled. "I'm afraid that goes for me too."

Saying her huggy doll wasn't hungry, Juanita came to the table without Dora. When all were seated, she reached her hands out to Hawk and Juanita.

"Will you offer our thanks tonight?" he asked.

"All right. Bow your head, Dep'ty. Dear God, thank You for this food and for this day and for Mama and Dep'ty Hawk and Dora and everyone and make us all better. A—men."

"Very nice," Hawk said, reluctant to let go of Anita's hand.

"Not everything that happened today was good, but God looked after us as He always does. We should always remember to thank Him for all His gifts," Anita said.

Juanita noticed her mother's new diamond ring. "That's pretty, Mama. That man who found Dora's shoe said you had a fortune. Does that mean you're rich?"

"No, Sweetie. He was wrong. We do not have riches, but we have good friends. They are worth much more than gold."

"So is being loved," Hawk told Juanita. "A lot of people around here love you and your mother. That ring shows I love her in a special way."

"We love you too, Dep'ty. Can we eat now?"

⁂

After the dishes were done, Anita invited Juanita to sit on the couch between her and Hawk. "We have something to tell you," Anita said.

"Wait! I want to get Dora."

Hawk smiled. "By all means. Everyone in the family should hear this."

Juanita returned with her huggy doll and climbed back onto the couch. "We're ready now."

Anita thought she was prepared to share their news with the whole world, but now that the time had come, she did not know how to tell her own daughter. When her eyes sent Hawk a mute appeal, he took one of Juanita's hands and spoke quietly.

"Your mother loves you very much, and so do I. We also love each other, and we want to be a family."

Juanita's eyes widened. "You mean get *married?*"

Anita nodded, uncertain what her daughter's reaction meant. "Yes, Sweetie."

Juanita threw both arms around Hawk's neck. Then, not to slight anyone, she hugged her mother and Dora as well. "Miss Toni is Josh and Mandy's stepmother, but they call her 'Mommy.' When you're my stepfather, can I call you Daddy?"

Obviously touched, Hawk smiled. "If that's what you want, of course."

Juanita was so excited she wanted to stay up past her bedtime, but soon she admitted she was tired. After Anita tucked her into bed, Hawk joined them to hear Juanita say her prayers. She asked God to bless just about everyone she knew in Rockdale by name, then added, "Thank You for sending us the dep'ty and making this the bestest day of my whole life."

When they returned to the living room, Anita tried to brush away her tears, but Hawk noticed. "Hey, what's this? Is the thought of marrying me so awful?"

"Oh, no—I agree with Juanita. This is the bestest day of my life too."

"And mine three." Hawk held Anita close for a moment, then sighed and drew back.

"What is the matter?"

"I was thinking how sad life must be for people like Bill Rankin. His concern about money has made him overlook life's true fortune."

"You are right. As much grief as he has caused, we should pray for that man."

Safely folded in Hawk's strong arms, Anita quietly offered thanks to God. He had given them salvation through His Son Jesus Christ, and now Anita and Hawk had also received a great fortune—a love which would continue to increase through all the years ahead.

epilogue

Small towns have long memories, and the story of a stranger who kidnapped a little girl in broad daylight passed almost immediately into Rockdale's folklore. Oddly enough, no one who told it mentioned the kidnapped girl and her mother were exotic Hispanic strangers themselves. They had become part of Rockdale now, and as such, anyone who tried to harm them had the whole community against them.

Anita and Juanita did not keep their Hispanic last names for long. Anita Sanchez became Mrs. Hawk Henson in an early summer wedding at Community Church, with Toni Trent serving as Anita's matron of honor.

By that time, their lives had undergone several changes. Hawk was promoted to chief deputy and moved into the condo next door to Mrs. Tarpley, where Anita and Juanita joined him after the wedding.

Even before he and Anita were married, Hawk filed a petition to adopt Juanita Sanchez.

"In my heart, you're my daughter already, but this will make it legal," Hawk told Juanita.

The little girl was delighted. "Now Dora and I will be Hensons too."

When Congressman Jeremy Winter heard Anita's story, he arranged an investigation into the deaths of her brother and her parents. He found out that the drug lords who were responsible had been in prison several years, and they had shown no interest in her after she fled to America. As Anita suspected, Juan Sanchez was the sole source of the threats she thought had come from Colombia.

Best of all, Anita's Aunt Rita had contacted the American

embassy in Barranquilla several years ago in an effort to find her niece, and both women now looked forward to the prospect of a family reunion in the near future.

In July, Bill Rankin went on trial in Texas on assorted counts of parole violations, impersonating a law officer, and attempted extortion. Following those proceedings, he would be returned to Alabama to face many of the same charges, plus the most serious of all, kidnapping.

Anita chose not to go to Texas for the trial, but the prosecuting attorney who took her deposition promised to keep her informed about the proceedings. Exactly six months from the day Juanita Sanchez had been kidnapped, a call from Texas cleared up the last remaining mystery concerning the fortune Bill Rankin thought Anita had taken.

"Deputy Henson asked me if the Texas police had investigated the manager of the storage unit where Juan Sanchez put the take from the robbery. It turns out they knew each other, and when he heard Juan Sanchez was dead, the manager opened the unit and took all the money. When Rankin showed up to get his share, the manager made up the story that a Hispanic woman had taken it. Rankin had seen your picture and assumed it must have been you."

"What happened to the money?"

"We're still working on that. My guess is the company will recover at least part of it."

"Does this change your case against Bill Rankin?"

"It confirms the reason he came after you. Don't worry, Mrs. Henson. Texas has enough on Rankin to put him away for a long time, not counting a sentence for the kidnapping charge."

Anita let out a sigh of relief. "Thank you for letting me know about this."

"Sure. I'll call again when the trial is over, but there's no doubt of the outcome."

Hawk came in just as Anita hung up the telephone. "From that smile, that call must have been good news."

"Very good. The Texas prosecutor says the police took your suggestion about checking on the storage unit manager, and thanks to you, they know he took the stolen money. The company could get some of it back."

Hawk smiled. "Great. Now we know what happened to your fortune."

"That money was never mine." Anita put her arms around Hawk. "My fortune is right here."

Author's Note

Although Anita Muños Sanchez is a fictional victim of domestic violence, she represents women everywhere who may need help to escape an abusive relationship. In real life, although most communities provide some kind of crisis counseling, many women may be unaware of these services or be unwilling to use them out of fear. Working with and praying for abused women can be a valuable ministry for Christian women. Even small acts of kindness can make a difference.

In the words of Dr. Amparo Vargas de Medina of Colombia, who has been a tireless campaigner against domestic violence in her own country and throughout Latin America: *"Las pequeñas cosa en las manos de Dios, Èl las vuelve grandes"*—God alone is able to take the smallest things and mold them into marvelous works.*

*Reprinted from the July 2003 issue of *Missions Mosaic*, published by Woman's Missionary Union, Birmingham, Alabama. Used by permission.

A Letter To Our Readers

Dear Reader:

In order that we might better contribute to your reading enjoyment, we would appreciate your taking a few minutes to respond to the following questions. We welcome your comments and read each form and letter we receive. When completed, please return to the following:

Fiction Editor
Heartsong Presents
PO Box 719
Uhrichsville, Ohio 44683

1. Did you enjoy reading *Anita's Fortune* by Kay Cornelius?
   ❑ Very much! I would like to see more books by this author!
   ❑ Moderately. I would have enjoyed it more if

   _____

   _____

   _____

2. Are you a member of **Heartsong Presents**? ❑ Yes ❑ No
   If no, where did you purchase this book? _____

   _____

3. How would you rate, on a scale from 1 (poor) to 5 (superior), the cover design? _____

4. On a scale from 1 (poor) to 10 (superior), please rate the following elements.

   ____ Heroine   ____ Plot
   ____ Hero   ____ Inspirational theme
   ____ Setting   ____ Secondary characters

5. These characters were special because?_____

_____

_____

6. How has this book inspired your life?_____

_____

_____

7. What settings would you like to see covered in future
   Heartsong Presents books? _____

_____

_____

8. What are some inspirational themes you would like to see
   treated in future books? _____

_____

_____

9. Would you be interested in reading other **Heartsong
   Presents** titles? ❑ Yes ❑ No

10. Please check your age range:
   ❑ Under 18   ❑ 18-24
   ❑ 25-34   ❑ 35-45
   ❑ 46-55   ❑ Over 55

Name_____

Occupation _____

Address _____

City_____ State_____ Zip_____

From Italy, with Love

4 stories in 1

Motivated by letters, four women travel to Italian cities and find love. Four American women are compelled to explore the historic country that their parents and grandparents called "home"—along the way finding God's plan for themselves. Authors include: Gail Gaymer Martin, DiAnn Mills, Melanie Panagiotopoulos, and Lois Richer.

Contempoary, paperback, 352 pages, 5 ³/₁₆"x 8"

Heartsong

HEARTSONG PRESENTS TITLES AVAILABLE NOW:

- ___HP213 *Picture of Love*, T. H. Murray
- ___HP217 *Odyssey of Love*, M. Panagiotopoulos
- ___HP218 *Hawaiian Heartbeat*, Y.Lehman
- ___HP221 *Thief of My Heart*, C. Bach
- ___HP222 *Finally, Love*, J. Stengl
- ___HP225 *A Rose Is a Rose*, R. R. Jones
- ___HP226 *Wings of the Dawn*, T. Peterson
- ___HP234 *Glowing Embers*, C. L. Reece
- ___HP242 *Far Above Rubies*, B. Melby & C. Wienke
- ___HP245 *Crossroads*, T. and J. Peterson
- ___HP246 *Brianna's Pardon*, G. Clover
- ___HP261 *Race of Love*, M. Panagiotopoulos
- ___HP262 *Heaven's Child*, G. Fields
- ___HP265 *Hearth of Fire*, C. L. Reece
- ___HP278 *Elizabeth's Choice*, L. Lyle
- ___HP298 *A Sense of Belonging*, T. Fowler
- ___HP302 *Seasons*, G. G. Martin
- ___HP305 *Call of the Mountain*, Y. Lehman
- ___HP306 *Piano Lessons*, G. Sattler
- ___HP317 *Love Remembered*, A. Bell
- ___HP318 *Born for This Love*, B. Bancroft
- ___HP321 *Fortress of Love*, M. Panagiotopoulos
- ___HP322 *Country Charm*, D. Mills
- ___HP325 *Gone Camping*, G. Sattler
- ___HP326 *A Tender Melody*, B. L. Etchison
- ___HP329 *Meet My Sister, Tess*, K. Billerbeck
- ___HP330 *Dreaming of Castles*, G. G. Martin
- ___HP337 *Ozark Sunrise*, H. Alexander
- ___HP338 *Somewhere a Rainbow*, Y. Lehman
- ___HP341 *It Only Takes a Spark*, P. K. Tracy
- ___HP342 *The Haven of Rest*, A. Boeshaar
- ___HP349 *Wild Tiger Wind*, G. Buck
- ___HP350 *Race for the Roses*, L. Snelling
- ___HP353 *Ice Castle*, J. Livingston
- ___HP354 *Finding Courtney*, B. L. Etchison

- ___HP361 *The Name Game*, M. G. Chapman
- ___HP377 *Come Home to My Heart*, J. A. Grote
- ___HP378 *The Landlord Takes a Bride*, K. Billerbeck
- ___HP390 *Love Abounds*, A. Bell
- ___HP394 *Equestrian Charm*, D. Mills
- ___HP401 *Castle in the Clouds*, A. Boeshaar
- ___HP402 *Secret Ballot*, Y. Lehman
- ___HP405 *The Wife Degree*, A. Ford
- ___HP406 *Almost Twins*, G. Sattler
- ___HP409 *A Living Soul*, H. Alexander
- ___HP410 *The Color of Love*, D. Mills
- ___HP413 *Remnant of Victory*, J. Odell
- ___HP414 *The Sea Beckons*, B. L. Etchison
- ___HP417 *From Russia with Love*, C. Coble
- ___HP418 *Yesteryear*, G. Brandt
- ___HP421 *Looking for a Miracle*, W. E. Brunstetter
- ___HP422 *Condo Mania*, M. G. Chapman
- ___HP425 *Mustering Courage*, L. A. Coleman
- ___HP426 *To the Extreme*, T. Davis
- ___HP429 *Love Ahoy*, C. Coble
- ___HP430 *Good Things Come*, J. A. Ryan
- ___HP433 *A Few Flowers*, G. Sattler
- ___HP434 *Family Circle*, J. L. Barton
- ___HP438 *Out in the Real World*, K. Paul
- ___HP441 *Cassidy's Charm*, D. Mills
- ___HP442 *Vision of Hope*, M. H. Flinkman
- ___HP445 *McMillian's Matchmakers*, G. Sattler
- ___HP449 *An Ostrich a Day*, N. J. Farrier
- ___HP450 *Love in Pursuit*, D. Mills
- ___HP454 *Grace in Action*, K. Billerbeck
- ___HP458 *The Candy Cane Calaboose*, J. Spaeth
- ___HP461 *Pride and Pumpernickel*, A. Ford
- ___HP462 *Secrets Within*, G. G. Martin
- ___HP465 *Talking for Two*, W. E. Brunstetter
- ___HP466 *Risa's Rainbow*, A. Boeshaar

(If ordering from this page, please remember to include it with the order form.)

Presents

Great Inspirational Romance at a Great Price!

Heartsong Presents books are inspirational romances in contemporary and historical settings, designed to give you an enjoyable, spirit-lifting reading experience. You can choose wonderfully written titles from some of today's best authors like Hannah Alexander, Andrea Boeshaar, Yvonne Lehman, Tracie Peterson, and many others.

When ordering quantities less than twelve, above titles are $3.25 each.
Not all titles may be available at time of order.

THE PELICAN SHAKESPEARE

GENERAL EDITOR ALFRED HARBAGE

KING LEAR

WILLIAM SHAKESPEARE

KING LEAR

EDITED BY ALFRED HARBAGE

PENGUIN BOOKS

Penguin Books Ltd, Harmondsworth,
Middlesex, England
Penguin Books, 40 West 23rd Street,
New York, New York 10010, U.S.A.
Penguin Books Australia Ltd, Ringwood,
Victoria, Australia
Penguin Books Canada Limited, 2801 John Street,
Markham, Ontario, Canada L3R 1B4
Penguin Books (N.Z.) Ltd, 182–190 Wairau Road,
Auckland 10, New Zealand

First published in *The Pelican Shakespeare* 1958
This revised edition first published 1970
Reprinted 1973, 1975, 1976, 1977, 1979, 1980 (twice),
1981 (twice), 1983 (twice)
First published in this television edition 1984

Library of Congress catalog card number: 75-98372

Printed in the United States of America by
Kingsport Press, Inc., Kingsport, Tennessee
Set in Monotype Ehrhardt

CONTENTS

PUBLISHER'S NOTE

Soon after the thirty-eight volumes forming *The Pelican Shakespeare* had been published, they were brought together in *The Complete Pelican Shakespeare*. The editorial revisions and new textual features are explained in detail in the General Editor's Preface to the one-volume edition. They have all been incorporated in the present volume. The following should be mentioned in particular:

The lines are not numbered in arbitrary units. Instead all lines are numbered which contain a word, phrase, or allusion explained in the glossarial notes. In the occasional instances where there is a long stretch of unannotated text, certain lines are numbered in italics to serve the conventional reference purpose.

The intrusive and often inaccurate place-headings inserted by early editors are omitted (as is becoming standard practise), but for the convenience of those who miss them, an indication of locale now appears as first item in the annotation of each scene.

In the interest of both elegance and utility, each speech-prefix is set in a separate line when the speaker's lines are in verse, except when these words form the second half of a pentameter line. Thus the verse form of the speech is kept visually intact, and turned-over lines are avoided. What is printed as verse and what is printed as prose has, in general, the authority of the original texts. Departures from the original texts in this regard have only the authority of editorial tradition and the judgment of the Pelican editors; and, in a few instances, are admittedly arbitrary.

SHAKESPEARE AND
HIS STAGE

William Shakespeare was christened in Holy Trinity Church, Stratford-upon-Avon, April 26, 1564. His birth is traditionally assigned to April 23. He was the eldest of four boys and two girls who survived infancy in the family of John Shakespeare, glover and trader of Henley Street, and his wife Mary Arden, daughter of a small landowner of Wilmcote. In 1568 John was elected Bailiff (equivalent to Mayor) of Stratford, having already filled the minor municipal offices. The town maintained for the sons of the burgesses a free school, taught by a university graduate and offering preparation in Latin sufficient for university entrance; its early registers are lost, but there can be little doubt that Shakespeare received the formal part of his education in this school.

On November 27, 1582, a license was issued for the marriage of William Shakespeare (aged eighteen) and Ann Hathaway (aged twenty-six), and on May 26, 1583, their child Susanna was christened in Holy Trinity Church. The inference that the marriage was forced upon the youth is natural but not inevitable; betrothal was legally binding at the time, and was sometimes regarded as conferring conjugal rights. Two additional children of the marriage, the twins Hamnet and Judith, were christened on February 2, 1585. Meanwhile the prosperity of the elder Shakespeares had declined, and William was impelled to seek a career outside Stratford.

The tradition that he spent some time as a country

7

teacher is old but unverifiable. Because of the absence of records his early twenties are called the "lost years," and only one thing about them is certain – that at least some of these years were spent in winning a place in the acting profession. He may have begun as a provincial trouper, but by 1592 he was established in London and prominent enough to be attacked. In a pamphlet of that year, *Groats-worth of Wit*, the ailing Robert Greene complained of the neglect which university writers like himself had suffered from actors, one of whom was daring to set up as a playwright:

. . . an vpstart Crow, beautified with our feathers, that with his *Tygers hart wrapt in a Players hyde*, supposes he is as well able to bombast out a blanke verse as the best of you: and beeing an absolute *Iohannes fac totum*, is in his owne conceit the onely Shake-scene in a countrey.

The pun on his name, and the parody of his line "O tiger's heart wrapped in a woman's hide" (*3 Henry VI*), pointed clearly to Shakespeare. Some of his admirers protested, and Henry Chettle, the editor of Greene's pamphlet, saw fit to apologize:

. . . I am as sory as if the originall fault had beene my fault, because my selfe haue seene his demeanor no lesse ciuill than he excelent in the qualitie he professes: Besides, diuers of worship haue reported his vprightnes of dealing, which argues his honesty, and his facetious grace in writting, that approoues his Art. (Prefatory epistle, *Kind-Harts Dreame*)

The plague closed the London theatres for many months in 1592–94, denying the actors their livelihood. To this period belong Shakespeare's two narrative poems, *Venus and Adonis* and *The Rape of Lucrece*, both dedicated to the Earl of Southampton. No doubt the poet was rewarded with a gift of money as usual in such cases, but he did no further dedicating and we have no reliable information on whether Southampton, or anyone else, became his regular patron. His sonnets, first mentioned in 1598 and published without his consent in 1609, are intimate without being

8

explicitly autobiographical. They seem to commemorate the poet's friendship with an idealized youth, rivalry with a more favored poet, and love affair with a dark mistress; and his bitterness when the mistress betrays him in conjunction with the friend; but it is difficult to decide precisely what the "story" is, impossible to decide whether it is fictional or true. The true distinction of the sonnets, at least of those not purely conventional, rests in the universality of the thoughts and moods they express, and in their poignancy and beauty.

In 1594 was formed the theatrical company known until 1603 as the Lord Chamberlain's men, thereafter as the King's men. Its original membership included, besides Shakespeare, the beloved clown Will Kempe and the famous actor Richard Burbage. The company acted in various London theatres and even toured the provinces, but it is chiefly associated in our minds with the Globe Theatre built on the south bank of the Thames in 1599. Shakespeare was an actor and joint owner of this company (and its Globe) through the remainder of his creative years. His plays, written at the average rate of two a year, together with Burbage's acting won it its place of leadership among the London companies.

Individual plays began to appear in print, in editions both honest and piratical, and the publishers became increasingly aware of the value of Shakespeare's name on the title pages. As early as 1598 he was hailed as the leading English dramatist in the *Palladis Tamia* of Francis Meres:

As *Plautus* and *Seneca* are accounted the best for Comedy and Tragedy among the Latines, so *Shakespeare* among the English is the most excellent in both kinds for the stage: for Comedy, witnes his *Gentlemen of Verona*, his *Errors*, his *Loue labors lost*, his *Loue labours wonne* [at one time in print but no longer extant, at least under this title], his *Midsummers night dream*, & his *Merchant of Venice*; for Tragedy, his *Richard the 2*, *Richard the 3*, *Henry the 4*, *King Iohn*, *Titus Andronicus*, and his *Romeo and Iuliet*.

9

The note is valuable both in indicating Shakespeare's prestige and in helping us to establish a chronology. In the second half of his writing career, history plays gave place to the great tragedies; and farces and light comedies gave place to the problem plays and symbolic romances. In 1623, seven years after his death, his former fellow-actors, John Heminge and Henry Condell, cooperated with a group of London printers in bringing out his plays in collected form. The volume is generally known as the First Folio.

Shakespeare had never severed his relations with Stratford. His wife and children may sometimes have shared his London lodgings, but their home was Stratford. His son Hamnet was buried there in 1596, and his daughters Susanna and Judith were married there in 1607 and 1616 respectively. (His father, for whom he had secured a coat of arms and thus the privilege of writing himself gentleman, died in 1601, his mother in 1608.) His considerable earnings in London, as actor-sharer, part owner of the Globe, and playwright, were invested chiefly in Stratford property. In 1597 he purchased for £60 New Place, one of the two most imposing residences in the town. A number of other business transactions, as well as minor episodes in his career, have left documentary records. By 1611 he was in a position to retire, and he seems gradually to have withdrawn from theatrical activity in order to live in Stratford. In March, 1616, he made a will, leaving token bequests to Burbage, Heminge, and Condell, but the bulk of his estate to his family. The most famous feature of the will, the bequest of the second-best bed to his wife, reveals nothing about Shakespeare's marriage; the quaintness of the provision seems commonplace to those familiar with ancient testaments. Shakespeare died April 23, 1616, and was buried in the Stratford church where he had been christened. Within seven years a monument was erected to his memory on the north wall of the chancel. Its portrait bust and the Droeshout engraving on the title page of the First Folio provide the only likenesses with an established claim to authenticity. The best verbal vignette was written by his rival Ben Jonson, the more impressive for being imbedded in a context mainly critical:

... I loved the man, and doe honour his memory (on this side idolatry) as much as any. Hee was indeed honest, and of an open and free nature: had an excellent Phantsie, brave notions, and gentle expressions.... (*Timber or Discoveries*, ca. 1623–30)

*

The reader of Shakespeare's plays is aided by a general knowledge of the way in which they were staged. The King's men acquired a roofed and artificially lighted theatre only toward the close of Shakespeare's career, and then only for winter use. Nearly all his plays were designed for performance in such structures as the Globe – a three-tiered amphitheatre with a large rectangular platform extending to the center of its yard. The plays were staged by daylight, by large casts brilliantly costumed, but with only a minimum of properties, without scenery, and quite possibly without intermissions. There was a rear stage gallery for action "above," and a curtained rear recess for "discoveries" and other special effects, but by far the major portion of any play was enacted upon the projecting platform, with episode following episode in swift succession, and with shifts of time and place signaled the audience only by the momentary clearing of the stage between the episodes. Information about the identity of the characters and, when necessary, about the time and place of the action was incorporated in the dialogue. No place-headings have been inserted in the present editions; these are apt to obscure the original fluidity of structure, with the emphasis upon action and speech rather than scenic background. (Indications of place are supplied in the footnotes.) The acting, including that of the youthful apprentices to the profession who performed the parts of women, was highly skillful, with a premium placed upon grace of gesture and beauty of diction. The audiences, a cross section of the general public, commonly numbered a thousand, sometimes more than two thousand. Judged by the type of plays they applauded, these audiences were not only large but also perceptive.

THE TEXTS OF THE PLAYS

About half of Shakespeare's plays appeared in print for the first time in the folio volume of 1623. The others had been published individually, usually in quarto volumes, during his lifetime or in the six years following his death. The copy used by the printers of the quartos varied greatly in merit, sometimes representing Shakespeare's true text, sometimes only a debased version of that text. The copy used by the printers of the folio also varied in merit, but was chosen with care. Since it consisted of the best available manuscripts, or the more acceptable quartos (although frequently in editions other than the first), or of quartos corrected by reference to manuscripts, we have good or reasonably good texts of most of the thirty-seven plays.

In the present series, the plays have been newly edited from quarto or folio texts, depending, when a choice offered, upon which is now regarded by bibliographical specialists as the more authoritative. The ideal has been to reproduce the chosen texts with as few alterations as possible, beyond occasional relineation, expansion of abbreviations, and modernization of punctuation and spelling. Emendation is held to a minimum, and such material as has been added, in the way of stage directions and lines supplied by an alternative text, has been enclosed in square brackets.

None of the plays printed in Shakespeare's lifetime were divided into acts and scenes, and the inference is that the author's own manuscripts were not so divided. In the folio collection, some of the plays remained undivided, some were divided into acts, and some were divided into acts and scenes. During the eighteenth century all of the plays were divided into acts and scenes, and in the Cambridge edition of the mid-nineteenth century, from which the influential Globe text derived, this division was more or less regularized and the lines were numbered. Many useful works of reference employ the act–scene–line apparatus thus established.

Since this act–scene division is obviously convenient, but is of very dubious authority so far as Shakespeare's own structural principles are concerned, or the original manner of staging his plays, a problem is presented to modern editors. In the present series the act–scene division is retained marginally, and may be viewed as a reference aid like the line numbering. A star marks the points of division when these points have been determined by a cleared stage indicating a shift of time and place in the action of the play, or when no harm results from the editorial assumption that there is such a shift. However, at those points where the established division is clearly misleading – that is, where continuous action has been split up into separate "scenes" – the star is omitted and the distortion corrected. This mechanical expedient seemed the best means of combining utility and accuracy.

THE GENERAL EDITOR

INTRODUCTION

The play begins with a moment of prose "exposition," an idle conversation about the partition of a kingdom and the bastardy of a son. Its tone is casual, jocular, polite. The son responds decorously to a social introduction. The speakers are wearing familiar masks. It is then as if these murmurs by the portal subsided at the opening of some old but half-remembered ceremony. All is ritual – heralding trumpet, formal procession, symbolic objects in coronet and map, a sequence of arbitrary yet strangely predictable acts. What can be made of it? Why should that patriarch who wishes to yield up his power and possessions require of the receivers declarations of love? Why should that maiden who honestly loves him respond only with declarations of her love of honesty? No logical reasons appear – ritual is ritual, its logic its own. Prose is yielding to poetry, "realism" to reality. *King Lear* is not true. It is an allegory of truth.

That its truths are not literal is the first thing about it discerned by the budding critical faculty. Everything is initially *patterned* – this one making obvious errors which he obviously will rue, these others emerging as the good and the evil in almost geometrical symmetry, with the inevitable sisters-three, the two elder chosen though wicked, the younger rejected though virtuous. Surely these are childish things! A defense has been offered by Tolstoy, in his valedictory judgment that the only truths conveyable in literature can be conveyed in the simplest folk-tale. But *King Lear* is not simple, and Tolstoy himself failed to see its relevance to his doctrine. Freud noticed its primitive features, and compared Goneril, Regan, and Cordelia to the caskets of lead, silver, and gold in *The Merchant of Venice*. He identified Cordelia as the benign, though resisted, call of death. Cordelia as the death-wish – *lovely and soothing death* – how suggestive this is! until we recognize that her identification as the life-wish might be equally suggestive. The value of such reflections lies in their reminder that the oldest story-patterns have the greatest power to touch off reverberations. No other framework than this parable-myth could have borne so well the weight of what Shakespeare was compelled to say.

The story of Lear and his three daughters was given written form four centuries before Shakespeare's birth. How much older its components may be we do not know. Cordelia in one guise or another, including Cinderella's, has figured in the folklore of most cultures, perhaps originally expressing what Emerson saw as the conviction of every human being of his worthiness to be loved and chosen, if only his *true* self were truly known. The figure of the ruler asking a question, often a riddle, with disastrous consequences to himself is equally old and dispersed. In his *Historia Regum Britanniae* (1136) Geoffrey of Monmouth converted folklore to history and established Lear and his daughters as rulers of ancient Britain, thus bequeathing them to the chronicles. Raphael Holinshed's (1587) declared that "Leir, the sonne of Baldud," came to the throne "in the yeare of the world 3105, at what time Joas reigned in Juda," but belief in the historicity of such British kings was now beginning to wane, and Shakespeare could deal freely with the record. He read the story also in John Higgins' lamentable verses in *The Firste part of the Mirour for Magistrates* (1574), and in Edmund Spenser's *Faerie Queene*, II, 10, 27–32. He knew, and may even have acted in, a bland dramatic version, *The True Chronicle History of King Leir*, published anonymously in 1605 but staged at least as early as 1594.

The printing of the old play may mark an effort to capitalize upon the staging of Shakespeare's, performed at court on December 26, 1606, and probably first brought out at the Globe playhouse sometime in 1605, although its allusion to "these late eclipses of the sun and moon" was not necessarily suggested by those of September and October of that year. The only certain anterior limit of date is March 16, 1603, when Samuel Harsnett's *Declaration of Egregious Popishe Impostures* was registered for publication. That this excursion in "pseudo-demonology" was available to Shakespeare is evident in various ways, most clearly in the borrowed inventory of devils imbedded in Edgar's jargon as Tom o' Bedlam. It is of small consequence to fix the date of *King Lear* so far as its relation to the older play is concerned, which must be reckoned as analogue rather than source, but if, as seems certain, it was composed in 1605 or early 1606, it belongs to the same season of the poet's growth as *The Tragedy of Macbeth*.

In its pre-Shakespearean forms, both those mentioned above and others, the Lear story remains rudimentary. The emphasis may vary in various recensions, depending upon whether the author was most interested in the inexpedience of subdividing a kingdom, the mutability of fortune, or, as in the older play, the rewards of Christian virtue; but all are alike in that they end happily for Lear, who is reconciled to Cordelia and restored to his throne. The fact that the story was sometimes followed by a sequel in which Cordelia was finally hounded to suicide by the broodlings of her wicked sisters has little bearing on a remarkable fact: Shakespeare alone and in defiance of precedent conducted Lear to ultimate misery. *Enter Lear, with Cordelia in his arms. . . . He dies.* These directions enclose a scene which demonstrates beyond any other in tragic literature the intransigence of poetic art – inventing the inevitable, investing horrifying things with beauty.

Compared with the tragedies of ancient Greece – and it is with these alone that one is tempted to compare it -- *King Lear* suggests the Gothic order. Its form is irregular and organic, determined seemingly by a series of upward thrusts of mounting internal energy. There is even a Gothic element of the grotesque, as when mock-beggar, jester, and king, reduced to common condition, hold their mad juridical proceedings in a storm-lashed shelter, or when crazed king and blinded subject exchange lamentations and puns! In the method of Lear's madness there is often a savage humor, more remarkable when all is said than his companioning with a Fool. It was the Fool, however, who seemed to the next age the unpardonable sin against classical decorum. In the 1680 adaptation by Nahum Tate he was expunged from the play, along with the tragic ending. Tate capped the concluding felicities of the pre-Shakespearean versions by huddling up a marriage between Edgar and Cordelia; yet his work held the stage throughout the eighteenth century. It is always ruefully remarked that the greatest critic of the age approved the adaptation, but in fairness we should add that it was not for literary reasons. The pain of Shakespeare's concluding scenes was simply too much for Dr Johnson; his response is preferable to that of those – fit for treasons, stratagems, and spoils – who can read these scenes unmoved.

The original play, or its approximation, was restored to the stage in the early nineteenth century, after it had begun to receive its critical due from the romantic essayists and poets. It is a poet's play. Keats saw in it the warrant for his conviction that truth and beauty are one, and, more surprisingly, recognized the choral and catalytic function of Lear's jester for the stroke of genius it is. Coleridge, Lamb, and Hazlitt also recorded illuminating judgments, and many critics since, of many different "schools," have said fine things about it.

The question now most frequently debated is whether the play is Christian and affirmative in spirit, or pagan and pessimistic. No work of art could endure the tugs of such a debate without being somewhat torn. "Pessimistic," like "optimistic," is a small word for a small thing, and *King Lear* is not small. It is sad, as all tragedies are sad. It is religious, as all great tragedies are religious. The exclusion of specific Christian reference, more consistent than in any other Shakespearean play of non-Christian setting, is in harmony with its Old Testament atmosphere (when "Joas reigned in Juda"), but it may reflect nothing more than evasion, in the printed text, of a recent Parliamentary ruling, which in effect labelled *God* in stage speech as blasphemy, *gods* as mere classical allusion. Although the play is rather inclusively than exclusively Christian, which can scarcely be deemed a fault, it shows obvious signs of its genesis in a Christian culture. To cite those involving a single character (other than Cordelia, who has often been viewed as a Christ-symbol), there is Edgar's persistence in returning good for evil, his preachments against the sin of despair, and his reluctance to kill except in trial by combat with its implied religious sanctions. Great questions are asked of the unseen powers – "Is there any cause in nature that makes these hard hearts?" – and these questions remain unanswered, but the silence which follows them should be viewed, here as in other contexts, as the substance of faith. On the human level, the implications of the play are more comforting than the data it abstracts. In our actual world, suffering is not always ennobling, evil not always self-consuming. In every scene where there is pain, there is someone who strives to relieve that pain. At the close, the merciless have all perished; the last sound we hear is the choral voices of the merciful.

The workers of evil are stylized in a way not quite typical of Shakespeare. He could not love these characters even as characters, except perhaps Edmund a little. To imitate the dominant animal imagery of the style, Cornwall is less repellent than Goneril and Regan only as the mad bull is less repellent than the hyena, they less repellent than Oswald only as the hyena is less repellent than the jackal. To the latter he failed to give even that engaging touch of the ludicrous he usually reserved for assistant villains. It is useless to speak of their "motivation." Like other aged parents Lear is no gift to good housewifery, and there is something poignantly familiar about such a one's trudging resentfully to the home of a second daughter. "Age is unnecessary." But to see a causal relationship between what he does to Goneril and Regan and what they do to him, or to interpret their aggression as normal revolt against parental domination, is simply to be perverse. The play deals directly, and in both its stories, with one indissoluble bond:

> We'll no more meet, no more see one another.
> But yet thou art my flesh, my blood, my daughter....

Eroded, it leaves no human bond secure. To argue that Edmund's conduct is attributable to humiliating illegitimacy, we must supply him with an "unconscious" and invoke its spectral evidence; there is no sign of sensitivity in his lines. Even that curious product of our times, the liberalism-gone-to-seed which automatically defends anything from treachery to sadism providing it savors of non-conformity, has found little to say for this insatiable quintet.

Shakespeare is not normally associated with hatred, but "a fierce hatred of cruelty and deceitful wickedness" informs *King Lear* – this the opinion of so pure an aesthetician as Benedetto Croce. Hazlitt has said, "It is then the best of all Shakespeare's plays, for it is the one in which he was most in earnest." A non-sequitur may lurk in this assertion, but we cannot deny its relevance. Our inescapable impression of the play is of its overwhelming sincerity. It says everything powerfully and everything twice – and always "what we feel, not what we ought to say." The language varies from the cryptic allusiveness of Lear's "mad" speeches to the biblical plainness of his pleas for forgiveness; and though it is often difficult, it is never ambiguous. Lamb has been much taken to task for declaring that "*Lear* is essentially impossible to be represented on a stage," but more often than not our experiences in the theatre confirm his view. There have been fine productions, but not very many: one touch of insincerity can rot everything away.

Those who now "introduce" this play must wish with Hazlitt, and with much more likelihood of greeting the wish of the reader, that they might resort to silence, since all that can be said will "fall short of the subject, or even what we ourselves conceive of it." Yet an effort must be made to state its theme, and to the present editor there seems no way of doing this except by focussing the gaze directly and continuously upon Lear himself.

"The King is coming." These words announce the first entrance of the tragic hero. Let us see him as he is, no pre-conceptions or critical rumors spoiling the innocence of our vision. Nothing about him suggests infirmity or decay. His magnitude and force are far greater than one's own. He issues commands with the assurance of instinct and lifelong custom. He holds a map in his hands like a Titan holding a kingdom. The kingdom spreads before us in his spacious utterance:

> Of all these bounds, even from this line to this,
> With shadowy forests and with champains riched,
> With plenteous rivers and wide-skirted meads,
> We make thee lady.

We make thee lady! Thus he disposes of a sector of the earth, this ring-giver, this warrior-leader, this chosen one, his only landlord God! Is it not passing fine . . . ? Here is no soft-brained *Senex*, but the archetypal *King*.

As such Lear symbolizes Mankind, and we will say nothing essential about him by reckoning up his years and growing glib about the symptoms of senile dementia. The king-figure surrogate is an understandable product of the human mind in its early attempts at abstraction, since the most imposing of single men best lends his image to the difficult concept of Man. His vicissitudes best epitomize the vicissitudes of all, since upon the highest altitude the sun shines brightest and the cold snow lies most deep. Early Renaissance drama was steeped in the tradition of this symbolic figure, sometimes still called *King* as well as *Mankind, Everyman, Genus Humanum,* and the like. He is always identifiable by his centrality in the action, and the mixed company he keeps – vices or flatterers on the one hand, virtues or truth-speakers on the other. And there stands Lear – Goneril and Regan to the left, Kent and Cordelia to the right.

But this is also a family gathering. There is the father, and there the servants and children of his house. The central figure is, and seems always more so as the play weaves its spell, not only archetypal King, Man, and Father, but particular king, man, and father. No symbol that remained purely symbol could so touch our emotions. To have children of his flesh and blood, the father must be flesh and blood – such as can be old, grow weary, feel cold and wet.

Only a few days of fictional time elapse, only a few hours in the theatre, so that Lear's first words still echo in our ears as we hear his last.

We make thee lady. . . . Let it be so, thy truth then be thy dower! . . . Peace, Kent! Come not between the dragon and his wrath. . . . The bow is bent and drawn; make from the shaft. . . . Therefore be gone. . . . Let me not stay a jot for dinner; go get it ready. . . . Call the clotpoll back.

Such are Lear's accents at the beginning. And at the close –

You must bear with me. . . . I am old and foolish. . . . Her voice was ever soft, gentle, and low. . . . Pray you undo this button. Thank you, sir.

He has learned a new language. We are required to accept this learning as good, but we are forbidden to rejoice.

The play is Lear's gethsemane, its great reality his suffering, which so draws us into itself that our conception of the work as a whole is formed in the crucible of our fear and pity. His anguish is kin with the anguish of Job, Prometheus, Oedipus, and other tragic projections of spirits in agony, but it retains its own peculiar quality. Its cause, its nature, and its meaning will always remain the imperfectly resolved crux of the play; and one can do no more than explain, with such confidence as one is able to muster, how these things appear to him.

To say that Lear gets what he deserves is to share the opinion of Goneril and Regan. (Some have even implied that Cordelia gets what she deserves, anaesthetizing their heads and hearts with obtuse moralisms suggested by the doctrine of "poetic justice.") What does Lear deserve? He is proud and peremptory, and it is better to be humble and temporizing, but there are occupational hazards in being a king, perhaps even in being a father. Is his charge not true that the world has lied to him, telling him he was wise before he was bearded, returning "yea and nay" to everything he said? His guilt is widely shared, and his "flaw" like that of Oedipus seems mysteriously hereditary. And it is linked inextricably with his virtues. We applaud the resurgence of youthful might that cuts down Cordelia's assassin. We admire the valor of his attempts (and they come quite early) to be patient, to compromise, to hold back womanish tears, to cling to his reason. Nothing is more moving than his bewildered attempts to meet "social" obligations as he kneels by Cordelia's body. We love his *manliness*. Pride has its value too.

Lear's errors stem from no corruption of heart. His rejection of Kent and Cordelia is the reflex of his attachment to them. The errors are not the man. The man is one who has valued and been valued by such as they. The things he wants – fidelity and love – are good things. That he should find them in his servant and his child seems to him an aspect of universal order. In his vocabulary, as distinct from Edmund's, such things are *natural*. His inability to distinguish between the false and the true, and his craving for visible displays, are not failings peculiar to him. "How much do you love me?" – few parents suppress this bullying question, spoken or unspoken, however much they may have felt its burden as children. It seems in the nature of some things that they always be learned too late, that as children we might have offered more, as parents demanded less. To punish a thankless child has the appearance of justice, to withdraw in one's age from the cares of state the appearance of wisdom, to dispose of one's goods by gift instead of testament the appearance of generosity. Plain men in their prime have been similarly deceived. Gloucester shakes his head sadly over Lear's injustice, folly, and selfishness as he duplicates his actions.

In the maimed but agile mind of the Fool faithfully dogging Lear's steps, his errors stand as an *idée fixe* and are harped upon with terrible iteration. We should not imitate the example. We may find more meaning in the excess of expiation. The purely physical suffering – denial of rest, exposure to wind and rain – is real, but it strikes the sufferer himself as little more than a metaphor. We may say that his spiritual suffering is in excess of his actual afflictions, that it is selfish and centrifugal, or a mere symptom of aged petulance, but if we do so, we are stopping our ears to the voice of Shakespeare and all his decent spokesmen. Lear's curse of Goneril is still alienating, like his treatment of Cordelia, but when he stands weeping before his cormorant daughters in whom he has put his faith, and they coolly and relentlessly strip him of every vestige of dignity, our hearts turn over. Humility may be good, but this humiliation is evil.

There is no *need* that this man be attended by a hundred knights, that his messenger be deferentially treated, or that his children offer him more than subsistence. His cause rests upon no more rational grounds than our powers of sympathy and imagination. "O reason not the need." As his every expectation is brutally defeated, and he looks in dazed recognition upon the world as it is instead of what he thought it was, of himself as he is instead of what he thought he was, we defer to his past illusions. He had never identified prestige merely as power, had never imagined that the visages of respect, kindliness, and love could contort into the hideous lines of icy contempt and sour indifference.

Lear's anguish now represents for us Man's horror and sense of helplessness at the discovery of evil – the infiltration of animality in the human world, naked cruelty and appetite. It is a fissure that threatens to widen infinitely, and we see Lear at the center of turbulence as it works its breakage in minds, in families, in nations, in the heavens themselves, interacting in dreadful concatenation.

The significance of Lear's response to his discovery is best seen in the light of Gloucester's. In Sidney's *Arcadia*, II, 10, the "storie of the Paphlagonian unkind King and his kinde sonne" repeats in essence the Lear legend, except that the children, false and true, are sons instead of daughters. By reducing the rank of Sidney's king and interweaving his parallel fate in alternate scenes, Shakespeare is able, amazingly, both further to universalize and further to particularize the experience of Lear. Gloucester also represents Man, but his distinction from Lear suggests the distinction between ordinary and extraordinary men. Gloucester is amiably confused about the tawdriness of his past, of which Edmund is the product, and sentimentally fumbling in the present. What appears in Lear as heroic error appears in him as gullibility. His fine moments are identical with those of a nameless serf of Cornwall's and an ancient tenant of his own – in the presence of cruelty he becomes kind and brave:

GLOUCESTER I am tied to th' stake, and I must stand the course.
REGAN Wherefore to Dover?
GLOUCESTER Because I would not see thy cruel nails
   Pluck out his poor old eyes.

Like Lear he is incorrupt of heart, and he grows in dignity, but his total response to vicious encroachment is something akin to apathy and surrender; his instinct is to retreat.

Not so with Lear. He batters himself to pieces against the fact of evil. Granted that its disruptive power has been unleashed by his own error, so that error itself partakes of evil, as he is shudderingly aware, yet he remains the great antagonist. Falsity, cruelty, injustice, corruption – their appalling forms swirl about him in phantasmic patterns. His instinct is to rip them from the universe, to annihilate all things if it is the only way to annihilate these things. His charges of universal hypocrisy: "handy-dandy, which is the justice, which is the thief?" – his denial of human responsibility: "None does offend, none – I say none!" – his indictment of life itself:

> Thou know'st, the first time that we smell the air
> We wawl and cry –

cancel their own nihilism, because they sound no acquiescence. Lear is the voice of protest. The grandeur of his spirit supplies the impotence of his body as he opposes to evil all that is left him to oppose – his molten indignation, his huge invectives, his capacity for feeling pain.

This quality of Lear seen in retrospect, his hunger after righteousness, gives magnitude to the concluding scenes. His spirit has been doubly lacerated by his own sense of guilt. He has failed "poor naked wretches" no different from himself, and he has wronged Cordelia. His remorse has found expression only in brief occasional utterances, welling up as it were against desperate efforts of containment, but its scalding power is revealed in his acts of abasement when he and Cordelia meet. The final episodes are all vitally linked. When the two are led in captive, we are made to look back upon their reunion, which he dreams of endlessly reenacting:

> When thou dost ask me blessing, I'll kneel down
> And ask of thee forgiveness;

then forward to their death:

> Upon such sacrifices, my Cordelia,
> The gods themselves throw incense.

The words help to effect that perfect coalescence of particular and general tragic experience achieved as he kneels beside her body. This is a father and his child who will come no more, the father remembering his own unkindness and the child's endearing ways. There is no melioration in his dying delusion that she still lives, no mention of an after-life. It is unspeakably sad. But it merges with a larger yet less devastating sadness. This is also a sacrifice, and although the somber tones of the survivors as they take up the burden of survival give it relevance to the future as well as the past, it is such a sacrifice as obliquely vindicates the gods if upon it they throw incense.

We know, not as an item of faith but of simple demonstrable fact, that we are greatly indebted for such wisdom as we have, that it was bought with "sacrifices." In the struggle of our kind against brutality, the great casualties, spiritual and even physical, have always been among those who have been best and those who have cared most. In the world of this play Cordelia has brought us the truest sense of human goodness, her words "No cause, no cause" the truest sense of moral beauty. She is the perfect offering. And so is Lear. She is best. He cares most for what is

26

best. The play ends as it begins in an allegorical grouping, commemorating humanity's long, agonized, and continuing struggle to be human. This larger meaning gives our tears the dignity of an act of ratification and gratitude: to these still figures we have pitied we owe the gift of feeling pity.

Harvard University   ALFRED HARBAGE

NOTE ON THE TEXT

In 1608 a version of *King Lear* appeared in a quarto volume sold by Nathaniel Butter at his shop at the Pied Bull. Its text was reproduced in 1619 in a quarto falsely dated 1608. Various theories have been offered to explain the nature of the Pied Bull text, the most recent being that it represents Shakespeare's rough draft carelessly copied, and corrupted by the faulty memories of actors who were party to the copying. In 1623 a greatly improved though "cut" version of the play appeared in the first folio, evidently printed from the quarto after it had been carefully collated with the official playhouse manuscript. The present edition follows the folio text, and although it adds in square brackets the passages appearing only in the quarto, and accepts fifty-three quarto readings, it follows the chosen text more closely than do most recent editions. However, deference to the quarto is paid in an appendix, where its alternative readings, both those accepted and those rejected, are listed. Few editorial emendations have been retained, but see I, ii, 21 *top* (Q & F 'to'), II, ii, 138 *contemnèd'st* (Q 'temnest'), III, vi, 25 *bourn* (Q 'broom'), III, vi, 67 *lym* (Q & F 'him'), IV, ii, 57 *to threat* (Q 'thereat'), IV, iii, 20 *seemed* (Q 'seeme'), 31 *moistened* (Q 'moistened her'). The quarto text is not divided into acts and scenes. The act and scene division here supplied marginally for reference purposes is that of the folio except that Act II, Scene ii of the latter has been subdivided into Scenes ii, iii, and iv. The continuity of the action here, and at several other misleadingly divided sections of the play, is indicated in the manner explained at the end of "The texts of the plays."

KING LEAR

KING LEAR

Enter Kent, Gloucester, and Edmund.   I, i

KENT I thought the King had more affected the Duke of 1
Albany than Cornwall.   2

GLOUCESTER It did always seem so to us; but now, in the
division of the kingdom, it appears not which of the
dukes he values most, for equalities are so weighed that 5
curiosity in neither can make choice of either's moiety. 6

KENT Is not this your son, my lord?

GLOUCESTER His breeding, sir, hath been at my charge. 8
I have so often blushed to acknowledge him that now I
am brazed to't.   10

KENT I cannot conceive you.   11

GLOUCESTER Sir, this young fellow's mother could;
whereupon she grew round-wombed, and had indeed,
sir, a son for her cradle ere she had a husband for her
her bed. Do you smell a fault?

KENT I cannot wish the fault undone, the issue of it being
so proper.   17

GLOUCESTER But I have a son, sir, by order of law, some
year elder than this who yet is no dearer in my account: 19
though this knave came something saucily to the world 20

I, i Room of state within King Lear's palace 1 *affected* warmly regarded
2 *Albany* i.e. Scotland (once ruled by 'Albanacte') 5 *equalities . . .
weighed* i.e. the portions weigh so equally 6 *curiosity . . . moiety* careful
analysis by neither can make him prefer the other's portion 8 *breeding*
rearing 10 *brazed* brazened 11 *conceive* understand (with pun following)
17 *proper* handsome 19 *account* estimation 20 *saucily* (1) impertinently,
(2) bawdily

31

before he was sent for, yet was his mother fair, there was
22   good sport at his making, and the whoreson must be
acknowledged. Do you know this noble gentleman,
Edmund?

EDMUND No, my lord.

GLOUCESTER My Lord of Kent. Remember him here-
after as my honorable friend.

EDMUND My services to your lordship.

KENT I must love you, and sue to know you better.

EDMUND Sir, I shall study deserving.

31   GLOUCESTER He hath been out nine years, and away he
32   shall again.

[Sound a] sennet.

The King is coming.

*Enter [one bearing a coronet, then] King Lear, [then
the Dukes of] Cornwall, [and] Albany, [next]
Goneril, Regan, Cordelia, and Attendants.*

LEAR

Attend the lords of France and Burgundy, Gloucester.

GLOUCESTER

I shall, my lord.   *Exit [with Edmund].*

LEAR

36   Meantime we shall express our darker purpose.
Give me the map there. Know that we have divided
38   In three our kingdom; and 'tis our fast intent
To shake all cares and business from our age,
Conferring them on younger strengths while we
Unburdened crawl toward death. Our son of Cornwall,
And you our no less loving son of Albany,
43   We have this hour a constant will to publish
44   Our daughters' several dowers, that future strife

---

22 *whoreson* (affectionate abuse, but literally applicable, like *knave* above)
31 *out* away (for training, or in military service) 32 s.d. *sennet* trumpet
flourish (heralding a procession) 36 *darker purpose* more secret intention
(to require declarations of affection) 38 *fast* firm 43 *constant . . . publish*
fixed intention to announce 44 *several* individual

May be prevented now. The princes, France and
    Burgundy,
Great rivals in our youngest daughter's love;
Long in our court have made their amorous sojourn,   47
And here are to be answered. Tell me, my daughters
(Since now we will divest us both of rule,
Interest of territory, cares of state),   50
Which of you shall we say doth love us most,
That we our largest bounty may extend
Where nature doth with merit challenge. Goneril,   53
Our eldest-born, speak first.

GONERIL

Sir, I love you more than word can wield the matter;   55
Dearer than eyesight, space, and liberty;   56
Beyond what can be valuèd, rich or rare;
No less than life, with grace, health, beauty, honor;
As much as child e'er loved, or father found;
A love that makes breath poor, and speech unable.   60
Beyond all manner of so much I love you.

CORDELIA [aside]

What shall Cordelia speak? Love, and be silent.

LEAR

Of all these bounds, even from this line to this,
With shadowy forests and with champains riched,   64
With plenteous rivers and wide-skirted meads,   65
We make thee lady. To thine and Albany's issues   66
Be this perpetual. – What says our second daughter,   67
Our dearest Regan, wife of Cornwall?

REGAN

I am made of that self mettle as my sister,
And prize me at her worth. In my true heart   70

---

47 *amorous sojourn* i.e. visit of courtship 50 *Interest* legal possession 53
nature . . . challenge natural affection matches other merits 55 *wield*
handle 56 *space* scope (for the exercise of *liberty*) 60 *breath* voice;
unable inadequate 64 *champains riched* plains enriched 65 *wide-skirted*
far spreading 66 *issues* descendants 67 *perpetual* in perpetuity 70
prize . . . worth value me at her value

71   I find she names my very deed of love;
     Only she comes too short, that I profess
     Myself an enemy to all other joys
74   Which the most precious square of sense possesses,
75   And find I am alone felicitate
     In your dear Highness' love.

CORDELIA [aside]   Then poor Cordelia;
     And yet not so, since I am sure my love 's
78   More ponderous than my tongue.

LEAR
     To thee and thine hereditary ever
     Remain this ample third of our fair kingdom,
81   No less in space, validity, and pleasure
     Than that conferred on Goneril. – Now, our joy,
83   Although our last and least; to whose young love
84   The vines of France and milk of Burgundy
85   Strive to be interest; what can you say to draw
     A third more opulent than your sisters? Speak.

CORDELIA
     Nothing, my lord.

LEAR Nothing?

CORDELIA Nothing.

LEAR
     Nothing will come of nothing. Speak again.

CORDELIA
     Unhappy that I am, I cannot heave
     My heart into my mouth. I love your Majesty
93   According to my bond, no more nor less.

LEAR
     How, how, Cordelia? Mend your speech a little,
     Lest you may mar your fortunes.

---

71 *my very deed of* the true fact of my   74 *Which . . . possesses* which the
most precise measurement by the senses holds to be most precious   75
felicitate made happy   78 *ponderous* weighty   81 *validity* value; *pleasure*
pleasing qualities   83 *least* smallest, youngest   84 *vines* vineyards; *milk*
pasture-lands (?)   85 *interest* concerned as interested parties   93 *bond*
obligation

CORDELIA   Good my lord,
You have begot me, bred me, loved me. I
Return those duties back as are right fit,   97
Obey you, love you, and most honor you.
Why have my sisters husbands if they say
They love you all? Haply, when I shall wed,
That lord whose hand must take my plight shall carry   101
Half my love with him, half my care and duty.
Sure I shall never marry like my sisters,
[To love my father all.]

LEAR
But goes thy heart with this?

CORDELIA   Ay, my good lord.

LEAR
So young, and so untender?

CORDELIA
So young, my lord, and true.

LEAR
Let it be so, thy truth then be thy dower!
For, by the sacred radiance of the sun,
The mysteries of Hecate and the night,   110
By all the operation of the orbs   111
From whom we do exist and cease to be,
Here I disclaim all my paternal care,
Propinquity and property of blood,   114
And as a stranger to my heart and me
Hold thee from this for ever. The barbarous Scythian,   116
Or he that makes his generation messes   117
To gorge his appetite, shall to my bosom
Be as well neighbored, pitied, and relieved,
As thou my sometime daughter.   120

KENT   Good my liege –

97 *Return . . . fit* i.e. am fittingly dutiful in return   101 *plight* pledge, troth-plight   110 *Hecate* infernal goddess, patroness of witches   111 *operation . . . orbs* astrological influences   114 *Propinquity* relationship; *property* i.e. common property, something shared   116 *Scythian* (proverbially barbarous)   117 *makes . . . messes* makes meals of his offspring   120 *sometime* former

LEAR

Peace, Kent!

122   Come not between the dragon and his wrath.
123   I loved her most, and thought to set my rest
124   On her kind nursery. – Hence and avoid my sight! –
125   So be my grave my peace as here I give

Her father's heart from her! Call France. Who stirs!
Call Burgundy. Cornwall and Albany,
With my two daughters' dowers digest the third;
Let pride, which she calls plainness, marry her.
I do invest you jointly with my power,

131   Preeminence, and all the large effects
132   That troop with majesty. Ourself, by monthly course,

With reservation of an hundred knights,
By you to be sustained, shall our abode
Make with you by due turn. Only we shall retain

136   The name, and all th' addition to a king. The sway,

Revenue, execution of the rest,
Belovèd sons, be yours; which to confirm,

139   This coronet part between you.

KENT   Royal Lear,

Whom I have ever honored as my king,
Loved as my father, as my master followed,
As my great patron thought on in my prayers –

LEAR

143   The bow is bent and drawn; make from the shaft.

KENT

144   Let it fall rather, though the fork invade

The region of my heart. Be Kent unmannerly
When Lear is mad. What wouldst thou do, old man?
Think'st thou that duty shall have dread to speak

---

122 *his* its   123 *set my rest* (1) risk my stake (a term in the card game pri-
mero), (2) rely for my repose   124 *nursery* nursing, care   125 *So . . . peace as*
let me rest peacefully in my grave only as   131 *effects* tokens   132 *Ourself*
I (royal plural)   136 *th' addition* honors and prerogatives   139 *coronet*
(symbol of rule; not necessarily the royal crown)   143 *make* make away
144 *fall* strike; *fork* two-pronged head

36

When power to flattery bows? To plainness honor 's
   bound
When majesty falls to folly. Reserve thy state,   149
And in thy best consideration check   150
This hideous rashness. Answer my life my judgment,   151
Thy youngest daughter does not love thee least,
Nor are those empty-hearted whose low sounds
Reverb no hollowness.   154

LEAR   Kent, on thy life, no more!

KENT
My life I never held but as a pawn   155
To wage against thine enemies; ne'er fear to lose it,   156
Thy safety being motive.   157

LEAR   Out of my sight!

KENT
See better, Lear, and let me still remain   158
The true blank of thine eye.   159

LEAR
Now by Apollo –

KENT   Now by Apollo, King,
Thou swear'st thy gods in vain.

LEAR   O vassal! Miscreant!   161
   [Grasping his sword.]

ALBANY, CORNWALL Dear sir, forbear!

KENT
Kill thy physician, and thy fee bestow
Upon the foul disease. Revoke thy gift,
Or, whilst I can vent clamor from my throat,
I'll tell thee thou dost evil.

LEAR   Hear me, recreant,   166
On thine allegiance, hear me!

---

149 *Reserve thy state* retain your kingly authority   150 *best consideration*
most careful deliberation   151 *Answer my life* i.e. I'll stake my life on
154 *Reverb no hollowness* i.e. do not reverberate (like a drum) as a result
of hollowness   155 *pawn* stake   156 *wage* wager, pit   157 *motive* the
moving cause   158 *still* always   159 *blank* center of the target (to guide
your aim truly)   161 *Miscreant* (1) rascal, (2) infidel   166 *recreant* traitor

168 That thou hast sought to make us break our vows,
169 Which we durst never yet, and with strained pride
170 To come betwixt our sentence and our power,
    Which nor our nature nor our place can bear,
172 Our potency made good, take thy reward.
    Five days we do allot thee for provision
174 To shield thee from disasters of the world,
    And on the sixth to turn thy hated back
    Upon our kingdom. If, on the tenth day following,
177 Thy banished trunk be found in our dominions,
    The moment is thy death. Away. By Jupiter,
    This shall not be revoked.

KENT
180 Fare thee well, King. Sith thus thou wilt appear,
    Freedom lives hence, and banishment is here.
      [To Cordelia]
    The gods to their dear shelter take thee, maid,
    That justly think'st and hast most rightly said.
      [To Regan and Goneril]
184 And your large speeches may your deeds approve,
185 That good effects may spring from words of love.
    Thus Kent, O princes, bids you all adieu;
187 He'll shape his old course in a country new.   *Exit.*
      Flourish. Enter Gloucester, with France and
      Burgundy; Attendants.

GLOUCESTER
Here's France and Burgundy, my noble lord.

LEAR
My Lord of Burgundy,
We first address toward you, who with this king
Hath rivalled for our daughter. What in the least

---

168 *That* in that, since   **169** *strained* excessive   **170** *To come . . . power*
i.e. to oppose my power to sentence   **172** *Our . . . good* if my power is to
be demonstrated as real   **174** *disasters* accidents   **177** *trunk* body   **180**
Sith since   **184** *approve* confirm   **185** *effects* consequences   **187** *shape*
. . . course keep to his customary ways (of honesty)

Will you require in present dower with her,
Or cease your quest of love?

BURGUNDY   Most royal Majesty,
I crave no more than hath your Highness offered,
Nor will you tender less.

LEAR   Right noble Burgundy,
When she was dear to us, we did hold her so;
But now her price is fallen. Sir, there she stands.
If aught within that little seeming substance,   198
Or all of it, with our displeasure pieced   199
And nothing more, may fitly like your Grace,
She's there, and she is yours.

BURGUNDY   I know no answer.

LEAR
Will you, with those infirmities she owes,   202
Unfriended, new adopted to our hate,
Dow'red with our curse, and strangered with our oath, 204
Take her, or leave her?

BURGUNDY   Pardon me, royal sir.
Election makes not up on such conditions.   206

LEAR
Then leave her, sir, for by the pow'r that made me
I tell you all her wealth. *[to France]* For you, great King,
I would not from your love make such a stray   209
To match you where I hate; therefore beseech you
T' avert your liking a more worthier way   211
Than on a wretch whom Nature is ashamed
Almost t' acknowledge hers.

FRANCE   This is most strange,
That she whom even but now was your best object,   214
The argument of your praise, balm of your age,   215
The best, the dearest, should in this trice of time

---

198 *seeming substance* i.e. nothing, mere shell   **199** *pieced* joined   **202** *owes*
owns   **204** *strangered with* made alien by   **206** *Election . . . conditions* no
choice is possible on such terms   **209** *make . . . stray* stray so far as   **211**
avert turn   **214** *best* favorite   **215** *argument* theme

217   Commit a thing so monstrous to dismantle
     So many folds of favor. Sure her offense
     Must be of such unnatural degree
220   That monsters it, or your fore-vouched affection
221   Fall'n into taint ; which to believe of her
222   Must be a faith that reason without miracle
     Should never plant in me.

    CORDELIA   I yet beseech your Majesty,
     If for I want that glib and oily art
225   To speak and purpose not since what I well intend
     I'll do't before I speak, that you make known
     It is no vicious blot, murder or foulness,
     No unchaste action or dishonorèd step,
     That hath deprived me of your grace and favor ;
     But even for want of that for which I am richer –
231   A still-soliciting eye, and such a tongue
     That I am glad I have not, though not to have it
     Hath lost me in your liking.

    LEAR   Better thou
     Hadst not been born than not t' have pleased me better.

    FRANCE
235   Is it but this ? A tardiness in nature
236   Which often leaves the history unspoke
     That it intends to do. My Lord of Burgundy,
     What say you to the lady ? Love 's not love
239   When it is mingled with regards that stands
     Aloof from th' entire point. Will you have her ?
     She is herself a dowry.

---

217 *to dismantle* so to strip off   **220** *That monsters it* as makes it monstrous (i.e. abnormal, freakish); *fore-vouched* previously sworn   **221** *taint* decay (with the implication that the affection, and the oath attesting it, were tainted in the first place)   **222** *reason . . . miracle* i.e. rational, unaided by miraculous, means of persuasion   **225** *purpose not* i.e. without intending to act in accordance with my words   **231** *still-soliciting* always-begging   **235** *tardiness in nature* natural reticence   **236** *history unspoke* actions unannounced   **239-40** *mingled . . . point* i.e. mixed with irrelevant considerations

BURGUNDY   Royal King,
  Give but that portion which yourself proposed,
  And here I take Cordelia by the hand,
  Duchess of Burgundy.

LEAR
  Nothing. I have sworn. I am firm.

BURGUNDY
  I am sorry then you have so lost a father
  That you must lose a husband.

CORDELIA   Peace be with Burgundy.
  Since that respects of fortune are his love,   248
  I shall not be his wife.

FRANCE
  Fairest Cordelia, that art most rich being poor,
  Most choice forsaken, and most loved despised,
  Thee and thy virtues here I seize upon.
  Be it lawful I take up what's cast away.
  Gods, gods! 'Tis strange that from their cold'st neglect
  My love should kindle to inflamed respect.   255
  Thy dow'rless daughter, King, thrown to my chance,
  Is queen of us, of ours, and our fair France.
  Not all the dukes of wat'rish Burgundy   258
  Can buy this unprized precious maid of me.   259
  Bid them farewell, Cordelia, though unkind.
  Thou losest here, a better where to find.   261

LEAR
  Thou hast her, France; let her be thine, for we
  Have no such daughter, nor shall ever see
  That face of hers again. Therefore be gone
  Without our grace, our love, our benison.   265
  Come, noble Burgundy.
        Flourish. Exeunt [Lear, Burgundy, Cornwall,
          Albany, Gloucester, and Attendants].

---

248 *respects* considerations **255** *inflamed respect* ardent regard **258**
wat'rish (1) watery, weak, (2) watered, diluted **259** *unprized* unvalued
261 *here* this place; *where* other place **265** *benison* blessing

41

FRANCE
   Bid farewell to your sisters.

CORDELIA

268   The jewels of our father, with washèd eyes
    Cordelia leaves you. I know you what you are;
270   And, like a sister, am most loath to call
271   Your faults as they are named. Love well our father.
272   To your professèd bosoms I commit him;
    But yet, alas, stood I within his grace,
274   I would prefer him to a better place.
    So farewell to you both.

REGAN
   Prescribe not us our duty.

GONERIL   Let your study
    Be to content your lord, who hath received you
278   At fortune's alms. You have obedience scanted,
279   And well are worth the want that you have wanted.

CORDELIA

280   Time shall unfold what plighted cunning hides,
281   Who covers faults, at last with shame derides.
    Well may you prosper.

FRANCE   Come, my fair Cordelia.

Exit France and Cordelia.

GONERIL Sister, it is not little I have to say of what most nearly appertains to us both. I think our father will hence to-night.

REGAN That's most certain, and with you; next month with us.

GONERIL You see how full of changes his age is. The observation we have made of it hath not been little. He

---

268 *jewels* i.e. things held precious (cf. l. 259); *washèd* tear-washed 270 *like a sister* i.e. with sisterly loyalty 271 *as . . . named* by their true names 272 *professèd* i.e. love-professing 274 *prefer* promote 278 *alms* small offerings 279 *worth . . . wanted* i.e. deserving no affection since you have shown no affection 280 *plighted* pleated, enfolded 281 *Who . . . derides* i.e. time at first conceals faults, then exposes them to shame

always loved our sister most, and with what poor judgment he hath now cast her off appears too grossly. 291

REGAN 'Tis the infirmity of his age; yet he hath ever but
slenderly known himself. 293

GONERIL The best and soundest of his time hath been but 294
rash; then must we look from his age to receive not alone
the imperfections of lŏng-ingraffed condition, but there- 296
withal the unruly waywardness that infirm and choleric
years bring with them.

REGAN Such unconstant starts are we like to have from 299
him as this of Kent's banishment.

GONERIL There is further compliment of leave-taking 301
between France and him. Pray you let us hit together; if 302
our father carry authority with such disposition as he
bears, this last surrender of his will but offend us. 304

REGAN We shall further think of it.

GONERIL We must do something, and i' th' heat. *Exeunt*. 306

*

Enter Bastard [Edmund, solus, with a letter]. I, ii

EDMUND
  Thou, Nature, art my goddess; to thy law 1
  My services are bound. Wherefore should I
  Stand in the plague of custom, and permit 3
  The curiosity of nations to deprive me, 4
  For that I am some twelve or fourteen moonshines 5

---

291 *grossly* crudely conspicuous 293 *known himself* i.e. been aware of what
he truly is 294 *of his time* period of his past life 296 *long-ingraffed* in-
grown, chronic; *therewithal* along with that 299 *unconstant starts* im-
pulsive moves 301 *compliment* formality 302 *hit* agree 304 *surrender* i.e.
yielding up of authority; *offend* harm 306 *i' th' heat* i.e. while the iron is hot
I, ii Within the Earl of Gloucester's castle 1 *Nature* i.e. the material and
mechanistic as distinct from the spiritual and heaven-ordained 3 *Stand
. . . custom* submit to the affliction of convention 4 *curiosity* nice distinctions 5 *For that* because; *moonshines* months

6   Lag of a brother? Why bastard? Wherefore base,

7   When my dimensions are as well compact,

8   My mind as generous, and my shape as true,

9   As honest madam's issue? Why brand they us
      With base? with baseness? Bastardy base? Base?

11   Who, in the lusty stealth of nature, take

12   More composition and fierce quality
      Than doth, within a dull, stale, tirèd bed,

14   Go to th' creating a whole tribe of fops

15   Got 'tween asleep and wake? Well then,
      Legitimate Edgar, I must have your land.
      Our father's love is to the bastard Edmund
      As to th' legitimate. Fine word, 'legitimate.'
      Well, my legitimate, if this letter speed,

20   And my invention thrive, Edmund the base
      Shall top th' legitimate. I grow, I prosper.
      Now, gods, stand up for bastards.

         Enter Gloucester.

GLOUCESTER
    Kent banished thus? and France in choler parted?

24   And the King gone to-night? prescribed his pow'r?

25   Confined to exhibition? All this done

26   Upon the gad? – Edmund, how now? What news?

EDMUND
    So please your lordship, none.

GLOUCESTER

28   Why so earnestly seek you to put up that letter?

EDMUND
    I know no news, my lord.

GLOUCESTER
    What paper were you reading?

EDMUND Nothing, my lord.

6 *Lag of* behind (in age)   7 *compact* fitted, matched   8 *generous* befitting the high-born   9 *honest* chaste   11 *lusty . . . nature* secrecy of natural lust   12 *composition* completeness of constitution, robustness; *fierce* mettlesome, thoroughbred   14 *fops* fools   15 *Got* begotten   20 *invention thrive* plot succeed   24 *prescribed* limited   25 *exhibition* an allowance, a pension   26 *gad* spur   28 *put up* put away

GLOUCESTER No? What needed then that terrible dispatch of it into your pocket? The quality of nothing
hath not such need to hide itself. Let's see. Come, if it
be nothing, I shall not need spectacles.

EDMUND I beseech you, sir, pardon me. It is a letter from
my brother that I have not all o'er-read; and for so much
as I have perused, I find it not fit for your o'erlooking.   38

GLOUCESTER Give me the letter, sir.

EDMUND I shall offend, either to detain or give it. The
contents, as in part I understand them, are to blame.   41

GLOUCESTER Let's see, let's see.

EDMUND I hope, for my brother's justification, he wrote
this but as an essay or taste of my virtue.   44

GLOUCESTER *(reads)* 'This policy and reverence of age   45
makes the world bitter to the best of our times; keeps our   46
fortunes from us till our oldness cannot relish them. I
begin to find an idle and fond bondage in the oppression   48
of aged tyranny, who sways, not as it hath power, but as   49
it is suffered. Come to me, that of this I may speak more.   50
If our father would sleep till I waked him, you should
enjoy half his revenue for ever, and live the beloved of   52
your brother,   Edgar.'

Hum! Conspiracy? 'Sleep till I waked him, you should
enjoy half his revenue.' My son Edgar! Had he a hand to
write this? A heart and brain to breed it in? When came
you to this? Who brought it?   57

EDMUND It was not brought me, my lord; there's the
cunning of it. I found it thrown in at the casement of my   59
closet.   60

GLOUCESTER You know the character to be your   61
brother's?

---

38 *o'erlooking* examination   **41** *to blame* blameworthy   **44** *essay* trial; *taste*
test   **45** *policy and reverence* policy of reverencing   **46** *the best of our times*
our best years   **48** *idle, fond* foolish (synonyms)   **49** *who sways* which rules
50 *suffered* allowed   **52** *revenue* income   **57** *to this* upon this   **59** *casement*
window   **60** *closet* room   **61** *character* handwriting

62 EDMUND If the matter were good, my lord, I durst swear
63   it were his; but in respect of that, I would fain think it
       were not.

  GLOUCESTER It is his.

  EDMUND It is his hand, my lord; but I hope his heart is
       not in the contents.

68 GLOUCESTER Has he never before sounded you in this
       business?

  EDMUND Never, my lord. But I have heard him oft main-
71   tain it to be fit that, sons at perfect age, and fathers
       declined, the father should be as ward to the son, and
       the son manage his revenue.

  GLOUCESTER O villain, villain! His very opinion in the
       letter. Abhorred villain, unnatural, detested, brutish
76   villain; worse than brutish! Go, sirrah, seek him. I'll
       apprehend him. Abominable villain! Where is he?

  EDMUND I do not well know, my lord. If it shall please
       you to suspend your indignation against my brother till
       you can derive from him better testimony of his intent,
81   you should run a certain course; where, if you violently
       proceed against him, mistaking his purpose, it would
       make a great gap in your own honor and shake in pieces
       the heart of his obedience. I dare pawn down my life for
85   him that he hath writ this to feel my affection to your
86   honor, and to no other pretense of danger.

  GLOUCESTER Think you so?

88 EDMUND If your honor judge it meet, I will place you
89   where you shall hear us confer of this and by an auri-
       cular assurance have your satisfaction, and that without
       any further delay than this very evening.

  GLOUCESTER He cannot be such a monster.

---

62 *matter* contents   **63** *in respect of that* i.e. considering what those contents
are; *fain* prefer to   **68** *sounded you* sounded you out   **71** *perfect age* prime
of life   **76** *sirrah* sir (familiar, or contemptuous, form)   **81** *run . . . course*
i.e. know where you are going   **85** *feel* feel out, test; *affection* attachment,
loyalty   **86** *pretense of danger* dangerous intention   **88** *judge it meet*
consider it fitting   **89–90** *by . . . assurance* i.e. by the proof of your own ears

[EDMUND Nor is not, sure.

GLOUCESTER To his father, that so tenderly and entirely
loves him. Heaven and earth!] Edmund, seek him out;
wind me into him, I pray you; frame the business after 96
your own wisdom. I would unstate myself to be in a due 97
resolution.

EDMUND I will seek him, sir, presently; convey the busi- 99
ness as I shall find means, and acquaint you withal. 100

GLOUCESTER These late eclipses in the sun and moon 101
portend no good to us. Though the wisdom of nature can 102
reason it thus and thus, yet nature finds itself scourged by 103
the sequent effects. Love cools, friendship falls off, 104
brothers divide. In cities, mutinies; in countries, dis- 105
cord; in palaces, treason; and the bond cracked 'twixt
son and father. This villain of mine comes under the pre- 107
diction, there's son against father; the King falls from
bias of nature, there's father against child. We have seen 109
the best of our time. Machinations, hollowness, treachery, and all ruinous disorders follow us disquietly to our
graves. Find out this villain, Edmund; it shall lose thee 112
nothing; do it carefully. And the noble and true-hearted
Kent banished; his offense, honesty. 'Tis strange. *Exit*.

EDMUND This is the excellent foppery of the world, that 115
when we are sick in fortune, often the surfeits of our own 116
behavior, we make guilty of our disasters the sun, the
moon, and stars; as if we were villains on necessity; fools
by heavenly compulsion; knaves, thieves, and treachers 119
by spherical predominance; drunkards, liars, and adul- 120

96 *wind me* worm; *frame* plan   97–98 *unstate . . . resolution* i.e. give everything to know for certain   99 *presently* at once; *convey* conduct   100 *withal*
therewith   101 *late* recent   102 *wisdom of nature* natural lore, science
102–04 *can . . . effects* i.e. can supply explanations, yet punitive upheavals in
nature (such as earthquakes) follow   103 *scourged* whipped   104 *sequent*
following   105 *mutinies* rebellions   107 *comes . . . prediction* i.e. is included
among these ill-omened things   109 *bias of nature* natural tendency
112–13 *lose thee nothing* i.e. you will not lose by it   115 *foppery* foolishness
116 *we are sick . . . surfeits* i.e. our fortunes grow sickly, often from the
excesses   119 *treachers* traitors   120 *spherical predominance* i.e. ascen-
dancy, or rule, of a particular sphere

terers by an enforced obedience of planetary influence;
and all that we are evil in, by a divine thrusting on. An

123 admirable evasion of whoremaster man, to lay his goatish
124 disposition on the charge of a star. My father compoun-
125 ded with my mother under the Dragon's Tail, and my
126 nativity was under Ursa Major, so that it follows I am
rough and lecherous. Fut! I should have been that I am,
had the maidenliest star in the firmament twinkled on
my bastardizing. Edgar –
      Enter Edgar.
130 and pat he comes, like the catastrophe of the old comedy.
131 My cue is villainous melancholy, with a sigh like Tom o'
Bedlam. – O, these eclipses do portend these divisions.
Fa, sol, la, mi.

EDGAR How now, brother Edmund; what serious con-
templation are you in?

EDMUND I am thinking, brother, of a prediction I read
this other day, what should follow these eclipses.

EDGAR Do you busy yourself with that?

139 EDMUND I promise you, the effects he writes of succeed
140 unhappily: [as of unnaturalness between the child and
the parent; death, dearth, dissolutions of ancient ami-
ties; divisions in state, menaces and maledictions
143 against king and nobles; needless diffidences, banish-
144 ment of friends, dissipation of cohorts, nuptial breaches,
and I know not what.

146 EDGAR How long have you been a sectary astronomical?
EDMUND Come, come,] when saw you my father last?
EDGAR The night gone by.

---

123 *goatish* lecherous 124 *compounded* (1) came to terms, (2) created
125, 126 *Dragon's Tail, Ursa Major* (constellations, cited because of the
suggestiveness of their names) 126 *nativity* birthday 130 *catastrophe*
conclusion 131–32 *Tom o' Bedlam* (a type of beggar, mad or pretending
to be, so named from the London madhouse, Bethlehem or 'Bedlam'
Hospital) 139–40 *succeed unhappily* unluckily follow 140 *unnaturalness*
unkindness, enmity 143 *diffidences* instances of distrust 144 *dissipation
of cohorts* melting away of supporters 146 *sectary astronomical* of the
astrological sect

EDMUND Spake you with him?

EDGAR Ay, two hours together.

EDMUND Parted you in good terms? Found you no displeasure in him by word nor countenance?   152

EDGAR None at all.

EDMUND Bethink yourself wherein you may have offended him; and at my entreaty forbear his presence until
some little time hath qualified the heat of his displeasure, 156
which at this instant so rageth in him that with the mis- 157
chief of your person it would scarcely allay.   158

EDGAR Some villain hath done me wrong.

EDMUND That's my fear. I pray you have a continent for- 160
bearance till the speed of his rage goes slower; and, as I
say, retire with me to my lodging, from whence I will
fitly bring you to hear my lord speak. Pray ye, go;   163
there's my key. If you do stir abroad, go armed.

EDGAR Armed, brother?

EDMUND Brother, I advise you to the best. Go armed. I
am no honest man if there be any good meaning toward
you. I have told you what I have seen and heard; but
faintly, nothing like the image and horror of it. Pray   169
you, away.

EDGAR Shall I hear from you anon?   170

EDMUND I do serve you in this business.   *Exit [Edgar].*
A credulous father, and a brother noble,
Whose nature is so far from doing harms
That he suspects none; on whose foolish honesty
My practices ride easy. I see the business.   175
Let me, if not by birth, have lands by wit;   176
All with me's meet that I can fashion fit.   *Exit.* 177

*

152 *countenance* expression, look   156 *qualified* moderated   157 *mischief*
injury   158 *allay* be appeased   160 *continent forbearance* cautious in-
accessibility   163 *fitly* conveniently   169 *image and horror* horrible true
picture   170 *anon* soon   175 *practices* plots   176 *wit* intelligence   177
meet proper, acceptable; *fashion fit* i.e. rig up, shape to the purpose

I, iii   *Enter Goneril and Steward [Oswald].*

GONERIL

Did my father strike my gentleman for chiding of his
fool?

OSWALD Ay, madam.

GONERIL

By day and night he wrongs me. Every hour
4   He flashes into one gross crime or other
That sets us all at odds. I'll not endure it.
6   His knights grow riotous, and himself upbraids us
On every trifle. When he returns from hunting,
I will not speak with him. Say I am sick.
9   If you come slack of former services,
10   You shall do well; the fault of it I'll answer.
[Horns within.]

OSWALD He's coming, madam; I hear him.

GONERIL

Put on what weary negligence you please,
13   You and your fellows. I'd have it come to question.
14   If he distaste it, let him to my sister,
Whose mind and mine I know in that are one,
16   [Not to be overruled. Idle old man,
That still would manage those authorities
That he hath given away. Now, by my life,
Old fools are babes again, and must be used
20   With checks as flatteries, when they are seen abused.]
Remember what I have said.

OSWALD   Well, madam.

GONERIL

And let his knights have colder looks among you.
What grows of it, no matter; advise your fellows so.

I, iii Within the Duke of Albany's palace 4 *crime* offense 6 *riotous*
boisterous 9 *come . . . services* i.e. serve him less well than formerly
10 *answer* answer for 13 *question* i.e. open issue, a thing discussed
14 *distaste* dislike 16 *Idle* foolish 20 *checks . . . abused* restraints in
place of cajolery when they (the old men) are seen to be deceived (about
their true state)

[I would breed from hence occasions, and I shall,   24
That I may speak.] I'll write straight to my sister
To hold my course. Prepare for dinner.   *Exeunt.*
    Enter Kent [disguised].   I, iv

KENT
  If but as well I other accents borrow
  That can my speech defuse, my good intent   2
  May carry through itself to that full issue   3
  For which I razed my likeness. Now, banished Kent,   4
  If thou canst serve where thou dost stand condemned,
  So may it come thy master whom thou lov'st
  Shall find thee full of labors.
    Horns within. Enter Lear, [Knight,] and Attendants.

LEAR Let me not stay a jot for dinner; go get it ready. 8
  [Exit an Attendant.] How now, what art thou?

KENT A man, sir.

LEAR What dost thou profess? What wouldst thou with 11
  us?

KENT I do profess to be no less than I seem, to serve him 12
  truly that will put me in trust, to love him that is honest,
  to converse with him that is wise and says little, to fear 14
  judgment, to fight when I cannot choose, and to eat no 15
  fish.

LEAR What art thou?

KENT A very honest-hearted fellow, and as poor as the
  King.

LEAR If thou be'st as poor for a subject as he's for a king,
  thou art poor enough. What wouldst thou?

KENT Service.

LEAR Who wouldst thou serve?

KENT You.

LEAR Dost thou know me, fellow?

24–25 *breed . . . speak* i.e. make an issue of it so that I may speak
I, iv 2 *defuse* disorder, disguise 3 *full issue* perfect result 4 *razed my likeness* erased my natural appearance 8 *stay* wait 11 *profess* do, work at (with pun following) 12 *profess* claim 14 *converse* associate 15 *judgment* i.e. God's judgment 15–16 *eat no fish* be a Protestant (anachronism) (?), avoid unmanly diet (?)

KENT No, sir, but you have that in your countenance
27 which I would fain call master.

LEAR What's that?

KENT Authority.

LEAR What services canst thou do?

31 KENT I can keep honest counsel, ride, run, mar a curious
tale in telling it, and deliver a plain message bluntly.
That which ordinary men are fit for I am qualified in,
and the best of me is diligence.

LEAR How old art thou?

KENT Not so young, sir, to love a woman for singing, nor
so old to dote on her for anything. I have years on my
back forty-eight.

LEAR Follow me; thou shalt serve me. If I like thee no
worse after dinner, I will not part from thee yet. Dinner,
41 ho, dinner! Where's my knave? my fool? Go you and
call my fool hither.   *[Exit an Attendant.]*
        Enter Steward [Oswald].
You, you, sirrah, where's my daughter?

OSWALD So please you –   *Exit.*

45 LEAR What says the fellow there? Call the clotpoll back.
[Exit Knight.] Where's my fool? Ho, I think the world's
asleep. *[Enter Knight.]* How now? Where's that
mongrel?

KNIGHT He says, my lord, your daughter is not well.

LEAR Why came not the slave back to me when I called
him?

KNIGHT Sir, he answered me in the roundest manner, he
would not.

LEAR He would not?

KNIGHT My lord, I know not what the matter is; but to
56 my judgment your Highness is not entertained with
that ceremonious affection as you were wont. There's a

---

27 *fain* like to   31 *keep honest counsel* keep counsel honestly, i.e. respect confidences; *curious* elaborate, embroidered (as contrasted with *plain*)   41 *knave* boy   45 *clótpoll* clodpoll, dolt   56 *entertained* rendered hospitality

great abatement of kindness appears as well in the
general dependants as in the Duke himself also and your
daughter.

LEAR Ha? Say'st thou so?

KNIGHT I beseech you pardon me, my lord, if I be mistaken; for my duty cannot be silent when I think your
Highness wronged.

LEAR Thou but rememb'rest me of mine own conception.   64
I have perceived a most faint neglect of late, which I have   65
rather blamed as mine own jealous curiosity than as a   66
very pretense and purpose of unkindness. I will look   67
further into't. But where's my fool? I have not seen
him this two days.

KNIGHT Since my young lady's going into France, sir,
the fool hath much pined away.

LEAR No more of that; I have noted it well. Go you and
tell my daughter I would speak with her. *[Exit Knight.]*
Go you, call hither my fool.   *[Exit an Attendant.]*
      Enter Steward [Oswald].

O, you, sir, you! Come you hither, sir. Who am I, sir?

OSWALD My lady's father.

LEAR 'My lady's father'? My lord's knave, you whoreson
dog, you slave, you cur!

OSWALD I am none of these, my lord; I beseech your
pardon.

LEAR Do you bandy looks with me, you rascal?   80
      [Strikes him.]

OSWALD I'll not be strucken, my lord.   81

KENT Nor tripped neither, you base football player.   82
      [Trips up his heels.]

LEAR I thank thee, fellow. Thou serv'st me, and I'll love
thee.

---

64 *rememb'rest* remind   65 *faint neglect* i.e. the *weary negligence* of I, iii, 12
66 *jealous curiosity* i.e. suspicious concern about trifles   67 *very pretense* true
intention   80 *bandy* volley, exchange   81 *strucken* struck   82 *football* (an
impromptu street and field game, held in low esteem)

85 KENT Come, sir, arise, away. I'll teach you differences.
Away, away. If you will measure your lubber's length
87 again, tarry; but away. Go to! Have you wisdom? So.
[Pushes him out.]

88 LEAR Now, my friendly knave, I thank thee. There's earnest of thy service.
[Gives money.] Enter Fool.

90 FOOL Let me hire him too. Here's my coxcomb.
[Offers Kent his cap.]

LEAR How now, my pretty knave? How dost thou?

FOOL Sirrah, you were best take my coxcomb.

KENT Why, fool?

FOOL Why? For taking one's part that's out of favor. Nay,
95 an thou canst not smile as the wind sits, thou'lt catch
cold shortly. There, take my coxcomb. Why, this fellow
97 has banished two on's daughters, and did the third a
blessing against his will. If thou follow him, thou must
99 needs wear my coxcomb. – How now, nuncle? Would I
had two coxcombs and two daughters.

LEAR Why, my boy?

FOOL If I gave them all my living, I'ld keep my coxcombs
myself. There's mine; beg another of thy daughters.

LEAR Take heed, sirrah – the whip.

FOOL Truth's a dog must to kennel; he must be whipped
106 out, when the Lady Brach may stand by th' fire and
stink.

108 LEAR A pestilent gall to me.

FOOL Sirrah, I'll teach thee a speech.

LEAR Do.

FOOL Mark it, nuncle.

Have more than thou showest,
Speak less than thou knowest,

85 *differences* distinctions in rank   87 *Go to!* . . . *wisdom* i.e. Get along! Do
you know what's good for you?   88 *earnest* part payment   90 *coxcomb* (cap
of the professional fool, topped with an imitation comb)   95 *smile . . . sits* i.e.
adapt yourself to prevailing forces   97 *banished* i.e. provided the means for
them to become alien to him   99 *nuncle* mine uncle   106 *Brach* hound
bitch   108 *gall* sore, source of irritation

Lend less than thou owest,   114
Ride more than thou goest,   115
Learn more than thou trowest,   116
Set less than thou throwest;   117
Leave thy drink and thy whore,
And keep in-a-door,
And thou shalt have more   120
Than two tens to a score.

KENT This is nothing, fool.

FOOL Then 'tis like the breath of an unfee'd lawyer – you 123
gave me nothing for't. Can you make no use of nothing,
nuncle?

LEAR Why, no, boy. Nothing can be made out of nothing.

FOOL *[to Kent]* Prithee tell him, so much the rent of his 127
land comes to; he will not believe a fool.

LEAR A bitter fool.

FOOL Dost thou know the difference, my boy, between a
bitter fool and a sweet one?   131

LEAR No, lad; teach me.

FOOL   [That lord that counselled thee
                To give away thy land,
             Come place him here by me –
                Do thou for him stand.   136
             The sweet and bitter fool
                Will presently appear;
             The one in motley here,
                The other found out there.   140

LEAR Dost thou call me fool, boy?

FOOL All thy other titles thou hast given away; that thou
wast born with.

---

114 *owest* borrow (?), own, keep (?) 115 *goest* walk 116 *Learn* hear,
listen to; *trowest* believe 117 *Set . . . throwest* stake less than you throw for
(i.e. play for odds) 120–21 *have . . . score* i.e. do better than break even
123 *breath* voice, counsel (reliable only when paid for) 127–28 *rent . . .
land* (nothing, since he has no land) 131 *bitter, sweet* satirical, non-satirical
136 *Do . . . stand* (the Fool thus identifying Lear as his own foolish
counsellor) 140 *found out* revealed (since Lear is the *born* fool as distinct
from himself, the fool in *motley*, professionally satirical)

KENT This is not altogether fool, my lord.

145 FOOL No, faith; lords and great men will not let me. If I had a monopoly out, they would have part on't. And ladies too, they will not let me have all the fool to my-
148 self; they'll be snatching.] Nuncle, give me an egg, and I'll give thee two crowns.

LEAR What two crowns shall they be?

FOOL Why, after I have cut the egg i' th' middle and eat up the meat, the two crowns of the egg. When thou clovest thy crown i' th' middle and gav'st away both
154 parts, thou bor'st thine ass on thy back o'er the dirt. Thou hadst little wit in thy bald crown when thou
156 gav'st thy golden one away. If I speak like myself in
157 this, let him be whipped that first finds it so.
158 [Sings] Fools had ne'er less grace in a year,
159 For wise men are grown foppish,
160 And know not how their wits to wear,
Their manners are so apish.

LEAR When were you wont to be so full of songs, sirrah?
163 FOOL I have used it, nuncle, e'er since thou mad'st thy daughters thy mothers; for when thou gav'st them the rod, and put'st down thine own breeches,
[Sings] Then they for sudden joy did weep,
And I for sorrow sung,
168 That such a king should play bo-peep
And go the fools among.
Prithee, nuncle, keep a schoolmaster that can teach thy fool to lie. I would fain learn to lie.
172 LEAR An you lie, sirrah, we'll have you whipped.

FOOL I marvel what kin thou and thy daughters are.

---

145 *let me* (i.e. be all fool, since they seek a share of folly)   148 *snatching* (like greedy courtiers seeking shares in royal patents of monopoly)   154 *bor'st . . . dirt* (thus foolishly reversing normal behavior)   156 *like myself* i.e. like a fool   157 *let . . . so* i.e. let him be whipped (as a fool) who mistakes this truth as my typical folly   158 *grace . . . year* favor at any time   159 *foppish* foolish   160 *their wits to wear* i.e. to use their intelligence   163 *used* practiced   168 *play bo-beep* i.e. act like a child   172 *An* if

They'll have me whipped for speaking true; thou'lt have
me whipped for lying; and sometimes I am whipped for
holding my peace. I had rather be any kind o' thing than
a fool, and yet I would not be thee, nuncle: thou hast
pared thy wit o' both sides and left nothing i' th' middle. 178
Here comes one o' the parings.

  Enter Goneril.

LEAR How now, daughter? What makes that frontlet on? 180
You are too much of late i' th' frown.

FOOL Thou wast a pretty fellow when thou hadst no need
to care for her frowning. Now thou art an O without a 183
figure. I am better than thou art now: I am a fool, thou
art nothing. *[to Goneril]* Yes, forsooth, I will hold my
tongue. So your face bids me, though you say nothing.
Mum, mum,

  He that keeps nor crust nor crum, 188
  Weary of all, shall want some. – 189
  [Points at Lear.]
That's a shealed peascod. 190

GONERIL
Not only, sir, this your all-licensed fool, 191
But other of your insolent retinue
Do hourly carp and quarrel, breaking forth 193
In rank and not-to-be-endurèd riots. Sir,
I had thought by making this well known unto you
To have found a safe redress, but now grow fearful, 196
By what yourself too late have spoke and done,
That you protect this course, and put it on 198
By your allowance; which if you should, the fault 199
Would not 'scape censure, nor the redresses sleep, 200
Which, in the tender of a wholesome weal, 201

---

178 *pared . . . middle* i.e. completely disposed of your wits (in disposing
of your power) 180 *frontlet* band worn across the brow; hence, frown
183–84 *O . . . figure* cipher without a digit to give it value 188 *crum* soft
bread within the crust 189 *want* need 190 *shealed* shelled, empty; *peascod* pea-pod 191 *all-licensed* all privileged 193 *carp* complain 196
safe sure 198 *put it on* instigate it 199 *allowance* approval 200 *redresses sleep* correction lie dormant 201 *tender of* care for; *weal* state

202 Might in their working do you that offense,
     Which else were shame, that then necessity
     Will call discreet proceeding.

FOOL For you know, nuncle,

206   The hedge-sparrow fed the cuckoo so long
207   That it's had it head bit off by it young.
208 So out went the candle, and we were left darkling.

LEAR Are you our daughter?

GONERIL
     I would you would make use of your good wisdom
211 (Whereof I know you are fraught) and put away
212 These dispositions which of late transport you
     From what you rightly are.

FOOL May not an ass know when the cart draws the horse?

215 Whoop, Jug, I love thee!

LEAR
     Does any here know me? This is not Lear.
     Does Lear walk thus? speak thus? Where are his eyes?
218 Either his notion weakens, his discernings
219 Are lethargied – Ha! Waking? 'Tis not so.
     Who is it that can tell me who I am?

FOOL Lear's shadow.

[LEAR
222 I would learn that; for, by the marks of sovereignty,
     Knowledge, and reason, I should be false persuaded
     I had daughters.

FOOL Which they will make an obedient father.]

LEAR Your name, fair gentlewoman?

202–04 *Might . . . proceeding* in their operation might be considered
humiliating to you but, under the circumstances, are merely prudent
206 *cuckoo* (an image suggesting illegitimacy as well as voraciousness,
since the cuckoo lays its eggs in the nests of other birds)   207 *it* its   208
darkling in the dark (like the dead hedge-sparrow and the threatened
Lear)   211 *fraught* freighted, laden   212 *dispositions* moods   215 *Jug*
Joan (evidently part of some catch-phrase)   218 *notion* understanding
219 *Ha! Waking* i.e. so I am really awake (presumably accompanied by
the 'business' of pinching himself)   222 *marks of sovereignty* evidences
that I am King (and hence the father of the princesses)

GONERIL

    This admiration, sir, is much o' th' savor   227
    Of other your new pranks. I do beseech you
    To understand my purposes aright.
    As you are old and reverend, should be wise.
    Here do you keep a hundred knights and squires,
    Men so disordered, so deboshed and bold   232
    That this our court, infected with their manners,
    Shows like a riotous inn. Epicurism and lust   234
    Makes it more like a tavern or a brothel
    Than a graced palace. The shame itself doth speak   236
    For instant remedy. Be then desired
    By her that else will take the thing she begs
    A little to disquantity your train,   239
    And the remainders that shall still depend   240
    To be such men as may besort your age,   241
    Which know themselves, and you.   242

LEAR   Darkness and devils!
    Saddle my horses; call my train together.
    Degenerate bastard, I'll not trouble thee: 244
    Yet have I left a daughter.

GONERIL

    You strike my people, and your disordered rabble
    Make servants of their betters.
        Enter Albany.

LEAR

    Woe that too late repents. – [O, sir, are you come?]
    Is it your will? Speak, sir. – Prepare my horses.
    Ingratitude! thou marble-hearted fiend,
    More hideous when thou show'st thee in a child
    Than the sea-monster.

ALBANY   Pray, sir, be patient.

---

227 *admiration* air of wonderment   232 *deboshed* debauched   234 *Epicurism* loose living   236 *graced* honored; *shame* disgrace   239 *disquantity your train* reduce the size of your retinue   240 *depend* be attached   241 *besort* befit   242 *Which know* i.e. who are aware of the status of   244 *Degenerate* unnatural, fallen away from kind

LEAR

253 Detested kite, thou liest.
254 My train are men of choice and rarest parts,
That all particulars of duty know
256 And in the most exact regard support
257 The worships of their name. O most small fault,
How ugly didst thou in Cordelia show!
259 Which, like an engine, wrenched my frame of nature
From the fixed place; drew from my heart all love
261 And added to the gall. O Lear, Lear, Lear!
Beat at this gate that let thy folly in
        [Strikes his head.]
And thy dear judgment out. Go, go, my people.

ALBANY

My lord, I am guiltless, as I am ignorant
Of what hath moved you.

LEAR   It may be so, my lord.
Hear, Nature, hear; dear goddess, hear:
Suspend thy purpose if thou didst intend
To make this creature fruitful.
Into her womb convey sterility,
Dry up in her the organs of increase,
271 And from her derogate body never spring
272 A babe to honor her. If she must teem,
273 Create her child of spleen, that it may live
274 And be a thwart disnatured torment to her.
Let it stamp wrinkles in her brow of youth,
276 With cadent tears fret channels in her cheeks,
277 Turn all her mother's pains and benefits
To laughter and contempt, that she may feel

---

253 *Detested kite* detestable bird of prey 254 *parts* accomplishments
256 *exact regard* careful attention, punctiliousness 257 *worships* honor
259 *engine* destructive contrivance of war 259–60 *wrenched . . . place* set
askew my natural structure, distorted my normal self 261 *gall* bitterness
271 *derogate* degraded 272 *teem* increase 273 *spleen* ill-humor, spite-
fulness 274 *thwart disnatured* perverse unnatural 276 *cadent* falling;
fret wear 277 *pains and benefits* care and offerings

How sharper than a serpent's tooth it is
To have a thankless child. Away, away !   *Exit.*

ALBANY
Now, gods that we adore, whereof comes this ?

GONERIL
Never afflict yourself to know more of it,
But let his disposition have that scope   283
As dotage gives it.
        Enter Lear.

LEAR
What, fifty of my followers at a clap ?
Within a fortnight ?

ALBANY   What's the matter, sir ?

LEAR
I'll tell thee. *[to Goneril]* Life and death, I am ashamed
That thou hast power to shake my manhood thus !
That these hot tears, which break from me perforce,   289
Should make thee worth them. Blasts and fogs upon
    thee !
Th' untented woundings of a father's curse   291
Pierce every sense about thee ! Old fond eyes,   292
Beweep this cause again I'll pluck ye out   293
And cast you, with the waters that you loose,   294
To temper clay. [Yea, is it come to this ?]   295
Ha ! Let it be so. I have another daughter,
Who I am sure is kind and comfortable.   297
When she shall hear this of thee, with her nails
She'll flay thy wolvish visage. Thou shalt find
That I'll resume the shape which thou dost think   300
I have cast off for ever.
        Exit [Lear with Kent and Attendants].

GONERIL   Do you mark that ?

---

283 *disposition* mood   289 *perforce* by force, against my will   291 *un-tented* untentable, too deep for treatment by a probe   292 *sense about* faculty possessed by; *fond* foolish   293 *Beweep this cause* if you weep over this matter   294 *loose* let loose   295 *temper* soften   297 *comfortable* ready to comfort   300 *shape* i.e. role of authority

ALBANY

302　I cannot be so partial, Goneril,
　　To the great love I bear you –

GONERIL

　　Pray you, content. – What, Oswald, ho!
　　[To Fool]
　　You, sir, more knave than fool, after your master!

306 FOOL Nuncle Lear, nuncle Lear, tarry. Take the fool
　　with thee.

　　　　　　A fox, when one has caught her,
　　　　　　And such a daughter,
310　　　　　Should sure to the slaughter,
311　　　　　If my cap would buy a halter.
312　　　　　So the fool follows after.　　　　　*Exit.*

GONERIL

313　This man hath had good counsel – a hundred knights!
314　'Tis politic and safe to let him keep
315　At point a hundred knights – yes, that on every dream,
316　Each buzz, each fancy, each complaint, dislike,
　　He may enguard his dotage with their pow'rs
318　And hold our lives in mercy. – Oswald, I say!

ALBANY

　　Well, you may fear too far.

GONERIL　　　　　　　　　　Safer than trust too far.

320　Let me still take away the harms I fear,
321　Not fear still to be taken. I know his heart.
　　What he hath uttered I have writ my sister.
　　If she sustain him and his hundred knights,
　　When I have showed th' unfitness –
　　　　Enter Steward [Oswald].　　　How now, Oswald?
　　What, have you writ that letter to my sister?

302–03 *partial . . . To* made partial . . . by　**306** *the fool* i.e. both your fool
and your folly　**310** *slaughter* hanging and quartering　**311, 312** *halter,
after* (pronounced 'hauter,' 'auter')　**313** *good counsel* i.e. from such
company (ironic)　**314** *politic* prudent　**315** *At point* in arms　**316** *buzz*
murmur　**318** *in mercy* at his mercy　**320** *still . . . harms* always eliminate
the sources of injury　**321** *still . . . taken* always to be overtaken (by them)

OSWALD Ay, madam.

GONERIL

Take you some company, and away to horse.   327
Inform her full of my particular fear,   328
And thereto add such reasons of your own
As may compact it more. Get you gone,   330
And hasten your return. *[Exit Oswald.]* No, no, my lord,
This milky gentleness and course of yours,   332
Though I condemn not, yet under pardon,
You are much more ataxked for want of wisdom   334
Than praised for harmful mildness.   335

ALBANY

How far your eyes may pierce I cannot tell;
Striving to better, oft we mar what's well.

GONERIL Nay then –

ALBANY Well, well; th' event.   *Exeunt.* 339

*

Enter Lear, Kent, and Fool.   I, v

LEAR Go you before to Gloucester with these letters. Acquaint my daughter no further with anything you know than comes from her demand out of the letter. If your 3 diligence be not speedy, I shall be there afore you.

KENT I will not sleep, my lord, till I have delivered your letter.   *Exit.*

FOOL If a man's brains were in's heels, were't not in danger of kibes?   8

LEAR Ay, boy.

FOOL Then I prithee be merry. Thy wit shall not go slip- 10 shod.

LEAR Ha, ha, ha.

327 *some company* an escort 328 *particular* own 330 *compact it more* substantiate it further 332 *milky . . . course* mildly gentle way 334 *ataxked* censured, taken to task 335 *harmful mildness* mildness that proves harmful 339 *th' event* the outcome, i.e. we shall see what happens
I, v The courtyard of Albany's palace 3 *demand out of* i.e. questioning provoked by reading 8 *kibes* chilblains 10 *wit . . . slipshod* intelligence (*brains*) shall not go slippered (because of *kibes*)

12 FOOL Shalt see thy other daughter will use thee kindly;
13   for though she's as like this as a crab 's like an apple, yet
     I can tell what I can tell.

LEAR What canst tell, boy?

FOOL She will taste as like this as a crab does to a crab.
     Thou canst tell why one's nose stands i' th' middle on's
     face?

LEAR No.

FOOL Why, to keep one's eyes of either side 's nose, that
     what a man cannot smell out he may spy into.

21 LEAR I did her wrong.

FOOL Canst tell how an oyster makes his shell?

LEAR No.

FOOL Nor I neither; but I can tell why a snail has a house.

LEAR Why?

FOOL Why, to put 's head in; not to give it away to his
27   daughters, and leave his horns without a case.

28 LEAR I will forget my nature. So kind a father! – Be my
     horses ready?

FOOL Thy asses are gone about 'em. The reason why the
31   seven stars are no moe than seven is a pretty reason.

LEAR Because they are not eight.

FOOL Yes indeed. Thou wouldst make a good fool.

34 LEAR To take 't again perforce – Monster ingratitude!

FOOL If thou wert my fool, nuncle, I'ld have thee beaten
     for being old before thy time.

LEAR How's that?

FOOL Thou shouldst not have been old till thou hadst
     been wise.

LEAR

    O, let me not be mad, not mad, sweet heaven!

---

12 *Shalt* thou shalt; *kindly* after her kind, i.e. in the same way as this
daughter 13 *crab* crab apple 21 *her* i.e. Cordelia (the first of the remarkable intimations of Lear's inner thoughts in this scene) 27 *horns* i.e.
snail's horns (with pun on cuckold's horns; the legitimacy of Goneril and
Regan being, figuratively, suspect throughout); *case* covering 28 *nature*
i.e. fatherly instincts 31 *moe* more 34 *perforce* by force

Keep me in temper; I would not be mad!   41
    [Enter a Gentleman.]
How now, are the horses ready?
GENTLEMAN Ready, my lord.
LEAR Come, boy.
FOOL
    She that's a maid now, and laughs at my departure,   45
    Shall not be a maid long, unless things be cut shorter.
                                Exeunt.

                        *

    Enter Bastard [Edmund] and Curan severally.   II, i
EDMUND Save thee, Curan.   1
CURAN And you, sir. I have been with your father, and
    given him notice that the Duke of Cornwall and Regan
    his Duchess will be here with him this night.
EDMUND How comes that?
CURAN Nay, I know not. You have heard of the news
    abroad – I mean the whispered ones, for they are yet but
    ear-kissing arguments?   8
EDMUND Not I. Pray you, what are they?
CURAN Have you heard of no likely wars toward, 'twixt   10
    the Dukes of Cornwall and Albany?
EDMUND Not a word.
CURAN You may do, then, in time. Fare you well, sir. *Exit.*
EDMUND
    The Duke be here to-night? The better best!   14
    This weaves itself perforce into my business.   15
    My father hath set guard to take my brother,
    And I have one thing of a queasy question   17

---

41 *in temper* properly balanced   45–46 *She . . . shorter* (an indecent gag
addressed to the audience, calculated to embarrass the maids who joined
in the laughter)
II, i The Earl of Gloucester's castle   1 *Save* God save   8 *ear-kissing
arguments* whispered topics   10 *likely* probable; *toward* impending
14 *better best* (hyperbole)   15 *perforce* of necessity (?), of its own accord (?)
17 *of . . . question* delicately balanced as to outcome, touch-and-go

18   Which I must act. Briefness and fortune, work!
      Brother, a word: descend. Brother, I say!
                Enter Edgar.
      My father watches. O sir, fly this place.
      Intelligence is given where you are hid.
      You have now the good advantage of the night.
      Have you not spoken 'gainst the Duke of Cornwall?
      He's coming hither; now i' th' night, i' th' haste,
      And Regan with him. Have you nothing said
26   Upon his party 'gainst the Duke of Albany?
27   Advise yourself.

EDGAR   I am sure on't, not a word.

EDMUND
      I hear my father coming. Pardon me:
29   In cunning I must draw my sword upon you.
30   Draw, seem to defend yourself; now quit you well. –
      Yield! Come before my father! Light ho, here! –
      Fly, brother. – Torches, torches! – So farewell.
                                        Exit Edgar.
      Some blood drawn on me would beget opinion
      Of my more fierce endeavor.
          [Wounds his arm.]   I have seen drunkards
      Do more than this in sport. – Father, father!
      Stop, stop! No help?
          Enter Gloucester, and Servants with torches.

GLOUCESTER
      Now, Edmund, where's the villain?

EDMUND
      Here stood he in the dark, his sharp sword out,
      Mumbling of wicked charms, conjuring the moon
      To stand auspicious mistress.

GLOUCESTER   But where is he?

---

18 *Briefness and fortune* decisive speed and good luck   26 *Upon his party
'gainst* i.e. reflecting upon his feud against   27 *Advise yourself* take
thought; *on't* of it   29 *In cunning* i.e. as a ruse   30 *quit you* acquit yourself

EDMUND
    Look, sir, I bleed.
GLOUCESTER   Where is the villain, Edmund?
EDMUND
    Fled this way, sir, when by no means he could –
GLOUCESTER
    Pursue him, ho! Go after.   *[Exeunt some Servants.]*
                            By no means what?
EDMUND
    Persuade me to the murder of your lordship;
    But that I told him the revenging gods
    'Gainst parricides did all the thunder bend;   46
    Spoke with how manifold and strong a bond
    The child was bound to th' father – sir, in fine,   48
    Seeing how loathly opposite I stood   49
    To his unnatural purpose, in fell motion   50
    With his preparèd sword he charges home
    My unprovided body, latched mine arm;   52
    And when he saw my best alarumed spirits   53
    Bold in the quarrel's right, roused to th' encounter,   54
    Or whether gasted by the noise I made,   55
    Full suddenly he fled.
GLOUCESTER   Let him fly far.
    Not in this land shall he remain uncaught;
    And found – dispatch. The noble Duke my master,   58
    My worthy arch and patron, comes to-night: 59
    By his authority I will proclaim it
    That he which finds him shall deserve our thanks,
    Bringing the murderous coward to the stake;
    He that conceals him, death.
EDMUND
    When I dissuaded him from his intent

---

46 *bend* aim   48 *in fine* finally   49 *loathly opposite* in loathing opposition
50 *fell* deadly   52 *unprovided* undefended; *latched* lanced, pierced   53
best alarumed fully aroused   54 *Bold . . . right* confident in the justice of the
cause   55 *gasted* struck aghast   58 *dispatch* (equivalent to 'death' or
'finis')   59 *arch* superior

65 And found him pight to do it, with curst speech
66 I threatened to discover him. He replied,
67 'Thou unpossessing bastard, dost thou think,
68 If I would stand against thee, would the reposal
   Of any trust, virtue, or worth in thee
70 Make thy words faithed? No. What I should deny
   (As this I would, ay, though thou didst produce
72 My very character) I'ld turn it all
73 To thy suggestion, plot, and damnèd practice;
74 And thou must make a dullard of the world,
75 If they not thought the profits of my death
76 Were very pregnant and potential spirits
   To make thee seek it.'
77 GLOUCESTER   O strange and fast'ned villain!
78 Would he deny his letter, said he? [I never got him.]
        Tucket within.
   Hark, the Duke's trumpets. I know not why he comes.
   All ports I'll bar; the villain shall not 'scape;
   The Duke must grant me that. Besides, his picture
   I will send far and near, that all the kingdom
   May have due note of him; and of my land,
   Loyal and natural boy, I'll work the means
85 To make thee capable.
        Enter Cornwall, Regan, and Attendants.
   CORNWALL
   How now, my noble friend? Since I came hither
87 (Which I can call but now) I have heard strange news.
   REGAN
   If it be true, all vengeance comes too short

---

65 *pight* determined, set; *curst* angry **66** *discover* expose **67** *unpossessing* having no claim, landless **68** *reposal* placing **70** *faithed* believed **72** *character* written testimony **73** *suggestion* instigation; *practice* devices **74** *make . . . world* i.e. consider everyone stupid **75** *not thought* did not think **76** *pregnant . . . spirits* teeming and powerful spirits, i.e. the devils which 'possess' him **77** *fast'ned* confirmed **78** *got* begot; **s.d.** *Tucket* (personal signature in trumpet notes) **85** *capable* i.e. legitimate, able to inherit **87** *call* i.e. say was

Which can pursue th' offender. How dost, my lord?

GLOUCESTER
O madam, my old heart is cracked, it's cracked.

REGAN
What, did my father's godson seek your life?
He whom my father named, your Edgar?

GLOUCESTER
O lady, lady, shame would have it hid.

REGAN
Was he not companion with the riotous knights
That tended upon my father?

GLOUCESTER
I know not, madam. 'Tis too bad, too bad.

EDMUND
Yes, madam, he was of that consort.   97

REGAN
No marvel then though he were ill affected.   98
'Tis they have put him on the old man's death,   99
To have th' expense and waste of his revenues.   100
I have this present evening from my sister
Been well informed of them, and with such cautions
That, if they come to sojourn at my house,
I'll not be there.

CORNWALL   Nor I, assure thee, Regan.
Edmund, I hear that you have shown your father
A childlike office.   106

EDMUND   It was my duty, sir.

GLOUCESTER
He did bewray his practice, and received   107
This hurt you see, striving to apprehend him.

CORNWALL
Is he pursued?

GLOUCESTER   Ay, my good lord.

---

97 *consort* company, set   98 *affected* disposed   99 *put* set   100 *expense and waste* wasteful expenditure   106 *childlike* filial   107 *bewray his practice* expose his plot

CORNWALL
  If he be taken, he shall never more
111 Be feared of doing harm. Make your own purpose,
  How in my strength you please. For you, Edmund,
113 Whose virtue and obedience doth this instant
  So much commend itself, you shall be ours.
  Natures of such deep trust we shall much need;
  You we first seize on.
EDMUND   I shall serve you, sir,
  Truly, however else.
GLOUCESTER   For him I thank your Grace.
CORNWALL
  You know not why we came to visit you?
REGAN
  Thus out of season, threading dark-eyed night.
120 Occasions, noble Gloucester, of some prize,
  Wherein we must have use of your advice.
  Our father he hath writ, so hath our sister,
123 Of differences, which I best thought it fit
124 To answer from our home. The several messengers
125 From hence attend dispatch. Our good old friend,
126 Lay comforts to your bosom, and bestow
127 Your needful counsel to our businesses,
128 Which craves the instant use.
GLOUCESTER   I serve you, madam.
  Your Graces are right welcome.   *Exeunt. Flourish.*

*

111 *of doing* lest he do   111–12 *Make . . . please* i.e. accomplish your purpose, making free use of my powers   113 *virtue and obedience* virtuous
obedience   120 *prize* price, importance   123 *differences* quarrels; *which*
(refers, indefinitely, to the whole situation)   124 *answer . . . home* cope with
away from home (where she need not receive Lear)   125 *attend dispatch*
i.e. await settlement of the business   126 *Lay . . . bosom* be consoled (about
your own trouble)   127 *needful* needed   128 *craves . . . use* requires immediate transaction (?), requires use of your counsel (?)

70

Enter Kent and Steward [Oswald], severally.   II, ii

OSWALD Good dawning to thee, friend. Art of this house ? 1

KENT Ay.

OSWALD Where may we set our horses ?

KENT I' th' mire.

OSWALD Prithee, if thou lov'st me, tell me.

KENT I love thee not.

OSWALD Why then, I care not for thee.

KENT If I had thee in Lipsbury Pinfold, I would make 8
thee care for me.

OSWALD Why dost thou use me thus ? I know thee not.

KENT Fellow, I know thee.

OSWALD What dost thou know me for ?

KENT A knave, a rascal, an eater of broken meats ; a base, 13
proud, shallow, beggarly, three-suited, hundred-pound, 14
filthy worsted-stocking knave ; a lily-livered, action- 15
taking, whoreson, glass-gazing, superserviceable, finical 16
rogue ; one-trunk-inheriting slave ; one that wouldst be a 17
bawd in way of good service, and art nothing but the
composition of a knave, beggar, coward, pander, and the 19
son and heir of a mongrel bitch ; one whom I will beat
into clamorous whining if thou deny'st the least syllable
of thy addition. 22

OSWALD Why, what a monstrous fellow art thou, thus to
rail on one that is neither known of thee nor knows thee !

KENT What a brazen-faced varlet art thou to deny thou
knowest me ! Is it two days ago since I tripped up thy
heels and beat thee before the King ? *[Draws his sword.]*

II, ii Before Gloucester's castle 1 *dawning* (perhaps indicating that it
is too early for 'good morning'); *Art . . . house* i.e. do you belong to this
household 8 *Lipsbury Pinfold* i.e. between the teeth (cant term: 'pen in
the region of the lips') 13 *broken meats* scraps 14 *three-suited* with
three suits (the wardrobe allowed serving-men); *hundred-pound* (the mini-
mal estate for anyone aspiring to gentility) 15 *worsted-stocking* (serving-
men's attire) 15–16 *action-taking* i.e. cowardly (resorting to law instead
of fighting) 16 *glass-gazing, superserviceable, finical* i.e. conceited, toady-
ing, foppish 17 *inheriting* possessing 17–18 *a bawd . . . service* i.e. a
pander, if pleasing your employer required it 19 *composition* composite
22 *addition* titles

Draw, you rogue, for though it be night, yet the moon
29   shines. I'll make a sop o' th' moonshine of you. You
30   whoreson cullionly barbermonger, draw!

OSWALD Away, I have nothing to do with thee.

KENT Draw, you rascal. You come with letters against the
33   King, and take Vanity the puppet's part against the
34   royalty of her father. Draw, you rogue, or I'll so car-
35   bonado your shanks. Draw, you rascal. Come your ways!

OSWALD Help, ho! Murder! Help!

37 KENT Strike, you slave! Stand, rogue! Stand, you neat
      slave! Strike!
        [Beats him.]

OSWALD Help, ho! Murder, murder!
        Enter Bastard [Edmund, with his rapier drawn],
          Cornwall, Regan, Gloucester, Servants.

EDMUND How now? What's the matter? Part!

41 KENT With you, goodman boy, if you please! Come, I'll
42   flesh ye; come on, young master.

GLOUCESTER Weapons? Arms? What's the matter here?

CORNWALL Keep peace, upon your lives. He dies that
    strikes again. What is the matter?

REGAN The messengers from our sister and the King.

CORNWALL What is your difference? Speak.

OSWALD I am scarce in breath, my lord.

49 KENT No marvel, you have so bestirred your valor. You
50   cowardly rascal, Nature disclaims in thee. A tailor made
      thee.

CORNWALL Thou art a strange fellow. A tailor make a
    man?

---

29 *sop o' th' moonshine* i.e. something that sops up moonshine through its
perforations   **30** *cullionly barbermonger* vile fop (i.e. always dealing with
hairdressers)   **33** *Vanity the puppet* i.e. Goneril (here equated with a stock
figure in morality plays, now dwindled into puppet shows)   **34** *carbonado*
(cut into strips or cubes)   **35** *your ways* get along   **37** *neat* primping   **41**
goodman boy (doubly contemptuous, since peasants were addressed as
'goodmen')   **42** *flesh ye* give you your first taste of blood   **49** *bestirred*
exercised   **50** *disclaims* claims no part

KENT A tailor, sir. A stonecutter or a painter could not 53
have made him so ill, though they had been but two
years o' th' trade.

CORNWALL
Speak yet, how grew your quarrel?

OSWALD This ancient ruffian, sir, whose life I have
spared at suit of his gray beard –   58

KENT Thou whoreson zed, thou unnecessary letter! My 59
lord, if you will give me leave, I will tread this unbolted 60
villain into mortar and daub the wall of a jakes with him. 61
Spare my gray beard? you wagtail.   62

CORNWALL
Peace, sirrah!
You beastly knave, know you no reverence?   64

KENT
Yes, sir, but anger hath a privilege.

CORNWALL
Why art thou angry?

KENT
That such a slave as this should wear a sword,
Who wears no honesty. Such smiling rogues as these
Like rats oft bite the holy cords atwain   69
Which are too intrinse t' unloose; smooth every passion 70
That in the natures of their lords rebel,   71
Being oil to fire, snow to the colder moods;   72
Renege, affirm, and turn their halcyon beaks   73
With every gale and vary of their masters,   74

---

53 *stonecutter* sculptor **58** *at suit of* on the plea of, moved to mercy by
59 *zed* (last and least useful of letters) **60** *unbolted* unsifted, crude **61**
jakes privy **62** *wagtail* (any of several birds whose tail-feathers wag or
bob, suggesting obsequiousness or effeminacy) **64** *beastly* beast-like,
irrational **69** *holy cords* sacred bonds (between parents and children,
husbands and wives, man and God) **70** *intrinse* intrinsic, inextricable;
smooth flatter, cater to **71** *rebel* (i.e. against reason and moral restraint)
72 *Being . . . moods* (i.e. feeders of intemperance) **73** *Renege* deny; *halcyon
beaks* kingfisher beaks (supposedly serving as weather vanes when the birds
were hung up by their necks) **74** *gale and vary* varying wind

Knowing naught, like dogs, but following.
76 A plague upon your epileptic visage!
77 Smile you my speeches, as I were a fool?
78 Goose, if I had you upon Sarum Plain,
79 I'd drive ye cackling home to Camelot.

CORNWALL
What, art thou mad, old fellow?

GLOUCESTER
How fell you out? Say that.

KENT
82 No contraries hold more antipathy
Than I and such a knave.

CORNWALL
Why dost thou call him knave? What is his fault?

KENT
His countenance likes me not.

CORNWALL
No more perchance does mine, nor his, nor hers.

KENT
Sir, 'tis my occupation to be plain:
I have seen better faces in my time
Than stands on any shoulder that I see
Before me at this instant.

CORNWALL   This is some fellow
Who, having been praised for bluntness, doth affect
92 A saucy roughness, and constrains the garb
Quite from his nature. He cannot flatter, he;
An honest mind and plain – he must speak truth.
An they will take it, so; if not, he's plain.
These kind of knaves I know which in this plainness
Harbor more craft and more corrupter ends

---

76 *epileptic* contorted in a grin (?) 77 *Smile you* smile you at, mock you
78 *Sarum Plain* Salisbury Plain (said to have been associated with geese,
but the allusion remains cryptic) 79 *Camelot* legendary seat of King
Arthur, variously sited at Winchester, near Cadbury, in Wales, etc.
82 *contraries* opposites 92–93 *constrains . . . nature* distorts the plain
fashion from its true nature, caricatures it

Than twenty silly-ducking observants   98
That stretch their duties nicely.   99

KENT
Sir, in good faith, in sincere verity,
Under th' allowance of your great aspect,   101
Whose influence, like the wreath of radiant fire   102
On flick'ring Phoebus' front –   103

CORNWALL   What mean'st by this?

KENT To go out of my dialect, which you discommend so   104
much. I know, sir, I am no flatterer. He that beguiled   105
you in a plain accent was a plain knave, which, for my
part, I will not be, though I should win your displeasure   107
to entreat me to't.

CORNWALL
What was th' offense you gave him?

OSWALD
I never gave him any.
It pleased the King his master very late   ,   111
To strike at me, upon his misconstruction;   112
When he, compact, and flattering his displeasure,   113
Tripped me behind; being down, insulted, railed,
And put upon him such a deal of man   115
That worthied him, got praises of the King   116
For him attempting who was self-subdued;   117
And, in the fleshment of this dread exploit,   118
Drew on me here again.

---

98 *silly-ducking observants* ludicrously bowing form-servers **99** *nicely*
fussily **101** *allowance* approval; *aspect* (1) appearance, (2) heavenly
position **102** *influence* astrological force **103** *Phoebus' front* sun's forehead (i.e. face) **104** *go . . . dialect* depart from my way of speaking **105**
He (the type of plain-speaker Cornwall has condemned) **107–08** *though
. . . to't* though I should persuade your disapproving self to beg me to do so
(? with *displeasure* sarcastically substituted for 'grace') **111** *very late*
quite recently **112** *misconstruction* misunderstanding **113** *compact* in
league with **115** *And put . . . man* i.e. affected such excessive manliness
116 *worthied* enhanced his worth **117** *For him . . . self-subdued* for assail-
ing him (Oswald) who chose not to resist **118** *fleshment of* bloodthirsti-
ness induced by

119 KENT   None of these rogues and cowards
        But Ajax is their fool.
      CORNWALL   Fetch forth the stocks!
121   You stubborn ancient knave, you reverent braggart,
        We'll teach you.
      KENT   Sir, I am too old to learn.
        Call not your stocks for me, I serve the King –
        On whose employment I was sent to you;
125   You shall do small respect, show too bold malice
126   Against the grace and person of my master,
        Stocking his messenger.
      CORNWALL
        Fetch forth the stocks. As I have life and honor,
        There shall he sit till noon.
      REGAN
        Till noon? Till night, my lord, and all night too.
      KENT
        Why, madam, if I were your father's dog,
        You should not use me so.
      REGAN   Sir, being his knave, I will.
      CORNWALL
133   This is a fellow of the selfsame color
134   Our sister speaks of. Come, bring away the stocks.
              Stocks brought out.
      GLOUCESTER
        Let me beseech your Grace not to do so.
        [His fault is much, and the good King his master
137   Will check him for't. Your purposed low correction
138   Is such as basest and contemnèd'st wretches
        For pilf'rings and most common trespasses
        Are punished with.]

119–20 *None . . . fool* i.e. the Ajax type, stupidly belligerent, is the favorite
butt of cowardly rogues like Oswald   121 *stubborn* rude; *reverent* aged
125 *malice* ill will   126 *grace* royal honor   133 *color* kind   134 *away* along
137 *check* rebuke; *purposed* intended   138 *contemnèd'st* most harshly
sentenced

The King his master needs must take it ill
That he, so slightly valued in his messenger,   142
Should have him thus restrained.

CORNWALL   I'll answer that.   143

REGAN
My sister may receive it much more worse,
To have her gentleman abused, assaulted,
[For following her affairs. Put in his legs.]
    [Kent is put in the stocks.]

CORNWALL
Come, my lord, away!
       Exit [with all but Gloucester and Kent].

GLOUCESTER
I am sorry for thee, friend. 'Tis the Duke's pleasure,
Whose disposition all the world well knows   149
Will not be rubbed nor stopped. I'll entreat for thee.   150

KENT
Pray do not, sir. I have watched and travelled hard.   151
Some time I shall sleep out, the rest I'll whistle.
A good man's fortune may grow out at heels.   153
Give you good morrow.   154

GLOUCESTER
The Duke's to blame in this. 'Twill be ill taken.   *Exit.*   155

KENT
Good King, that must approve the common saw,   156
Thou out of heaven's benediction com'st   157
To the warm sun.
Approach, thou beacon to this under globe,   159
That by thy comfortable beams I may

---

142 *slightly valued in* i.e. little respected in the person of   143 *answer* answer for   149 *disposition* inclination   150 *rubbed* deflected (bowling term)   151 *watched* gone sleepless   153 *A good . . . heels* i.e. it is no disgrace to decline in fortune   154 *Give* God give   155 *taken* received   156 *approve* demonstrate the truth of; *saw* saying, proverb   157–58 *Thou . . . sun* (proverb, meaning from better to worse, i.e. from heavenly shelter to earthly exposure – 'the heat of the day')   159 *beacon . . . globe* i.e. the sun (here viewed as benign)

161 Peruse this letter. Nothing almost sees miracles
     But misery. I know 'tis from Cordelia,
     Who hath most fortunately been informed
164 Of my obscurèd course. And shall find time
165 From this enormous state, seeking to give
166 Losses their remedies. – All weary and o'erwatched,
167 Take vantage, heavy eyes, not to behold
168 This shameful lodging. Fortune, good night;
169 Smile once more; turn thy wheel.
              [Sleeps.]
II, iii   *Enter Edgar.*
     EDGAR
     I heard myself proclaimed,
2   And by the happy hollow of a tree
     Escaped the hunt. No port is free, no place
     That guard and most unusual vigilance
5   Does not attend my taking. Whiles I may 'scape,
6   I will preserve myself; and am bethought
     To take the basest and most poorest shape
     That ever penury, in contempt of man,
     Brought near to beast: my face I'll grime with filth,
10   Blanket my loins, elf all my hairs in knots,
11   And with presented nakedness outface
     The winds and persecutions of the sky.
13   The country gives me proof and precedent
14   Of Bedlam beggars, who, with roaring voices,
15   Strike in their numbed and mortified bare arms
16   Pins, wooden pricks, nails, sprigs of rosemary;

161–62 *Nothing . . . misery* i.e. miraculous aid is seldom seen (or searched for?) except by the miserable **164** *obscurèd* disguised **164–66** *And . . . remedies* (incoherent: perhaps corrupt, or perhaps snatches read from the letter) **165** *enormous state* monstrous situation **166** *Losses* reverses **167** *vantage* i.e. advantage of sleep **168** *lodging* (in the stocks) **169** *wheel* (Fortune's wheel was represented as vertical. Kent is at its bottom.)
II, iii **2** *happy hollow* i.e. lucky hiding-place **5** *attend my taking* contemplate my capture **6** *bethought* in mind **10** *elf* tangle (into 'elf-locks') **11** *presented* a show of **13** *proof* example **14** *Bedlam* (see I, ii, 131–32n.) **15** *Strike* stick; *mortified* deadened to pain **16** *pricks* skewers

And with this horrible object, from low farms,   17
Poor pelting villages, sheepcotes, and mills,   18
Sometimes with lunatic bans, sometime with prayers,   19
Enforce their charity. Poor Turlygod, poor Tom,   20
That's something yet : Edgar I nothing am.   21

Exit.

Enter Lear, Fool, and Gentleman.   II, iv

LEAR
'Tis strange that they should so depart from home,
And not send back my messenger.

GENTLEMAN   As I learned,
The night before there was no purpose in them   3
Of this remove.   4

KENT   Hail to thee, noble master.

LEAR Ha !
Mak'st thou this shame thy pastime ?

KENT   No, my lord.

FOOL Ha, ha, he wears cruel garters. Horses are tied by 7
the heads, dogs and bears by th' neck, monkeys by th'
loins, and men by th' legs. When a man 's over-lusty at 9
legs, then he wears wooden nether-stocks.   10

LEAR
What's he that hath so much thy place mistook
To set thee here ?

KENT   It is both he and she,
Your son and daughter.

LEAR No.

KENT Yes.

LEAR No, I say.

KENT I say yea.

[LEAR No, no, they would not.

17 *object* picture   18 *pelting* paltry   19 *bans* curses   20 *Turlygod* (un-
identified, but evidently another name for a Tom o' Bedlam)   21 *Edgar* i.e.
as Edgar
II, iv   3 *purpose* intention   4 *remove* removal   7 *cruel* painful (with pun
on 'crewel,' a yarn used in garters)   9–10 *over-lusty at legs* i.e. too much on
the go (?), or too much given to kicking (?)   10 *nether-stocks* stockings (as
distinct from 'upper-stocks' or breeches)

KENT Yes, they have.]

LEAR
By Jupiter, I swear no!

KENT
By Juno, I swear ay!

LEAR   They durst not do't;
They could not, would not do't. 'Tis worse than murder
23 To do upon respect such violent outrage.
24 Resolve me with all modest haste which way
Thou mightst deserve or thy impose this usage,
Coming from us.

KENT   My lord, when at their home
27 I did commend your Highness' letters to them,
Ere I was risen from the place that showed
My duty kneeling, came there a reeking post,
30 Stewed in his haste, half breathless, panting forth
From Goneril his mistress salutations;
32 Delivered letters, spite of intermission,
33 Which presently they read; on whose contents
34 They summoned up their meiny, straight took horse,
Commanded me to follow and attend
The leisure of their answer, gave me cold looks;
And meeting here the other messenger,
Whose welcome I perceived had poisoned mine,
Being the very fellow which of late
40 Displayed so saucily against your Highness,
41 Having more man than wit about me, drew;
42 He raised the house with loud and coward cries.
Your son and daughter found this trespass worth
The shame which here it suffers.

45 FOOL Winter's not gone yet, if the wild geese fly that way.

---

23 *To . . . outrage* i.e. to show such outrageous disrespect 24 *Resolve* enlighten; *modest* seemly 27 *commend* entrust 30 *Stewed* steaming 32 *spite of intermission* in disregard of its being an interruption 33 *presently* immediately; *on* on the strength of 34 *meiny* attendants 40 *Displayed* showed off 41 *man* manhood; *wit* sense 42 *raised* aroused 45 *Winter's . . . way* i.e. the ill season continues according to these signs (with Cornwall and Regan equated with *wild geese*, proverbially evasive)

Fathers that wear rags
  Do make their children blind,   47
But fathers that bear bags   48
  Shall see their children kind.
Fortune, that arrant whore,   50
Ne'er turns the key to th' poor.   51
But for all this, thou shalt have as many dolors for thy 52
daughters as thou canst tell in a year.   53

LEAR
O, how this mother swells up toward my heart! 54
Hysterica passio, down, thou climbing sorrow; 55
Thy element's below. Where is this daughter?   56

KENT
With the Earl, sir, here within.

LEAR   Follow me not;
Stay here.   *Exit.*

GENTLEMAN
Made you no more offense but what you speak of?

KENT None.

How chance the King comes with so small a number?

FOOL An thou hadst been set i' th' stocks for that question, thou'dst well deserved it.

KENT Why, fool?

FOOL We'll set thee to school to an ant, to teach thee
there's no laboring i' th' winter. All that follow their 66
noses are led by their eyes but blind men, and there's not
a nose among twenty but can smell him that's stinking.
Let go thy hold when a great wheel runs down a hill, lest
it break thy neck with following. But the great one that
goes upward, let him draw thee after. When a wise man

47 *blind* (to their fathers' needs)   48 *bags* (of gold)   50 *Fortune . . . whore*
(because so fickle and callous)   51 *turns the key* i.e. opens the door   52
dolors sorrows (with pun on 'dollars,' continental coins)   53 *tell* count
54, 55 *mother, Hysterica passio* hysteria (the popular and the medical
terms)   56 *element* proper place   66 *no laboring . . . winter* (Lear, accompanied by *so small a number,* is equated with winter bereft of workers, such
as ants)   66-68 *All . . . stinking* i.e. almost anyone can smell out a person
decayed in fortune

gives thee better counsel, give me mine again. I would
73 have none but knaves follow it since a fool gives it.

That sir which serves and seeks for gain,
75   And follows but for form,
76   Will pack when it begins to rain
              And leave thee in the storm.
            But I will tarry ; the fool will stay,
              And let the wise man fly.
80   The knave turns fool that runs away ;
81   The fool no knave, perdy.

KENT Where learned you this, fool ?

83 FOOL Not i' th' stocks, fool.

Enter Lear and Gloucester.

LEAR
    Deny to speak with me ? They are sick, they are weary,
85 They have travelled all the night ? Mere fetches,
86 The images of revolt and flying off !
    Fetch me a better answer.

GLOUCESTER   My dear lord,
88 You know the fiery quality of the Duke,
    How unremovable and fixed he is
    In his own course.

LEAR   Vengeance, plague, death, confusion !
    Fiery ? What quality ? Why, Gloucester, Gloucester,
    I'ld speak with the Duke of Cornwall and his wife.

GLOUCESTER
    Well, my good lord, I have informed them so.

LEAR
    Informed them ? Dost thou understand me, man ?

GLOUCESTER
    Ay, my good lord.

---

73 *none but knaves* (here and in what follows the Fool repudiates his advice
to abandon Lear) 75 *form* show 76 *pack* be off 80 *The knave . . . away*
i.e. faithlessness is the true folly 81 *perdy* I swear (from '*par dieu*') 83
fool (persiflage, but also a term of honour; cf. V, iii, 306n.) 85 *fetches*
counterfeit reasons, false likenesses of truth 86 *images* true likenesses;
flying off revolt 88 *quality* disposition

LEAR

The King would speak with Cornwall. The dear father
Would with his daughter speak, commands – tends –   97
    service.
Are they informed of this? My breath and blood!
Fiery? The fiery Duke, tell the hot Duke that –
No, but not yet. May be he is not well.
Infirmity doth still neglect all office   101
Whereto our health is bound. We are not ourselves   102
When nature, being oppressed, commands the mind
To suffer with the body. I'll forbear;
And am fallen out with my more headier will   105
To take the indisposed and sickly fit
For the sound man. – Death on my state! Wherefore
Should he sit here? This act persuades me   108
That this remotion of the Duke and her   109
Is practice only. Give me my servant forth.   110
Go tell the Duke and 's wife I'ld speak with them!
Now, presently! Bid them come forth and hear me,   112
Or at their chamber door I'll beat the drum
Till it cry sleep to death.   114

GLOUCESTER

I would have all well betwixt you.   *Exit.*

LEAR

O me, my heart, my rising heart! But down!
FOOL Cry to it, nuncle, as the cockney did to the eels when 117
she put 'em i' th' paste alive. She knapped 'em o' th' cox- 118
combs with a stick and cried, 'Down, wantons, down!' 119
'Twas her brother that, in pure kindness to his horse,
buttered his hay.   121

---

97 *tends* attends, awaits (?), tenders, offers (?) 101 *all office* duties 102
Whereto . . . bound to which, in health, we are bound 105 *headier* head-
strong 108 *he* i.e. Kent 109 *remotion* remaining remote, inaccessible
110 *practice* trickery 112 *presently* immediately 114 *cry* pursue with
noise (like a pack or 'cry' of hounds) 117 *cockney* city-dweller 118
paste pastry pie; *knapped* rapped 119 *wantons* i.e. frisky things 121
buttered his hay (another example of rustic humor at the expense of cockney
inexperience)

Enter Cornwall, Regan, Gloucester, Servants.

LEAR
Good morrow to you both.

CORNWALL   Hail to your Grace.
Kent here set at liberty.

REGAN
I am glad to see your Highness.

LEAR
Regan, I think you are. I know what reason
I have to think so. If thou shouldst not be glad,
126   I would divorce me from thy mother's tomb,
Sepulchring an adultress. *[to Kent]* O, are you free?
Some other time for that. – Beloved Regan,
Thy sister's naught. O Regan, she hath tied
Sharp-toothed unkindness, like a vulture, here.
I can scarce speak to thee. Thou'lt not believe
132   With how depraved a quality – O Regan!

REGAN
133   I pray you, sir, take patience. I have hope
You less know how to value her desert
135   Than she to scant her duty.

LEAR   Say? How is that?

REGAN
I cannot think my sister in the least
Would fail her obligation. If, sir, perchance
She have restrained the riots of your followers,
'Tis on such ground, and to such wholesome end,
As clears her from all blame.

LEAR
My curses on her!

REGAN   O, sir, you are old;
142   Nature in you stands on the very verge

126–27 *divorce . . . adultress* i.e. refuse to be buried with your mother
since such a child as you must have been conceived in adultery   132 *how
. . . quality* i.e. what innate depravity   133 *have hope* i.e. suspect   135
scant (in effect, a double negative; 'do' would be more logical though less
emphatic)   142–43 *Nature . . . confine* i.e. your life nears the limit of its
tenure

Of his confine. You should be ruled, and led
By some discretion that discerns your state   144
Better than you yourself. Therefore I pray you
That to our sister you do make return ;
Say you have wronged her.

LEAR   Ask her forgiveness ?
Do you but mark how this becomes the house :   148
'Dear daughter, I confess that I am old.
    [Kneels.]
Age is unnecessary. On my knees I beg
That you'll vouchsafe me raiment, bed, and food.'

REGAN
Good sir, no more. These are unsightly tricks.
Return you to my sister.

LEAR [rises]   Never, Regan.
She hath abated me of half my train,   154
Looked black upon me, struck me with her tongue
Most serpent-like upon the very heart.
All the stored vengeances of heaven fall
On her ingrateful top ! Strike her young bones,   158
You taking airs, with lameness.   159

CORNWALL   Fie, sir, fie !

LEAR
You nimble lightnings, dart your blinding flames
Into her scornful eyes ! Infect her beauty,
You fen-sucked fogs drawn by the pow'rful sun   162
To fall and blister –   163

REGAN   O the blessed gods !
So will you wish on me when the rash mood is on.

LEAR
No, Regan, thou shalt never have my curse.
Thy tender-hefted nature shall not give   166

144 *some discretion . . . state* someone discerning enough to recognize your
condition 148 *the house* household or family decorum 154 *abated*
curtailed 158 *ingrateful top* ungrateful head 159 *taking* infectious
162 *fen-sucked* drawn up from swamps 163 *fall and blister* strike and raise
blisters (such as those of smallpox) 166 *tender-hefted* swayed by tender-
ness, gently disposed

Thee o'er to harshness. Her eyes are fierce, but thine
Do comfort, and not burn. 'Tis not in thee
To grudge my pleasures, to cut off my train,
170 To bandy hasty words, to scant my sizes,
171 And, in conclusion, to oppose the bolt
Against my coming in. Thou better know'st
173 The offices of nature, bond of childhood,
174 Effects of courtesy, dues of gratitude.
Thy half o' th' kingdom hast thou not forgot,
Wherein I thee endowed.
176 REGAN   Good sir, to th' purpose.
        Tucket within.
LEAR
Who put my man i' th' stocks?
CORNWALL   What trumpet 's that?
REGAN
178 I know't – my sister's. This approves her letter,
That she would soon be here.
        Enter Steward [Oswald].   Is your lady come?
LEAR
180 This is a slave, whose easy-borrowèd pride
181 Dwells in the fickle grace of her he follows.
182 Out, varlet, from my sight.
CORNWALL   What means your Grace?
LEAR
Who stocked my servant? Regan, I have good hope
Thou didst not know on't.
        Enter Goneril.   Who comes here? O heavens!
If you do love old men, if your sweet sway
186 Allow obedience, if you yourselves are old,
187 Make it your cause. Send down, and take my part.

---

170 *bandy* volley; *sizes* allowances   **171** *oppose the bolt* i.e. bar the door
173 *offices of nature* natural duties   **174** *Effects* actions   **176** *purpose* point
178 *approves* confirms   **180** *easy-borrowèd* acquired on small security   **181**
grace favor   **182** *varlet* low fellow   **186** *Allow* approve   **187** *Make . . . cause*
i.e. make my cause yours

[To Goneril]
Art not ashamed to look upon this beard?
O Regan, will you take her by the hand?

GONERIL
Why not by th' hand, sir? How have I offended?
All's not offense that indiscretion finds   191
And dotage terms so.

LEAR   O sides, you are too tough!   192
Will you yet hold? How came my man i' th' stocks?

CORNWALL
I set him there, sir; but his own disorders
Deserved much less advancement.   195

LEAR   You? Did you?

REGAN
I pray you, father, being weak, seem so.   196
If till the expiration of your month
You will return and sojourn with my sister,
Dismissing half your train, come then to me.
I am now from home, and out of that provision
Which shall be needful for your entertainment.   201

LEAR
Return to her, and fifty men dismissed?
No, rather I abjure all roofs, and choose
To wage against the emnity o' th' air,   204
To be a comrade with the wolf and owl,
Necessity's sharp pinch. Return with her?   206
Why, the hot-blooded France, that dowerless took   207
Our youngest born, I could as well be brought
To knee his throne, and, squire-like, pension beg   209
To keep base life afoot. Return with her?

---

191 *indiscretion finds* ill judgment detects as such   **192** *sides* breast (which
should burst with grief)   **195** *less advancement* i.e. more abasement   **196**
seem so i.e. act the part   **201** *entertainment* lodging   **204** *wage* fight   **206**
Necessity's sharp pinch (a summing up of the hardships previously listed)
207 *hot-blooded* choleric (cf. I, ii, 23)   **209** *knee* kneel at; *squire-like* like an
attendant

211 Persuade me rather to be slave and sumpter
212 To this detested groom.

GONERIL   At your choice, sir.

LEAR

I prithee, daughter, do not make me mad.
I will not trouble thee, my child ; farewell.
We'll no more meet, no more see one another.
But yet thou art my flesh, my blood, my daughter ;
Or rather a disease that's in my flesh,
Which I must needs call mine. Thou art a boil,
219 A plague-sore, or embossèd carbuncle
In my corrupted blood. But I'll not chide thee.
Let shame come when it will, I do not call it.
222 I do not bid the thunder-bearer shoot,
223 Nor tell tales of thee to high-judging Jove.
Mend when thou canst, be better at thy leisure ;
I can be patient, I can stay with Regan,
I and my hundred knights.

REGAN   Not altogether so.
I looked not for you yet, nor am provided
For your fit welcome. Give ear, sir, to my sister ;
229 For those that mingle reason with your passion
Must be content to think you old and so –
But she knows what she does.

LEAR   Is this well spoken ?

REGAN

232 I dare avouch it, sir. What, fifty followers ?
Is it not well ? What should you need of more ?
234 Yea, or so many, sith that both charge and danger
Speak 'gainst so great a number ? How in one house
Should many people, under two commands,
Hold amity ? 'Tis hard, almost impossible.

---

211 *sumpter* packhorse 212 *groom* i.e. Oswald 219 *embossèd* risen to a
head 222 *thunder-bearer* i.e. Jupiter 223 *high-judging* judging from on
high 229 *mingle . . . passion* interpret your passion in the light of reason
232 *avouch* swear by 234 *sith that* since; *charge* expense

GONERIL
     Why might not you, my lord, receive attendance
     From those that she calls servants, or from mine?
REGAN
     Why not, my lord? If then they chanced to slack ye,   240
     We could control them. If you will come to me
     (For now I spy a danger), I entreat you
     To bring but five-and-twenty. To no more
     Will I give place or notice.   244
LEAR
     I gave you all.
REGAN   And in good time you gave it.
LEAR
     Made you my guardians, my depositaries,   246
     But kept a reservation to be followèd   247
     With such a number. What, must I come to you
     With five-and-twenty? Regan, said you so?
REGAN
     And speak't again, my lord. No more with me.
LEAR
     Those wicked creatures yet do look well-favored   251
     When others are more wicked; not being the worst
     Stands in some rank of praise.   253
        [To Goneril]   I'll go with thee.
     Thy fifty yet doth double five-and-twenty,
     And thou art twice her love.   255
GONERIL   Hear me, my lord.
     What need you five-and-twenty? ten? or five?
     To follow in a house where twice so many
     Have a command to tend you?
REGAN   What need one?

240 *slack* neglect 244 *notice* recognition 246 *depositaries* trustees
247 *kept . . . to be* stipulated that I be 251 *well-favored* comely 253
Stands . . . praise i.e. is at least relatively praiseworthy 255 *her love* i.e. as
loving as she

LEAR

259 O reason not the need ! Our basest beggars
260 Are in the poorest thing superfluous.
261 Allow not nature more than nature needs,
      Man's life is cheap as beast's. Thou art a lady :
263 If only to go warm were gorgeous,
      Why, nature needs not what thou gorgeous wear'st,
      Which scarcely keeps thee warm. But, for true need –
      You heavens, give me that patience, patience I need.
      You see me here, you gods, a poor old man,
      As full of grief as age, wretched in both.
      If it be you that stirs these daughters' hearts
270 Against their father, fool me not so much
      To bear it tamely ; touch me with noble anger,
      And let not women's weapons, water drops,
      Stain my man's cheeks. No, you unnatural hags !
      I will have such revenges on you both
      That all the world shall – I will do such things –
      What they are, yet I know not ; but they shall be
      The terrors of the earth. You think I'll weep.
      No, I'll not weep.
          Storm and tempest.
      I have full cause of weeping, but this heart
280 Shall break into a hundred thousand flaws
281 Or ere I'll weep. O fool, I shall go mad !
             Exeunt [Lear, Fool, Kent, and Gloucester].

CORNWALL

Let us withdraw ; 'twill be a storm.

REGAN

This house is little ; the old man and 's people
Cannot be well bestowed.

---

259 *reason* analyze   **260** *Are . . . superfluous* i.e. have some poor possession not utterly indispensable   **261** *than nature needs* i.e. than life needs for mere survival   **263–65** *If . . . warm* i.e. if to be dressed warmly (i.e. for need) were considered sufficiently gorgeous, you would not need your present attire, which is gorgeous rather than warm   **270** *fool* play with, humiliate   **280** *flaws* fragments   **281** *Or ere* before

GONERIL

  'Tis his own blame; hath put himself from rest   285
  And must needs taste his folly.

REGAN

  For his particular, I'll receive him gladly,   287
  But not one follower.

GONERIL   So am I purposed.   288

  Where is my Lord of Gloucester?

CORNWALL

  Followèd the old man forth.
      [Enter Gloucester.]   He is returned.

GLOUCESTER

  The King is in high rage.

CORNWALL   Whither is he going?

GLOUCESTER

  He calls to horse, but will I know not whither.

CORNWALL

  'Tis best to give him way; he leads himself.

GONERIL

  My lord, entreat him by no means to stay.

GLOUCESTER

  Alack, the night comes on, and the high winds
  Do sorely ruffle. For many miles about   296
  There's scarce a bush.

REGAN   O, sir, to willful men
  The injuries that they themselves procure
  Must be their schoolmasters. Shut up your doors.
  He is attended with a desperate train,
  And what they may incense him to, being apt   301
  To have his ear abused, wisdom bids fear.

CORNWALL

  Shut up your doors, my lord; 'tis a wild night.
  My Regan counsels well. Come out o' th' storm.   *Exeunt.*

*

285 *hath . . . rest* i.e. is responsible for leaving his resting place with her (?),
is self-afflicted (?) 287 *particular* own person 288 *purposed* determined
296 *ruffle* rage 301-02 *apt . . . abused* i.e. predisposed to listen to ill counsel

III, i   *Storm still. Enter Kent and a Gentleman severally.*

KENT
Who's there besides foul weather?

GENTLEMAN
2   One minded like the weather, most unquietly.

KENT
I know you. Where's the King?

GENTLEMAN
4   Contending with the fretful elements;
       Bids the wind blow the earth into the sea,
6   Or swell the curlèd waters 'bove the main,
7   That things might change or cease; [tears his white hair,
8   Which the impetuous blasts, with eyeless rage,
       Catch in their fury and make nothing of;
10   Strives in his little world of man to outscorn
       The to-and-fro-conflicting wind and rain.
12   This night, wherein the cub-drawn bear would couch,
13   The lion and the belly-pinchèd wolf
       Keep their fur dry, unbonneted he runs,
15   And bids what will take all.]

KENT   But who is with him?

GENTLEMAN
       None but the fool, who labors to outjest
       His heart-struck injuries.

KENT   Sir, I do know you,
18   And dare upon the warrant of my note
19   Commend a dear thing to you. There is division,
       Although as yet the face of it is covered
       With mutual cunning, 'twixt Albany and Cornwall;
22   Who have – as who have not, that their great stars

III, i An open heath   **2** *minded . . . unquietly* i.e. in disturbed mood   **4**
Contending quarrelling   **6** *main* mainland   **7** *change* revert to chaos (?),
improve (?)   **8** *eyeless* (1) blind, (2) invisible   **10** *little world* (the 'microcosm,' which is disturbed like the great world or 'macrocosm')   **12** *cub-
drawn* cub-sucked (and hence ravenous)   **13** *belly-pinchèd* famished
15 *take all* (the cry of the desperate gambler in staking his last)   **18** *warrant
. . . note* assurance of my knowledge   **19** *Commend . . . thing* entrust a
precious matter   **22** *that* whom; *stars* destinies

Throned and set high ? – servants, who seem no less,   23
Which are to France the spies and speculations   24
Intelligent of our state. What hath been seen,   25
Either in snuffs and packings of the Dukes,   26
Or the hard rein which both of them have borne   27
Against the old kind King, or something deeper,
Whereof, perchance, these are but furnishings –   29
[But, true it is, from France there comes a power   30
Into this scatterèd kingdom, who already,   31
Wise in our negligence, have secret feet
In some of our best ports and are at point
To show their open banner. Now to you :
If on my credit you dare build so far   35
To make your speed to Dover, you shall find
Some that will thank you, making just report
Of how unnatural and bemadding sorrow   38
The King hath cause to plain.   39
I am a gentleman of blood and breeding,
And from some knowledge and assurance offer
This office to you.]   42

GENTLEMAN
  I will talk further with you.
KENT   No, do not.
  For confirmation that I am much more
  Than my out-wall, open this purse and take   45
  What it contains. If you shall see Cordelia,
  As fear not but you shall, show her this ring,
  And she will tell you who that fellow is
  That yet you do not know. Fie on this storm !
  I will go seek the King.

GENTLEMAN
  Give me your hand. Have you no more to say ?

23 *Throned* have throned; *no less* i.e. truly so   24 *speculations* spies   25
Intelligent supplying intelligence   26 *snuffs* quarrels; *packings* intrigues
27 *hard rein . . . borne* i.e. harsh curbs . . . exercised   29 *furnishings* pretexts
30 *power* army   31 *scatterèd* divided   35 *my credit* trust in me; *build* take
constructive action   38 *bemadding sorrow* maddening grievances   39 *plain*
lament   42 *office* service   45 *out-wall* surface appearance

KENT

52   Few words, but, to effect, more than all yet:
53   That when we have found the King – in which your pain
      That way, I'll this – he that first lights on him
      Holla the other.   *Exeunt [severally].*

*

III, ii   *Storm still. Enter Lear and Fool.*

   LEAR
      Blow, winds, and crack your cheeks. Rage, blow.
2   You cataracts and hurricanoes, spout
3   Till you have drenched our steeples, drowned the cocks.
4   You sulph'rous and thought-executing fires,
5   Vaunt-couriers of oak-cleaving thunderbolts,
      Singe my white head. And thou, all-shaking thunder,
      Strike flat the thick rotundity o' th' world,
8   Crack Nature's moulds, all germains spill at once,
      That makes ingrateful man.
10 FOOL   O nuncle, court holy-water in a dry house is better
      than this rain-water out o' door. Good nuncle, in; ask
      thy daughters blessing. Here's a night pities neither
      wise men nor fools.

   LEAR
      Rumble thy bellyful. Spit, fire. Spout, rain.
      Nor rain, wind, thunder, fire are my daughters.
16   I tax not you, you elements, with unkindness.
      I never gave you kingdom, called you children;
18   You owe me no subscription. Then let fall
19   Your horrible pleasure. Here I stand your slave,
      A poor, infirm, weak, and despised old man.

      52 *to effect* in their import   **53** *pain* pains, care
      III, ii The same   **2** *hurricanoes* water-spouts   **3** *cocks* weathercocks
      4 *thought-executing fires* i.e. flashes of lightning swift as thought (?),
      dazing, benumbing the mind (?)   **5** *Vaunt-couriers* heralds   **8** *moulds* (in
      which Nature's creations are formed); *germains* seeds   **10** *court holy-water*
      flattery (slang)   **16** *tax* charge   **18** *subscription* deference   **19** *pleasure*
      will

But yet I call you servile ministers,   21
That will with two pernicious daughters join
Your high-engendered battles 'gainst a head   23
So old and white as this. O, ho ! 'tis foul.

FOOL He that has a house to put 's head in has a good
headpiece.

    The codpiece that will house   27
      Before the head has any,
    The head and he shall louse :   29
      So beggars marry many.   30
    The man that makes his toe   31
      What he his heart should make
    Shall of a corn cry woe,
      And turn his sleep to wake.

For there was never yet fair woman but she made   35
mouths in a glass.
    Enter Kent.

LEAR
No, I will be the pattern of all patience ;
I will say nothing.

KENT Who's there ?

FOOL Marry, here's grace and a codpiece ; that's a wise
man and a fool.

KENT
Alas, sir, are you here ? Things that love night
Love not such nights as these. The wrathful skies
Gallow the very wanderers of the dark   44
And make them keep their caves. Since I was man,   45

---

21 *ministers* agents **23** *high-engendered battles* heavenly battalions **27–30**
The codpiece . . . many (the moral of the rime is that improvident cohabita-
tion spells penury) **27** *codpiece* padded gusset at the crotch of the breeches
(slang for penis) **29** *he* it **30** *many* (head-lice and body-lice, accompany-
ing poverty) **31–34** *The man . . . wake* (a parallel instance of misery
deriving from reckless impulse: to transpose the tender and precious
heart and the tough and base toe is to invite injury; with *heart* also suggesting Cordelia) **35–36** *made . . . glass* i.e. posed before a mirror (irrelevant, except as vanity is a form of folly, the Fool's general theme) **44**
Gallow frighten **45** *keep their caves* i.e. keep under cover

46 Such sheets of fire, such bursts of horrid thunder,
   Such groans of roaring wind and rain, I never
48 Remember to have heard. Man's nature cannot carry
   Th' affliction nor the fear.

LEAR   Let the great gods
50 That keep this dreadful pudder o'er our heads
51 Find out their enemies now. Tremble, thou wretch,
   That hast within thee undivulgèd crimes
   Unwhipped of justice. Hide thee, thou bloody hand,
54 Thou perjured, and thou simular of virtue
   That art incestuous. Caitiff, to pieces shake,
56 That under covert and convenient seeming
57 Has practiced on man's life. Close pent-up guilts,
58 Rive your concealing continents and cry
59 These dreadful summoners grace. I am a man
   More sinned against than sinning.

KENT   Alack, bareheaded?
61 Gracious my lord, hard by here is a hovel;
   Some friendship will it lend you 'gainst the tempest.
63 Repose you there, while I to this hard house
   (More harder than the stones whereof 'tis raised,
65 Which even but now, demanding after you,
   Denied me to come in) return, and force
67 Their scanted courtesy.

LEAR   My wits begin to turn.
   Come on, my boy. How dost, my boy? Art cold?
   I am cold myself. Where is this straw, my fellow?
70 The art of our necessities is strange,
   And can make vile things precious. Come, your hovel.
   Poor fool and knave, I have one part in my heart

---

46 *horrid* horrible   48 *carry* bear   50 *pudder* turmoil   51 *Find . . . enemies*
i.e. discover sinners (by their show of fear)   54 *simular* counterfeit   56
seeming hypocrisy   57 *practiced on* plotted against; *Close* secret   58 *Rive*
split, break through; *continents* containers, covers   59 *summoners* arresting
officers of ecclesiastical courts; *grace* mercy   61 *Gracious my lord* my
gracious lord   63 *house* household (both building and occupants)   65
demanding after inquiring for   67 *scanted* stinted   70 *art* magic skill (as in
alchemy)

That's sorry yet for thee.

FOOL [sings]

> He that has and a little tiny wit,
>> With, heigh-ho, the wind and the rain,
> Must make content with his fortunes fit   76
>> Though the rain it raineth every day.

LEAR True, boy. Come, bring us to this hovel.

Exit [with Kent].

FOOL This is a brave night to cool a courtesan. I'll speak a 79
prophecy ere I go:

> When priests are more in word than matter;   81
> When brewers mar their malt with water;   82
> When nobles are their tailors' tutors,   83
> No heretics burned, but wenches' suitors;   84
> When every case in law is right,
> No squire in debt nor no poor knight;
> When slanders do not live in tongues,
> Nor cutpurses come not to throngs;
> When usurers tell their gold i' th' field,   89
> And bawds and whores do churches build –
> Then shall the realm of Albion   91
> Come to great confusion.   92
> Then comes the time, who lives to see't,
> That going shall be used with feet.   94

This prophecy Merlin shall make, for I live before his 95
time.   *Exit.*

*

76 *make . . . fit* i.e. reconcile himself to his fortunes   79 *brave* fine   81
are . . . matter i.e. can outshine the gospel message (At present their ability
to speak is quite unworthy of their theme.)   82 *mar* i.e. dilute (At present
they dilute water with malt, producing very small beer.)   83 *are . . . tutors*
i.e. are no longer subservient to fashion (Each subsequent line also reverses
the present state of affairs.)   84 *burned* (pun on contracting venereal
disease); *wenches' suitors* i.e. libertines   89 *tell* count; *i' th' field* (instead
of in secret places)   91 *Albion* England   92 *confusion* ruin (ironic: an
edifice of abuses is 'ruined' by reform)   94 *going . . . feet* walking will
be done with feet (the humor of anticlimax, but suggesting a return to
normality)   95 *Merlin* (a legendary magician associated with King Arthur,
who reigned later than King Lear)

III, iii   *Enter Gloucester and Edmund.*

GLOUCESTER Alack, alack, Edmund, I like not this unnatural dealing. When I desired their leave that I might
3   pity him, they took from me the use of mine own house,
charged me on pain of perpetual displeasure neither to
5   speak of him, entreat for him, or any way sustain him.

EDMUND Most savage and unnatural.

7 GLOUCESTER Go to; say you nothing. There is division
8   between the Dukes, and a worse matter than that. I have
received a letter this night – 'tis dangerous to be spoken
10   – I have locked the letter in my closet. These injuries the
11   King now bears will be revenged home; there is part of a
12   power already footed; we must incline to the King. I will
13   look him and privily relieve him. Go you and maintain
talk with the Duke, that my charity be not of him perceived. If he ask for me, I am ill and gone to bed. If I die
for it, as no less is threatened me, the King my old mas-
17   ter must be relieved. There is strange things toward,
Edmund; pray you be careful.   *Exit.*

EDMUND
19   This courtesy forbid thee shall the Duke
Instantly know, and of that letter too.
21   This seems a fair deserving, and must draw me
That which my father loses – no less than all.
The younger rises when the old doth fall.   *Exit.*

*

III, iv   *Enter Lear, Kent, and Fool.*

KENT
1   Here is the place, my lord. Good my lord, enter.
The tyranny of the open night's too rough

III, iii Within Gloucester's castle **3** *pity* have mercy upon **5** *entreat*
plead **7** *division* contention **8** *worse* more serious **10** *closet* chamber
11 *home* thoroughly **12** *power* army; *footed* landed; *incline to* side with
13 *look* search for; *privily* secretly **17** *toward* imminent **19** *courtesy* kind
attention (to Lear) **21** *fair deserving* i.e. action that should win favor
III, iv Before a hovel on the heath **1** *Good my lord* my good lord

For nature to endure.
    Storm still.
LEAR   Let me alone.
KENT
  Good my lord, enter here.
LEAR   Wilt break my heart?   4
KENT
  I had rather break mine own. Good my lord, enter.
LEAR
  Thou think'st 'tis much that this contentious storm
  Invades us to the skin. So 'tis to thee,
  But where the greater malady is fixed   8
  The lesser is scarce felt. Thou'dst shun a bear;
  But if thy flight lay toward the roaring sea,
  Thou'dst meet the bear i' th' mouth. When the mind's 11
    free,
  The body's delicate. The tempest in my mind
  Doth from my senses take all feeling else
  Save what beats there. Filial ingratitude,
  Is it not as this mouth should tear this hand
  For lifting food to't? But I will punish home.   16
  No, I will weep no more. In such a night
  To shut me out! Pour on; I will endure.
  In such a night as this! O Regan, Goneril,
  Your old kind father, whose frank heart gave all –   20
  O, that way madness lies; let me shun that.
  No more of that.
KENT   Good my lord, enter here.
LEAR
  Prithee go in thyself; seek thine own ease.
  This tempest will not give me leave to ponder
  On things would hurt me more, but I'll go in.
    [To the Fool]
  In, boy; go first. You houseless poverty –   26

---

4 *break my heart* i.e. by removing the distraction of mere physical distress
8 *fixed* lodged 11 *i' th' mouth* i.e. in the teeth; *free* free of care 16 *home*
i.e. to the hilt 20 *frank* liberal 26 *houseless* unsheltered

Nay, get thee in. I'll pray, and then I'll sleep. *Exit [Fool].*
Poor naked wretches, wheresoe'er you are,
That bide the pelting of this pitiless storm,
How shall your houseless heads and unfed sides,

31 Your looped and windowed raggedness, defend you
From seasons such as these? O, I have ta'en

33 Too little care of this! Take physic, pomp;
Expose thyself to feel what wretches feel,

35 That thou mayst shake the superflux to them
And show the heavens more just.

37 EDGAR *[within]* Fathom and half, fathom and half! Poor
Tom!

    Enter Fool.

FOOL Come not in here, nuncle; here's a spirit. Help me,
help me!

KENT
Give me thy hand. Who's there?

FOOL A spirit, a spirit. He says his name's poor Tom.

KENT
What art thou that dost grumble there i' th' straw?
Come forth.

    Enter Edgar [as Tom o' Bedlam].

45 EDGAR Away! the foul fiend follows me. Through the
46 sharp hawthorn blow the winds. Humh! go to thy bed
and warm thee.

LEAR Didst thou give all to thy daughters? And art thou
come to this?

EDGAR Who gives anything to poor Tom? whom the foul
fiend hath led through fire and through flame, through
ford and whirlpool, o'er bog and quagmire; that hath

53 laid knives under his pillow and halters in his pew, set
54 ratsbane by his porridge, made him proud of heart, to

---

31 *looped* loopholed 33 *Take physic, pomp* i.e. cure yourself, you vain-
glorious ones 35 *superflux* superfluities 37 *Fathom and half* (nautical
cry in taking soundings, perhaps suggested by the deluge) 45–46 *Through
... winds* (cf. ll. 93–94; a line from a ballad) 46–47 *go ... thee* (evidently a
popular retort; cf. *Taming of the Shrew*, Ind., i, 7–8) 53, 54 *knives
halters, ratsbane* (temptations to suicide) 53 *pew* a gallery or balcony

ride on a bay trotting horse over four-inched bridges, to 55
course his own shadow for a traitor. Bless thy five wits, 56
Tom 's acold. O, do, de, do, de, do, de. Bless thee from
whirlwinds, star-blasting, and taking. Do poor Tom 58
some charity, whom the foul fiend vexes. There could I
have him now – and there – and there again – and there –
    Storm still.

LEAR
    Has his daughters brought him to this pass? 61
    Couldst thou save nothing? Wouldst thou give 'em all?
FOOL Nay, he reserved a blanket, else we had been all 63
shamed.

LEAR
    Now all the plagues that in the pendulous air 65
    Hang fated o'er men's faults light on thy daughters! 66
KENT
    He hath no daughters, sir.
LEAR
    Death, traitor! Nothing could have subdued nature
    To such a lowness but his unkind daughters.
    Is it the fashion that discarded fathers
    Should have thus little mercy on their flesh? 71
    Judicious punishment – 'twas this flesh begot
    Those pelican daughters. 73
EDGAR Pillicock sat on Pillicock Hill. Alow, alow, loo, loo! 74
FOOL This cold night will turn us all to fools and madmen.
EDGAR Take heed o' th' foul fiend; obey thy parents;
    keep thy words' justice; swear not; commit not with 77

---

55 *ride . . . bridges* i.e. take mad risks   56 *course . . . traitor* chase his own
shadow as an enemy   58 *star-blasting* i.e. becoming the victim of malig-
nant stars; *taking* pestilence   61 *pass* evil condition   63 *blanket* (to cover
his nakedness)   65 *pendulous* ominously suspended   66 *Hang . . . faults*
i.e. destined to chastise sins   71 *have . . . flesh* i.e. torture themselves   73
pelican i.e. feeding upon the parent's blood (a supposed habit of this
species of bird)   74 *Pillicock . . . Hill* (probably from a nursery rhyme;
'Pillicock' is a pet name for a child); *Alow . . . loo* (hunting cry?)   77
justice i.e. dependability; *commit not* (i.e. adultery)

man's sworn spouse; set not thy sweet heart on proud
array. Tom's acold.

LEAR What hast thou been?

EDGAR A servingman, proud in heart and mind; that
82 curled my hair, wore gloves in my cap; served the lust of
my mistress' heart, and did the act of darkness with her;
swore as many oaths as I spake words, and broke them in
the sweet face of heaven. One that slept in the contriving
of lust, and waked to do it. Wine loved I deeply, dice
87 dearly; and in woman out-paramoured the Turk. False
88 of heart, light of ear, bloody of hand; hog in sloth, fox in
stealth, wolf in greediness, dog in madness, lion in prey.
90 Let not the creaking of shoes nor the rustling of silks be-
tray thy poor heart to woman. Keep thy foot out of
92 brothels, thy hand out of plackets, thy pen from lenders'
books, and defy the foul fiend. Still through the haw-
94 thorn blows the cold wind; says suum, mun, nonny.
95 Dolphin my boy, boy, sessa! let him trot by.

Storm still.

96 LEAR Thou wert better in a grave than to answer with thy
uncovered body this extremity of the skies. Is man no
98 more than this? Consider him well. Thou ow'st the
worm no silk, the beast no hide, the sheep no wool, the
100 cat no perfume. Ha! here's three on's are sophisticated.
101 Thou art the thing itself; unaccommodated man is no
102 more but such a poor, bare, forked animal as thou art.
103 Off, off, you lendings! Come, unbutton here.

[Begins to disrobe.]

---

82 *gloves . . . cap* (a fashion among Elizabethan gallants) 87 *out-
paramoured the Turk* outdid the Sultan in mistress-keeping 88 *light of
ear* i.e. attentive to flattery and slander 90 *creaking, rustling* (both
considered seductively fashionable sounds) 92 *plackets* slits in skirts
92–93 *pen . . . books* (in signing for loans) 94 *suum . . . nonny* (the refrain
of the wind?) 95 *Dolphin . . . trot by* (variously explained as cant phrases
or ballad refrain, equivalent to 'Let it go') 96 *answer* bear the brunt of
98 *ow'st* have borrowed from 100 *cat* civet cat; *sophisticated* altered by
artifice 101 *unaccommodated* unpampered 102 *forked* two-legged 103
lendings borrowed coverings

FOOL Prithee, nuncle, be contented; 'tis a naughty night 104
to swim in. Now a little fire in a wild field were like an 105
old lecher's heart – a small spark, all the rest on's body
cold. Look, here comes a walking fire.
    Enter Gloucester with a torch.

EDGAR This is the foul Flibbertigibbet. He begins at cur- 108
few, and walks till the first cock. He gives the web and 109
the pin, squints the eye, and makes the harelip; mildews 110
the white wheat, and hurts the poor creature of earth. 111
      Swithold footed thrice the 'old; 112
      He met the nightmare, and her nine fold; 113
          Bid her alight 114
          And her troth plight, 115
      And aroint thee, witch, aroint thee! 116

KENT
    How fares your Grace?

LEAR What's he?

KENT
    Who's there? What is't you seek?

GLOUCESTER
    What are you there? Your names?

EDGAR Poor Tom, that eats the swimming frog, the toad,
the todpole, the wall-newt and the water; that in the fury 122
of his heart, when the foul fiend rages, eats cow-dung
for sallets, swallows the old rat and the ditch-dog, drinks 124
the green mantle of the standing pool; who is whipped 125
from tithing to tithing, and stock-punished and im- 126
prisoned; who hath had three suits to his back, six

---

104 *naughty* evil   105 *wild* barren   108 *Flibbertigibbet* (a dancing devil);
curfew (9 p.m.)   109 *first cock* (midnight)   109–10 *web . . . pin* cataract of
the eye   110 *squints* crosses   111 *white* ripening   112 *Swithold* St Withold
(Anglo-Saxon exorcist); *footed* walked over; *'old* wold, uplands   113
nightmare incubus, demon; *fold* offspring   114 *alight* i.e. from the horse
she was afflicting   115 *her troth plight* plight her troth, pledge her good
intentions   116 *aroint thee* be gone (a direct command, concluding the
charm)   122 *todpole* tadpole; *water* water-newt   124 *sallets* salads; *ditch-
dog* (carcass)   125 *mantle* scum; *standing* stagnant   126 *tithing* a ten-
family district within a parish; *stock-punished* placed in the stocks

shirts to his body,
     Horse to ride, and weapon to wear,
130   But mice and rats, and such small deer,
     Have been Tom's food for seven long year.
132 Beware my follower! Peace, Smulkin, peace, thou fiend!

GLOUCESTER
What, hath your Grace no better company?

EDGAR
The prince of darkness is a gentleman.
135 Modo he's called, and Mahu.

GLOUCESTER
Our flesh and blood, my lord, is grown so vile
137 That it doth hate what gets it.

EDGAR   Poor Tom's acold.

GLOUCESTER
139 Go in with me. My duty cannot suffer
T' obey in all your daughters' hard commands.
Though their injunction be to bar my doors
And let this tyrannous night take hold upon you,
Yet have I ventured to come seek you out
And bring you where both fire and food is ready.

LEAR
First let me talk with this philosopher.
What is the cause of thunder?

KENT
Good my lord, take his offer; go into th' house.

LEAR
148 I'll talk a word with this same learnèd Theban.
149 What is your study?

EDGAR
150 How to prevent the fiend, and to kill vermin.

---

130 *deer* game (adapted from lines in the romance *Bevis of Hampton*)   132, 135 *Smulkin, Modo, Mahu* (devils described in Harsnett's *Declaration*, 1603)   137 *gets* begets (a reference to Edgar, Goneril, and Regan)   139 *suffer* permit   148 *Theban* (an unexplained association of Thebes with philosophy, i.e. science)   149 *study* i.e. scientific specialty   150 *prevent* thwart

LEAR
    Let me ask you one word in private.
KENT
    Importune him once more to go, my lord.
    His wits begin t' unsettle.
GLOUCESTER   Canst thou blame him?
        Storm still.
    His daughters seek his death. Ah, that good Kent,
    He said it would be thus, poor banished man!
    Thou sayest the King grows mad – I'll tell thee, friend,
    I am almost mad myself. I had a son,
    Now outlawed from my blood; he sought my life   158
    But lately, very late. I loved him, friend,
    No father his son dearer. True to tell thee,
    The grief hath crazed my wits. What a night's this!
    I do beseech your Grace –
LEAR   O, cry you mercy, sir.   162
    Noble philosopher, your company.
EDGAR Tom's acold.
GLOUCESTER
    In, fellow, there, into th' hovel; keep thee warm.
LEAR
    Come, let's in all.
KENT   This way, my lord.
LEAR   With him!
    I will keep still with my philosopher.
KENT
    Good my lord, soothe him; let him take the fellow.   168
GLOUCESTER
    Take him you on.   169
KENT
    Sirrah, come on; go along with us.
LEAR
    Come, good Athenian.   171

---

158 *outlawed . . . blood* proscribed as no child of mine   **162** *cry you mercy*
I beg your pardon   **168** *soothe* humor   **169** *you on* along with you   **171**
Athenian i.e. philosopher

GLOUCESTER
    No words, no words! Hush.
173 EDGAR   Child Rowland to the dark tower came;
174   His word was still, 'Fie, foh, and fum,
              I smell the blood of a British man.'   *Exeunt.*

*

III, v   *Enter Cornwall and Edmund.*

CORNWALL I will have my revenge ere I depart his house.

2 EDMUND How, my lord, I may be censured, that nature
3   thus gives way to loyalty, something fears me to think of.

CORNWALL I now perceive it was not altogether your
5   brother's evil disposition made him seek his death; but a
     provoking merit, set awork by a reproveable badness in
     himself.

EDMUND How malicious is my fortune that I must repent
     to be just! This is the letter which he spoke of, which
10   approves him an intelligent party to the advantages of
     France. O heavens, that this treason were not! or not I
     the detector!

CORNWALL Go with me to the Duchess.

EDMUND If the matter of this paper be certain, you have
     mighty business in hand.

CORNWALL True or false, it hath made thee Earl of
     Gloucester. Seek out where thy father is, that he may be
     ready for our apprehension.

19 EDMUND *[aside]* If I find him comforting the King, it
20   will stuff his suspicion more fully. – I will persever in

---

173 *Child* (i.e. a candidate for knighthood); *Rowland* Roland of the Charle-
magne legends (the line perhaps from a lost ballad)   174 *His word was
still* i.e. his repeated word, his motto, was always   174–75 *Fie . . . man*
(absurdly heroic)

III, v Within Gloucester's castle   2 *censured* judged   3 *something fears me*
frightens me somewhat   5–7 *a provoking . . . himself* i.e. evil justice incited
by evil (a case of poison driving out poison)   10 *approves* proves; *intelligent . . . advantages* spying partisan on behalf   19 *comforting* aiding
20 *persever* persevere

my course of loyalty, though the conflict be sore between that and my blood.   22
CORNWALL I will lay trust upon thee, and thou shalt find 23
a dearer father in my love.   *Exeunt.*

*

Enter Kent and Gloucester.   III, vi
GLOUCESTER Here is better than the open air; take it
thankfully. I will piece out the comfort with what addition I can. I will not be long from you.
KENT All the power of his wits have given way to his
impatience. The gods reward your kindness.   5
                              Exit [Gloucester].
     Enter Lear, Edgar, and Fool.
EDGAR Frateretto calls me, and tells me Nero is an angler 6
in the lake of darkness. Pray, innocent, and beware the   7
foul fiend.
FOOL Prithee, nuncle, tell me whether a madman be a
gentleman or a yeoman.   10
LEAR
A king, a king.
FOOL No, he's a yeoman that has a gentleman to his son;
for he's a mad yeoman that sees his son a gentleman   13
before him.
LEAR
To have a thousand with red burning spits
Come hizzing in upon 'em –   16
[EDGAR The foul fiend bites my back.

22 *blood* natural feelings   23 *lay . . . thee* trust you (?), reward you with
a place of trust (?)
III, vi Within a cottage near Gloucester's castle   5 *impatience* rage
6 *Frateretto* (a devil mentioned in Harsnett's *Declaration*); *Nero* (in
Rabelais, Trajan was the angler, Nero a fiddler, in Hades)   7 *innocent*
hapless victim, plaything   10 *yeoman* a property owner, next in rank to
a gentleman (The allusion is to self-penalizing indulgence of one's children.)
13 *sees* i.e. sees to it   16 *hizzing* hissing (Lear is musing on vicious military
retaliation)

FOOL He's mad that trusts in the tameness of a wolf, a
horse's health, a boy's love, or a whore's oath.

LEAR

20   It shall be done; I will arraign them straight.
        [To Edgar]
        Come, sit thou here, most learned justice.
        [To the Fool]
        Thou, sapient sir, sit here. Now, you she-foxes –

23 EDGAR Look, where he stands and glares. Want'st thou
24   eyes at trial, madam?

25   Come o'er the bourn, Bessy, to me.

    FOOL   Her boat hath a leak,
                    And she must not speak
                Why she dares not come over to thee.

    EDGAR The foul fiend haunts poor Tom in the voice of a
30   nightingale. Hoppedance cries in Tom's belly for two
31   white herring. Croak not, black angel; I have no food
        for thee.

KENT

33 How do you, sir? Stand you not so amazed.
    Will you lie down and rest upon the cushions?

LEAR

    I'll see their trial first. Bring in their evidence.
        [To Edgar]
    Thou, robèd man of justice, take thy place.
        [To the Fool]
    And thou, his yokefellow of equity,
38 Bench by his side. *[to Kent]* You are o' th' commission;
    Sit you too.

    EDGAR Let us deal justly.

---

20 *arraign* bring to trial   **23** *he* Lear (?), one of Edgar's 'devils' (?)   **24**
eyes such eyes (?), spectators (?)   **25** *bourn* brook (Edgar's line is from a
popular song; the Fool's are a ribald improvisation)   **30** *nightingale* i.e.
the fool; *Hoppedance* (a devil mentioned in Harsnett's *Declaration* as
'Hobberdidance')   **31** *white* unsmoked (in contrast with *black angel*, i.e.
smoked devil)   **33** *amazed* bewildered   **38** *commission* those commissioned
as King's justices

> Sleepest or wakest thou, jolly shepherd?
>> Thy sheep be in the corn;   42
> And for one blast of thy minikin mouth   43
>> Thy sheep shall take no harm.
Purr, the cat is gray.   45

LEAR Arraign her first. 'Tis Goneril, I here take my oath before this honorable assembly, kicked the poor king her father.

FOOL Come hither, mistress. Is your name Goneril?

LEAR She cannot deny it.

FOOL Cry you mercy, I took you for a joint-stool.   51

LEAR
And here's another, whose warped looks proclaim
What store her heart is made on. Stop her there!
Arms, arms, sword, fire! Corruption in the place!   54
False justicer, why hast thou let her 'scape?]

EDGAR Bless thy five wits!

KENT
O pity! Sir, where is the patience now
That you so oft have boasted to retain?

EDGAR [aside]
My tears begin to take his part so much   59
They mar my counterfeiting.   60

LEAR
The little dogs and all,
Tray, Blanch, and Sweetheart – see, they bark at me.

EDGAR Tom will throw his head at them. Avaunt, you curs.
> Be thy mouth or black or white,
> Tooth that poisons if it bite;
> Mastiff, greyhound, mongrel grim,

---

42 *corn* wheatfield   43 *one . . . mouth* one strain on your delicate shepherd's pipe (?)   45 *gray* (gray cats were among the forms supposedly assumed by devils)   51 *Cry . . . joint-stool* (a cant expression for 'Pardon me for failing to notice you,' but two joint-stools – cf. *warped*, l. 52 – were probably the actual stage objects arraigned as Goneril and Regan)   54 *Corruption . . . place* i.e. bribery in the court   59 *takes his part* i.e. fall on his behalf   60 *counterfeiting* i.e. simulating madness

67   Hound or spaniel, brach or lym,
68   Or bobtail tike, or trundle-tail –
              Tom will make him weep and wail;
              For, with throwing thus my head,
71   Dogs leaped the hatch, and all are fled.
72 Do, de, de, de. Sessa! Come, march to wakes and fairs
73 and market towns. Poor Tom, thy horn is dry.

LEAR Then let them anatomize Regan. See what breeds
about her heart. Is there any cause in nature that makes
these hard hearts? *[to Edgar]* You, sir, I entertain for
one of my hundred; only I do not like the fashion of
78 your garments. You will say they are Persian; but let
them be changed.

KENT
Now, good my lord, lie here and rest awhile.

LEAR
Make no noise, make no noise; draw the curtains.
So, so. We'll go to supper i' th' morning.

FOOL And I'll go to bed at noon.

Enter Gloucester.

GLOUCESTER
Come hither, friend. Where is the King my master?

KENT
Here, sir, but trouble him not; his wits are gone.

GLOUCESTER
Good friend, I prithee take him in thy arms.
I have o'erheard a plot of death upon him.
There is a litter ready; lay him in't
And drive toward Dover, friend, where thou shalt meet
Both welcome and protection. Take up thy master.
If thou shouldst dally half an hour, his life,

---

67 *brach* hound bitch; *lym* bloodhound **68** *bobtail . . . trundle-tail* short-tailed cur or long-tailed **71** *hatch* lower half of a 'Dutch door' **72** *Sessa* (interjection, equivalent to 'Away!'); *wakes* parish feasts **73** *Poor . . . dry* (Edgar expresses his exhaustion in his role, by an allusion to the horns proffered by Toms o' Bedlam in begging drink) **78** *Persian* (Persian costume was reputedly gorgeous. Ironically, or in actual delusion, Lear refers thus to Edgar's rags, as he refers to bed curtains in l. 81.)

With thine and all that offer to defend him,
Stand in assurèd loss. Take up, take up,
And follow me, that will to some provision   94
Give thee quick conduct.   95
[KENT   Oppressèd nature sleeps.
This rest might yet have balmed thy broken sinews,   96
Which, if convenience will not allow,   97
Stand in hard cure.   98
        [To the Fool] Come, help to bear thy master.
Thou must not stay behind.]
GLOUCESTER   Come, come, away!
                                Exeunt [all but Edgar].

[EDGAR
When we our betters see bearing our woes,   100
We scarcely think our miseries our foes.   101
Who alone suffers suffers most i' th' mind,
Leaving free things and happy shows behind;   103
But then the mind much sufferance doth o'erskip   104
When grief hath mates, and bearing fellowship.   105
How light and portable my pain seems now,   106
When that which makes me bend makes the King bow.
He childed as I fatherèd. Tom, away.
Mark the high noises, and thyself bewray   109
When false opinion, whose wrong thoughts defile thee,   110
In thy just proof repeals and reconciles thee.   111
What will hap more to-night, safe 'scape the King!   112
Lurk, lurk.]   [Exit.]   113

                        *

94 *provision* supplies 95 *conduct* guidance 96 *balmed* healed; *sinews*
nerves 97 *convenience* propitious circumstances 98 *Stand . . . cure* will
be hard to cure 100 *our woes* woes like ours 101 *our foes* i.e. our peculiar
foes (they seem rather a part of universal misery) 103 *free* carefree;
shows scenes 104 *sufferance* suffering 105 *bearing fellowship* enduring
has company 106 *portable* bearable 109 *Mark . . . noises* i.e. heed the
rumors concerning those in power (?); *bewray* reveal 110 *wrong thoughts*
misconceptions 111 *In . . . reconciles thee* i.e. upon your vindication
recalls you and makes peace with you 112 *What . . . more* whatever more
happens 113 *Lurk* i.e. keep covered

III, vii   *Enter Cornwall, Regan, Goneril, Bastard [Edmund],*
            and Servants.

CORNWALL *[to Goneril]* Post speedily to my lord your
husband; show him this letter. The army of France is
landed. *[to Servants]* Seek out the traitor Gloucester.
                              [Exeunt some Servants.]

REGAN Hang him instantly.

GONERIL Pluck out his eyes.

CORNWALL Leave him to my displeasure. Edmund, keep
7   you our sister company. The revenges we are bound to
     take upon your traitorous father are not fit for your be-
     holding. Advise the Duke where you are going, to a most
10   festinate preparation. We are bound to the like. Our
11   posts shall be swift and intelligent betwixt us. Farewell,
12   dear sister; farewell, my Lord of Gloucester.
          Enter Steward [Oswald].
     How now? Where's the King?

OSWALD
My Lord of Gloucester hath conveyed him hence.
Some five or six and thirty of his knights,
16   Hot questrists after him, met him at gate;
     Who, with some other of the lord's dependants,
     Are gone with him toward Dover, where they boast
     To have well-armèd friends.

CORNWALL   Get horses for your mistress.
                                        Exit [Oswald].

GONERIL
Farewell, sweet lord, and sister.

CORNWALL
Edmund, farewell.   *[Exeunt Goneril and Edmund.]*
              Go seek the traitor Gloucester,
Pinion him like a thief, bring him before us.
                              [Exeunt other Servants.]

III, vii Within Gloucester's castle   7 *bound* required   10 *festinate* speedy
11 *intelligent* informative   12 *Lord of Gloucester* (as now endowed with
his father's title and estates)   16 *questrists* seekers

Though well we may not pass upon his life   23
Without the form of justice, yet our power
Shall do a court'sy to our wrath, which men   25
May blame, but not control.
    Enter Gloucester and Servants.
                      Who's there, the traitor?

REGAN
Ingrateful fox, 'tis he.

CORNWALL
Bind fast his corky arms.   28

GLOUCESTER
What means your Graces? Good my friends, consider
You are my guests. Do me no foul play, friends.

CORNWALL
Bind him, I say.
    [Servants bind him.]

REGAN   Hard, hard! O filthy traitor.

GLOUCESTER
Unmerciful lady as you are, I'm none.

CORNWALL
To this chair bind him. Villain, thou shalt find –
    [Regan plucks his beard.]

GLOUCESTER
By the kind gods, 'tis most ignobly done
To pluck me by the beard.

REGAN
So white, and such a traitor?

GLOUCESTER   Naughty lady,   36
These hairs which thou dost ravish from my chin
Will quicken and accuse thee. I am your host.   38
With robber's hands my hospitable favors   39
You should not ruffle thus. What will you do?   40

CORNWALL
Come, sir, what letters had you late from France?   41

---

23 *pass upon* issue a sentence against   25 *do a court'sy to* i.e. defer to, act in
conformity with   28 *corky* (because aged)   36 *Naughty* evil   38 *quicken*
come to life   39 *favors* features   40 *ruffle* tear at   41 *late* of late

REGAN
42   Be simple-answered, for we know the truth.

CORNWALL
And what confederacy have you with the traitors
44   Late footed in the kingdom?

REGAN
To whose hands you have sent the lunatic King.
Speak.

GLOUCESTER
47   I have a letter guessingly set down,
Which came from one that's of a neutral heart,
And not from one opposed.

CORNWALL   Cunning.

REGAN   And false.

CORNWALL
Where hast thou sent the king?

GLOUCESTER
To Dover.

REGAN
52   Wherefore to Dover? Wast thou not charged at peril –

CORNWALL
Wherefore to Dover? Let him answer that.

GLOUCESTER
54   I am tied to th' stake, and I must stand the course.

REGAN
Wherefore to Dover?

GLOUCESTER
Because I would not see thy cruel nails
Pluck out his poor old eyes; nor thy fierce sister
58   In his anointed flesh stick boarish fangs.
The sea, with such a storm as his bare head
60   In hell-black night endured, would have buoyed up

---

42 *Be simple-answered* i.e. give plain answers 44 *footed* landed 47
guessingly i.e. tentatively, not stated as an assured fact 52 *charged at peril*
ordered on peril of your life 54 *course* coursing (as by a string of dogs
baiting a bear or bull tied in the pit) 58 *anointed* (as king) 60 *buoyed*
surged

114

And quenched the stellèd fires.   61
Yet, poor old heart, he holp the heavens to rain.   62
If wolves had at thy gate howled that stern time,
Thou shouldst have said, 'Good porter, turn the key.'   64
All cruels else subscribe. But I shall see   65
The wingèd vengeance overtake such children.   66

CORNWALL
See't shalt thou never. Fellows, hold the chair.
Upon these eyes of thine I'll set my foot.

GLOUCESTER
He that will think to live till he be old,   69
Give me some help. – O cruel! O you gods!

REGAN
One side will mock another. Th' other too.   71

CORNWALL
If you see vengeance –

1. SERVANT   Hold your hand, my lord!
I have served you ever since I was a child;
But better service have I never done you
Than now to bid you hold.

REGAN   How now, you dog?

1. SERVANT
If you did wear a beard upon your chin,
I'ld shake it on this quarrel. What do you mean!   77

CORNWALL
My villain!   78
    [Draw and fight.]

1. SERVANT
Nay, then, come on, and take the chance of anger.

61 *stellèd* starry   62 *holp* helped   64 *turn the key* i.e. let them come in to shelter   65 *All . . . subscribe* i.e. at such times all other cruel creatures give way, agree to renounce their cruelty (?)   66 *wingèd* heavenly (?), swift (?)   69 *will think* hopes, expects   71 *mock* i.e. subject to ridicule (because of the contrast)   77 *shake it* (as Regan has done with Gloucester's – an act of extreme defiance); *on this quarrel* in this cause; *What . . . mean* i.e. how dare you (The words are given to Regan by most editors, but they are no more 'un-servantlike,' than those which precede them.)   78 *My villain* i.e. my serf (with play on its more modern meaning)

REGAN

    Give me thy sword. A peasant stand up thus ?
    [She takes a sword and runs at him behind,] kills him.

1 . SERVANT

    O, I am slain ! My lord, you have one eye left
82 To see some mischief on him. O !

CORNWALL

    Lest it see more, prevent it. Out, vile jelly.
    Where is thy lustre now ?

GLOUCESTER

    All dark and comfortless. Where's my son Edmund ?
86 Edmund, enkindle all the sparks of nature
87 To quit this horrid act.

REGAN   Out, treacherous villain ;

    Thou call'st on him that hates thee. It was he
89 That made the overture of thy treasons to us ;
    Who is too good to pity thee.

GLOUCESTER

91 O my follies ! Then Edgar was abused.
    Kind gods, forgive me that, and prosper him.

REGAN

    Go thrust him out at gates, and let him smell
    His way to Dover.   *Exit [one] with Gloucester.*
94   How is't, my lord ? How look you ?

CORNWALL

    I have received a hurt. Follow me, lady.
    Turn out that eyeless villain. Throw this slave
    Upon the dunghill. Regan, I bleed apace.
    Untimely comes this hurt. Give me your arm.   *Exeunt.*

[2 . SERVANT

    I'll never care what wickedness I do,
    If this man come to good.

3 . SERVANT   If she live long,

---

82 *mischief* injury   86 *nature* natural feeling   87 *quit* requite, avenge; *horrid* horrible   89 *overture* disclosure   91 *abused* wronged   94 *How look you* i.e. how looks it with you, what is your condition

And in the end meet the old course of death,   101
Women will all turn monsters.

2 . SERVANT
Let's follow the old Earl, and get the bedlam
To lead him where he would. His roguish madness   104
Allows itself to anything.   *[Exit.]*

3 . SERVANT
Go thou. I'll fetch some flax and whites of eggs
To apply to his bleeding face. Now heaven help him.
                                        Exit.]

                        *

    Enter Edgar.   IV, i

EDGAR
Yet better thus, and known to be contemned,   1
Than still contemned and flattered. To be worst,
The lowest and most dejected thing of fortune,   3
Stands still in esperance, lives not in fear.   4
The lamentable change is from the best;
The worst returns to laughter. Welcome then,   6
Thou unsubstantial air that I embrace:
The wretch that thou hast blown unto the worst
Owes nothing to thy blasts.   9
    Enter Gloucester and an Old Man.
                        But who comes here?
My father, poorly led? World, world, O world!   10
But that thy strange mutations make us hate thee,   11
Life would not yield to age.

OLD MAN   O my good lord,
I have been your tenant, and your father's tenant,
These fourscore years.

---

101 *meet . . . death* i.e. die a natural death   104–05 *His roguish . . . anything*
i.e. his being an irresponsible wanderer allows him to do anything
IV, i A path leading from Gloucester's castle   1 *contemned* despised   3
dejected cast down, abased   4 *esperance* hope   6 *The worst . . . laughter* i.e.
the worst extreme is the point of return to happiness   9 *nothing* i.e. nothing
good (and hence he is free of debt)   10 *poorly* poor-like, i.e. like a blind
beggar (?)   11–12 *But . . . age* i.e. were it not for your hateful mutability,
we would never be reconciled to old age and death

GLOUCESTER
Away, get thee away. Good friend, be gone.
16   Thy comforts can do me no good at all;
17   Thee they may hurt.
OLD MAN   You cannot see your way.
GLOUCESTER
18   I have no way, and therefore want no eyes;
I stumbled when I saw. Full oft 'tis seen
20   Our means secure us, and our mere defects
Prove our commodities. O dear son Edgar,
22   The food of thy abusèd father's wrath,
23   Might I but live to see thee in my touch
I'ld say I had eyes again!
OLD MAN   How now? Who's there?
EDGAR [aside]
O gods! Who is't can say 'I am at the worst'?
I am worse than e'er I was.
OLD MAN   'Tis poor mad Tom.
EDGAR [aside]
27   And worse I may be yet. The worst is not
So long as we can say 'This is the worst.'
OLD MAN
Fellow, where goest?
GLOUCESTER   Is it a beggarman?
OLD MAN
Madman and beggar too.
GLOUCESTER
31   He has some reason, else he could not beg.
I' th' last night's storm I such a fellow saw,
33   Which made me think a man a worm. My son

---

16 *comforts* ministrations   17 *hurt* do injury (since they are forbidden)
18 *want* need   20–21 *Our means . . . commodities* i.e. prosperity makes us
rash, and sheer affliction proves a boon   22 *food* i.e. the object fed upon;
abusèd deceived   23 *in* i.e. by means of   27–28 *The worst . . . worst* (because
at the very worst there will be no such comforting thought)   31 *reason*
powers of reason   33–34 *My son . . . mind* (because it was actually he –
a natural touch)

Came then into my mind, and yet my mind
Was then scarce friends with him. I have heard more
    since.
As flies to wanton boys are we to th' gods;   36
They kill us for their sport.

EDGAR *[aside]*   How should this be?
Bad is the trade that must play fool to sorrow,
Ang'ring itself and others. – Bless thee, master.   39

GLOUCESTER
Is that the naked fellow?

OLD MAN   Ay, my lord.

GLOUCESTER
Then prithee get thee gone. If for my sake
Thou wilt o'ertake us hence a mile or twain
I' th' way toward Dover, do it for ancient love;   43
And bring some covering for this naked soul,
Which I'll entreat to lead me.

OLD MAN   Alack, sir, he is mad.

GLOUCESTER
'Tis the time's plague when madmen lead the blind.   46
Do as I bid thee, or rather do thy pleasure.   47
Above the rest, be gone.

OLD MAN
I'll bring him the best 'parel that I have,   49
Come on't what will.   *Exit.*

GLOUCESTER
Sirrah naked fellow –

EDGAR
Poor Tom's acold. *[aside]* I cannot daub it further.   52

GLOUCESTER
Come hither, fellow.

EDGAR *[aside]*
And yet I must. – Bless thy sweet eyes, they bleed.

36 *wanton* irresponsibly playful   39 *Ang'ring* offending   43 *ancient love*
i.e. such love as formerly bound master and man (nostalgic)   46 *time's*
plague i.e. malady characteristic of these times   47 *thy pleasure* as you
please   49 *'parel* apparel   52 *daub it* lay it on, act the part

GLOUCESTER
    Know'st thou the way to Dover?

EDGAR Both stile and gate, horseway and footpath. Poor
    Tom hath been scared out of his good wits. Bless thee,
    good man's son, from the foul fiend. [Five fiends have
59 been in poor Tom at once: of lust, as Obidicut; Hobbi-
60 didence, prince of dumbness; Mahu, of stealing; Modo,
61 of murder; Flibbertigibbet, of mopping and mowing,
    who since possesses chambermaids and waiting women.
    So, bless thee, master.]

GLOUCESTER
    Here, take this purse, thou whom the heavens' plagues
65 Have humbled to all strokes. That I am wretched
66 Makes thee the happier. Heavens, deal so still!
67 Let the superfluous and lust-dieted man,
68 That slaves your ordinance, that will not see
    Because he does not feel, feel your pow'r quickly;
    So distribution should undo excess,
    And each man have enough. Dost thou know Dover?

EDGAR Ay, master.

GLOUCESTER
73 There is a cliff, whose high and bending head
74 Looks fearfully in the confinèd deep.
    Bring me but to the very brim of it,
    And I'll repair the misery thou dost bear
    With something rich about me. From that place
    I shall no leading need.

EDGAR   Give me thy arm.
    Poor Tom shall lead thee.   *Exeunt*.

                          *

59 *Obidicut* Hoberdicut (a devil mentioned in Harsnett's *Declaration*, as are
the four following) 60 *dumbness* muteness (Shakespeare identifies each
devil with some form of possession) 61 *mopping and mowing* grimaces,
affected facial expressions 65 *humbled to* reduced to bearing humbly
66 *happier* i.e. less wretched 67 *superfluous* possessed of superfluities;
lust-dieted i.e. whose desires are feasted 68 *slaves your ordinance* sub-
ordinates your injunction (to share) 73 *bending* overhanging 74 *in . . .
deep* i.e. to the sea hemmed in below

Enter Goneril, Bastard [Edmund], and Steward   IV, ii
[Oswald].

GONERIL

Welcome, my lord. I marvel our mild husband
Not met us on the way.   2
[*To Oswald*]   Now, where's your master?

OSWALD

Madam, within, but never man so changed.
I told him of the army that was landed:
He smiled at it. I told him you were coming:
His answer was, 'The worse.' Of Gloucester's treachery
And of the loyal service of his son
When I informed him, then he called me sot   8
And told me I had turned the wrong side out.
What most he should dislike seems pleasant to him;
What like, offensive.   11

GONERIL [*to Edmund*] Then shall you go no further.
It is the cowish terror of his spirit,   12
That dares not undertake. He'll not feel wrongs   13
Which tie him to an answer. Our wishes on the way   14
May prove effects. Back, Edmund, to my brother.
Hasten his musters and conduct his pow'rs.   16
I must change names at home, and give the distaff   17
Into my husband's hands. This trusty servant
Shall pass between us. Ere long you are like to hear
(If you dare venture in your own behalf)
A mistress's command. Wear this. Spare speech.   21
[*Gives a favor.*]
Decline your head. This kiss, if it durst speak,
Would stretch thy spirits up into the air.

IV, ii Before Albany's palace 2 *Not met* has not met 8 *sot* fool 11
What like what he should like 12 *cowish* cowardly 13 *undertake* engage
14 *an answer* retaliation 14–15 *Our wishes . . . effects* i.e. our wishes, that
you might supplant Albany, may materialize 16 *musters* enlistments;
conduct his pow'rs lead his army 17 *change names* i.e. exchange the name of
'mistress' for 'master'; *distaff* spinning-staff (symbol of the housewife)
21 *mistress's* (at present she plays the role of master, but, mated with
Edmund, she would again *change names*)

24   Conceive, and fare thee well.

EDMUND
    Yours in the ranks of death.   *Exit.*

GONERIL   My most dear Gloucester.
    O, the difference of man and man :
    To thee a woman's services are due ;
28   My fool usurps my body.

OSWALD   Madam, here comes my lord.
                                    [Exit.]

    Enter Albany.

GONERIL
29   I have been worth the whistle.

ALBANY   O Goneril,
    You are not worth the dust which the rude wind
31   Blows in your face. [I fear your disposition :
    That nature which contemns its origin
33   Cannot be borderèd certain in itself.
34   She that herself will sliver and disbranch
35   From her material sap, perforce must wither
    And come to deadly use.

GONERIL
    No more ; the text is foolish.

ALBANY
    Wisdom and goodness to the vile seem vile ;
39   Filths savor but themselves. What have you done ?
    Tigers not daughters, what have you performed ?
    A father, and a gracious agèd man,
42   Whose reverence even the head-lugged bear would lick,
43   Most barbarous, most degenerate, have you madded.

---

24 *Conceive* (1) understand, (2) quicken (with the seed I have planted in you)   **28** *usurps* wrongfully occupies   **29** *worth the whistle* i.e. valued enough to be welcomed home ('not worth the whistle' applying proverbially to a 'poor dog')   **31** *fear your disposition* distrust your nature   **33** *borderèd certain* safely contained (it will be unpredictably licentious)   **34** *sliver*, *disbranch* cut off   **35** *material sap* sustaining stock, nourishing trunk   **39** *savor* relish   **42** *head-lugged* dragged with a head-chain (hence, surly); *lick* i.e. treat with affection   **43** *degenerate* unnatural; *madded* maddened

Could my good brother suffer you to do it?
A man, a prince, by him so benefited!
If that the heavens do not their visible spirits   46
Send quickly down to tame these vile offenses,
It will come,   48
Humanity must perforce prey on itself,
Like monsters of the deep.]

GONERIL   Milk-livered man,   50
    That bear'st a cheek for blows, a head for wrongs;
Who hast not in thy brows an eye discerning   52
Thine honor from thy suffering; [that not know'st
Fools do those villains pity who are punished   54
Ere they have done their mischief. Where's thy drum?   55
France spreads his banners in our noiseless land,   56
With plumèd helm thy state begins to threat,   57
Whilst thou, a moral fool, sits still and cries   58
'Alack, why does he so?']

ALBANY   See thyself, devil:
Proper deformity seems not in the fiend   60
So horrid as in woman.

GONERIL   O vain fool!
[ALBANY
Thou changèd and self-covered thing, for shame   62
Bemonster not thy feature. Were't my fitness   63
To let these hands obey my blood,   64
They are apt enough to dislocate and tear
Thy flesh and bones. Howe'er thou art a fiend,
A woman's shape doth shield thee.

---

46 *visible* made visible, material 48 *It* i.e. chaos 50 *Milk-livered* i.e.
spiritless 52–53 *discerning . . . suffering* distinguishing between dishonor
and tolerance 54 *Fools* i.e. only fools 55 *drum* i.e. military preparation 56 *noiseless* i.e. unaroused 57 *helm* war-helmet 58 *moral* moral-
izing 60 *Proper* i.e. fair-surfaced 62 *changèd* transformed (diabolically,
as in witchcraft); *self-covered* i.e. your natural self overwhelmed by
evil (?), devil disguised as woman (?) 63 *Bemonster . . . feature* i.e. do
not exchange your human features for a monster's; *my fitness* fit for me
64 *blood* passion

GONERIL

68   Marry, your manhood – mew!]
         Enter a Messenger.

[ALBANY What news?]

MESSENGER

    O, my good lord, the Duke of Cornwall's dead,
71   Slain by his servant, going to put out
    The other eye of Gloucester.

ALBANY   Gloucester's eyes?

MESSENGER

73   A servant that he bred, thrilled with remorse,
    Opposed against the act, bending his sword
    To his great master; who, thereat enraged,
76   Flew on him, and amongst them felled him dead;
    But not without that harmful stroke which since
78   Hath plucked him after.

ALBANY   This shows you are above,
79   You justicers, that these our nether crimes
80   So speedily can venge. But, O poor Gloucester,
    Lost he his other eye?

MESSENGER   Both, both, my lord.
82   This letter, madam, craves a speedy answer.
    'Tis from your sister.

GONERIL *[aside]*   One way I like this well;
    But being widow, and my Gloucester with her,
85   May all the building in my fancy pluck
86   Upon my hateful life. Another way
87   The news is not so tart. – I'll read, and answer.   *[Exit.]*

---

68 *Marry* (oath, derived from 'By Mary'); *your manhood – mew* i.e. 'What a man!' followed by a contemptuous interjection (?), mew up (contain) this display of manliness (?)   71 *going to* about to   73 *bred* reared; *thrilled with remorse* in the throes of pity   76 *amongst them* i.e. aided by the others 78 *plucked him after* drawn him along (to death)   79 *justicers* dispensers of justice; *nether crimes* sins committed here below 80 *venge* avenge 82 *craves* requires 85–86 *May . . . life* i.e. may make my life hateful by destroying my dream-castles 86 *Another way* the other way (alluded to in l. 83, probably the removal of Cornwall as an obstacle to sole reign with Edmund) 87 *tart* distasteful

ALBANY
  Where was his son when they did take his eyes?
MESSENGER
  Come with my lady hither.
ALBANY   He is not here.
MESSENGER
  No, my good lord; I met him back again.   90
ALBANY
  Knows he the wickedness?
MESSENGER
  Ay, my good lord. 'Twas he informed against him,
  And quit the house on purpose, that their punishment
  Might have the freer course.
ALBANY   Gloucester, I live
  To thank thee for the love thou show'dst the King,
  And to revenge thine eyes. Come hither, friend.
  Tell me what more thou know'st.   *Exeunt.*

                         *

      [*Enter Kent and a Gentleman.*   IV, iii
KENT Why the King of France is so suddenly gone back
     know you no reason?
GENTLEMAN Something he left imperfect in the state,   3
     which since his coming forth is thought of, which imports 4
     to the kingdom so much fear and danger that his per- 5
     sonal return was most required and necessary.   6
KENT
  Who hath he left behind him general?
GENTLEMAN The Marshal of France, Monsieur La Far.
KENT Did your letters pierce the Queen to any demon-   9
     stration of grief?

90 *back* going back
IV, iii A meeting place at Dover   3 *imperfect . . . state* i.e. rift in affairs
of state   4 *imports* means   5 *fear* uneasiness   6 *most* most urgently
9 *pierce* goad

GENTLEMAN

Ay, sir. She took them, read them in my presence,
12   And now and then an ample tear trilled down
Her delicate cheek. It seemed she was a queen
14   Over her passion, who, most rebel-like,
Sought to be king o'er her.

KENT   O, then it movèd her?

GENTLEMAN

Not to a rage. Patience and sorrow strove
17   Who should express her goodliest. You have seen
Sunshine and rain at once – her smiles and tears
19   Were like, a better way : those happy smilets
That played on her ripe lip seemed not to know
What guests were in her eyes, which parted thence
As pearls from diamonds dropped. In brief,
23   Sorrow would be a rarity most belovèd,
If all could so become it.

KENT   Made she no verbal question?

GENTLEMAN

25   Faith, once or twice she heaved the name of father
Pantingly forth, as if it pressed her heart ;
Cried 'Sisters, sisters, shame of ladies, sisters !
Kent, father, sisters ? What, i' th' storm i' th' night ?
29   Let pity not be believed !' There she shook
The holy water from her heavenly eyes,
31   And clamor moistened ; then away she started
To deal with grief alone.

KENT   It is the stars,
33   The stars above us govern our conditions ;
34   Else one self mate and make could not beget
35   Such different issues. You spoke not with her since?

---

12 *trilled* trickled   14 *who* which   17 *goodliest* i.e. most becomingly   19
Were . . . way i.e. improved upon that spectacle   23 *rarity* gem   25–26
heaved . . . forth uttered . . . chokingly   29 *Let pity* let it for pity (?)   31
clamor moistened i.e. mixed, and thus muted, lamentation with tears   33
govern our conditions determine our characters   34 *Else . . . make* otherwise
the same husband and wife   35 *issues* children

GENTLEMAN No.
KENT
  Was this before the King returned?
GENTLEMAN   No, since.
KENT
  Well, sir, the poor distressèd Lear's i' th' town;
  Who sometime, in his better tune, remembers   39
  What we are come about, and by no means
  Will yield to see his daughter.
GENTLEMAN   Why, good sir?
KENT
  A sovereign shame so elbows him; his own unkindness,   42
  That stripped her from his benediction, turned her   43
  To foreign casualties, gave her dear rights   44
  To his dog-hearted daughters – these things sting
  His mind so venomously that burning shame
  Detains him from Cordelia.
GENTLEMAN   Alack, poor gentleman.
KENT
  Of Albany's and Cornwall's powers you heard not?
GENTLEMAN
  'Tis so; they are afoot.   49
KENT
  Well, sir, I'll bring you to our master Lear
  And leave you to attend him. Some dear cause   51
  Will in concealment wrap me up awhile.
  When I am known aright, you shall not grieve
  Lending me this acquaintance. I pray you go
  Along with me.   *Exeunt.*]

                                    *

39 *better tune* i.e. more rational state, less jangled   42 *sovereign* overruling; *elbows* jogs   43 *stripped* cut off (cf. *disbranch*, IV, ii, 34); *benediction* blessing   44 *casualties* chances   49 *'Tis so* i.e. I have to this extent   51 *dear cause* important purpose

IV, iv *Enter, with Drum and Colors, Cordelia, Gentleman [Doctor], and Soldiers.*

CORDELIA

Alack, 'tis he ! Why, he was met even now
As mad as the vexed sea, singing aloud,
3 Crowned with rank fumiter and furrow weeds,
4 With hardocks, hemlock, nettles, cuckoo flow'rs,
5 Darnel, and all the idle weeds that grow
6 In our sustaining corn. A century send forth !
Search every acre in the high-grown field
And bring him to our eye.   *[Exit an Officer.]*
8   What can man's wisdom
9 In the restoring his bereavèd sense ?
10 He that helps him take all my outward worth.

DOCTOR

There is means, madam.
12 Our foster nurse of nature is repose,
13 The which he lacks. That to provoke in him
14 Are many simples operative, whose power
Will close the eye of anguish.

CORDELIA   All blessed secrets,
16 All you unpublished virtues of the earth,
17 Spring with my tears ; be aidant and remediate
In the good man's distress. Seek, seek for him,
Lest his ungoverned rage dissolve the life
20 That wants the means to lead it.

Enter Messenger.

MESSENGER   News, madam.
The British pow'rs are marching hitherward.

IV, iv A field near Dover **3** *fumiter* fumitory; *furrow weeds* (those that appear after ploughing?) **4** *hardocks* (variously identified as burdock, 'hoar dock,' 'harlock,' etc.) **5** *Darnel* tares; *idle* useless **6** *sustaining corn* life-giving wheat; *century* troop of a hundred men **8** *can* i.e. can accomplish **9** *bereavèd* bereft **10** *outward worth* material possessions **12** *foster* fostering **13** *provoke* induce **14** *simples operative* medicinal herbs, sedatives **16** *unpublished virtues* i.e. little-known benign herbs **17** *Spring* grow; *remediate* remedial **20** *wants* lacks; *means* i.e. power of reason; *lead it* govern it (the rage)

CORDELIA
   'Tis known before. Our preparation stands
   In expectation of them. O dear father,
   It is thy business that I go about.
   Therefore great France   25
   My mourning, and importuned tears hath pitied. 26
   No blown ambition doth our arms incite,   27
   But love, dear love, and our aged father's right.
   Soon may I hear and see him !   *Exeunt.*

*

Enter Regan and Steward [Oswald].   IV, v

REGAN
   But are my brother's pow'rs set forth ?
OSWALD   Ay, madam.
REGAN
   Himself in person there ?
OSWALD   Madam, with much ado.   2
   Your sister is the better soldier.
REGAN
   Lord Edmund spake not with your lord at home ?
OSWALD No, madam.
REGAN
   What might import my sister's letter to him ?   6
OSWALD I know not, lady.
REGAN
   Faith, he is posted hence on serious matter.   8
   It was great ignorance, Gloucester's eyes being out, 9
   To let him live. Where he arrives he moves
   All hearts against us. Edmund, I think, is gone,
   In pity of his misery, to dispatch

---

25 *Therefore* therefor, because of that   26 *importuned* importunate   27
blown swollen
IV, v At Gloucester's castle   2 *much ado* great bother   6 *import* bear as
its message   8 *is posted* has sped   9 *ignorance* error

13   His nighted life ; moreover, to descry
      The strength o' th' enemy.
OSWALD
      I must needs after him, madam, with my letter.
REGAN
      Our troops set forth to-morrow. Stay with us.
      The ways are dangerous.
OSWALD   I may not, madam.
18   My lady charged my duty in this business.
REGAN
      Why should she write to Edmund ? Might not you
20   Transport her purposes by word ? Belike,
      Some things – I know not what. I'll love thee much,
      Let me unseal the letter.
OSWALD   Madam, I had rather –
REGAN
      I know your lady does not love her husband,
24   I am sure of that ; and at her late being here
25   She gave strange eliads and most speaking looks
26   To noble Edmund. I know you are of her bosom.
OSWALD I, madam ?
REGAN
      I speak in understanding – y' are, I know't –
29   Therefore I do advise you take this note :
      My lord is dead ; Edmund and I have talked,
31   And more convenient is he for my hand
32   Than for your lady's. You may gather more.
33   If you do find him, pray you give him this ;
      And when your mistress hears thus much from you,
35   I pray desire her call her wisdom to her.
      So fare you well.
      If you do chance to hear of that blind traitor,

---

13 *nighted* benighted, blinded   18 *charged* strictly ordered   20 *Transport her purposes* convey her intentions; *Belike* probably   24 *late* recently   25 *eliads* amorous glances   26 *of her bosom* in her confidence   29 *take this note* note this   31 *convenient* appropriate   32 *gather more* i.e. draw your own conclusions   33 *this* this word, this reminder   35 *call* recall

Preferment falls on him that cuts him off.   38

OSWALD

Would I could meet him, madam! I should show
What party I do follow.

REGAN   Fare thee well.   *Exeunt.*

*

Enter Gloucester and Edgar.   IV, vi

GLOUCESTER

When shall I come to th' top of that same hill?

EDGAR

You do climb up it now. Look how we labor.

GLOUCESTER

Methinks the ground is even.

EDGAR   Horrible steep.
Hark, do you hear the sea?

GLOUCESTER   No, truly.

EDGAR

Why, then, your other senses grow imperfect
By your eyes' anguish.   6

GLOUCESTER   So may it be indeed.
Methinks thy voice is altered, and thou speak'st
In better phrase and matter than thou didst.

EDGAR

Y' are much deceived. In nothing am I changed
But in my garments.

GLOUCESTER   Methinks y' are better spoken.

EDGAR

Come on, sir; here's the place. Stand still. How fearful
And dizzy 'tis to cast one's eyes so low!
The crows and choughs that wing the midway air   13
Show scarce so gross as beetles. Halfway down   14

---

38 *Preferment* advancement
IV, vi An open place near Dover 6 *anguish* affliction 13 *choughs* jack-
daws; *midway* i.e. halfway down 14 *gross* large

15   Hangs one that gathers sampire – dreadful trade ;
      Methinks he seems no bigger than his head.
      The fishermen that walk upon the beach
18   Appear like mice ; and yond tall anchoring bark,
19   Diminished to her cock ; her cock, a buoy
      Almost too small for sight. The murmuring surge
21   That on th' unnumb'red idle pebble chafes
      Cannot be heard so high. I'll look no more,
23   Lest my brain turn, and the deficient sight
24   Topple down headlong.

GLOUCESTER   Set me where you stand.

EDGAR
      Give me your hand. You are now within a foot
      Of th' extreme verge. For all beneath the moon
27   Would I not leap upright.

GLOUCESTER   Let go my hand.
      Here, friend, 's another purse ; in it a jewel
29   Well worth a poor man's taking. Fairies and gods
      Prosper it with thee. Go thou further off ;
      Bid me farewell, and let me hear thee going.

EDGAR
      Now fare ye well, good sir.

GLOUCESTER   With all my heart.

EDGAR [aside]
33   Why I do trifle thus with his despair
      Is done to cure it.

GLOUCESTER   O you mighty gods !
          [He kneels.]
      This world I do renounce, and in your sights
      Shake patiently my great affliction off.
37   If I could bear it longer and not fall

15 *sampire* samphire (aromatic herb used in relishes) 18 *anchoring* anchored 19 *Diminished . . . cock* reduced to the size of her cockboat 21 *unnumb'red idle pebble* i.e. barren reach of countless pebbles 23 *the deficient sight* i.e. my dizziness 24 *Topple* topple me 27 *upright* i.e. even upright, let alone forward 29 *Fairies* (the usual wardens of treasure) 33 *Why . . . trifle* i.e. the reason I toy with (*done* in l. 34 being redundant) 37–38 *fall . . . with* i.e. rebel against (irreligiously)

To quarrel with your great opposeless wills,   38
My snuff and loathèd part of nature should   39
Burn itself out. If Edgar live, O bless him!
Now, fellow, fare thee well.
    [He falls forward and swoons.]

EDGAR   Gone, sir – farewell.
And yet I know not how conceit may rob   42
The treasury of life when life itself
Yields to the theft. Had he been where he thought,   44
By this had thought been past. Alive or dead?
Ho you, sir! Friend! Hear you, sir? Speak!
Thus might he pass indeed. Yet he revives.
What are you, sir?

GLOUCESTER   Away, and let me die.

EDGAR
Hadst thou been aught but gossamer, feathers, air,
So many fathom down precipitating,   50
Thou'dst shivered like an egg; but thou dost breathe,
Hast heavy substance, bleed'st not, speak'st, art sound.
Ten masts at each make not the altitude   53
Which thou hast perpendicularly fell.
Thy life's a miracle. Speak yet again.   55

GLOUCESTER
But have I fall'n, or no?

EDGAR
From the dread summit of this chalky bourn.   57
Look up a-height. The shrill-gorged lark so far   58
Cannot be seen or heard. Do but look up.

GLOUCESTER
Alack, I have no eyes.
Is wretchedness deprived that benefit
To end itself by death? 'Twas yet some comfort

38 *opposeless* not to be opposed   39 *My snuff . . . nature* i.e. the guttering and hateful tag end of my life   42 *conceit* imagination   44 *Yields to* i.e. welcomes   50 *precipitating* falling   53 *at each* end to end   55 *life* survival   57 *bourn* boundary, headland   58 *a-height* on high; *gorged* throated

63   When misery could beguile the tyrant's rage
      And frustrate his proud will.

EDGAR   Give me your arm.

65   Up – so. How is't ? Feel you your legs ? You stand.

GLOUCESTER
      Too well, too well.

EDGAR   This is above all strangeness.
      Upon the crown o' th' cliff what thing was that
      Which parted from you ?

GLOUCESTER   A poor unfortunate beggar.

EDGAR
      As I stood here below, methought his eyes
      Were two full moons ; he had a thousand noses,

71   Horns whelked and waved like the enridgèd sea.

72   It was some fiend. Therefore, thou happy father,

73   Think that the clearest gods, who make them honors
      Of men's impossibilities, have preservèd thee.

GLOUCESTER
      I do remember now. Henceforth I'll bear
      Affliction till it do cry out itself
      'Enough, enough, and die.' That thing you speak of,
      I took it for a man. Often 'twould say
      'The fiend, the fiend' – he led me to that place.

EDGAR
80   Bear free and patient thoughts.

      Enter Lear [mad, bedecked with weeds].

                                    But who comes here ?

81   The safer sense will ne'er accommodate

82   His master thus.

83 LEAR No, they cannot touch me for coining ; I am the
      King himself.

63 *beguile* outwit 65 *Feel* test 71 *whelked* corrugated; *enridgèd* blown
into ridges 72 *happy father* lucky old man 73 *clearest* purest 73–74
who . . . impossibilities i.e. whose glory it is to do for man what he cannot do
for himself 80 *free* (of despair) 81 *safer* saner; *accommodate* accoutre
82 *His* its 83 *touch* i.e. interfere with; *coining* minting coins (a royal
prerogative)

EDGAR

O thou side-piercing sight!

LEAR Nature 's above art in that respect. There's your 86
press money. That fellow handles his bow like a crow- 87
keeper. Draw me a clothier's yard. Look, look, a mouse! 88
Peace, peace; this piece of toasted cheese will do't.
There's my gauntlet; I'll prove it on a giant. Bring up 90
the brown bills. O, well flown, bird. I' th' clout, i' th' 91
clout – hewgh! Give the word. 92

EDGAR Sweet marjoram. 93

LEAR Pass.

GLOUCESTER

I know that voice.

LEAR Ha! Goneril with a white beard? They flattered me
like a dog, and told me I had the white hairs in my beard 97
ere the black ones were there. To say 'ay' and 'no' to 98
everything that I said! 'Ay' and 'no' too was no good 99
divinity. When the rain came to wet me once, and the
wind to make me chatter; when the thunder would not
peace at my bidding; there I found 'em, there I smelt
'em out. Go to, they are not men o' their words. They
told me I was everything. 'Tis a lie – I am not ague-proof. 104

GLOUCESTER

The trick of that voice I do well remember. 105

---

86 *Nature . . . respect* i.e. a born king is above a made king in legal immunity (cf. the coeval debate on the relative merits of poets of nature, i.e.
born, and poets of art, i.e. made by self-effort)   87 *press money* i.e. the
'king's shilling' (token payment on military impressment or enlistment)
87–88 *crow-keeper* i.e. farmhand warding off crows   88 *clothier's yard* i.e.
arrow (normally a yard long)   90 *gauntlet* armored glove (hurled as challenge); *prove it on* maintain it against   91 *brown bills* varnished halberds;
well flown (hawking cry); *clout* bull's-eye (archery term)   92 *word* pass-
word   93 *Sweet marjoram* (herb, associated with treating madness?)   97
like a dog i.e. fawningly; *I . . . beard* i.e. I was wise   98 *To say . . . 'no'* i.e. to
agree   99–100 *no good divinity* i.e. bad theology (For 'good divinity' cf. 2
Corinthians i, 18: 'But as God is true, our word to you was not yea and nay';
also Matthew v, 36–37, James v, 12.)   104 *ague-proof* proof against chills
and fever   105 *trick* peculiarity

Is't not the King?

LEAR   Ay, every inch a king.
When I do stare, see how the subject quakes.
108   I pardon that man's life. What was thy cause?
Adultery?
Thou shalt not die. Die for adultery? No.
The wren goes to't, and the small gilded fly
112   Does lecher in my sight.
Let copulation thrive; for Gloucester's bastard son
Was kinder to his father than my daughters
115   Got 'tween the lawful sheets.
116   To't, luxury, pell-mell, for I lack soldiers.
Behold yond simp'ring dame,
118   Whose face between her forks presages snow,
119   That minces virtue, and does shake the head
120   To hear of pleasure's name.
121   The fitchew nor the soilèd horse goes to't
With a more riotous appetite.
123   Down from the waist they are Centaurs,
Though women all above.
125   But to the girdle do the gods inherit,
Beneath is all the fiend's.
There's hell, there's darkness, there is the sulphurous
pit; burning, scalding, stench, consumption. Fie, fie,
129   fie! pah, pah! Give me an ounce of civet; good apothe-
cary, sweeten my imagination! There's money for thee.

GLOUCESTER
O, let me kiss that hand.
132   LEAR   Let me wipe it first; it smells of mortality.

---

108 *cause* case   112 *lecher* copulate   115 *Got* begotten   116 *luxury*
lechery; *for . . . soldiers* (and therefore a higher birth rate)   118 *Whose
. . . snow* i.e. whose face (mien) presages snow (frigidity) between her forks
(legs)   119 *minces* mincingly affects   120 *pleasure's name* i.e. the very name
of sexual indulgence   121 *fitchew* polecat, prostitute; *soilèd* pastured   123
Centaurs (lustful creatures of mythology, half-human and half-beast)
125 *girdle* waist; *inherit* possess   129 *civet* musk perfume   132 *mortality*
death

GLOUCESTER
> O ruined piece of nature; this great world   133
> Shall so wear out to naught. Dost thou know me?

LEAR I remember thine eyes well enough. Dost thou
> squiny at me? No, do thy worst, blind Cupid; I'll not   136
> love. Read thou this challenge; mark but the penning of it.

GLOUCESTER
> Were all thy letters suns, I could not see.

EDGAR *[aside]*
> I would not take this from report – it is,   139
> And my heart breaks at it.

LEAR Read.

GLOUCESTER
> What, with the case of eyes?   142

LEAR O, ho, are you there with me? No eyes in your head,   143
> nor no money in your purse? Your eyes are in a heavy
> case, your purse in a light; yet you see how this world   145
> goes.

GLOUCESTER
> I see it feelingly.   147

LEAR What, art mad? A man may see how this world goes
> with no eyes. Look with thine ears. See how yond justice
> rails upon yond simple thief. Hark in thine ear: change   150
> places and, handy-dandy, which is the justice, which is   151
> the thief? Thou hast seen a farmer's dog bark at a beggar?

GLOUCESTER Ay, sir.

LEAR And the creature run from the cur. There thou
> mightst behold the great image of authority – a dog 's   155
> obeyed in office.
> Thou rascal beadle, hold thy bloody hand!   157

133–34 *this . . . naught* i.e. the universe (macrocosm) will decay like this
man (microcosm) (cf. III, i, 10n.) 136 *squiny* squint 139 *take* accept
142 *case* sockets 143 *are . . . me* is that the situation 145 *case* plight (pun)
147 *feelingly* (1) only by touch, (2) by feeling pain 150 *simple* mere 151
handy-dandy (old formula used in the child's game of choosing which
hand) 155 *great image* universal symbol 155–56 *a dog's . . . office* i.e.
man bows to authority regardless of who exercises it 157 *beadle* parish
constable

Why dost thou lash that whore? Strip thy own back.
159 Thou hotly lusts to use her in that kind
160 For which thou whip'st her. The usurer hangs the
     cozener.
161 Through tattered clothes small vices do appear;
     Robes and furred gowns hide all. Plate sin with gold,
163 And the strong lance of justice hurtless breaks;
164 Arm it in rags, a pygmy's straw does pierce it.
165 None does offend, none – I say none! I'll able 'em.
166 Take that of me, my friend, who have the power
     To seal th' accuser's lips. Get thee glass eyes
168 And, like a scurvy politician, seem
     To see the things thou dost not. Now, now, now, now!
     Pull off my boots. Harder, harder! So.

EDGAR
171 O, matter and impertinency mixed;
     Reason in madness.

LEAR
     If thou wilt weep my fortunes, take my eyes.
     I know thee well enough; thy name is Gloucester.
     Thou must be patient. We came crying hither;
     Thou know'st, the first time that we smell the air
     We wawl and cry. I will preach to thee. Mark.

GLOUCESTER
     Alack, alack the day.

LEAR
     When we are born, we cry that we are come
180 To this great stage of fools. – This' a good block.
181 It were a delicate stratagem to shoe
182 A troop of horse with felt. I'll put't in proof,

---

159 *lusts* wish (suggestive form of 'lists'); *kind* i.e. same act 160 *The usurer . . . cozener* i.e. the great cheat, some moneylending judge, sentences to death the little cheat 161 *appear* show plainly 163 *hurtless* without hurting 164 *Arm . . . rags* i.e. armored (cf. *Plate*, l. 162) only in rags 165 *able* authorize 166 *that* (i.e. the assurance of immunity) 168 *scurvy politician* vile opportunist 171 *matter and impertinency* sense and nonsense 180 *block* felt hat (?) 181 *delicate* subtle 182 *in proof* to the test

And when I have stol'n upon these son-in-laws,
Then kill, kill, kill, kill, kill, kill!
    Enter a Gentleman [with Attendants].

GENTLEMAN
O, here he is! Lay hand upon him. – Sir,
Your most dear daughter –

LEAR
No rescue? What, a prisoner? I am even
The natural fool of fortune. Use me well;   188
You shall have ransom. Let me have surgeons;
I am cut to th' brains.   190

GENTLEMAN   You shall have anything.

LEAR
No seconds? All myself?
Why, this would make a man a man of salt,   192
To use his eyes for garden waterpots,
[Ay, and laying autumn's dust.] I will die bravely,
Like a smug bridegroom. What, I will be jovial!   195
Come, come, I am a king; masters, know you that?

GENTLEMAN
You are a royal one, and we obey you.

LEAR Then there's life in't. Come, an you get it, you shall 198
get it by running. Sa, sa, sa, sa!   199
    Exit [running, followed by Attendants].

GENTLEMAN
A sight most pitiful in the meanest wretch,
Past speaking of in a king. Thou hast one daughter
Who redeems Nature from the general curse   202
Which twain have brought her to.   203

EDGAR
Hail, gentle sir.

---

188 *natural fool* born plaything   190 *cut* wounded   192 *salt* i.e. all tears
195 *smug bridegroom* spruce bridegroom (the image suggested by the
secondary meaning of *bravely*, i.e. handsomely, and the sexual suggestion
of *will die*)   198 *life* (and therefore 'hope')   199 *Sa . . . sa* (hunting and
rallying cry)   202 *general curse* universal condemnation   203 *twain* i.e.
the other two

204 GENTLEMAN   Sir, speed you. What's your will?
    EDGAR
205   Do you hear aught, sir, of a battle toward?
    GENTLEMAN
206   Most sure and vulgar. Every one hears that
      Which can distinguish sound.
    EDGAR   But, by your favor,
      How near's the other army?
    GENTLEMAN
209   Near and on speedy foot. The main descry
      Stands on the hourly thought.
    EDGAR   I thank you, sir. That's all.
    GENTLEMAN
      Though that the Queen on special cause is here,
      Her army is moved on.
    EDGAR   I thank you, sir. *Exit [Gentleman]*.
    GLOUCESTER
      You ever-gentle gods, take my breath from me;
214   Let not my worser spirit tempt me again
      To die before you please.
    EDGAR   Well pray you, father.
    GLOUCESTER
      Now, good sir, what are you?
    EDGAR
217   A most poor man, made tame to fortune's blows,
218   Who, by the art of known and feeling sorrows,
219   Am pregnant to good pity. Give me your hand;
220   I'll lead you to some biding.
    GLOUCESTER   Hearty thanks.
221   The bounty and the benison of heaven
        To boot, and boot.

---

204 *speed* God speed 205 *toward* impending 206 *sure and vulgar* commonly known certainty 209 *on speedy foot* rapidly marching 209–10 *main . . . thought* sight of the main body is expected hourly 214 *worser spirit* i.e. bad angel 217 *tame* submissive 218 *art . . . sorrows* i.e. lesson of sorrows painfully experienced 219 *pregnant* prone 220 *biding* biding place 221 *benison* blessing

Enter Steward [Oswald].

OSWALD   A proclaimed prize ! Most happy ;   222
  That eyeless head of thine was first framed flesh   223
  To raise my fortunes. Thou old unhappy traitor,
  Briefly thyself remember. The sword is out   225
  That must destroy thee.

GLOUCESTER   Now let thy friendly hand   226
  Put strength enough to't.
    [Edgar interposes.]

OSWALD   Wherefore, bold peasant,
  Dar'st thou support a published traitor ? Hence,   228
  Lest that th' infection of his fortune take
  Like hold on thee. Let go his arm.

EDGAR
  Chill not let go, zir, without vurther 'casion.   231

OSWALD
  Let go, slave, or thou diest.

EDGAR Good gentleman, go your gait, and let poor voke 233
pass. An chud ha' bin zwaggered out of my life, 'twould 234
not ha' bin zo long as 'tis by a vortnight. Nay, come not
near th' old man. Keep out, che vore ye, or Ise try 236
whether your costard or my ballow be the harder. Chill 237
be plain with you.

OSWALD Out, dunghill !
    [They fight.]

EDGAR Chill pick your teeth, zir. Come. No matter vor 240
your foins.   241
    [Oswald falls.]

OSWALD
  Slave, thou hast slain me. Villain, take my purse.   242

---

222 *proclaimed prize* i.e. one with a price on his head; *happy* lucky   **223**
framed flesh born, created   **225** *thyself remember* i.e. pray, think of your soul
226 *friendly* i.e. unconsciously befriending   **228** *published* proclaimed   **231**
Chill I'll (rustic dialect); *vurther 'casion* further occasion   **233** *gait* way;
voke folk   **234** *An chud* if I could; *zwaggered* swaggered, bluffed   **236** *che
vore* I warrant, assure; *Ise* I shall   **237** *costard* head; *ballow* cudgel   **240**
Chill pick i.e. I'll knock out   **241** *foins* thrusts   **242** *Villain* serf

If ever thou wilt thrive, bury my body,
244 And give the letters which thou find'st about me
To Edmund Earl of Gloucester. Seek him out
246 Upon the English party. O, untimely death!
Death!
[He dies.]

EDGAR
248 I know thee well. A serviceable villain,
249 As duteous to the vices of thy mistress
As badness would desire.

GLOUCESTER   What, is he dead?

EDGAR
Sit you down, father; rest you.
Let's see these pockets; the letters that he speaks of
May be my friends. He's dead; I am only sorry
254 He had no other deathsman. Let us see.
255 Leave, gentle wax and manners: blame us not
256 To know our enemies' minds. We rip their hearts;
257 Their papers is more lawful.
Reads the letter.

'Let our reciprocal vows be remembered. You have
259 many opportunities to cut him off. If your will want not,
time and place will be fruitfully offered. There is nothing done, if he return the conqueror. Then am I the
262 prisoner, and his bed my gaol; from the loathed warmth
whereof deliver me, and supply the place for your labor.

264   'Your (wife, so I would say) affectionate servant,
'Goneril.'

266 O indistinguished space of woman's will —
A plot upon her virtuous husband's life,
268 And the exchange my brother! Here in the sands

---

244 *letters* letter; *about* upon   246 *party* side   248 *serviceable* usable   249
duteous ready to serve   254 *deathsman* executioner   255 *Leave, gentle wax*
by your leave, kind seal (formula used in opening sealed documents)   256
To know i.e. for growing intimate with   257 *Their papers* i.e. to rip their
papers   259 *want not* is not lacking   262 *gaol* jail   264 *would* wish to   266
indistinguished unlimited; *will* desire   268 *exchange* substitute

Thee I'll rake up, the post unsanctified   269
Of murderous lechers; and in the mature time   270
With this ungracious paper strike the sight   271
Of the death-practiced Duke. For him 'tis well   272
That of thy death and business I can tell.

GLOUCESTER
The King is mad. How stiff is my vile sense,   274
That I stand up, and have ingenious feeling   275
Of my huge sorrows! Better I were distract;   276
So should my thoughts be severed from my griefs,
And woes by wrong imaginations lose   278
The knowledge of themselves.
        Drum afar off.

EDGAR   Give me your hand.
Far off methinks I hear the beaten drum.
Come, father, I'll bestow you with a friend.   *Exeunt.* 281

*

Enter Cordelia, Kent, [Doctor,] and Gentleman.   IV, vii

CORDELIA
O thou good Kent, how shall I live and work
To match thy goodness? My life will be too short
And every measure fail me.

KENT
To be acknowledged, madam, is o'erpaid.
All my reports go with the modest truth;   5
Nor more nor clipped, but so.   6

CORDELIA   Be better suited.
These weeds are memories of those worser hours.   7
I prithee put them off.

269 *rake up* cover, bury 270 *in the mature* at the ripe 271 *strike* blast
272 *death-practiced* whose death is plotted 274 *stiff* obstinate; *vile sense*
i.e. hateful consciousness 275 *ingenious feeling* i.e. awareness 276
distract distracted 278 *wrong imaginations* i.e. delusions 281 *bestow*
lodge
IV, vii The French camp near Dover 5 *go conform* 6 *clipped* i.e. less
(curtailed); *suited* attired 7 *weeds* clothes; *memories* reminders

KENT   Pardon, dear madam.
9   Yet to be known shortens my made intent.
10 My boon I make it that you know me not
11 Till time and I think meet.

CORDELIA
    Then be't so, my good lord.
        [To the Doctor]   How does the King?

DOCTOR
    Madam, sleeps still.

CORDELIA
    O you kind gods,
15 Cure this great breach in his abusèd nature!
16 Th' untuned and jarring senses, O, wind up
17 Of this child-changèd father!

DOCTOR   So please your Majesty
    That we may wake the King? He hath slept long.

CORDELIA
    Be governed by your knowledge, and proceed
20 I' th' sway of your own will. Is he arrayed?
        Enter Lear in a chair carried by Servants.

GENTLEMAN
    Ay, madam. In the heaviness of sleep
    We put fresh garments on him.

DOCTOR
    Be by, good madam, when we do awake him.
    I doubt not of his temperance.

[CORDELIA   Very well.
        [Music.]

DOCTOR
    Please you draw near. Louder the music there.]

---

9 *Yet . . . intent* i.e. to reveal myself just yet would mar my plan   10 *My boon
. . . it* the reward I ask is   11 *meet* proper   15 *abusèd* confused, disturbed
16 *jarring* discordant; *wind up* tune   17 *child-changèd* (1) changed to a
child, (2) changed by his children (suggesting 'changeling,' wherein
mental defect is associated with the malignance of witches)   20 *I' th'
sway of* according to

CORDELIA
> O my dear father, restoration hang
> Thy medicine on my lips, and let this kiss
> Repair those violent harms that my two sisters   28
> Have in thy reverence made.   29

KENT   Kind and dear princess.

CORDELIA
> Had you not been their father, these white flakes   30
> Did challenge pity of them. Was this a face   31
> To be opposed against the jarring winds?
> [To stand against the deep dread-bolted thunder?   33
> In the most terrible and nimble stroke
> Of quick cross lightning to watch, poor perdu,   35
> With this thin helm?] Mine enemy's dog,   36
> Though he had bit me, should have stood that night
> Against my fire; and wast thou fain, poor father,   38
> To hovel thee with swine and rogues forlorn
> In short and musty straw? Alack, alack,   40
> 'Tis wonder that thy life and wits at once
> Had not concluded all. – He wakes. Speak to him.

DOCTOR
> Madam, do you; 'tis fittest.

CORDELIA
> How does my royal lord? How fares your Majesty?

LEAR
> You do me wrong to take me out o' th' grave.
> Thou art a soul in bliss; but I am bound
> Upon a wheel of fire, that mine own tears   47
> Do scald like molten lead.

CORDELIA   Sir, do you know me?

---

28 *harms* wounds   **29** *reverence* reverend person   **30** *flakes* strands of hair
31 *challenge* demand   **33** *deep dread-bolted* deep-voiced and full of
dreadful bolts   **35** *perdu* (1) expendable outpost (military term), (2)
lost one   **36** *helm* military helmet; here, thin hair   **38** *fain* glad   **40**
short scanty (?), tramped to fragments (?)   **47** *wheel of fire* (implement
combining the tortures of breaking and burning, figuring in medieval
visions of hell)

LEAR

You are a spirit, I know. Where did you die?

CORDELIA

50   Still, still, far wide!

DOCTOR

He's scarce awake. Let him alone awhile.

LEAR

Where have I been? Where am I? Fair daylight?

53   I am mightily abused. I should e'en die with pity
To see another thus. I know not what to say.
I will not swear these are my hands. Let's see —
I feel this pin prick. Would I were assured
Of my condition.

CORDELIA   O look upon me, sir,
And hold your hand in benediction o'er me.
You must not kneel.

LEAR   Pray, do not mock me.

60   I am a very foolish fond old man,
Fourscore and upward, not an hour more nor less;
And, to deal plainly,
I fear I am not in my perfect mind.
Methinks I should know you, and know this man;
Yet I am doubtful, for I am mainly ignorant
What place this is; and all the skill I have
Remembers not these garments; nor I know not
Where I did lodge last night. Do not laugh at me;
For, as I am a man, I think this lady
To be my child Cordelia.

70 **CORDELIA**   And so I am! I am!

LEAR

Be your tears wet? Yes, faith. I pray weep not.
If you have poison for me, I will drink it.
I know you do not love me; for your sisters
Have (as I do remember) done me wrong.
You have some cause, they have not.

50 *wide* off the mark   53 *abused* confused

CORDELIA   No cause, no cause.

LEAR
  Am I in France?

KENT   In your own kingdom, sir.

LEAR
  Do not abuse me.   77

DOCTOR
  Be comforted, good madam. The great rage
  You see is killed in him; [and yet it is danger
  To make him even o'er the time he has lost.]   80
  Desire him to go in. Trouble him no more
  Till further settling.   82

CORDELIA
  Will't please your Highness walk?

LEAR   You must bear with me.
  Pray you now, forget and forgive. I am old and foolish.
                    Exeunt. [Manent Kent and Gentleman.]

[GENTLEMAN Holds it true, sir, that the Duke of Cornwall was so slain?

KENT Most certain, sir.

GENTLEMAN Who is conductor of his people?

KENT As 'tis said, the bastard son of Gloucester.

GENTLEMAN They say Edgar, his banished son, is with
  the Earl of Kent in Germany.

KENT Report is changeable. 'Tis time to look about; the
  powers of the kingdom approach apace.   93

GENTLEMAN The arbitrement is like to be bloody. Fare   94
  you well, sir.   *[Exit.]*

KENT
  My point and period will be throughly wrought,   96
  Or well or ill, as this day's battle 's fought. *Exit.]* 97

                        *

77 *abuse* deceive 80 *even o'er* fill in 82 *settling* calming 93 *powers*
armies 94 *arbitrement* decisive action 96 *My point . . . wrought* i.e. my
destiny will be completely worked out 97 *Or* either

                        147

V, i   *Enter, with Drum and Colors, Edmund, Regan,*
          Gentleman, and Soldiers.

EDMUND

1   Know of the Duke if his last purpose hold,
2   Or whether since he is advised by aught
     To change the course. He's full of alteration
4   And self-reproving. Bring his constant pleasure.

                                    [Exit an Officer.]

REGAN

5   Our sister's man is certainly miscarried.

EDMUND

6   'Tis to be doubted, madam.

REGAN   Now, sweet lord,

7   You know the goodness I intend upon you.
     Tell me, but truly – but then speak the truth –
     Do you not love my sister?

9 EDMUND   In honored love.

REGAN

     But have you never found my brother's way
11   To the forfended place?

[EDMUND   That thought abuses you.

REGAN

12   I am doubtful that you have been conjunct
     And bosomed with her, as far as we call hers.]

EDMUND

     No, by mine honor, madam.

REGAN

     I never shall endure her. Dear my lord,
     Be not familiar with her.

EDMUND   Fear me not.
     She and the Duke her husband!

V, i An open place near the British camp   **s.d.** *Drum and Colors* drummer
and standard-bearers   **1** *Know* learn; *last purpose hold* most recent intention
(i.e. to fight) holds good   **2** *advised* induced   **4** *constant pleasure* firm
decision   **5** *miscarried* met with mishap   **6** *doubted* feared   **7** *goodness I*
intend boon I plan to confer   **9** *honored* honorable   **11** *forfended* forbidden; *abuses* deceives   **12–13** *doubtful . . . hers* i.e. fearful you have been
intimately linked with her both in mind and body

Enter, with Drum and Colors, Albany, Goneril,
   Soldiers.

[GONERIL [*aside*]
   I had rather lose the battle than that sister
   Should loosen him and me.]   19

ALBANY
   Our very loving sister, well bemet.   20
   Sir, this I heard : the King is come to his daughter,
   With others whom the rigor of our state   22
   Forced to cry out. [Where I could not be honest,   23
   I never yet was valiant. For this business,
   It touches us as France invades our land,   25
   Not bolds the King with others, whom I fear   26
   Most just and heavy causes make oppose.

EDMUND
   Sir, you speak nobly.]

REGAN   Why is this reasoned ?   28

GONERIL
   Combine together 'gainst the enemy ;
   For these domestic and particular broils   30
   Are not the question here.   31

ALBANY   Let's then determine
   With th' ancient of war on our proceeding.   32

[EDMUND
   I shall attend you presently at your tent.]   33

REGAN
   Sister, you'll go with us ?

GONERIL No.

REGAN
   'Tis most convenient. Pray go with us.   36

19 *loosen* separate 20 *bemet* met 22 *rigor* tyranny 13 *honest* honorable
25 *touches us as* concerns me because 26–27 *Not bolds . . . oppose* i.e. but
not because he supports the King and others whose truly great grievances
arouse them to arms 28 *reasoned* argued 30 *particular broils* private
quarrels 31 *question* issue 32 *th' ancient of war* i.e. seasoned officers
33 *presently* immediately 36 *convenient* fitting; *with us* (i.e. with her rather
than Edmund as each leads an 'army' from the stage)

GONERIL

37   O ho, I know the riddle. – I will go.

Exeunt both the Armies.

Enter Edgar.

EDGAR *[to Albany]*

38   If e'er your Grace had speech with man so poor,
Hear me one word.

ALBANY *[to those departing]*

I'll overtake you. *[to Edgar]* Speak.

EDGAR

Before you fight the battle, ope this letter.

41   If you have victory, let the trumpet sound
For him that brought it. Wretched though I seem,

43   I can produce a champion that will prove

44   What is avouchèd there. If you miscarry,
Your business of the world hath so an end,

46   And machination ceases. Fortune love you.

ALBANY

Stay till I have read the letter.

EDGAR   I was forbid it.
When time shall serve, let but the herald cry,
And I'll appear again.

ALBANY

50   Why, fare thee well. I will o'erlook thy paper.

Exit [Edgar].

Enter Edmund.

EDMUND

51   The enemy's in view; draw up your powers.

52   Here is the guess of their true strength and forces

53   By diligent discovery; but your haste
Is now urged on you.

54   ALBANY   We will greet the time.   *Exit.*

---

37 *riddle* (i.e. the reason for Regan's strange demand)   38 *had speech* i.e. has condescended to speak   41 *sound* sound a summons   43 *prove* (in trial by combat)   44 *avouchèd* charged   46 *machination* i.e. all plots and counterplots   50 *o'erlook* look over   51 *powers* troops   52 *guess* estimate 53 *discovery* reconnoitering   54 *greet* i.e. meet the demands of

EDMUND

To both these sisters have I sworn my love;
Each jealous of the other, as the stung   56
Are of the adder. Which of them shall I take?
Both? One? Or neither? Neither can be enjoyed,
If both remain alive. To take the widow
Exasperates, makes mad her sister Goneril;
And hardly shall I carry out my side,   61
Her husband being alive. Now then, we'll use
His countenance for the battle, which being done, 63
Let her who would be rid of him devise
His speedy taking off. As for the mercy
Which he intends to Lear and to Cordelia –
The battle done, and they within our power,
Shall never see his pardon; for my state   68
Stands on me to defend, not to debate.   *Exit.*

*

           Alarum within. Enter, with Drum and Colors, Lear,   V, ii
           [held by the hand by] Cordelia; and Soldiers [of
           France], over the stage and exeunt.
           Enter Edgar and Gloucester.

EDGAR

Here, father, take the shadow of this tree
For your good host. Pray that the right may thrive.
If ever I return to you again,
I'll bring you comfort.
GLOUCESTER   Grace go with you, sir.   4
                                     Exit [Edgar].
        Alarum and retreat within. Enter Edgar.

56 *jealous* suspicious   61 *hardly . . . side* with difficulty shall I play my part
(as Goneril's lover, or as a great power in England?)   63 *countenance*
backing   68–69 *my state . . . debate* i.e. my status depends upon my strength,
not my arguments
V, ii An open place near the field of battle   4 s.d. *Alarum and retreat*
(trumpet sounds, signalling the beginning and the ending of a battle)

EDGAR

Away, old man ! Give me thy hand. Away !
6   King Lear hath lost, he and his daughter ta'en.
Give me thy hand. Come on.

GLOUCESTER

8   No further, sir. A man may rot even here.

EDGAR

9   What, in ill thoughts again ? Men must endure
Their going hence, even as their coming hither ;
11   Ripeness is all. Come on.

GLOUCESTER   And that's true too.   *Exeunt.*

V, iii   *Enter, on conquest, with Drum and Colors, Edmund ;*
Lear and Cordelia as prisoners ; Soldiers, Captain.

EDMUND

Some officers take them away. Good guard
2   Until their greater pleasures first be known
3   That are to censure them.

CORDELIA   We are not the first
4   Who with best meaning have incurred the worst.
For thee, oppressèd king, I am cast down ;
Myself could else outfrown false Fortune's frown.
Shall we not see these daughters and these sisters ?

LEAR

No, no, no, no ! Come, let's away to prison.
We two alone will sing like birds i' th' cage.
10   When thou dost ask me blessing, I'll kneel down
And ask of thee forgiveness. So we'll live,
12   And pray, and sing, and tell old tales, and laugh
At gilded butterflies, and hear poor rogues
Talk of court news ; and we'll talk with them too –
Who loses and who wins ; who's in, who's out –

6 *ta'en* captured 8 *rot* i.e. die 9 *ill* i.e. suicidal; *endure* put up with,
suffer through 11 *Ripeness* i.e. the time decreed by the gods for the fruit
to fall from the branch
V, iii 2 *greater pleasures* i.e. the desires of those in higher command
3 *censure* judge 4 *meaning* intentions 10-11 *When . . . forgiveness* (cf.
IV, vii, 57–59) 12-14 *laugh . . . news* view with amusement bright
ephemera, such as gallants preoccupied with court gossip

And take upon 's the mystery of things   16
As if we were God's spies ; and we'll wear out,   17
In a walled prison, packs and sects of great ones   18
That ebb and flow by th' moon.
EDMUND   Take them away.
LEAR
Upon such sacrifices, my Cordelia,   20
The gods themselves throw incense. Have I caught thee ?
He that parts us shall bring a brand from heaven   22
And fire us hence like foxes. Wipe thine eyes.
The goodyears shall devour them, flesh and fell,   24
Ere they shall make us weep ! We'll see 'em starved first.
Come.   *Exeunt [Lear and Cordelia, guarded].*
EDMUND Come hither, captain ; hark.
Take thou this note.
       [Gives a paper.] Go follow them to prison.
One step I have advanced thee. If thou dost
As this instructs thee, thou dost make thy way
To noble fortunes. Know thou this, that men
Are as the time is. To be tender-minded   31
Does not become a sword. Thy great employment   32
Will not bear question. Either say thou'lt do't,   33
Or thrive by other means.
CAPTAIN   I'll do't, my lord.
EDMUND
About it ; and write happy when th' hast done.   35
Mark, I say instantly, and carry it so
As I have set it down.

16–17 *take . . . spies* i.e. contemplate the wonder of existence as if with divine
insight, seek eternal rather than temporal truths   17 *wear out* outlast
18–19 *packs . . . moon* i.e. partisan and intriguing clusters of *great ones* who
gain and lose power monthly   20–21 *Upon . . . incense* i.e. the gods themselves are the celebrants at such sacrificial offerings to love as we are
22–23 *He . . . foxes* i.e. to separate us, as foxes are smoked out and scattered,
would require not a human but a heavenly torch   24 *goodyears* (un-
defined forces of evil); *fell* hide   31 *as the time is* (i.e. ruthless in war)
32 *become* befit   33 *bear question* admit discussion   35 *write happy*
consider yourself fortunate

[CAPTAIN
    I cannot draw a cart, nor eat dried oats –
    If it be man's work, I'll do't.]   *Exit*
      Flourish. Enter Albany, Goneril, Regan, Soldiers.

ALBANY
    Sir, you have showed to-day your valiant strain,
    And fortune led you well. You have the captives
42 Who were the opposites of this day's strife.
    I do require them of you, so to use them
44 As we shall find their merits and our safety
    May equally determine.

EDMUND   Sir, I thought it fit
    To send the old and miserable King
47 To some retention [and appointed guard];
    Whose age had charms in it, whose title more,
49 To pluck the common bosom on his side
50 And turn our impressed lances in our eyes
    Which do command them. With him I sent the Queen,
    My reason all the same ; and they are ready
53 To-morrow, or at further space, t' appear
54 Where you shall hold your session. [At this time
    We sweat and bleed, the friend hath lost his friend,
56 And the best quarrels, in the heat, are cursed
57 By those that feel their sharpness.
    The question of Cordelia and her father
    Requires a fitter place.]

ALBANY   Sir, by your patience,
60 I hold you but a subject of this war,
    Not as a brother.

61 REGAN   That's as we list to grace him.
    Methinks our pleasure might have been demanded
    Ere you had spoke so far. He led our powers,

---

42 *opposites of* enemies in   44 *merits* deserts   47 *some . . . guard* detention
under duly appointed guards   49 *pluck . . . bosom* draw popular sympathy
50 *turn . . . eyes* i.e. make our conscripted lancers turn on us   53 *space*
interval   54 *session* trials   56 *best quarrels* worthiest causes   57 *sharpness*
i.e. painful effects   60 *subject of* subordinate in   61 *list to grace* please to
honor

Bore the commission of my place and person,
The which immediacy may well stand up   65
And call itself your brother.

GONERIL   Not so hot!
In his own grace he doth exalt himself
More than in your addition.   68

REGAN   In my rights
By me invested, he compeers the best.   69

ALBANY
That were the most if he should husband you.   70

REGAN
Jesters do oft prove prophets.

GONERIL   Holla, holla!
That eye that told you so looked but asquint. 72

REGAN
Lady, I am not well; else I should answer
From a full-flowing stomach. General,   74
Take thou my soldiers, prisoners, patrimony;   75
Dispose of them, of me; the walls is thine.   76
Witness the world that I create thee here
My lord and master.

GONERIL   Mean you to enjoy him?

ALBANY
The let-alone lies not in your good will.   79

EDMUND
Nor in thine, lord.

ALBANY   Half-blooded fellow, yes.   80

REGAN [to Edmund]
Let the drum strike, and prove my title thine. 81

ALBANY
Stay yet; hear reason. Edmund, I arrest thee

65 *immediacy* i.e. present status (as my deputy) 68 *your addition* honors
conferred by you 69 *compeers* equals 70 *most* i.e. most complete investi-
ture in your rights; *husband* wed 72 *asquint* cross-eyed, crookedly 74
stomach anger 75 *patrimony* inheritance 76 *walls is thine* i.e. you have
stormed the citadel (myself) 79 *let-alone* permission 80 *Half-blooded*
i.e. by birth only half noble 81 *Let . . . thine* i.e. fight and win for yourself
my rights in the kingdom

83   On capital treason ; and, in thy attaint,
       This gilded serpent.
              [Points to Goneril.] For your claim, fair sister,
       I bar it in the interest of my wife.
86   'Tis she is subcontracted to this lord,
87   And I, her husband, contradict your banes.
88   If you will marry, make your loves to me ;
       My lady is bespoke.

89 GONERIL   An interlude !

    ALBANY
       Thou art armed, Gloucester. Let the trumpet sound.
       If none appear to prove upon thy person
       Thy heinous, manifest, and many treasons,
       There is my pledge.
93   *[Throws down a glove.]* I'll make it on thy heart,
94   Ere I taste bread, thou art in nothing less
       Than I have here proclaimed thee.

    REGAN   Sick, O sick !

    GONERIL *[aside]*
96   If not, I'll ne'er trust medicine.

    EDMUND
       There's my exchange.
              [Throws down a glove.] What in the world he is
       That names me traitor, villain-like he lies.
99   Call by the trumpet. He that dares approach,
       On him, on you, who not ? I will maintain
       My truth and honor firmly.

    ALBANY
       A herald, ho !

    [EDMUND   A herald, ho, a herald !]

83 *in thy attaint* i.e. as party to your corruption (cf. the *serpent* of Eden)
86 *subcontracted* i.e. engaged, though previously married (sarcastic play on
'precontracted,' a legal term applied to one facing an impediment to
marriage because previously engaged to another) 87 *contradict your banes*
forbid your banns, i.e. declare an impediment 88 *loves* love-suits 89 *An
interlude* a quaint playlet (equivalent to saying 'How dramatic!' or 'How
comical!') 93 *make* prove 94 *nothing less* i.e. no respect less guilty 96
medicine i.e. poison 99 *trumpet* trumpeter

ALBANY
  Trust to thy single virtue; for thy soldiers,   103
  All levied in my name, have in my name
  Took their discharge.

REGAN   My sickness grows upon me.

ALBANY
  She is not well. Convey her to my tent.

                         [Exit Regan, attended.]

    Enter a Herald.

  Come hither, herald. Let the trumpet sound,
  And read out this.

[CAPTAIN Sound, trumpet!]

    A trumpet sounds.

HERALD *(reads)* 'If any man of quality or degree within   110
  the lists of the army will maintain upon Edmund, sup-   111
  posed Earl of Gloucester, that he is a manifold traitor,
  let him appear by the third sound of the trumpet. He is
  bold in his defense.'

[EDMUND Sound!]

    First trumpet.

HERALD Again!

    Second trumpet.

  Again!

    Third trumpet.

    Trumpet answers within.

    Enter Edgar, armed [at the third sound, a Trumpeter
    before him].

ALBANY
  Ask him his purposes, why he appears
  Upon this call o' th' trumpet.

HERALD   What are you?
  Your name, your quality, and why you answer
  This present summons?

EDGAR   Know my name is lost,
  By treason's tooth bare-gnawn and canker-bit;   122

103 *single virtue* unaided prowess 110 *degree* rank 111 *lists* muster
122 *canker-bit* eaten, as by the rose-caterpillar

Yet am I noble as the adversary
I come to cope.

ALBANY   Which is that adversary?

EDGAR
What's he that speaks for Edmund Earl of Gloucester?

EDMUND
Himself. What say'st thou to him?

EDGAR   Draw thy sword.
That, if my speech offend a noble heart,
Thy arm may do thee justice. Here is mine.

129   Behold it is my privilege,
The privilege of mine honors,
My oath, and my profession. I protest –

132   Maugre thy strength, place, youth, and eminence,
133   Despite thy victor sword and fire-new fortune,
134   Thy valor and thy heart – thou art a traitor,
False to thy gods, thy brother, and thy father,
136   Conspirant 'gainst this high illustrious prince,
137   And from th' extremest upward of thy head
138   To the descent and dust below thy foot
139   A most toad-spotted traitor. Say thou 'no,'
140   This sword, this arm, and my best spirits are bent
To prove upon thy heart, whereto I speak,
Thou liest.

142   EDMUND   In wisdom I should ask thy name,
But since thy outside looks so fair and warlike,
144   And that thy tongue some say of breeding breathes,
145   What safe and nicely I might well delay
By rule of knighthood I disdain and spurn.
147   Back do I toss these treasons to thy head,

129–31 *it . . . profession* i.e. wielding this sword is the privilege of my knightly honor, oath, and function **132** *Maugre* in spite of **133** *fire-new* brand-new **134** *heart* courage **136** *Conspirant* in conspiracy **137** *extremest upward* uppermost extreme **138** *descent and dust* i.e. all that intervenes from the head to the dust **139** *toad-spotted* i.e. exuding venom like a toad **140** *bent* directed **142** *wisdom* prudence **144** *some say* some assay, i.e. proof (?), one might say (?) **145** *safe and nicely* cautiously and punctiliously **147** *treasons* accusations of treason

With the hell-hated lie o'erwhelm thy heart,   148
Which – for they yet glance by and scarcely bruise – 149
This sword of mine shall give them instant way
Where they shall rest for ever. Trumpets, speak!
    Alarums. Fight. [Edmund falls.]

ALBANY
Save him, save him.   152

GONERIL   This is practice, Gloucester.
By th' law of war thou wast not bound to answer
An unknown opposite. Thou art not vanquished,
But cozened and beguiled.   155

ALBANY   Shut your mouth, dame,
Or with this paper shall I stop it. – Hold, sir. –   156
    [To Goneril]
Thou worse than any name, read thine own evil.
No tearing, lady! I perceive you know it.

GONERIL
Say if I do – the laws are mine, not thine.
Who can arraign me for't?   159

ALBANY   Most monstrous! O,
Know'st thou this paper?

GONERIL   Ask me not what I know. *Exit.*

ALBANY
Go after her. She's desperate; govern her.   162
                              [Exit an Officer.]

EDMUND
What you have charged me with, that have I done,
And more, much more. The time will bring it out.
'Tis past, and so am I. – But what art thou
That hast this fortune on me? If thou'rt noble,   166
I do forgive thee.

---

148 *hell-hated* hateful as hell   **149–51** *Which . . . ever* i.e. the accusations of
treason, now flying about harmlessly, will be routed into you with my sword-
thrust and lodge there permanently   **152** *Save him* spare him (cf. l. 156);
practice trickery   **155** *cozened* cheated   **156** *Hold* wait (If addressed to
Edmund, this suggests a motive for the *Save him* of l. 152: i.e. Albany hopes
to obtain a confession.)   **159** *mine* (i.e. as ruler)   **162** *govern* control   **166**
fortune on i.e. victory over

167 EDGAR   Let's exchange charity.
    I am no less in blood than thou art, Edmund;
169 If more, the more th' hast wronged me.
    My name is Edgar and thy father's son.
171 The gods are just, and of our pleasant vices
    Make instruments to plague us.
173 The dark and vicious place where thee he got
    Cost him his eyes.
    EDMUND   Th' hast spoken right; 'tis true.
175 The wheel is come full circle; I am here.
    ALBANY
176 Methought thy very gait did prophesy
    A royal nobleness. I must embrace thee.
    Let sorrow split my heart if ever I
    Did hate thee, or thy father.
    EDGAR   Worthy prince, I know't.
    ALBANY
    Where have you hid yourself?
    How have you known the miseries of your father?
    EDGAR
    By nursing them, my lord. List a brief tale;
    And when 'tis told, O that my heart would burst!
    The bloody proclamation to escape
185 That followed me so near (O our lives' sweetness,
    That we the pain of death would hourly die
    Rather than die at once!) taught me to shift
    Into a madman's rags, t' assume a semblance
189 That very dogs disdained; and in this habit
190 Met I my father with his bleeding rings,
    Their precious stones new lost; became his guide,
    Led him, begged for him, saved him from despair;

---

167 *charity* forgiveness and love   169 *If more* if greater (since legitimate)
171 *of our pleasant* out of our pleasurable   173 *place* i.e. the bed of adultery;
got begot   175 *wheel* (of fortune); *here* (at its bottom)   176 *prophesy*
promise   185–86 *O . . . die* i.e. how sweet is life that we would prefer to
suffer death-pangs hourly   189 *habit* attire   190 *rings* sockets

Never – O fault ! – revealed myself unto him
Until some half hour past, when I was armed,   194
Not sure, though hoping of this good success,
I asked his blessing, and from first to last
Told him our pilgrimage. But his flawed heart –   197
Alack, too weak the conflict to support –
'Twixt two extremes of passion, joy and grief,
Burst smilingly.

EDMUND   This speech of yours hath moved me,
And shall perchance do good ; but speak you on –
You look as you had something more to say.

ALBANY
If there be more, more woeful, hold it in,
For I am almost ready to dissolve,   204
Hearing of this.

[EDGAR   This would have seemed a period   205
To such as love not sorrow ; but another,   206
To amplify too much, would make much more,
And top extremity.
Whilst I was big in clamor, came there in a man,   209
Who, having seen me in my worst estate,   210
Shunned my abhorred society ; but then, finding
Who 'twas that so endured, with his strong arms
He fastened on my neck, and bellowed out
As he'd burst heaven, threw him on my father,
Told the most piteous tale of Lear and him
That ever ear received ; which in recounting
His grief grew puissant, and the strings of life   217
Began to crack. Twice then the trumpets sounded,
And there I left him tranced.   219

ALBANY   But who was this ?

194 *armed* in armor 197 *our pilgrimage* of our journey; *flawed* cracked
204 *dissolve* melt into tears 205 *a period* the limit 206–08 *another . . .
extremity* i.e. another sorrow, too fully described, would exceed the limit
209 *big in clamor* loud in lamentation 210 *estate* state 217 *puissant*
powerful 219 *tranced* insensible

EDGAR
    Kent, sir, the banished Kent; who in disguise
221   Followed his enemy king and did him service
    Improper for a slave.]
            Enter a Gentleman [with a bloody knife].
GENTLEMAN
    Help, help! O, help!
EDGAR   What kind of help?
ALBANY   Speak, man.
EDGAR
    What means this bloody knife?
224 GENTLEMAN   'Tis hot, it smokes.
    It came even from the heart of – O, she's dead.
ALBANY
    Who dead? Speak, man.
GENTLEMAN
    Your lady, sir, your lady; and her sister
    By her is poisonèd; she confesses it.
EDMUND
229   I was contracted to them both. All three
230   Now marry in an instant.
EDGAR   Here comes Kent.
        Enter Kent.
ALBANY
    Produce the bodies, be they alive or dead.
                            [Exit Gentleman.]
    This judgment of the heavens, that makes us tremble,
    Touches us not with pity. – O, is this he?
234   The time will not allow the compliment
235   Which very manners urges.
KENT   I am come
    To bid my king and master aye good night.
    Is he not here?

---

221 *enemy* inimical **224** *smokes* steams **229** *contracted* engaged **230**
marry (i.e. in death) **234** *compliment* ceremony **235** *very manners* i.e.
sheer decency

ALBANY   Great thing of us forgot! 237
   Speak, Edmund, where's the King? and where's
     Cordelia?
     Goneril and Regan's bodies brought out.
   Seest thou this object, Kent? 239

KENT
   Alack, why thus?

EDMUND   Yet Edmund was beloved. 240
   The one the other poisoned for my sake,
   And after slew herself.

ALBANY
   Even so. Cover their faces.

EDMUND
   I pant for life. Some good I mean to do, 244
   Despite of mine own nature. Quickly send –
   Be brief in it – to th' castle, for my writ 246
   Is on the life of Lear and on Cordelia.
   Nay, send in time.

ALBANY   Run, run, O run!

EDGAR
   To who, my lord? Who has the office? Send 249
   Thy token of reprieve.

EDMUND
   Well thought on. Take my sword;
   Give it the captain.

EDGAR   Haste thee for thy life. *[Exit Officer.]*

EDMUND
   He hath commission from thy wife and me
   To hang Cordelia in the prison and
   To lay the blame upon her own despair
   That she fordid herself. 256

ALBANY
   The gods defend her! Bear him hence awhile.
                       [Edmund is borne off.]

---

237 *thing* matter; *of* by **239** *object* sight **240** *Yet* despite all **244** *pant for life* i.e. gasp for life's breath **246** *writ* i.e. order of execution **249** *office* commission **256** *fordid* destroyed

*Enter Lear, with Cordelia in his arms [, Gentleman,
and others following].*

LEAR
Howl, howl, howl! O, you are men of stones.
Had I your tongues and eyes, I'ld use them so
That heaven's vault should crack. She's gone for ever.
I know when one is dead, and when one lives.
She's dead as earth. Lend me a looking glass.
263 If that her breath will mist or stain the stone,
Why then she lives.

264 **KENT**   Is this the promised end?

EDGAR
265 Or image of that horror?

ALBANY   Fall and cease.

LEAR
This feather stirs; she lives! If it be so,
267 It is a chance which does redeem all sorrows
That ever I have felt.

KENT   O my good master.

LEAR
Prithee away.

EDGAR   'Tis noble Kent, your friend.

LEAR
A plague upon you murderers, traitors all;
I might have saved her; now she's gone for ever.
Cordelia, Cordelia, stay a little. Ha,
What is't thou say'st? Her voice was ever soft,
Gentle, and low – an excellent thing in woman.
I killed the slave that was a-hanging thee.

GENTLEMAN
'Tis true, my lords, he did.

LEAR   Did I not, fellow?
277 I have seen the day, with my good biting falchion
I would have made them skip. I am old now,

---

263 *stone* i.e. glass   264 *promised end* i.e. doomsday   265 *image* duplicate;
Fall and cease i.e. strike once and for all, make an end of things   267
redeem atone for   277 *falchion* small sword slightly hooked

And these same crosses spoil me. Who are you?   279
Mine eyes are not o' th' best, I'll tell you straight.   280

KENT

If Fortune brag of two she loved and hated,   281
One of them we behold.

LEAR

This is a dull sight. Are you not Kent?   283

KENT   The same:
Your servant Kent; where is your servant Caius?   284

LEAR

He's a good fellow, I can tell you that.
He'll strike, and quickly too. He's dead and rotten.

KENT

No, my good lord; I am the very man.

LEAR

I'll see that straight.   288

KENT

That from your first of difference and decay   289
Have followed your sad steps.

LEAR   You are welcome hither.

KENT

Nor no man else. All's cheerless, dark, and deadly.   291
Your eldest daughters have fordone themselves,   292
And desperately are dead.   293

LEAR   Ay, so I think.

ALBANY

He knows not what he says; and vain is it
That we present us to him.

EDGAR   Very bootless.   295

---

279 *crosses* adversities; *spoil me* i.e. sap my strength   **280** *tell you straight* admit (?), recognize you in a moment (?)   **281** *two* (i.e. Lear, and a hypothetical second extreme example of Fortune's cruelty with whom he may be equated); *loved and hated* i.e. favored, then victimized   **283** *sight* eyesight (instinctively Lear shuns the admission that he is dazed and weeping) **284** *Caius* (Kent's alias)   **288** *see that straight* understand that in a moment **289** *difference and decay* change and decline in fortune   **291** *Nor no man else* i.e. no, nor anyone else   **292** *fordone* destroyed   **293** *desperately* in a state of despair   **295** *bootless* useless

Enter a Messenger.

MESSENGER
Edmund is dead, my lord.

ALBANY   That's but a trifle here.
You lords and noble friends, know our intent.
298   What comfort to this great decay may come
Shall be applied. For us, we will resign,
During the life of this old Majesty,
To him our absolute power; *[to Edgar and Kent]* you to
    your rights,
302   With boot and such addition as your honors
Have more than merited. All friends shall taste
The wages of their virtue, and all foes
The cup of their deservings. – O, see, see!

LEAR
306   And my poor fool is hanged: no, no, no life?
Why should a dog, a horse, a rat, have life,
And thou no breath at all? Thou'lt come no more,
Never, never, never, never, never.
Pray you undo this button. Thank you, sir.
Do you see this? Look on her! Look her lips,
Look there, look there –
    He dies.

EDGAR   He faints. My lord, my lord –
KENT
Break, heart, I prithee break!

EDGAR   Look up, my lord.
KENT
314   Vex not his ghost. O, let him pass! He hates him
315   That would upon the rack of this tough world
Stretch him out longer.

EDGAR   He is gone indeed.

298 *What . . . come* i.e. whatever means of aiding this ruined great one
presents itself 302 *boot* good measure; *addition* titles, advancement in
rank 306 *fool* i.e. Cordelia ('Fool' was often a term of affection, and sometimes, as in Erasmus and elsewhere in Shakespeare, of praise – an ironic
commentary upon self-seeking 'worldly wisdom.') 314 *Vex . . . ghost* do
not trouble his departing spirit 315 *rack* instrument of torture

KENT

The wonder is he hath endured so long ;
He but usurped his life.   318

ALBANY

Bear them from hence. Our present business
Is general woe.
        [To Kent and Edgar] Friends of my soul, you twain
Rule in this realm, and the gored state sustain.

KENT

I have a journey, sir, shortly to go.
My master calls me ; I must not say no.

EDGAR

The weight of this sad time we must obey,   324
Speak what we feel, not what we ought to say.
The oldest hath borne most ; we that are young
Shall never see so much, nor live so long.
                            Exeunt with a dead march.

318 *usurped* possessed contrary to (natural) law   324 *obey* i.e. accept

APPENDIX: THE QUARTO TEXT

The present edition, as explained in the "Note on the text," adheres closely to the folio version of the play. The quarto version, although inferior in the main, is of great literary interest. The essential material for a comparison of the verbal features of the two versions is here supplied.

Mechanically, the quarto text is very defective: stage directions are often lacking and the speakers are confusingly designated; the punctuation is bad; and the verse is often printed as prose, the prose as verse. Omitted from the quarto but included in the folio are passages totalling approximately 100 lines, appearing in the present edition at the following points:

I, i, 40–45 *while . . . now*   49–50 *Since . . . state*   64–65 *and . . .*
   rivers   83–85 *to whose . . . interest*   88–89 *Nothing . . . Nothing*
   162 *Dear sir, forbear*
I, ii 107–12 *This villain . . . graves*   160–65 *I pray . . . brother*
I, iv, 252 *Pray . . . patient*   265 *Of . . . you*   313–24 *This man . . .*
   Oswald
II, iv, 6 *No, my lord*   21 *By Juno . . . ay*   45–53 *Winter's . . . year*
   93–94 *Well . . . man*   98 *Are . . . blood*   135–40 *Say . . . blame*
   291–92 *Whither . . . horse*
III, i, 22–29 *Who have . . . furnishings*
III, ii, 79–96 *This . . . time*
III, iv, 17–18 *In . . . endure*   26–27 *In, boy . . . sleep*   37–38
   Fathom . . . Tom
III, vi, 12–14 *No . . . him*   83 *And . . . noon*
IV, i, 6–9 *Welcome . . . blasts*
IV, ii, 25 *My . . . Gloucester*
IV, vi, 162–67 *Plate . . . lips*
V, ii, 11 *And . . . too*

V, iii, 76 *Dispose . . . thine* 89 *An interlude* 145 *What . . . delay*
223 *Speak, man* 311–12 *Do . . . there*

On the other hand, included in the quarto but omitted from the
folio are passages totalling approximately 283 lines – inserted in
square brackets in the present edition at the following points:

I, i, 104   I, ii, 93–95, 140–47   I, iii, 16–20, 24–25   I, iv, 133–48,
222–25, 248, 295   II, i, 78   II, ii, 136–40, 146   II, iv, 18–19
III, i, 7–15, 30–42   III, vi, 17–55, 95–99, 100–13   III, vii, 99–
107   IV, i, 58–63   IV, ii, 31–50, 53–59, 62–68, 69   IV, iii, 1–55
IV, vi, 194   IV, vii, 24–25, 33–36, 79–80, 85–97   V, i, 11–13,
18–19, 23–28, 33   V, iii, 38–39, 47, 54–59, 102, 109, 115, 205–22.

In addition, the following words in the present edition represent
insertions from the quarto: I, i, 214 *best*   289 *not*   I, ii, 127 *Fut*
129 *Edgar*   130 *and*   166 *Go armed*   II, i, 71 *ay*   II, iii, 15 *bare*
III, iv, 127 *had*   IV, vii, 24 *not*   V, i, 16 *me*

The wording of the quarto text differs from that of the folio
in hundreds of instances. In the present edition a quarto reading
has been substituted for a folio reading only when the latter makes
poor or obviously inferior sense. The list of such substitutions
follows, with the adopted quarto readings in italics followed by the
folio readings in roman. (In this appendix the readings of the
quarto as well as the folio are given in modern spelling.)

I, i, 5 *equalities* qualities   74 *possesses* professes   170 *sentence*
sentences   188 *Gloucester* Cordelia   206 *on* in   221 *Fall'n* Fall
225 *well* will   248 *respects of fortune* respect and fortunes   302
hit sit
I, iv, 1 *well* will   93 *Kent. Why, fool* Lear. Why, my boy   163 *e'er*
(from 'euer') ere   169 *fools* fool   194 *endurèd* endured   334
atasked at task
II, i, 70 *I should* should I   79 *why* where   87 *strange news* strangeness   115 *Natures* Nature's
II, ii, 21 *clamorous* clamors   70 *too* t'   73 *Renege* Revenge   74
gale gall   118 *dread* dead   125 *respect* respects
II, iv, 2 *messenger* messengers   30 *panting* painting   33 *whose*
those   126 *mother's* mother   181 *fickle* 'fickly'
III, ii, 3 *drowned* drown

III, iv, 52 *ford* sword   86 *deeply* dearly   109 *till the* at   126 *stock-punished* stocked, punished

III, v, 24 *dearer* dear

III, vi, 68 *tike* tight   75 *makes* make

IV, i, 41 *Then prithee get thee gone* Get thee away

IV, ii, 75 *thereat enraged* threat-enraged   79 *justicers* justices

IV, iv, 18 *distress* desires

IV, vi, 17 *walk* walked   71 *enridgèd* enragèd   83 *coining* crying   161 *small* great   201 *one* a

V, i, 46 *love* loves

V, iii, 83 *attaint* arrest   84 *sister* sisters   97 *he is* he's   161 *Goneril* Bastard (i.e. Edmund)   278 *them* him

Omitted from the above list are a few instances of variation in which a folio misprint would have been detectable without reference to the quarto. Omitted from the following list are numerous instances of slight variation between quarto and folio in the use of articles, prepositions, elision, number, tense, etc., in which the literary interest is small. In all such instances the folio has been followed in the present edition, as well as in the variations listed below. Here the adopted folio readings are in italics followed by the quarto readings in roman. The great majority of the latter are, by common consent, inferior, but while these cast suspicion upon all, the fact remains that a certain number are not inferior to the folio readings and may represent what Shakespeare actually wrote. Marked with stars are the quarto readings which seem to the present editor best able to compete with the folio readings when judged from a purely literary point of view.

I, i, 20 *to* into   34 *the* my   35 *lord* liege   37 *Give me the map there. Know that we have divided* *The map there. Know we have divided   38 *fast* first   39 *from our age* of our state   40 *Conferring* Confirming   *strengths* years   45 *The princes* The two great princes   53 *Where nature doth with merit challenge* Where merit doth most challenge it   55 *love* do love   62 *speak* do   64 *shadowy* shady   68 *of Cornwall* *to Cornwall? Speak   69 *of that self mettle as my sister* of the selfsame mettle that my sister is   72 *comes too* came   78 *ponderous* richer   82 *conferred* confirmed   83 *our last and least* the last, not least in our dear love   85 *draw* win   86 *sisters? Speak* sisters   90 *Nothing will* How? Nothing can   94 *How, how, Cordelia* Go to, Go to   95 *you* it 108 *Let* Well, let 118 *shall to my bosom* shall 130 *with* in 135 *shall* still 149 *falls* *stoops *Reserve thy state* *Reverse thy doom 156 *ne'er* nor 157 *motive* the motive 161 *Miscreant* Recreant 163 *Kill* Do. Kill 164 *gift* doom 166 *Hear me, recreant* Hear me 168 *That* Since *vows* vow 169 *strained* strayed 173 *Five* Four 174 *disasters* *diseases 175 *sixth* fifth 180 *Fare* Why, fare 181 *Freedom* Friendship 182 *dear shelter* protection 190 *this* a 193 *Most royal* Royal 194 *hath* what 200 *more* else 202 *Will* Sir, will 204 *Dow'red* Covered 214 *whom* that 216 *The best, the dearest* Most best, most dearest 223 *Should* Could 226 *make known* may know 228 *unchaste* *unclean 230 *richer* rich 232 *That* As 233 *Better* Go, to, go to. Better 235 *but* no more but 239 *regards* respects 241 *a dowry* and dower *King* Lear 258 *of* in 259 *Can* Shall 271 *Love* Use 276 *duty* duties 280 *plighted* pleated 281 *with shame* shame them 283 *not little* not a little 291 *grossly* gross 305 *of it* on't

I, ii, 10 *With base? with baseness? Bastardy base? Base* With base, base bastardy 15 *then* the 18 *legitimate. Fine word, 'legitimate'* legitimate 24 *prescribed* subscribed 38 *o'erlooking* liking 45 *policy and reverence* policy 68 *before* heretofore 70 *heard him oft* often heard him 72 *declined* declining 76 *sirrah* sir *I'll* I 85 *that he hath writ* he hath wrote 86 *other* further 100 *find* see 103 *reason it* reason 118 *on* by 120 *spherical* spiritual 124 *on* to *a star* stars 129 *bastardizing* bastardy 130 *pat* out 131 *Tom o'* them of 132–33 *divisions. Fa, sol, la, mi* divisions 138 *with* about 139 *writes* writ 148 *The night* Why, the night 150 *Ay, two* Two

I, iii, 13 *fellows* fellow servants *to* in 14 *distaste* dislike 18 *my* our 21 *have said* tell you *Well* Very well 26 *course* *very course *Prepare* Go prepare

I, iv, 20 *be'st* be 30 *canst thou* canst 43 *You, you* You 68 *my* this 72 *noted it well* noted it 75 *you, sir, you* you sir, you sir *hither, sir* hither 78–79 *your pardon* you pardon me 81 *strucken* struck 85 *sir, arise, away* sir 87 *Go to! Have you wisdom? So* You have wisdom 97 *did* done 106 *the Lady Brach* Lady o' the Brach 111 *nuncle* uncle 122 *Kent* Lear 123 *'tis like* like 125 *nuncle* uncle 131 *sweet one* sweet fool 158 *grace* wit 160 *And* They *to wear* do wear 172 *lie, sirrah* lie 181 *You* *Methinks you 183 *frowning* *frown 188 *nor crust* neither crust 204 *Will* Must 205 *know* trow 210 *I would* Come, sir, I would *your* that   212 *transport* transform   216 *This* Why, this   219 *Ha! Waking? 'Tis* Sleeping or waking? Ha! Sure 'tis   227 *This admiration, sir* Come, sir, this admiration   229 *To understand* Understand   236 *graced* great   237 *then* thou   248 *Woe* We   *repents* repent's   261 *Lear, Lear, Lear* Lear, Lear   266 *Hear* Hark   280 *Away, away* Go, go, my people   282 *more of it* the cause   294 *loose* make   296 *Ha! Let it be so. I have another daughter* *Let it be so. Yet have I left a daughter   301 *ever* ever. Thou shalt, I warrant thee   *that* that, my lord   304 *Pray you, content. – What, Oswald, ho* Come, sir, no more   306 *tarry* tarry and   331 *No, no,* Now   333 *condemn* dislike

I, v, 4 *afore* before   10 *not* ne'er   14 *can tell what* can what   15 *What canst tell, boy* Why, what canst thou tell, my boy   17 *canst* canst not   *i' th' middle on's* in the middle of his   31 *moe* more   33 *Yes indeed* Yes   38 *till* before   40 *O, let me not be mad, not mad, sweet heaven* O, let me not be mad, sweet heaven. I would not be mad   42 *How now, are* Are   45 *that's a* that is   46 *unless* except

II, i, 3–4 *Regan his Duchess* his Duchess   4 *this* to   7 *they* there   8 *ear-kissing* *ear-bussing   11 *the* the two   13 *may do* may   18 *I must act. Briefness* must ask briefness   *work* help   23 *Cornwall* Cornwall ought   27 *yourself* your –   30 *Draw, seem* Seem   31 *ho* here   32 *Fly, brother* Fly, brother, fly   39 *Mumbling* Warbling   40 *stand* stand's   43 *him, ho* him   46 *the thunder* *their thunders   52 *latched* lanched   56 *Full* But   62 *coward* caitiff   68 *would the reposal* could the reposure   73 *practice* pretence   76 *spirits* *spurs   77 *O strange* *Strong   78 *letter, said he* letter   90 *O madam Madam* it's cracked *is cracked   97 *he was of that consort* he was   100 *th' expense and waste* the waste and spoil   120 *prize* poise

II, ii, 1 *dawning* even   5 *lov'st* love   15–16 *action-taking* action-taking knave. A   16 *superserviceable, finical* superfinical   21 *deny'st* deny   28 *night, yet* night   29 *You* Draw, you   32 *come with* bring   39 *Murder, murder* Murder! help   40 *matter? Part* matter   54 *they* he   55 *years o' th' trade* hours at the trade   64 *know you* you have   69 *atwain* in twain   72 *Being* *Bring   *the* *their   79 *drive* send   84 *fault* offense   90 *some* a   94 *An honest mind and plain* He must be plain   100 *faith* sooth   101 *great* grand   103 *mean'st* mean'st thou   113 *compact* conjunct   120 *Fetch* Bring   121 *ancient* miscreant   122 *Sir, I* I

127 *Stocking* Stopping   133 *color* nature   141 *King his master needs must* King must   142 *he* he's   147 *Cornwall. Come, my lord, away* *Regan. Come, my good lord, away   152 *out* on't   155 *taken* took

II, iii, 1 *heard* hear   10 *hairs in* hair with   19 *Sometimes* Sometime

II, iv, 3 *purpose in them* purpose   5 *Ha* How   7 *he* look, he   8 *heads* heels   25 *impose* purpose   34 *meiny* men   57 *here within* within   58 *here* there   59 *but* than   60 *None* no   61 *number* train   68 *twenty* a hundred   70 *following* following it   71 *upward* up the hill   74 *which serves and seeks* that serves   83 *stocks, fool* stocks   85 *have travelled all the night* travelled hard to-night   91 *Fiery? What quality* What fiery quality   97 *commands – tends – service* *commands her service   99 *Fiery? The fiery Duke* Fiery Duke   *that* that Lear   111 *Go tell* Tell   116 *O me, my heart, my rising heart! But down* O my heart, my heart   118 *knapped* rapped   132 *With* Of   135 *scant* slack   143 *his* *her   148 *you but* you   153 *Never* No   163 *blister* blast her pride   164 *mood is on* *mood –   186 *you yourselves* yourselves   189 *will you* wilt thou   217 *that's in* that lies within   227 *looked* look   230 *you* you are   251 *look* seem   258 *need* needs   267 *man* fellow   272 *And let* O let   293 *best* good   295 *high* *bleak   296 *ruffle* rustle   297 *scarce* not

III, i, s.d. *severally* at several doors   1 *Who's there besides* What's there beside   4 *elements* element   18 *note* art   20 *is* be   48 *that* *your   53–54 *King – in which your pain* That way, I'll this King – I'll this way, you that

III, ii, 5 *of* *to   7 *Strike* Smite   16 *tax* task   18 *Then* Now then   22 *will* have   *join* joined   42 *are* sit   49 *fear* force   50 *pudder* pother   54 *simular* simular man   55 *to* in   58 *concealing continents* concealed centers   64 *harder than the stones* hard than is the stone   71 *And* *That   73 *That's sorry* That sorrows   74 *has and* has   77 *Though* For   78 *boy* my good boy

III, iii, 4 *perpetual* their   12 *footed* landed   13 *look* seek   15 *If I* Though I   17 *strange things* some strange thing   23 *The* Then   *doth* do

III, iv, 4 *enter here* enter   6 *contentious* tempestuous   16 *home* sure   22 *enter here* enter   29 *storm* night   46 *blow the winds* *blows the cold wind   *Humh! go* Go   *bed* *cold bed   48 *Didst thou give all to thy* Hast given all to thy two   54 *porridge* pottage   57 *acold. O, do, de, do, de, do, de* acold   60 *there – and there again – and there* and there again   61 *Has his* What, his

173

62 *Wouldst* Didst   66 *light* fall   74 *Alow, alow, loo, loo* Alo, lo, lo   77 *words' justice* *words justly   94 *says suum, mun* hay   96 *Thou* Why, thou   *a* thy   98 *more than* *more but   100 *Ha! here's* here's   104 *contented; 'tis* content; this is   108 *foul* foul fiend   110 *squints* *squemes (i.e. squinies?)   132 *Smulkin* Snulbug   148 *same* most   152 *him once more* him   162 *mercy, sir* mercy   173 *tower came* town come

III, v, 9 *letter which* *letter   11 *this* his

III, vi, 68 *Or bobtail* *Bobtail   69 *him* them   71 *leaped* *leap   72 *Do, de, de, de. Sessa* Loudla doodla   76 *these hard hearts* this hardness   78 *You will* You'll   *Persian* Persian attire   80 *here and rest* here   82 *So, so. We'll go to supper i' th' morning* So, so, so. We'll go to supper i' th' morning. So, so, so   93 *up, take up* up the King

III, vii, 3 *traitor* villain   23 *Though well* Though   32 *I'm none* I am true   42 *answered* answerer   53 *answer* first answer   58 *stick* *rash (meaning 'rip')   59 *bare* lowed   62 *rain* rage   63 *stern* *dearn (meaning 'drear')   65 *subscribe* *subscribed   73 *served you* served   79 *Nay* Why   81 *you have* *yet have you   86 *enkindle* unbridle   87 *treacherous villain* villain

IV, i, 4 *esperance* experience   9 *But who comes* Who's   10 *poorly led* parti, eyd (*sic*)   14 *These fourscore years* This fourscore –   17 *You* Alack, sir, you   36 *flies to* flies are to th'   45 *Which* Who   52 *daub* dance   54 *And yet I must. – Bless* Bless   57–58 *thee, good man's son* the good man

IV, ii, 17 *names* *arms   28 *My fool* A fool   *body* bed   29 *whistle* whistling   60 *seems* *shows   73 *thrilled* thralled

IV, iv, 10 *helps* can help   26 *importuned* important

IV, v, 15 *him, madam* him   40 *party* Lady

IV, vi, 1 *I* we   8 *In* With   46 *sir! Friend* sir   51 *Thou'dst* Thou hadst   65 *How is't* How   73 *make them* made their   78 *'twould* would it   89 *this piece of* this   91–92 *I' th' clout, i' th' clout* in the air, hah   96 *Goneril with a white beard* Goneril, ha Regan   104 *ague-proof* argue-proof   127 *sulphurous* sulphury   128 *consumption* consummation   130 *sweeten* *to sweeten   132 *Let me* Here   138 *thy* the   *see* see one   148 *this* the   150–51 *change places and, handy-dandy* Handy-dandy   159 *Thou* Thy blood   161 *clothes* rags   169 *Now, now, now, now* No, now   177 *wawl* wail   *Mark* Mark me   182 *felt. I'll put't in proof* felt   186 *dear daughter – dear –* 192 *a man a man* a man   195 *smug bridegroom* bridegroom   198 *Come* Nay   199 *running. Sa, sa,* *sa, sa* running   207 *sound* sense   217 *tame to* lame by   224 *old* most   237 *ballow* bat   246 *English* *British   252 *these* his   264 *servant* *servant, and for you her own for venture (*sic*)   277 *severed* *fencèd

IV, vii, 16 *jarring* hurrying   32 *opposed* exposed   *jarring* *warring   36 *enemy's* injurious   58 *hand* hands   59 *You* No, sir, you   *mock me* mock   61 *upward, not an hour more nor less* upward   70 *I am! I am* I am   79 *killed* cured   84 *Pray you* Pray

V, i, 21 *heard* hear   36 *Pray* Pray you   46 *And machination ceases. Fortune* Fortune   52 *true* great

V, ii, 1 *tree* bush

V, iii, 8 *No, no, no, no* No, no   25 *starved* starve   43 *I* We   62 *might* should   68 *addition* advancement   78 *him* him then   81 *thine* good   90 *Gloucester. Let the trumpet sound* Gloucester   91 *person* head   93 *make* prove   96 *medicine* poison   99 *the* thy   105 *My* This   110–11 *within the lists* in the host   113 *by* at   120 *name, your* name and   124 *cope* *cope withal   129–30 *my privilege, The privilege of mine honors* the privilege of my tongue   136 *Conspirant* Conspicuate   138 *below thy foot* beneath thy feet   144 *tongue* being   146 *rule* right   147 *Back* Here   152 *practice* *mere practice   153 *war* *arms   155 *Shut* *Stop   156 *stop* *stopple   *it. – Hold, sir* it   157 *name* thing   172 *plague* *scourge   174 *right; 'tis true* truth   186 *we* with   191 *Their* The   197 *our* my   223 *help! O, help* help   225 *of –* O, she's dead of   226 *Who dead? Speak, man* Who, man? Speak   228 *poisonèd; she confesses* poisoned; she hath confessed   232 *judgment* justice   233 *is this* 'tis   252 *Edgar* Albany   258 *Howl, howl, howl* Howl, howl, howl, howl   270 *you murderers* your murderous   274 *woman* women   281 *brag* bragged   *and* or   283 *This is a dull sight. Are* Are   289 *first* life   306 *no, no, no* no, no   308 *Thou'lt* O, thou wilt   309 *Never, never, never, never, never* Never, never, never   310 *sir* sir. o, o, o, o   316 *He* O, he   324 *Edgar* Albany   326 *hath* *have